I0691976

MINDFIRE

MINDFIRE

ALLEN STEADHAM

Power Alone Does Not Make a Hero or Villain

AMBASSADOR INTERNATIONAL
GREENVILLE, SOUTH CAROLINA & BELFAST, NORTHERN IRELAND

www.ambassador-international.com

Mindfire

ISBN: 978-1-62020-908-0
eISBN: 978-1-62020-921-9
Library of Congress Control Number: 2019938623

Cover Design & Typesetting by Hannah Nichols
Ebook Conversion by Anna Riebe Raats
Edited by Daphne Self

AMBASSADOR INTERNATIONAL
Emerald House
411 University Ridge, Suite B14
Greenville, SC 29601, USA
www.ambassador-international.com

AMBASSADOR BOOKS
The Mount
2 Woodstock Link
Belfast, BT6 8DD, Northern Ireland, UK
www.ambassadormedia.co.uk

The colophon is a trademark of Ambassador, a Christian publishing company.

"The hardest thing to learn in life is which bridge to cross and which to burn."
- David Russell

1

SWEATING FROM HER BRISK WALK across the Digby College campus in record-breaking near-ninety-degree July heat, Leia Hamilton dragged herself into an empty seat towards the back of the large Jason V. Frederick lecture hall, which wasn't well-lit or properly ventilated. The building itself must have been at least twenty-five to thirty years old. The acoustics carried well enough but also made it seem like all sound escaped from a human-sized tin can. Students were always tempted to sleep but their success often depended on the teacher.

Professor Angela Merrick, whom Leia had nicknamed "Professor Doom," scowled and deliberately made direct eye contact with Leia but said nothing, continuing her lecture. The professor radiated confidence and something else, Leia wasn't sure what. The professor's long black hair was often worn in a bun like today but sometimes she wore it down. Leia believed the professor would be very beautiful if she didn't always project a certain amount of tension. It had given her worry lines that made her look a few years older than she probably was.

Thirty minutes later, Josh Manning saw Leia escaping her first class of the day. Mentally noting her distressed expression, he whirled her around and kissed her passionately in front of the other class escapees in the hallway. He was red-haired, even taller than Leia and lanky. He also had more than a bit of Southern charm to accompany his slight Alabama drawl. Suddenly, he pulled back, confused and concerned.

"Your skin is, like, really hot!" Josh put his hand on her forehead. "You have a fever or something?"

"I'm fine," Leia pulled back and glared at Josh. "Now what are you doing? You said you'd keep things mellow on-campus!"

"You looked like you needed cheering up," Josh said.

Leia facepalmed. And a moment later, she grabbed his arms in a rage.

"What is wrong with you?" Leia screamed. "Save that stuff for when we're alone!"

"Oh yeah, that's subtle," Josh replied. "Do you think anyone didn't hear you just now? All I did was kiss you!"

"SHUT UP!" Leia shouted.

As Leia said that, her eyes became a bright, transfixing glare. And the outer halo of that glow burned like the hottest flames. Combined with her angry expression, it terrified him.

Josh stumbled backwards into a wall, shocked and afraid. He closed his eyes and shook his head a couple of times, as though not accepting what his eyes had seen.

"What's—what is it? What's wrong?" Leia asked.

"N-nothing! I must be seeing things," Josh said. "Um . . . for a second there, it looked like your eyes were glowing and . . . on fire."

"What?" Leia said, her eyes widening.

"I gotta, uh, go. I'll, um, I'll call you later. Maybe. I think!"

Josh, at first, briskly walked then ran down the hallway past the other students who apparently hadn't seen what he had. Then he almost collided with a couple of students on his way to the exit.

———

He acted like he'd seen a monster! Leia couldn't understand it at all.

In all the years she'd known him, Josh had never reacted like this and certainly never looked at her with such fear. Still stunned and hurt, Leia walked out of the building, feeling like a child who had lost their favorite toy. Slowly, she made her way out to one of the grass-covered hills nearby and sat down under the shade of a tree. Her thoughts took her back to the first time that she and Josh met.

"You're pretty tall for a girl!" Josh had said.

With her arms at her sides and fists clenched, Leia turned around and faced him. She was angry to the point of near-tears. Her left cheek was red from a recent punch, her lip was split, and some blood was drying on her right cheek.

Josh was tall but not as tall as Leia. He had a mop of red hair, freckles and was thin and scrawny. He wore thick glasses, a loud yellow t-shirt and green shorts.

"Are you gonna mess with me, too?" Leia had snarled.

They were nine years old at the time. She was standing next to the playground swings after school. He was next to the slide. The sun and clouds were overhead and there was no breeze on this late spring afternoon. A pair of female joggers were running through the neighborhood on the other side of the playground.

Leia's muddied white t-shirt sleeve was stretched and torn and there was dirt all over her blue shorts. There were fresh scrapes on her legs and arms.

"You're hurt!" Josh had said. "Are you okay?"

His concern was disarming. Still, Leia wasn't ready to completely drop her guard.

"You don't wanna fight?" she had asked.

"Why would I wanna fight you? I don't even know you," Josh had said. "What happened?"

"All the boys want to fight me 'cause I'm tall and I look strong," Leia said. "I like to play sports and I'm not all girly, so they treat me like a boy. And the girls won't help me 'cause if they do, the boys'll mess with them, too."

Leia spat out a little blood.

"What's your name?" Leia had asked. "And . . . why are you being nice to me?"

"I'm Josh. And like I said, I don't know you. Why should I be mean to you?"

"Okay, thanks. I'm Leia."

"Where do you live, Leia? I'll walk you home, hold your books, and stuff. And if more boys mess with you, I'll fight them for you."

Leia arched her left eyebrow at Josh.

"You can fight?" Leia had wondered aloud.

"Are you kidding? Everyone picks on me because I look scrawny," Josh replied. "But it's easy to beat someone when they underestimate you."

Leia's respect for Josh increased. He wasn't just nice, he was smart, too.

As Josh walked over, picked up her books and put them back in her scuffed and dirty backpack, Leia finally relaxed and allowed herself a genuine smile.

"Lean on me, Leia, I'll carry your backpack."

"You sure?" Leia asked.

"I'm stronger than I look," Josh said. "Just tell me where to take you."

Leia put her left arm around Josh's neck and let him support her as they walked home through the neighborhood.

Seven years had passed and the two continued to remain friends, entering middle then high school. Josh had grown to surpass Leia's height, tamed his hair into an actual style, and began wearing contacts. Leia had developed a womanly figure and left behind her tomboy days. She had also gained some popularity from her participation in track and volleyball. Josh had joined the basketball team and developed into quite the student. He and Leia had a regular routine of studying together. In fact, they were near-inseparable.

So, Leia didn't know whether to be happy or furious as Josh kissed her in the semi-crowded Digby High library. Her first kiss.

Probably his, too.

It was awkward at first but not unpleasant, so Leia didn't pull away. A moment later, it was over and she regained her senses. Leia looked around. If anyone was amused or offended, they didn't bother to show it. The other students continued about whatever they were doing, although Leia thought she saw one of the female librarians suppressing a smile as she checked in books at the counter.

"Wh-what—why did you do that??" Leia whispered loudly.

"'Cause I like you," Josh answered, not quite whispering. "You're my best friend, you're really pretty and I want you to be my girlfriend."

"Me . . . your girlfriend?" Leia whispered, shocked and impressed by his forthright manner.

"The way I see it, we're supposed to be together, Leia."

"Not following your math here, cowboy."

"Oh, come on! We've been there for each other, every day, for how long?" Josh said. "Don't tell me the kiss didn't feel right to you."

Leia said nothing. She was embarrassed to admit he was right.

"You kissed me back," Josh whispered.

"When did I do that?!" Leia said, no longer whispering.

"Those first few seconds were all me. But you pulled me close and kept going."

He was right. She blushed. Then she looked down to try and hide it. And inwardly, she smiled.

"Fine," Leia declared.

"What?"

"I'll be your girlfriend."

Three more years had passed. Josh was now living in an efficiency apartment near Digby College and working part-time at the local Burger Empire. Josh had decided to pursue an advertising degree. By his junior year in high school, Josh had been designing ads for the school newspaper while taking a journalism class. His sometimes-blunt social style translated well into his advertising style. He had a knack for making ads that people would talk about and remember, even if they were odd.

Leia looked at Josh sleeping on the fold-out bed in his apartment. She sat next to him and stroked his hair. The moonlight shone through the blinds revealing a surprisingly organized apartment. Josh had a few framed paintings and pictures on the walls, gifts from his mother. There was a medium-sized television on top of a wide wooden half-dresser. He kept all of his school materials to the left of the television on the dresser. The back half of the apartment contained the kitchen, dining area and bathroom. His "kitchen" was comprised of a small refrigerator and a microwave. It wasn't much but it was his home away from home.

Leia had come by after finishing her shift at Skippy's Pizza. It wasn't unusual for Leia to go for a late-night dinner or snack. But tonight, as on many occasions, Leia wanted to spend her time with Josh instead.

Leia smiled as she thought of how far their relationship had progressed in a decade's time. This was the man she'd given her heart to. He was the one who had protected and supported her. She knew he loved her with all his heart.

Sure, he had his faults. He could be loud and obnoxious, say the worst things at the worst times. He often didn't know when to quit. They could argue about almost anything. But he was sincere and honest, a good man, devoted to her happiness. Leia thought about her parents then.

When am I gonna tell them? What *am I gonna tell them? Call me crazy but I don't think "Mom, Dad, Josh and I aren't just boyfriend and girlfriend anymore" will go over so well. Would it help if I told them that he's the man I want to spend my life with?* She had thought back then.

Now, in the present, Leia sat on the hill, her eyes looking blankly at the sky as her reverie ended. Leia had continued to avoid telling her parents how close her relationship with Josh had become, even though on some level, she knew Mom was probably keenly aware of it. What was there to discuss? Leia and Josh had chosen this together.

Leia blinked back tears. She was assaulted once again by the mental image of Josh staring at her in abject horror and fear today.

How could this happen? How could Josh, of all people, look at me like that? Like a stranger!

It reminded her of the look one of her childhood bullies had given her after she'd broken his arm, a look of shock and disbelief.

Doesn't he know everything about me by now? Hasn't he accepted me unconditionally? Is he rejecting me now, after all we've been through?

Leia wiped the tears from her eyes and forced herself to stand up. She looked around at the numerous students sitting nearby or walking to class.

The worst thing any of you have to face is whatever class you have. I wish I could say the same. I wish Josh were here holding me . . . or even kissing me. Yeah, that would be nice.

Leia sighed and forced herself to start walking to her next class.

2

BIOLOGY AND ECONOMICS DISAPPEARED INTO a surreal fog for Leia. Mentally, she just wasn't there. It didn't help that she didn't have any friends in those classes, no one to help anchor her to reality.

"Miss Hamilton?" a woman's voice called. "Leia?"

Leia lifted her head up and saw Professor Janice Martinez staring at her in the hallway with deep brown eyes expressing concern past strands of Martinez's blond bangs. Professor Martinez was in her early forties, a few inches over five feet tall with shoulder-length hair. She'd returned from maternity leave at the beginning of the summer semester, a month ago, and was still wearing loose-fitting clothes. At the moment, she was looking at Leia like she would at one of her children.

"Yes, ma'am?" Leia replied.

"You look like someone who could use a friend," Professor Martinez said. "Am I right? May I ask what's troubling you? I don't have any more classes for the day, so if you want to talk . . . ?"

Leia smiled.

"It's . . . it's not that big a deal," Leia said. "I just had a misunderstanding with my boyfriend."

"That must have been some misunderstanding then," Professor Martinez said. "You look like you lost something really important."

"It's just . . . he's never been scared of me before," Leia said. "And I don't know why. I don't know what I did."

Professor Martinez put her arm around Leia and they started walking towards her office across the hallway. And they talked along the way. Not about Josh. Not yet. It was safer for Leia to complain about Professor Merrick. As they entered her office and Martinez closed the door behind them, she handed Leia a red rubber ball small enough to fit in her fist.

"This is my stress ball. Just squeeze it while you tell me what's bothering you," Martinez said. "I promise what you say will just be between us, okay?"

Leia nodded and began squeezing the little red ball in her right hand as she sat down on one of the professor's wooden office chairs.

The small office had yellow walls that were sparsely decorated with a clock and the professor's framed college degrees. There was an open window behind the professor's desk that was letting in a slight breeze. The desk had numerous framed photos on it as well as the professor's laptop, an empty coffee cup and several small stacks of paper. The professor's briefcase leaned against a half-bookcase filled with historical reference books and literary works.

"Don't feel too bad about Angela—I mean, Professor Merrick," Martinez said. "She's a hard one to figure out but she's exceptional at her job. She started here a little after I did, about three years ago. And you should know, she pushes all her students, not just you."

"I don't know why but somehow that makes me feel better," Leia replied.

"But that's not really what's bugging you," Martinez continued. "What's your boyfriend's name?"

"Josh," Leia said.

Leia shared her thoughts and feelings with Professor Martinez, who listened with patience born from years of practice. Leia noticed the framed pictures on Martinez's desk. A tall muscular man with close-cropped black hair in a U.S. Army uniform. A chubby teenage girl with shoulder-length brown hair who had Martinez's eyes and smile standing next to a younger boy who looked a lot like Martinez's husband. Next to that picture was one of her precious-looking baby daughter. The man in the picture looked very confident, completely devoted and in love. Like Josh did until that awful moment this morning.

That mental picture shattered Leia's emotional walls. All of the frustration and pain came pouring out at once. Leia knew she needed this. She didn't question why she trusted this professor, she just did. Eventually, Leia calmed down and finished telling Martinez what was troubling her.

"You were pretty mad at him for a minute there," Martinez added. "Maybe you just surprised him with your intensity."

"Maybe . . . but . . . " Leia said, closing her eyes and tensing in frustration. "What was that whole thing about thinking I had a fever and the way my eyes looked—"

Leia heard a small pop and a crack. She opened her eyes and looked at her fist. Wisps of black smoke escaped as she opened her fist and the half-melted ball dropped to the floor.

"What?" Leia exclaimed.

"Are you alright?" Martinez said. "Let me see your hand!"

Surprised flashed across the professor's face to see that Leia's hand wasn't injured and there were no marks on it at all. It was warm but not unusually so.

"I'm sorry, Leia, I've never seen any kind of ball do that. Are you sure you're alright?"

"Yeah," Leia replied. "I really don't know what happened."

"I'm . . . just glad you're okay," Martinez added. "That's really strange."

Somehow, that ball melted because of her, even if she didn't know how or why. Still, she was glad Professor Martinez didn't look scared of her at least, unlike Josh.

Leia quickly excused herself, walked out of the office and closed the door behind her. She decided to head into work early.

———

Five hours later, the green "i" in "Skippy's Pizza" flickered on the neon sign above the entranceway. Customers talked and dined in the booths or at their tables as "I Ran" by A Flock of Seagulls played over the speakers. The restaurant lighting was dimmed in the customer area to provide a comfortable atmosphere while it was well-lit behind the counter and in the cooking area. Skippy's was a local restaurant, so the owner had chosen to put pictures and even flyers from local events and bands around the counter and on the walls.

Tonight, Leia was at the register taking orders. She normally didn't mind this aspect of her job, it gave her a chance to talk with people as they ordered their food. But as usual, there were difficult customers.

"Are you saying you won't put that on my pizza?" the fifty-something man demanded. He was tall, very muscular, and smelled of beer and cigarettes.

"I'm sorry, sir, but we don't have grilled salmon as an ingredient here at Skippy's. I'll gladly substitute one of our other ingredients," Leia said.

"Like what?" he replied, curious but not yet satisfied.

"Well, sir, we have pepperoni, Italian sausage, hamburger, ham, spinach, barbecued chicken, Roma tomatoes—"

"Standard pizza toppings," the man interrupted gruffly.

"Yes, sir," Leia continued, smiling but holding her ground. "Just tell me what you'd like and I'll have it made for you."

"I want grilled salmon!" he shouted. "Let me talk to your manager, miss!"

Miffed, Leia pointed to her nametag. "I am the manager . . . sir!"

"Are you kidding me? You're just some kid barely out of high school! How can you be manager?"

Leia had had quite enough. Channeling every bit of self-confidence she could muster, she stood to her full six foot height and stared the man in the eyes.

"I have attempted to accommodate you, sir," Leia insisted, slamming her fist onto the counter next to the cash register. "I have explained that we do not carry grilled salmon at this or any of our locations and I have offered you an alternative, which you have refused. As the manager of this business, I have the right to refuse service to anyone . . . including you. You are preventing other customers from ordering, customers who know and understand what our regular ingredients are. So, sir, I must ask you to leave!"

It was then that Leia noticed that not only was the middle-aged man staring at her in fear, but so were the other six people near the counter and the two couples sitting at booths.

"What *are* you??" the man said. "You ain't normal!"

Leia turned around and saw the same frightened look in her co-workers' eyes. Then she noticed the four pizza cutters and two butcher knives suspended in mid-air around her, pointing towards the man.

In one of the butcher knives, close to the left side of her head, she saw a reflection of her face. Her eyes were glowing and on fire . . . yet they didn't hurt.

When she looked down and lifted her fist from the counter, she was further shocked to see the impression of her fist permanently embedded into the countertop and cracks spider-webbing from the impression. A pit opened in her stomach and she almost became nauseous. With her concentration shattered, the hovering objects fell to the floor. Then Leia collapsed to her knees, trembling with adrenaline and fear. She closed her eyes and all the sounds in the room were drowned out by the roar of a building tidal wave in her ears.

The sounds of employees and customers alike as they ran out of the building were barely heard.

Sometime later, she wasn't sure how long, Leia recovered her composure, her senses relented and most of her strength returned. Leia looked up and saw that she was alone.

"Leave. Now!" a female voice said. Leia didn't hear it with her ears. It seemed to be in her head. "The police have been called. You have to get out of there, now!"

The voice was familiar, though Leia couldn't identify who it was. But clearly, whoever spoke to her was worried about her. Leia stood up and exited the back door of the restaurant. Hearing sirens a few blocks away, she started running down back alleyways to avoid being seen out on the street.

"It'll be alright," the woman's voice soothed in Leia's head. "But you should get home. Only tell your parents. They'll understand."

Am I nuts? Is that it? Maybe Josh was right, I have a fever and I'm hallucinating!

"I wish that were true, girl," the voice added. "But sometimes the truth is harsher and more difficult to deal with."

Who are you??

"Someone with . . . abilities like you," the voice said. "I want to help you."

Why? Everyone else is scared of me! Are you just interested in me because I have powers? Why are you doing this?

"You mean much more to me than your powers, Leia Hamilton. I'll explain everything someday. I promise."

Still somewhat disoriented, Leia began to cry, feeling overwhelmed as it dawned on her what had happened. There was so much she still didn't understand.

"They fear you because you have power," the voice continued after a short pause. "It separates you from them, it makes you better than them. And they know it."

I'm not better than anyone.

"Really?" the voice said, ripe with sarcasm. "You could have turned that drunkard into a torch or impaled everyone in there with sharp objects. You could have crushed their skulls!"

Shut up! Leia thought, agonized by the callous imagery. *I'd never do that!*

The voice laughed.

"I was like you once," the voice added. "Young, hopelessly naïve, and idealistic. I hope you can maintain that illusion. I had to learn the hard way."

Who are you?

The voice went silent as Leia reached her home and went inside.

3

HER MOM OPENED THE FRONT door before Leia could insert her key. Her wavy dark brown hair parted in the middle as it gently framed her face and flowed over her shoulders and down to the middle of her back. When she has been Leia's age, she had been a Latina model. Looking at her now, even wearing a blue robe over her white nightgown, Leia didn't doubt it one bit. Regardless of the weight her mom had gained since those days, she maintained a gorgeous complexion, had crystal blue eyes, high cheeks that curved gently down to her chin and an impressive hourglass figure. Her natural beauty surpassed the need to wear makeup.

Had she not abandoned the beginnings of fame and likely a lucrative career, Mom would probably be a household name as a supermodel. But she had instead chosen to love Leia's father, Steve, and raise Leia, who wasn't even her biological daughter. That made her Mom as far as Leia was concerned.

"Are you alright, Leia? You're breathing pretty hard and you look . . . spooked."

Spooked? After what just happened, I guess that's as good a description as any.

"I'm pretty beat, Mom. I'm just gonna go to bed."

"You sure? It'll only take a minute to warm up some water for herbal tea. It'll—"

"No. Thanks, really," Leia said. "I just need sleep."

"Alright."

She was nowhere near ready to talk about any of this. As much as she wanted to cry or scream or just accept the hug and silent acceptance she knew Mom would provide, Leia had to find some way to make sense of this first.

Walking down the hall towards her room, Leia knew the voice in her head sounded so very familiar.

Who is this woman helping me? Is she a good person or a bad person?

"You could have turned that drunkard into a torch or impaled everyone in there with sharp objects. You could have crushed their skulls!"

Deep inside, she knew the voice was right. And it frightened her.

Leia stopped and looked at the pictures on the wall. There was the family portrait taken four years ago. She'd never really looked at it before, seen the pride in her parents' eyes towards Leia and her sister, the love they felt for their children. Leia felt her own pride swell and perhaps a twinge of jealousy at how utterly cute her sister could be without even trying.

Mom and Dad's wedding picture was proof positive of how svelte her mom looked in her modeling days. Another picture showed Leia and her dad fishing. Next to it was a picture of Dad's best friend, Uncle John. He was smiling and standing next to some nice sports car from the 1980s.

In every picture I've seen of them, Dad was always so happy and goofy around Uncle John. Dad said that, in the days before he met Mom, he and Uncle John used to get in fights with people, coming home with cuts and bruises. But they'd just laugh it off with a drink while sharing stories.

Leia admired their friendship. Leia wished she'd been able to get to know Uncle John. But he'd died in some kind of work-related accident before she was born.

Did Uncle John ever get married and have kids? Mom and Dad don't really talk about his life outside the friendship. He worked on cars and motorcycles and raced them for fun. But what did he do as a job? I guess I'll never know.

Leia felt Mom's gaze even though she wasn't facing her. When she caught a quick glance, she saw the compassion in Mom's eyes and demeanor. It looked like she was waiting for Leia to start any discussion. It was one of the things she loved about her mom. With a small sigh, Leia forced herself to finish the walk to her room.

What's gonna happen next? If the cops talk to any of my coworkers, they'll tell them what happened. Will the cops believe them? Will they come for me to ask me questions? Will they arrest me?

Leia laughed in spite of her mood.

What are they gonna charge me with? Lifting sharp objects with my mind? Using those objects to threaten a customer? Somehow, I don't think they've written laws to cover that kinda stuff.

Leia closed the door behind her. She sat down on her bed and stared out the window.

How am I gonna face Misha or any of the others at work again? Or the regulars who come by all the time? They all looked at me the same way Josh looked at me, so scared—like I was really a demon, a monster!

I only saw my reflection for a few seconds, but how could that have been me? How did I do that? Was that really me? I'm scared of what I saw, so I get why they were, too!

What am I? How did I get these . . . abilities? And how do I get rid of them?

"You'll never get rid of them," the voice interjected. "You were born with this. It's in your blood. But you're only now becoming mature enough, physically, to access these powers."

I'll never get rid of them? I can't control them! I'll be a danger to myself and everyone around me!

"That's not what's bothering you," the voice continued. "You know you can gain control. You're worried about what people will think of you."

I think that's a legitimate concern! Outside of my family, I can't imagine people just accepting me with these . . . these powers.

"Not even Lover Boy?"

You know about my boyfriend?!

"I'm a telepath. Of course, I know about Josh."

You know too much about me. And Josh . . . when he saw me change before . . . he got scared like everyone else, so . . . I dunno.

"He's going to have to accept you, to a certain degree," the voice said. "He's going to be a part of your life from now on."

What, you can read the future, too?

"Nevermind, that's a topic for another time. Look, Leia, you'll be surprised who will accept you, outside of your family. You'll find out who your friends really are."

Thanks . . . I think.

"I've done what I can to help you," the voice reassured. "I'm going to use my abilities to help you get some sleep. You'll see, things will be better tomorrow."

And with that, Leia succumbed to the voice's power, collapsed to her pillow and entered a deep, dreamless sleep.

The next morning, walking the hallways of the Frederick V. Jason Building, Leia's eyes scanned all over for Misha, but she couldn't find her. Then, slender yet familiar arms grabbed her from behind. She already knew it was Josh. His cologne had announced his presence before he could.

Has he forgotten what happened or has he changed his mind? How strange but I won't complain! Is this what the voice meant?

Grateful even for the possibility, she turned around, pulled Josh close and professed her love through a long kiss in front of everyone. She didn't care anymore, she was going to take the risk and show her feelings to him. After a few seconds of being surprised, Josh relaxed.

"That was nice," Josh said, smiling. "But . . . I thought you didn't want us doing that on campus—"

"That's not important anymore," Leia answered. "We're what's important. I don't want you to feel distant from me."

Josh stood there for several seconds with his mouth open. Then he looked at her with a confused expression.

"Who are you and what have you done with the real Leia Hamilton?"

"I know this isn't how I normally handle things, Josh. But I love you and when I think about it, it's not good to try and hide something like that."

"You're right."

"Um, I've got my Ethics class in a few minutes, but can we meet at the coffeehouse before I go to work tonight?" Leia added.

"Sounds good. Are you gonna be okay till then?"

"I think I can manage," Leia answered with a bit too much bravado.

Hours later, Leia waited for Josh at the bustling Greenback's Coffee. The massive coffeehouse was teeming with dozens of her fellow students. Most of them were sitting at booths with laptops and tablets, taking advantage of the free wi-fi as they enjoyed their java and snacks.

Plowing through the front door a minute later, Josh almost ran over someone before he located Leia with his eyes.

"Am I late?" Josh asked as he plopped down in the booth.

"No, cowboy, I got here early," Leia replied, smiling.

"Was there something you wanted to talk about?"

"He's going to have to accept you, to a certain degree," Leia recalled the voice saying. *"He's going to be a part of your life from now on."*

"Not really," Leia answered, still smiling. "Can't I just enjoy your company before I have to go to work?"

Josh brightened considerably when he heard that.

"Of course! I could just sit here and bask in your glow for hours."

"I have a glow?" Leia joked.

"Well, I was speaking figuratively but yeah. Your personality, who you are, your feelings, I love it. You radiate who you are. Maybe not everyone can see it but I do."

"He's going to be a part of your life from now on." The words kept replaying in Leia's thoughts.

What did she mean by that? Does she know I want to marry him? Has she been following him around, too? Does she know he's planning to propose to me or something? What else could it be?

"Earth to Leia," Josh said. "I know you were named after Princess Leia but you don't have to be in a galaxy far, far away."

"Sorry," Leia replied, taking a sip of the cappuccino she'd ordered. "Lost in thought."

For Josh, Leia had ordered Greenbacks' signature "Endurance Test" coffee: four shots of espresso added to an over-roasted house blend. He had almost finished the drink.

"About what?" Josh asked. "You know I'm a good listener."

Maybe he'll understand. I've got to try and start somewhere.

"What would you do if you could, I dunno, fly? How would you handle it? What would you do?"

He leaned back and pondered on it for a few seconds. He took a final sip of his "Endurance Test."

"I'd use it," he said. "I'd go around and help people. And I'd use my flying ability to impress you!"

Leia smiled at that and semi-blushed.

"For real? You'd go superhero?" she replied. "How would you deal with people knowing you could fly?"

"Well, I'd do like the comics and make up an identity. I'd either wear a mask or a helmet or something. That way, people couldn't recognize me when I flew around and saved the world."

"A complete secret identity, huh? Wouldn't it be hard, leading two lives? One where you're a normal guy who goes to school and works, and another where you're going around saving the world?"

"Do you think about it when you open a door for someone? Or when you warn someone to watch out if something's falling or help catch someone's arm when they slip and are about to fall down? You just do it and life goes on, right?"

Now it was Leia's turn to carefully consider what Josh had said. Then she smiled, thanked him for his answer and changed the topic.

Thirty minutes later, Leia walked cautiously towards Skippy's Pizza. Her anxiety slowly grew as she got closer to the front door of her workplace. She still hadn't seen Misha anywhere on campus. But that wasn't entirely unusual in a bustling student population, especially as distracted as Leia had been today.

"Hey, Leia!" Misha waved enthusiastically as Leia entered Skippy's.

"Misha . . . hey," Leia replied, confused. "Everything okay?"

"Sure, why wouldn't it be?"

Leia tried to smile as she looked at her friend. Misha Breyer was shorter and thinner than Leia, with short curly brown hair and amber eyes. This time of year, Misha sported a deep tan. She was always a bundle of barely-held-in-check energy, which translated well for making food in a high-traffic pizza joint. It helped that the customers liked her, and she always showed up early to the job.

"Um, so . . . last night—" Leia started to say.

"Oh, it's cool," Misha interrupted. "I didn't mind covering for you. It was a slow night anyway."

Leia blinked twice, unsure she'd heard Misha correctly.

"What?" Leia asked.

"Wow, you really were out of it, weren't you?" Misha added. "You told me you weren't feeling well, asked me to cover as manager the last couple of hours and you went home."

That's not what happened! What in the world?

"You still kinda look under the weather, Leia. Are you sure you're okay to work today? I can handle it if—"

"I'll be fine," Leia insisted. "I'll go change into my uniform."

"Sure, boss."

As Leia changed clothes in the ladies' restroom, she tried to make sense of things.

She doesn't remember last night! No, that's not right. She just remembers it differently! How is that possible?

"Do you really want to know the answer to that question?" the voice returned.

Do you ever leave my head, lady? I feel like you're stalking me! I don't get any privacy, you can just butt in whenever you want!

"I'd think that you'd find some comfort in having someone with you who understands you. Besides, I try not to be invasive. I only talk to you when you need to know something."

Leia sighed.

You did this somehow, didn't you? You changed Misha's memories about last night!

"Not just Misha's," the voice said. "Everyone who witnessed it, including the police who were called. I even fixed the counter you smashed, so there's no evidence of anything unusual happening last night. You have nothing to worry about anymore."

Who are you that you could do that? I know you helped me, and I'm grateful, but you messed with all those people's minds! You even made Josh forget!

"Would you rather I killed them all? Because that was my alternative. I've done it before."

What?

Suddenly, Leia could tell the presence behind the voice had departed.

And just like that, she's gone. But now I know she's a murderer . . . who's stalking me and talks to me in my mind. She's a bigger threat to everyone than I am! What am I going to do?

Leia walked to the counter and visually confirmed what the voice had said, that the surface had been completely repaired. It looked as if the entire counter had been taken apart and reformed from scratch with the same materials. Technically, it was impossible, but there it was in front of her. She decided to take Misha up on her offer to cover for her that evening. Leia was starting to feel sick after all.

4

BLACK FOX LEAPED FROM THE third floor of the office building and landed feet first on the hood of the speeding Mustang, severely denting the metal. Before now, she had been nearly invisible to the car's occupants. Her mostly black body-hugging costume helped her blend into the shadows.

Now, she quickly crouched down and stared menacingly through her golden metal fox mask at the men inside the vehicle. Her long and wavy black hair was blowing wildly in the wind, effectively blocking the driver's view. It didn't bother her at all that they were careening through the streets at ninety miles per hour.

"You get one chance!" Black Fox screamed at the men. "Pull over and no one gets hurt!"

The passenger, a wiry blond who couldn't have been more than eighteen, pulled a pistol out of his gray jacket and pointed it directly at Black Fox. At the same time, the driver, a bald African-American man in his early twenties, tried to shake her off of the car and bounced off of a curb by mistake. The impact threw the passenger's aim off as he fired. The bullet pierced the windshield and her left shoulder instead of her heart, where the passenger had been aiming.

More enraged than hurt, Black Fox summoned a sword to her right hand, its blade made entirely of flames. She plunged her sun saber all the way through the hood and engine, causing it to belch black smoke, flames and electrical currents.

Black Fox leaped off the vehicle as its momentum threw it into a parked SUV. She rolled several times and then stood up. As Black Fox stepped forward, she grabbed her shoulder and doubled over in agony. She visibly fought the urge to scream, feeling as though she might pass out.

Just then, the nearby shadows coalesced into the silhouette of a man. The silhouette caught Black Fox and helped steady her. Then it became a young biracial man with close-cropped, curly dark brown hair. He was wearing a form-fitting charcoal-gray costume and black boots.

"How bad is it?" the young man asked.

"It'll heal in a few minutes," Black Fox replied. "I'll be okay."

"You were lucky that man didn't kill you, Mother," he said.

"That *boy* is around the same age as you," Black Fox insisted. "And I told you not to call me Mother in public! I'm Black Fox and you're Shadow. That's all people need to know."

"Don't you think people will figure it out?"

"It will be a lot less likely to happen if you keep your Shadow form. And do as I've instruct—"

At that moment, Black Fox realized she'd made a dangerous mistake. With razor-sharp focus via her enhanced senses, Black Fox's perception of time slowed to a crawl. She pushed past all the other noises and heard the crisp sound of a gun's trigger being pulled back by one of the still-conscious thugs. Instantly, she determined the man's target by the proximity and position of the gun. With no time to explain and fueled by adrenaline and fear for her son's life, Black Fox propelled herself into Shadow with all her might. She fully intended to shield him by taking a shot in the abdomen or chest.

But then the bullet stopped in mid-air. Black Fox and Shadow tumbled out of its range and slammed hard against a parked truck. Black Fox took the brunt of the impact in her back and injured shoulder. The blinding pain knocked her unconscious.

———————

Shadow pointed at the younger man and both the gun and his hand were wrapped in the shadows from the ground, squeezed so tight he was unable to fire. More shadows wrapped around his legs and held him in place.

"Are you alright?" a young woman's voice shouted.

Shadow turned towards the voice. It belonged to the most beautiful-looking woman he'd ever seen. Wearing ordinary clothes, she was close in age to him. But she had glowing eyes made of flame.

"I'm fine but my—but Black Fox is injured," he replied.

"You're Black Fox and Shadow?" she exclaimed, amazed.

"Yes," Shadow answered.

"Whoa," the woman breathed the word.

"Thanks for the save," Shadow said warmly. "I haven't seen you before. You're a T.K. Very cool."

"A what?"

"T.K. You're a telekinetic. You move things with your thoughts."

"Yeah."

"Shouldn't we call an ambulance for Black Fox?"

"Not necessary," Shadow added. "She heals very fast. She'll be up in a few minutes and you'd never know she was hurt."

"You mean she really has powers? It's not the suit?" The woman looked down at Black Fox.

"It's a bit complicated. But the suit's just to hide her identity. She really is part-fox."

"Incredible. She's your mom, isn't she?"

Shadow nodded in agreement. "Don't tell anybody."

Shadow couldn't help staring at her. And she noticed.

"What's so interesting?" she asked.

"Sorry," he answered. "I've just never seen anyone with those before."

"Those? What are you talking about?"

"Your horns."

She just stared at Shadow in confusion for a solid ten seconds.

"Pardon me?" she asked.

"You know, your horns?" Shadow pointed at her head.

He watched her reach up towards her head with both hands and touch solid bone extending about one-inch wide and six inches tall, right above the left and right sides of her hairline, just above her forehead. They curved back to follow the contours of her skull. Her eyes widened.

"You didn't know?" Shadow realized. "I'm sorry."

"This—how'm I gonna deal with this? I'm a total freak now! I look like a demon!"

"Maybe you have control over the transformation," Shadow wondered. "While she's in Black Fox form, Mother has foxlike eyes and teeth. But she can revert to human form at will. Maybe you can make them disappear?"

Disappear? Okay, what've I got to lose? Horns, disappear!

Leia didn't feel any change to the bone horns. But she did feel an intense sensation of vertigo that sent her falling forwards.

When that feeling abated a couple of minutes later, Leia found herself in Shadow's arms while Black Fox was conscious and looking at her with deep concern. A few onlookers had located the source of all of the excitement but they wisely kept their distance.

"Leia?" Black Fox asked.

"You know me?" Leia replied, groggily.

"I'm a friend of your parents. Are you alright?"

"Did it work?"

"What?" Black Fox apparently had no idea what Leia was talking about.

"The horns," Shadow interjected.

"They're still there," Black Fox replied. "I take it you were trying to make them go away?"

Leia nodded. "I feel kinda sick," she added. "I guess I overexerted myself."

"We'll get you back to our place after we turn these criminals over to the authorities," Black Fox sympathized. "I think we need to run some tests and make sure you're alright."

"What . . . what did they do?" Leia asked.

"They murdered two people as part of their gang initiation," Black Fox answered. "Thanks to you, they can answer for their crimes."

An hour later, Leia was lying down on a couch in Black Fox's personal residence, a house several miles from where they'd met. Shadow had carried Leia, following Black Fox to their van. Shadow resumed human form and drove their vehicle home while his mother stayed with Leia in the back seat. During the drive, she had felt her new horns become smaller and now they were just one-inch tall stubs.

Leia's right arm was sore where Black Fox had drawn blood twenty minutes earlier.

Between all four blood draws, the urine test, and this persistent wooziness, this has turned into one rotten night. And who has a full biochemical lab in the middle of their house? Oh, yeah, a superhero. Duh.

Shadow walked in. He was wearing a blue t-shirt, jeans and tennis shoes. From what Leia could see, the rest of the house looked normal. She had seen at least three bedrooms on the way to the living room area. Most of the one-story house was painted either off-white or tan and the carpeting was deep brown. The kitchen had a wooden floor. Leia had been surprised to see a few pictures of Uncle John on one of the walls.

Black Fox knows my parents and Uncle John? That can't be a coincidence. Who is she?

"Are you feeling any better, Leia? Can I get you some water or something?" Shadow asked.

"No thanks," Leia replied. "I don't think I'm up for anything right now."

"How about some company then?"

He seems so normal now. And he's sweet.

"Is Shadow your real name?"

"No. My name is Dane."

"That's a good name, I like it," Leia said. "So . . . you're mixed?"

"Yeah, my dad's white," Dane said.

She nodded. Then she considered something else.

"He's a superhero, too?" Leia asked.

"He was a superhero, yeah," Dane replied.

"Was?"

"He's dead. He died protecting my mother and her teammates."

"Oh! I'm so sorry."

"I guess you could say he saved me, too," Dane added. "Neither of them knew I was along for the ride at the time."

Black Fox walked in. She was still in costume but she'd removed her mask and resumed human form. She looked tired but she tried to smile. At last, Leia recognized her.

"Aunt Dana? You're Black Fox?"

"Hi Leia. I'm glad you remember me. It's been a long time."

Leia's memories flashed back to her childhood momentarily.

"I was seven, I think. You mean the boy with you, the one I played with back then, that was Dane?"

"Yes," Dana replied, smiling widely now. Then she looked down and her smile faded.

"What's wrong?" Leia asked.

"I'm sorry, I just don't know a good way to tell you this," Dana added.

"What, am I dying or something?" Leia wasn't sure whether to be reassured or insulted when Dana briefly looked amused.

"No, nothing like that," Dana chuckled.

"Okay, well, what is it then?"

Leia looked to Dane when his mother didn't answer right away. Dane shrugged innocently.

"Leia, you're three months pregnant."

"What?" Leia suddenly felt faint, her mouth hanging open.

Several seconds passed as Leia replayed the words "you're three months pregnant" in her mind at least a dozen times.

"You really didn't know, did you?" Dana continued. "I didn't think so. You wouldn't have put yourself in danger otherwise."

"You're sure about this?" Leia replied timidly.

"I was as surprised as you. Your symptoms raised a flag with me, so I wanted to eliminate that as a possibility except I couldn't. I ran both the urine and blood tests and then used some rather sophisticated scanning equipment. There's no doubt."

"He's going to be a part of your life from now on," Leia remembered the voice's words in her thoughts again.

"She knew!" Leia blurted out.

"What?" Dana asked. "Who knew? What are you talking about?"

"Ever since the first night that I used my powers, there's been this voice in my head, a woman," Leia clarified.

"Go on, please," Dana urged cautiously.

"She's helped me a whole lot since then but she's kinda scary, too. And she told me that my boyfriend was going to be a part of my life from now on, so—"

Leia's eyes widened as she looked down at her belly and placed both hands on it.

"Waitasecond! I'm gonna have a baby?" she realized. "There's a kid in there? I'm—I'm gonna be a mom?"

Leia covered her eyes with her hands and leaned back on the couch.

Well, I guess I can't put off telling them about me and Josh anymore.

"Dane, will you go make us some tea?" Dana asked.

Dane left the room and Dana pulled a chair to the couch and sat down next to Leia.

We were supposed to finish college, get married and then have kids. Not the other way around!?

"Don't worry, it's not the end of the world," Dana said. "I know from experience, you can have a healthy baby and make the rest of your life come together."

"My life has been a complete mess lately," Leia replied. "This is just . . . icing on the cake."

"You have wonderful parents, they'll help support you," Dana reassured. "So will I. And the father—"

Hey, Josh! Good news, I've got super powers, I look like a demon, and I'm having your baby! Wanna get married?

Leia laughed at the thought. Then she closed her eyes and sighed.

"He'll probably be happy," Leia added. "We love each other."

"That's good. So, what's the problem?" Dana asked.

"He doesn't know about my powers. He saw a manifestation of them, but I think she made him forget it."

"She—that voice? She's a telepath then?"

Leia nodded. The woman behind the voice still scared her.

"A very powerful telepath," Leia replied. "She erased or changed the memories of everyone who saw me use my powers that night."

"Oh my!" Dana cast her eyes heavenward, then stood and paced the floor.

"What? You act like you know her?" Leia added.

"If she's who I think she is, then I do. And that's very, very bad."

"Why?"

"She's an extremely dangerous and psychotic woman, what we'd call a supervillain. Her name is Malevolence."

Just the mention of that name sent a chill down Leia's spine.

"Why would she even know me, much less be helping me?" Leia asked.

"I can tell you why," Dana replied. "But you won't like it."

"Just tell me, Aunt Dana. I need to know!"

"She's your biological mother."

5

DANE FOX WALKED INTO THE kitchen, put fresh water in the kettle and began heating it on the stove. Then he leaned against the nearest counter.

He knew that Mother wanted to talk to Leia alone. He figured that made sense. Still, he wished he could be of more help than just making tea that they probably wouldn't end up drinking.

Dane sighed.

It was frustrating, knowing that Leia had a boyfriend already and that she was pregnant with his child. He chided himself for thinking he'd ever had a chance with her romantically. After all, they hadn't seen each other since they were kids. But she had become such a beautiful woman! And he thought she looked amazing when she used her powers. He had hoped for the possibility, since they knew each other, and both had powers.

Dane looked out the kitchen window into the moonlit sky.

The memory was still so vivid. Fourteen-year-old Dane had just motioned with his hands and made the shadows on the wall leap into the air and obey his will. He even made them dance across his skin and obscure his identity before he made them return to the wall.

He had never seen his mother so shocked, but that fear had rapidly transitioned into joy. "Your degree of control is incredible, Dane! When did you realize you could do this?"

42

"Um, I first noticed the shadows respond about a year ago, but I thought my mind was playing tricks on me, so I didn't make a big deal out of it," Dane had replied. "Not too long after that, I started sensing the shadows. Then I imagined ways I could shape them, just in my thoughts, and it happened for real."

"Why didn't you tell me till now? I'm not upset or anything, but I am confused," Mother had wondered.

"I wanted to make sure I could control it first." Dane had answered. "And . . . I wanted to impress you."

Mother pulled him into a hug.

"I am very impressed! How could I not be? My precious son, you have an incredible gift—power over shadows and maybe even light itself. And you've learned to control it on your own, in a year? You have a very disciplined mind, just like your father."

"Do you think he'd be proud, too?" Dane had asked.

Mother withdrew some from the hug, her hands resting on her son's shoulders.

"Yes, he certainly would be proud, and he'd tell you as much. Then he'd proceed to give you his theory about how your power worked."

Mother gave a slight chuckle and her smile made Dane think she was reliving memories of her time with Dad.

"And about fifteen minutes later, you might wish you hadn't told him anything," she had continued. "But he had his charms, much as you do."

"Mother, I'd always imagined that one day I'd have powers like yours—fox powers," Dane had said. "Is any part of you disappointed that I'm . . . different?"

Mother's expression subtly shifted, becoming more thoughtful, as she considered her son's words.

"Disappointed? No. A little surprised? Maybe. But as strange as this may sound, you're young. You may develop werefox traits later in your life . . . or you may not."

"Mother, is it—no, nevermind," he had said, looking down.

"What is it?" Dana had asked, concerned.

"Well . . . with these powers—or powers like yours, how is it possible to have a normal life? I want to fall in love someday . . . maybe get married, have a family. Is that possible?"

He saw his mother wrinkle her nose in discomfort when he said "get married," then she calmed her reaction. Dane knew she disliked marriage but he had never asked her why. At the same time, he wanted to be honest about his feelings and aspirations in life.

"Listen to me carefully, Dane. Having powers, whether my type or yours, doesn't make you any less human. What you want is normal and yes, it is possible!"

"But?"

Mother had smiled at that.

"But you will have to take precautions," she had continued. "When you fall in love—and you will fall in love—it would be better to find someone who also has powers. If they don't have powers, they'll have to be a special person to accept and love you, despite your gifts."

"You mean, if I become a superhero like you?"

"It would be irresponsible not to use your abilities to help the world," she had replied, nodding. "But I'll train you myself and I won't go easy on you. I won't let you go solo until I'm sure you're ready."

"I understand."

"Your training will take a long time because I won't have it interfere with your school or other parts of your life. And in the meantime, you can't tell anyone about your powers. Do you understand me, Dane?"

"Yes, Mother."

The high-pitched whine of the kettle startled Dane out of his reverie. He walked over to the stove and turned off the burner. Then he poured the bubbling hot water into two mugs, inserting one tea bag in each so they could steep.

His cell phone made the sound of an arrow hitting a target, his notification for receiving a new text. He took the phone out of his pocket. It was MaidenPerth contacting him via his internet nickname of ShaDo3.

MaidenPerth: U bizy?

ShaDo3: kinda. wzup?

MaidenPerth: Need team 4 WB9K.

ShaDo3: can it wait? need 2 do smthing.

MaidenPerth: how long?

ShaDo3: An hour?

MaidenPerth: ...

MaidenPerth: ok. but only 4 u. don't b late!

ShaDo3: ok

MaidenPerth was a twenty-five-year-old woman named Amanda Franklin. As her nickname suggested, she lived in Perth, Australia. She and Dane had met through a Massive Multiplayer Online Role-Playing Game (MMORPG) called "War Blades 9000" and used a visual chat client in combination with the game.

Amanda was tall and curvy, fair-skinned with freckles and red hair. Dane enjoyed Amanda's forthrightness and quirky sense of humor.

They were both attending college. However, neither of them had any plans to leave their countries to meet in person. This arrangement gave them the illusion of a relationship without any real consequences. The only downside was the same as the advantage: there was no chance of this relationship progressing beyond what it was.

Dane looked at the kettle and the steeping tea in the cups. He listened to Leia and his mother talking in the other room.

How could I consider falling for Leia so easily? If she were available and interested, would that be "cheating" on Amanda? I—I didn't even think about Amanda once I saw Leia—it was like I was in a dream.

He'd believed that Leia could better understand him because she had powers. That chance for a real relationship, according to the standards Mother had set, made him forget about everything and everyone else. He wanted someone he could love and who could love him back, someone he could build a future with. Someone with powers.

But how realistic is that? Leia isn't available.

He knew he needed to let go of any romantic inclinations he had towards her. However, that wouldn't be easy. He thought she was an incredible young woman.

The talking in the other room stopped. Dane decided that it was an opportune time to go back in there with the tea.

"Dane, thanks for making the tea but I need you to walk Leia home."

"Of course, Mother," Dane replied, setting down the cups on the counter.

Dane stood at the door as Mother gave Leia a gentle hug. He sympathized with how stunned and bewildered she seemed. Her walk was slightly unsteady, so he was ready to assist her if needed. He opened the door for her and assured Mother of her safety with one look. Even so, he didn't need to look back to know she was still watching him and Leia.

———————

Fifteen minutes later, Dane and Leia were within sight of the Hamilton residence. He glanced at her every so often.

"Thanks for doing this, Dane. I didn't think I was okay enough to walk home alone."

"Oh, it's my pleasure," he replied. "You've had to take in a lot tonight."

You think? I don't have to be a telepath to figure out that he likes me. Should I be flattered or disturbed? Think I'll go with flattered. But I don't want him to get the wrong idea.

The well-lit neighborhood was relatively new in Digby, probably less than five years old. There were new-looking vehicles in the driveways and children's toys, wading pools and bicycles in the yards. It was an upper middle-class area. At one house, a middle-aged white man watered his yard while talking with his teenaged son. A thirty-something Asian man and woman in matching blue outfits ran by. A twenty-something African-American man with his long, straightened hair tied back in a ponytail worked at repairing his SUV while his Hispanic wife sat in a chair on their porch talking with him and paying attention to their newborn child.

"This is gonna change everything," Leia said, looking down at her stomach. "Having a kid."

Dane kept walking beside her, but he was silent. The temperature had dropped some since the sun set. However, the breeze was still warm.

"Do you think your mom is gonna tell my folks?" Leia looked at Dane.

"No, she'll let you do it," Dane replied. "But she'll call them or stop by tomorrow to make sure."

"Ah, she's that kind of mom. I imagine you didn't get away with a whole lot."

Dane looked down as they walked, a self-conscious smile crossing his face.

"That's an understatement," he answered. "After what happened to Dad, you could say she was very protective of me."

"Mind telling me what happened?" Leia asked.

"No, I don't mind. Mother was part of a team of superheroes called The AR-MEN. They had a headquarters that my dad and—the team leader constructed out of an asteroid. My dad was a scientific genius who developed a lot of revolutionary tech for the team. High speed shuttles, advanced armor, a teleporter system—"

Leia's eyes widened, both in amazement and curiosity.

"Seriously? A real teleporter?" she blurted. "Like, one second you're on Earth and another, you're in space?"

"It took more than a second, from what Mother told me. But yeah, that's basically how it worked."

Leia noticed Dane's contemplative silence. He looked sad.

"One of their most powerful enemies attacked them on the station," he shared. "His name was Killer Knight. Insanely strong, invulnerable and a tactical guru. He damaged key systems to trap everyone on the satellite. Then he knocked out Crusader, the leader, and was going to kill Mother and two other heroines, Medsnake and Flamia. But Dad flew into him at full speed in his armor and took him into another part of the satellite."

Dane choked on that last word. Leia pulled him into a friendly hug.

"I'm sorry, Dane. I shouldn't have asked."

"No, I want you to know."

"Why?"

"With our lifestyle, I don't make many friends. And I want to be your friend . . . again."

Leia hugged him more tightly. A tear ran down her right cheek.

"I could use a friend like you right now," she said. "One who knows I have super powers, an evil super-bio-mother and a baby on the way. No secrets."

"No secrets," Dane agreed. "And thanks."

They walked for about a block without saying anything.

"Dad took Killer Knight away from the rest of the team into a very damaged portion of the satellite," Dane continued. "He remotely fixed the teleporter and sent Mother, Crusader, and the others back to Earth. Then, Dad self-destructed the whole satellite with a series of nuclear charges. Neither of them survived."

"A hero," Leia said, with tears in her eyes. "Your dad's such a hero!"

"Yeah," Dane considered, forcing a smile.

Leia was grateful that Dane waited for a moment outside as she walked up to her front door. She tried to wipe away her tears but didn't quite succeed. She looked back at him and smiled, silently thanking him.

6

AT THE HAMILTON'S HOUSE, THE living room was bright with lamp light. The muted-blue walls, in combination with the illumination, provided a calming feel. A flat screen television was mounted on the wall by the stereo system. The kitchen and dining areas were dark but the aromas of cooked meatloaf, buttered corn, dinner rolls and something sweet, like a freshly baked pie, filled the room. The air conditioner was keeping the house well-cooled, the way Sue preferred. She had been trying to relax on the sofa but stood up when her husband entered the room.

"Is everything okay?" Steve asked.

"I'm worried about her, Steve," Sue replied. "Something happened yesterday but she won't talk about it."

"She's always kept to herself, ever since she was a teenager."

"Earlier than that, actually. But this is different. She's scared."

Sue watched her husband hang up his jacket in the closet, remove his tie and unfasten his shirt's top button. She knew he was taking time to consider her words.

"What makes you think she's scared about something?" he wondered aloud.

Standing in front of her, Steve gently ran his right hand through her long hair. She craved his attention but didn't want to change the topic.

"She smells scared," she continued. "And, though I'm not sure, I think I picked up another very familiar scent on her. It's faint—"

She watched his tender and loving expression solidify into that of a battle-hardened soldier. Standing at more than six feet tall, her husband possessed an intimidating musculature, even softened by two decades of marriage. To her, the only signs that he was no longer that warrior was the beginnings of a belly, a roundness to his jawline plus the work clothes he was wearing. He looked into her eyes as though he already knew her answer to his next question.

"Whose scent?" he asked.

Sue sighed. "I can't be one hundred percent certain, but it really smells like . . . Leia's mother."

"How recent?"

Sue narrowed her gaze at Steve.

"You know what I'd have to do to find out," she said. "And you know the risk if I do."

"Yes, but we have to know, right?"

"Let me try something else first. I think Leia will open up to me if I ask the right questions."

"Okay. Given the risks, I guess that's a good alternative. Whatever that woman wants with Leia can't be good."

Sue considered several possibilities and felt tension building in her temples. She massaged them lightly with her fingertips.

"I can't believe I'm about to say this," she interjected. "But . . . what if she just wants a relationship with her daughter?"

Steve closed his eyes and laughed but there was no humor in his voice. When he opened his eyes again, they looked haunted.

"After all these years keeping her distance . . . " he responded.

He rubbed his eyes. Seeing his distress, Sue hugged him warmly from behind and leaned her head against his back. She felt him start to relax but then he tensed up more than before.

"Do you honestly think that murdering psychopath will just sit down with us, have tea, and talk out our issues?" Steve asserted, bitterly. "Do you think she'll work with us towards a mutually beneficial arrangement?"

"Of course not. I . . . look, we're not the same people we were back when you were dating her. We've settled down, raised a family. We can't charge into battle like we used to."

"I know. But I'm not going to let her take and twist Leia into something she's not, something horrible."

"And how would you stop her, Steve? She's probably the strongest telepath in the world. How do you know she's not already in contact with Leia?"

That notion seemed to rattle Steve. He walked away from her for a moment. She figured he was trying to regain his composure. She walked up to Steve and faced him. Sue put her right hand to his left cheek and looked at him. Her touch and presence comforted him.

"This fight isn't going to be won by brute strength, Steve. It's going to be won in Leia's heart. You wanted your daughter when that woman didn't. And somehow, you convinced her mother to go through with the pregnancy. You saved Leia's life. Then you brought Leia into your home, showed her love and helped her become the young adult she is now."

"I couldn't have done it alone. I asked my nineteen-year old girlfriend to become a wife and mother at the same time, to raise another woman's child. And for reasons that still escape me, you said yes."

She took his hands in hers and put them over her heart. She hoped her eyes projected her love and compassion at him the way she was feeling it.

"I saw the man I love accept responsibility for a child he hadn't planned," she answered. "How could I not do everything I could to help you? Besides, Leia's a great kid."

"I asked you to give up a lot."

"I'll let you in on a little secret, mister. Modeling pays well but there's a lot of downsides to being someone else's clothes hanger. Plus, my 'other career' fighting crime would have either cost me my job or my life eventually. In comparison, being your wife and raising your kids . . . I can't even tell you how rewarding that's been. That's why I feel confident enough to talk to Leia about this."

Steve put his right hand to the left side of Sue's face and brushed back her hair. Then he smiled.

"This is the first time I've thought about her in years," Steve said. "I guess I let it get to me."

"I think you're allowed that," she replied. "But you don't have to stay that way. Everything will work out, you know."

"Yeah, I do know. I don't miss it, that life, anymore."

"Me, either. Always in danger, getting hurt. Losing people."

Steve closed his eyes. Sue knew the distant, hurt look on his face well.

"Losing John was the worst. I thought I was going to lose my mind, too."

"You almost did. If you'd have remained a superhero, there wouldn't have been much difference between you and the ones you were fighting."

"I'm just glad your mother was able to get through to you," Steve added.

"You mean she offered sanity when our lives were falling apart," Sue considered with a nod. "She was a good witness for Christ."

"And you were a good witness to me. I was able to put down my sun saber and focus on what's more important. By accepting Jesus, I didn't lose anything. Instead, that decision really gave our marriage, and parenting, what we needed to succeed."

"Twenty years next month would seem to back you up on that," Sue said with a smile.

———————

All talking abruptly ceased as Leia entered the living room. Leia could see that her father was pleased that she was safe and Mom looked concerned.

Just then, a wave of dizziness washed over Leia and she felt like she was going to fall again. No sooner had she blinked than Mom was there helping her, steadying her.

"I've got you, Leia," Mom soothed. "Just relax."

"How'd you do that?" Leia asked.

"Later. Let's get you—"

As Leia's position shifted, so did her hair.

"—horns?" Sue wondered.

"You like 'em? They just showed up tonight," Leia added woozily.

Leia then threw up on the floor. Reacting automatically as a parental team, Dad went to get something to clean up the mess and Mom helped Leia to the bathroom.

Leia's sister, Tanya, came downstairs to see what was going on. Tanya was about eight inches shorter than Leia and thirty pounds heavier. In many ways, she looked like a thinner version of Mom at fifteen years old. She was wearing blue jeans and a white t-shirt. Her long brown hair flowed over her shoulders. Tanya didn't say anything but she obviously wanted to help.

Tanya followed her mother and sister to the bathroom. It took about ten minutes for Leia's nausea to relent.

"You're pregnant," Mom declared. "And Josh is the father?"

Leia nodded, unsure what else to say.

"How long have you known? Does he know?"

"I only found out tonight, so Josh doesn't know yet. Aun--Black Fox ran some tests on me and verified it."

"How did you meet Black Fox?" Mom asked, concerned but otherwise unfazed. "And why did she run tests on you?"

"I was on my way home from work and they were in trouble," Leia said. "I . . . helped her—and Shadow."

"You helped *them*—how?"

"Shadow says I'm a telekinetic. I stopped a bullet from hitting Black Fox while she was saving him."

"A telekinetic," Mom repeated.

Leia fought the nausea and looked up at Mom curiously.

"You're not very surprised to hear this . . . are you?"

"We're kind of overdue to talk about this subject."

Then Mom closed her eyes and concentrated. Seconds later, feline ears emerged from her hairline at about the same positions as Leia's horns. When Mom opened her eyes, they were also cat-like, and light brown fur had begun to rapidly grow on her face and arms. A thick and bushy light brown tail began to sway behind her.

"I used to be a superhero called The Cat," Mom clarified. "That's how I met your father."

Tanya's jaw was wide open in amazement as she beheld her mother in this altered state. Equally stunned, a realization dawned on Leia.

"Does—does Dad have powers, too?" Leia asked.

"Yes."

"Then why is my biological mom a supervillain? Black Fox—Aunt Dana told me."

"Dana never was one for subtlety," Mom sighed. "But maybe it's best to finally deal with this. You deserve to hear that bit of history from your father."

Then Mom concentrated again and reverted to her former appearance.

———

Minutes later, in the living room and facing his daughters, Steve Hamilton's thoughts were twenty-one years in the past on a day when the wind was blowing particularly hard. Then again, at the time, he was fifteen stories in the air and hovering between buildings. So was she.

He was wearing his Crusader costume, a dark blue, form-fitting sleeveless top with light yellow gloves that covered half his forearms. He also wore a black belt and blue leggings with black and white boots. But the signature piece of his costume was his tan-colored, face-covering mask which rose to pointed tips like dull horns on each side, with sideways triangles for eye holes.

She was wearing a sleeveless black evening dress that hugged her curves while her skirt flowed with the wind. She didn't see the need to wear a mask.

"I came alone, like you asked," Crusader said. "Angela, is that you?"

"Angela was the weakling you had no use for, outside of your bed," the woman said scornfully. "I am what she bloomed into. I am Malevolence!"

Physically, Malevolence looked enough like Angela, about a foot shorter than Steve with a pear-shaped build. But her normally long black hair had unnatural, glowing red highlights and her eyes were also glowing and pupil-less. Her thin lips were covered in blood-red lipstick and Angela's gentle and happy expression had been replaced by one of spite and anger. Malevolence radiated raw telepathic power.

"What happened to you?" he asked. "And why Malevolence?"

"I am what you made me, Steven," Malevolence said. "It's funny, really. You valued that I was normal before, ordinary. But that was also the reason you ended our relationship after only a few weeks. Maybe you were right to. I wasn't strong enough to remain with you."

"What does that mean? I haven't seen you in months! I broke things off because I didn't want you to be targeted by my enemies. You just left without another word."

"As you can see, you no longer have to worry about me. I have powers of my own," Malevolence boasted. "I can now hear the thoughts of everyone within miles, should I wish. And I could bring these buildings down on top of you. You are strong, my once-love, but I have surpassed you!"

Then her confident look faltered. For a few seconds, she looked like the vulnerable and considerate woman Crusader had started falling in love with.

"But I need to discuss . . . an important matter with you," Malevolence continued.

"Alright," Crusader responded.

"I carry your child, Steven."

"What? Are you sure?"

"It was the creation of this child that led to the manifestation of my powers. The spark of biochemical activity caused by this pregnancy had the side-effect of igniting my latent abilities and supercharging them. I would thank you if the experience hadn't been so horrible. At first, I couldn't block out all the voices. So many voices, in my mind, all at once! I started to lose myself in the middle of all of them."

For a moment, he was speechless. What she was telling him was both extraordinary and overwhelming.

"I'm sorry," he replied. "I had no idea any of that could happen. And you're right . . . it's my fault."

"I had to reach within and find my true inner strength, tap into the power you had given me," Malevolence added. "And I did it, I silenced the other voices. I hear only the ones I wish to hear. And I have complete control over my telekinesis. All it took was becoming Malevolence."

Crusader felt a compassion and a sadness he'd never known in looking at his former girlfriend. He realized how huge the gap between them had become. And in that moment, he felt the tremendous loss of what they'd shared for such a brief time.

"Is that pity I feel from you, Steven? You know how I feel about people's pity!"

"No, not pity. Guilt."

"It's too late for guilt. You should get over that as I have my past life. Let's talk about what's important."

He nodded. "The child."

"Yes. Personally, I have no use for a child. I have other plans. But I have no antipathy towards her, either."

"Her? It's a girl?"

"Yes."

Crusader's thoughts were racing, trying to find a solution to this crisis. Then he had an idea.

"Alright, Malevolence, I'll make you a deal, one that I think we can all live with."

"A deal? What do you have to offer me?"

"If you take this child to term and give birth to her, I'll keep her and raise her. I'll also support and help you through the pregnancy."

"You think you can raise a baby, Steven? Do you have any experience with children?".

"I think I'll do whatever I have to. I don't have any experience with other people's kids but this is mine."

She half-smiled, but he could see the skepticism behind it.

"Admirable but a bit naïve," she scoffed. "You can't do this alone."

"I won't be alone," he replied.

She raised an eyebrow at that.

"Once—no, *if* I have this child, I will not raise her with you."

"I didn't mean you."

Malevolence stared at Crusader for a moment.

"I see! You're bedding Cat now," Malevolence said. "Trying for a litter?"

Crusader was not amused. But he said nothing. Malevolence sighed.

"Oh, lighten up, Crusader, it's a joke. But can she raise my child?"

"I don't know, I'll have to ask for her help. But I think she will."

"You're taking a pretty huge gamble over a baby you just learned about. Most guys would be happy to be rid of the problem, but you're not. Why?"

"She's our child and I want her, more than anything."

Although Malevolence didn't respond verbally, she was visibly touched by the sentiment. "I'm going to need just a little more convincing, Steven. Is there anything more you can bring to the table, so to speak?"

Crusader concentrated briefly, pained by his stress but determined to resolve this. Once he reached a decision, he looked up at Malevolence.

"After the pregnancy . . . after you've given me this daughter . . . if you go away and create a new life for yourself, avoid criminal activity . . . then I'll overlook the crimes you've committed as Malevolence and let you go free. You'll have a clean slate."

Malevolence took a few minutes to consider Crusader's offer in silence.

"Very well, I accept your terms, Steven. Congratulations. You're going to be a father!"

In the present, Leia Hamilton stared at her father in amazement. "She had changed so much, yet you somehow reached her and convinced her to have me. I really had no idea!"

"You were that important to me. And somehow, deep down, I knew she was sincere. She didn't want to harm you. I just gave her reasons not to."

"You fought for me, even though it wasn't a physical fight. That means a lot to me."

"Sue fought for you, too. She was younger than you when I asked her to marry me and help raise you."

Leia looked at Mom with surprise. She nodded in acknowledgment of what her husband had said. Leia hugged her to show her gratitude. Then Leia looked back at her father.

"You said Malevolence's real name was Angela. What was her last name?"

"Merrick."

Leia was utterly stunned. "You mean Professor Merrick is my biological mother??"

"Professor? She works at Digby College?"

"She's my statistics professor! I've always called her 'Professor Doom' because she gives off this . . . air. No wonder she paid such attention to me!"

"I think she's been keeping an eye on me, even protecting me," Leia said. "Maybe all of my life!"

7

JOSH MANNING WAS USED TO sleeping in most mornings. His first class was at noon. So, it was a surprise to be woken up by a gentle but persistent knocking on his apartment door instead of an alarm. He recognized the knocking style, too. It was Leia! He quickly stood up and grabbed a shirt and blue jeans.

"I'll be right there!"

Josh took a quick shot of mouthwash, spat it out in the sink, and ran his comb through his short hair. Then he walked over and answered the door with a smile.

"Leia! Is this more of your 'I don't want to be distant from you' campaign?" Josh said. "Because I—"

One look at Leia vanquished whatever else Josh was going to say. Her hair was a mess, she looked like she hadn't slept and wanted to cry. Instinctively, Josh just put his arms around her and held her. She held him back tightly. They didn't say anything for several minutes.

"Thanks," she offered. "You don't know just how much I needed that."

"I'm starting to get an idea," he replied. "C'mon in, you look like you need to sit down."

He turned on the lamp by the door and Leia sat down on his fold-out bed. Without thinking, she leaned forward and ran her hands through her hair.

"Are those bone hair clips?" he asked.

"Oh, forgot about those," She started to laugh but she stopped herself as they turned into sobs.

"What *happened* to you?" Josh wondered. "I've never seen you like this."

"Me, either. Sorry, I'm a little loopy. Didn't really sleep last night."

"Please, I want to help, Leia. Tell me what you can."

"I guess I'll start with the good news."

"I can handle good news. Tell me the good news."

"We're having a baby," Leia said, looking in his eyes.

"Whoa," Josh said. "Seriously? You're pregnant?"

"Three months. And I'm keeping it."

Josh looked deeply into Leia's eyes. He could see so much in them, so much she wanted to tell him.

"I'm going to fight for this kid, like Dad did for me," Leia said. "No matter what happens."

There were so many layers of emotional pain and longing to this woman he loved. It was nearly overwhelming to see her like this but it also brought out Josh's protective side.

"Then I'll fight alongside you," Josh said. "We'll make this work."

"Don't say that. You don't know everything about me yet."

"What do I need to know? I love you and you're having my kid. We'll get married and—"

"Josh, stop. Nothing would make me happier than to be your wife, but you need to know what you're getting into."

"I do? I've spent practically every day with you since we were kids. I know your moods, your likes, your dislikes, your fears—"

He watched as Leia concentrated, causing horns to grow from her head. In seconds, they extended upward by a foot, becoming two inches thick and c-shaped on each side, forming sharp tips at their ends. Her eyes became flame. Josh gasped and held his breath as she transformed.

"When I asked you about super powers, there was a reason," Leia admitted. "Look, I'm not a demon or anything. I'm human like you. But I have these powers."

He didn't know what to expect next as Leia gestured at yesterday's newspaper sitting on a table near them. His jaw dropped as she lifted her hand and at the same time, the periodical floated upward, matching her movements. Somehow, she was doing this with her mind.

He was relieved when Leia stood up and her eyes returned to normal. She picked up his metal world globe and began spinning it between her hands out of nervousness.

"I inherited this. I found out that both of my parents have powers, too," she continued. "And our child will have half of my genes, so he or she may have powers someday. None of this manifested in me until a few days ago."

Josh struggled to comprehend the magnitude of what Leia had just shared with him. It would be unbelievable if he hadn't witnessed it with his own eyes. And yet, she was the woman he loved, the one who meant everything to him. No matter how strange or frightening these powers of hers were, they weren't her fault, they were a part of her. And they didn't change the fact that she loved him, too. Her actions showed that she didn't want to hide this from him. They also revealed that she didn't want to hide this pregnancy or anything else from him. He knew she had come to him for help and understanding.

How could he turn her away? That wasn't possible.

"Whew! That's a whole lot you had dropped on you. And then you're pregnant, too."

Josh could see how tense and nervous Leia was. As she gripped the globe more tightly between both hands, she effortlessly crunched it like an accordion. Josh's mouth dropped open again.

"Um, looks like I'm really strong, too?" Leia said, sheepishly.

He searched for something to say to alleviate her embarrassment and awkwardness.

"I see that," he broached. "I've always wanted an art piece. Now I have one."

"I'm gonna have to get a handle on these powers fast," Leia dropped the globe. "If that had been you in my arms . . . I don't know what I'd do."

The imagery had the desired impact. They both stared at the crushed globe for several seconds in abject silence.

"You will get control of these . . . these gifts you have, Leia. You'll fight for it and you'll win."

"Why do you believe in me so much?" she asked.

"Do you even need to ask?" Josh took her into his arms.

"No. I guess I don't."

———————

Leia felt hope for the first time since learning about her pregnancy and her mother's identity. She was brimming with love for Josh.

"We'll just have to imagine the ring," he suggested.

"What?"

Is he about to—he's not—?

"Leia Cassandra Hamilton, will you marry me?"

In her heart, she swooned. But the reality of their circumstances did not elude her, either.

Nah, I'm gonna kick the father of my child to the curb. What do you think I'm gonna say, cowboy?

"Absolutely," she responded.

She grinned as he did a self-congratulatory fist pump.

"Alright!" he continued. "So, which parents do you wanna tell first?"

"My folks already know about the baby, and our engagement won't be a surprise to them. We'd better tell your folks."

He nodded. "Okay, that's cool. I just gotta ask one thing first."

"Anything."

"Can you make your horns go back down again?"

Suddenly self-conscious again, she put her hand to one of her horns. Abashed, she looked up at him with a lopsided smile.

"Oh yeah, I look . . . pretty bad right now, don't I?" she asked.

"Well, I'm not exactly in top form myself," he conceded. "Let's do a little fashion damage control before we give my parents a coronary."

"Deal!"

Soon, Leia reverted her horns to their smaller size. Presently, she was working on her hair in Josh's bathroom. Josh had taken a short shower and changed clothes. He was munching on some warmed-up toaster pastries and watching a game show in the living room.

Alright, "Professor." I think it's time we had a chat on my terms.

"Hello, Leia," Malevolence answered.

You're enjoying all of this, aren't you?

"Not all of it. I don't enjoy your suffering. But as I tried to warn you, life isn't always what we want it to be."

Why all the mystery? Why not just tell me you're my biological mother? Why pretend to be my professor and all that?

"As you surmised, I've been watching you ever since I gave you to your father. And I've protected you all this time."

Leia stiffened at that revelation.

Protected me? How?

"Do you remember in fourth grade when that little barbarian came after you with a chain?"

He swung too hard and hit himself in the head with it!

"He didn't swing too hard, I gave it a push. He could have seriously injured you."

Leia was stunned. Her mouth gaped.

He was in a coma for a week! I think he got brain damage.

"That would require having a brain, dear."

Leia could feel her temper flaring at Malevolence's insensitivity.

That's not funny! He was just a kid!

"And you're my daughter. Anyone who seriously threatens you deserves what they get."

Leia clenched her fists and her jaw, trying to restrain her ire.

I'm really starting to not like you.

"I don't need you to like me. And I'm not here to be your friend."

Why are *you here?*

"Do you remember three years ago, after you'd just learned to drive and that car side-swiped yours in the rain?"

Instinctively, Leia nodded.

We rolled once and came to a stop facing traffic. An eighteen-wheeler couldn't stop in time. If he hadn't made his truck jackknife, we'd have all died!

"He didn't have time to react. I caused the truck to jackknife."

Leia felt as if ice water had been thrown on her. A chill ran through her and ire turned to outrage.

I can't believe this! That man and the people in the car next to us died!

"But you survived. That's all that's important to me. I even saved your 'Mom' and little sister."

Thank you for that . . . but I wish it didn't come at such a high cost.

"Wishes are like greeting cards, Leia. They feel good but ultimately get thrown away."

Leia knew she had reached the limits of her patience.

Go away. Please.

"All right, Leia, I'll go. But I only came because you called."

Leia leaned forward and let her head rest against the bathroom mirror. Josh walked over, still holding a toaster pastry in his left hand.

"What is it?"

"I forgot to tell you something," Leia admitted. "My bio-mom is a super villain."

Josh blinked several times, taking in this latest revelation from Leia.

"Pop Tart?" Josh asked, offering Leia the toaster pastry.

8

"Did you really have to tell her so much, Dana?"

"Tell me the part she didn't need to know, Steve."

Across the room, Sue rolled her eyes. She could see where this was going.

"I'm going to make some coffee," Sue offered.

The kitchen seemed much more inviting than the living room. In fact, anywhere seemed more inviting than within listening distance of her two former teammates from The AR-MEN. And yet with her powers, she couldn't help but overhear them.

"Look, I understand what you were trying to do," Steve insisted. "But Leia's delicate right now."

"You think I don't know that?" Dana replied. "I performed the pregnancy tests. I saw the state of mind she was in. But she's not some flower. She's powerful! She saved Dane and me without a thought for herself."

"It's the 'without a thought for herself' part that worries me."

"Well, she can't help what she inherited, can she, Steve?"

Sue could picture Dana winking with that slight jibe to Steve.

"Anyway, now that she knows she's pregnant, I know she won't be asking to join me and Dane fighting crime," Dana continued. "So, what are you really worried about?"

There was a brief silence. Sue figured Steve was probably staring at Dana in frustration.

69

"I see. This is about Angela," Dana continued. "We need to find out what her plans are for Leia. Or at least find out where she's staying."

"We know she's a statistics professor at Digby," Steve added. "She's even using her real name."

"That's pretty bold of her. Oh, let me guess! She's *Leia's* statistics professor, right? And she's probably been in the background for quite a while."

"Yes."

"This complicates things," Dana said. "It means everything about Leia is personal to her. She'll be a lot more invested in how this turns out. And she'll be a lot more dangerous."

"My thoughts exactly," Steve agreed.

"Okay, thanks for the lead, Steve. I'll go check out Digby and see what turns up."

"You know she'll be expecting one of us," Steve shared. "She's probably been monitoring Leia's thoughts."

Sue walked out of the kitchen but didn't approach either her husband or Dana. She observed as Dana headed towards the door, turned and smiled at Steve. Her eyes were in fox-form and her teeth were feral.

"Yeah, but she's not infallible," Dana added. "The confident ones always leave clues and make mistakes. And I have my own . . . resources."

"Good hunting," Steve replied.

"Take care, Steve. Sue, I'll take a raincheck on the coffee."

Sue nodded at Dana, who exited the house. She made eye contact with her husband.

"You heard everything?" Steve asked.

Sue just looked at Steve with her hands on her hips.

"Right," he conceded. "Sorry."

"Are you sure that was a wise move?"

"Dana was going to go after Angela anyway. But she's less likely to go postal on a college campus while doing research on her target."

"You're not giving her enough credit, Steve. She hasn't stayed alive all these years as Black Fox by making rookie mistakes. She probably knows you're trying to protect her. Just like Angela knows you'll make a move now that you know she's here."

Steve tightened the fist he was making with his right hand. Sue put her arms around him and looked in his eyes.

"No offense, love, but you're not a superhero anymore. Your tactics are a little rusty."

"I was just trying to minimize the risk to Dana.".

"That's fine but all it does is delay the inevitable. You're not so rusty that you don't know what's coming. That's why you're so on-edge."

"Angela's coming to us," Steve realized. "And very soon."

"Very soon," Sue repeated.

"It's time to pray like never before, to protect Leia and show us what to do."

Sue saw the near-desperate mix of emotions in his eyes and body language. She took his hand and looked in his eyes. She nodded and smiled gently. When she saw him return her smile, she pulled him close.

———

Alyssa Manning looked pleased but confused. A real estate agent in her mid-fifties, her blond hair, woven flawlessly into a silky, thick bun, was liberally streaked with white, giving it an almost frosted appearance. She had big, bright green eyes behind small and thin wire-rimmed glasses, a long narrow nose and full lips painted candy red with lipstick. She was wearing a white blouse, light brown skirt and matching jacket.

When Josh had called her, she was in-between appointments showing houses to potential buyers. But despite her Type A personality, Alyssa was always willing to drop everything for her only child. So, she had rescheduled her afternoon appointments to make time to meet with Josh and Leia.

"You want to get married? Now?" she asked. "I know you two are close, that you love each other. But why the rush for marriage . . . unless . . . there's a baby?"

"There is," Josh admitted.

Alyssa looked over her glasses at Josh and then Leia, almost as if to see if they were playing a joke on her. When she could tell they were serious, she exhaled slowly. Alyssa smiled, gestured to Leia, and hugged her.

"I guess you decided you were ready, huh?" Alyssa whispered softly in Leia's ear. "That's okay. There's no one for my Josh but you. I've known that for a long time."

Alyssa pulled back a little but kept her hands on Leia's arms. She looked at Leia's belly.

"How far along are you?"

"Three months," Leia replied.

"Wow, you two—my first grandbaby! Josh, you have no idea what you're in for, son. But don't worry, Leia, between me and your mom, I think we can give you a pretty good idea what to expect."

"Thanks so much, Mrs. Manning."

"Uh-uh! You call me Alyssa from now on, Leia."

Alyssa noticed Josh walking over to a nearby window. She knew her son well. It looked like he was reacting to something he saw outside. But then he shrugged and joined her and Leia back in the living room.

———————

Black Fox crouched down, hiding between the bushes and the outer wall of the house. For now, she was content to simply wait and listen to Leia's and Alyssa Manning's conversation inside the house via her enhanced hearing. As the minutes passed, she looked down at the metal object resting in her gloved hand. Just seeing the device reminded her of when Silver Knight had given it to her twenty years ago.

That night, Dana Fox had watched as her boyfriend, John Covington, who was also Silver Knight, finished work on the last circuit board of the device. Seeing him work so intently, blocking out the rest of the world in order to concentrate, was often nerve-wracking. He wouldn't talk, eat or move from his workspace for hours at a time. She had learned to bring magazines or books to prevent complete boredom.

The metal warehouse they were in was surprisingly massive for how little was stored within it. She knew John liked his privacy and security. There had been only a handful of lights on. He had told her the rest were kept off to save on electricity. She'd noticed that he also hadn't done any decorating whatsoever. There had been four large work desks containing numerous diagnostic and other tools, several chairs, a small refrigerator and a microwave oven. A large box fan helped circulate air into the warehouse from outside and kept the temperature reasonable.

Finally, she had seen John place the cover onto the silver device, clicked a button on something Dana recognized as an electronics scanner and observed the readouts. Then he'd put both of the devices down, turned towards Dana and smiled.

"It's done!" John had said.

"Did you make a time machine? Because I want my two hours back, hon."

"Sorry about that. But when I tell you what this is, you'll thank me."

"That's a tall claim. Prove it."

"I made it for you, Dana, in case you ever have to face Malevolence one-on-one. This is a telepathic scrambler."

Dana had looked blankly at John for several seconds. "What? Why? Malevolence isn't a threat now, she's—"

"I know. She's having Steve's kid and living with him and Sue. *That's* gotta be a cheery living arrangement. I feel bad for Sue."

Dana had walked away from John, her arms folded, saddened.

"I know Angela changed a lot when her powers emerged, but I'm still having a hard time seeing her as a bloodthirsty killer."

"Tell that to the Marquez brothers. She used her telekinesis to crush every bone in their bodies simultaneously, just to make an example to other bosses in the area."

"That was before she made the deal with Steve. She was insane."

"Dana, she's still insane! I know she was your best friend for years and you think you know her but you don't. I faced her and I barely made it out of that confrontation alive."

She had watched as John walked right up to her and looked her in the eyes.

"I've known Angela for even longer than you. I love her like a sister. But the fact is, she's not Angela anymore. I don't know if Angela even exists in the madness that Malevolence occupies."

"Stop it, John," Dana had requested, clenching her fists.

"Malevolence is a monster, Dana. And she scares me."

"Stop!" Dana fought back tears. "I don't want to hear anymore."

A silent gulf filled the room between them for several minutes.

"Even if she's under control right now . . . let's say she honors Steve's deal and disappears after she has this kid. Do you think that's going to end her threat? She'll be back someday, just as powerful, if not *more* powerful. With this kid, she even has a reason to come back! All I've done is made insurance against that possibility. Maybe I'm wrong and she won't come back. That'd be great. But if she does, this is a way to stop her without killing her . . . which is more than she'd do for us."

"It won't kill her?"

"No. It should only disrupt her powers, as long as the field from this device is active. She won't be able to read thoughts or move objects with her mind. It would be like trying to concentrate during a bad headache, it's almost impossible. It might even knock her unconscious. But it won't kill her."

Black Fox cast away the memories and mentally reviewed what John had shown her about how to operate the device, which was surprisingly simple. She looked up to the bright afternoon sky for a moment.

John, I wish you hadn't been right. Malevolence has returned for her daughter just like you said she would.

Angela, even after all you've done and all that's come between us, I wish there was another way.

Just then, Black Fox sensed an energy in the air, almost electrical but not quite. Then it faded. Black Fox could feel her heart beating faster now but it was offset by a pang of anxiety.

This is one of those times I wish I had Steve and Sue—or even Sidra and Tina—for backup, in prime form like they were back then. Heck, I'd take 'em like they are right now! But that's not gonna happen, so I'd better just deal with it.

Black Fox sensed the energy once more. This time there was no doubt whose presence it was. She smiled savagely, anticipating her prey. Then the smile faded.

Dane, if all goes well, I'll see you tonight and we'll celebrate. If not, I'm glad I didn't bring you this time . . . and I hope you'll forgive me.

Josh wondered how long his mother and Leia would talk about pregnancy. To pass the time, since he had absolutely no point of reference for this discussion, he had started making a mental count of how many times they used the terms "baby," "pregnant," "pregnancy," "morning sickness" and "stretch marks." So far, the highest total was for "baby" with seventeen mentions, followed by "pregnant" with thirteen.

"The most important thing is to enjoy this time, Leia," his mom said. "Sure, you'll have nausea and mood swings and your body's going to change. But that's okay. It's all for your baby. I—"

A change came over his mom then. Her expression went blank for a few seconds. Then it was replaced by a hungry grin that revealed perfectly straight and polished white teeth. Her eyes, previously soft with maternal happiness and concern, became like glittering diamonds: beautiful yet hardened by time and heat.

"Hi Josh, I'm Angela, Leia's mother," his mom declared. "I thought it was time we met."

"Are you crazy?" Leia demanded of the woman. "What are you doing? Why did you take over his mom?"

"You didn't mind when I took over Professor Martinez and let you sob to your heart's content, did you?" his mother replied, her voice dripping in sarcasm.

"That was you?"

"What—what's going on?" Josh said, horrified. "What's happened to my mom?"

"Relax, kid," his mother snapped. "I'm not going to hurt your mom. I'm just projecting my thoughts through her mind and body. When I'm done, she won't remember any of this. Want me to get some refreshments, Leia? She keeps sodas in the fridge and a stash of those yummy fudge marshmallow cookies you like in the cabinet."

Josh looked at Leia, his mouth agape. He glanced from his mother to his fiancée and back, trying to comprehend what was going on. His mouth felt dry and a chill shot down his spine. The sweet mother he had always known never spoke so dismissively. Her eyes had never looked so cold or ferocious. As impossible as it seemed, the woman before him was no longer Mom and he had no idea why or what had changed.

"My biological mother is a *telepath*," Leia explained. "She can read people's thoughts or control their actions with her mind. So, Malevolence, what do you want?"

"Your bio-mom's name is Malevolence?"

"Supervillain, remember?"

"Does this ever get easier?" he asked.

"Who are you asking? My life was *normal* a week ago!"

The woman who was yet wasn't his mother reclaimed his attention by clearing her throat. Both he and Leia turned to look.

"Like I said, I thought Josh and I should talk," Malevolence said. "He's going to be your husband. He's the father of my grandchild."

"Fine," he replied. "What do you want to talk about, Ma'am?"

"Oh, don't worry about being formal with me. Angela is fine," Malevolence answered. "I wanted to tell you, I've been impressed with your loyalty to my daughter and the depth of your feelings for her. I also want you to know that I totally support this union between you two."

It was at that moment that a dark-skinned masked woman in black came crashing through the front window, armed with a flaming sword.

"Black Fox?" Leia shouted.

The woman Leia had called Black Fox landed on both feet, slid to a halt, and walked confidently over the broken glass towards Malevolence/his mother.

"Sorry about the mess. I had a feeling if I followed Leia, I'd find you," Black Fox said.

"Hmmm, breaking and entering," Malevolence replied. "Are you going to beat up Leia's future mother-in-law, too?"

Black Fox pulled a small metal cylinder from her glove, held her right thumb above a button on the device and smiled.

"Years ago, Silver Knight made this for me in case I ever had to face you," Black Fox added. "He called it a telepathic scrambler."

Josh didn't know what to expect when Black Fox pushed a button on the cylinder. It began to glow. Just then, Leia grabbed him and he could feel some kind of change in the air. He wondered if she was trying to protect him somehow.

He saw Malevolence/Mom put her hands to her head, recoiling as if in intense pain. She let loose a blood-curdling scream as everything in the room started flying away. He could feel the raw energy projecting outward from her, but she did not appear to be in control anymore. The nearby walls shattered as easily as the glass had.

―――――――

Black Fox had not expected this reaction. She thought the device might simply cripple Malevolence's powers or knock her out. Then again, she thought, the device had sat dormant for twenty years. Perhaps it was no longer working correctly?

Black Fox tried to dodge the debris but the telekinetic storm lifted her up and blew her backwards, making her completely vulnerable. As four large glass shards inflicted mortal wounds and debris threatened to crush and bury her, her final thoughts were of her son.

―――――――

Just then, the house's gas line ruptured and its explosion mushroomed into the houses on either side. For Leia, it was like watching a demonic pit open up, engulfing the whole area in flames.

While the firestorm raged around them, the telekinetic shield she had placed around Josh and herself held but the strain was incredible. Words failed her as she fought back the blistering heat and the flames that feverishly attacked the invisible bubble that kept her and her fiancé alive. She helped Josh stand up and they moved slowly through the red-hot remains of the house. Each step forward was like trying to walk outside during a hurricane. Fire, smoke, dust and debris were everywhere. The only thing truly intact about the house was its foundation.

As they made it to the driveway and past the burning skeletons of cars, Leia was finally able to drop her shield. Sweating from the sweltering heat, Leia could feel her arms shaking from the effort she'd just made and dull throbs signaled the beginnings of a headache. But those weren't important to Leia at the moment. Now that they had survived, she could allow herself to comprehend the sheer magnitude of what had just occurred. With a feeling inside that she'd never forget, Leia sat down on the sidewalk next to Josh, put her face in her hands and began to sob uncontrollably.

Neighbors had gathered in the street. Some were amazed, some were gawking, others were aghast, looking helpless. And a few were brave enough to run into the less damaged but still-burning houses to help survivors. Sirens from emergency vehicles grew louder as they approached.

She lifted her head up from her hands to look at Josh. He just stood there in shock, watching his house slowly burn to the ground. It surprised her when he inched forward on unsteady legs and began to speak.

"M-Mom?" he uttered. "Mom!"

Her heart went out to him as she observed him taking a few steps forward in an almost robot-like walk. But she was not prepared to see him suddenly break into a dash towards the inferno.

"No!" she screamed.

Leia reached out with her right arm, fully extending her fingers in Josh's direction. He stopped like a fly caught in amber and then she dragged him backwards, away from the danger.

"Let me go!" he cried. "She's in there! Mom's still in there!"

"Josh—"

"She needs me!"

"Josh, she's—she's gone!"

Leia spotted Black Fox's golden mask on the ground, dented and blotched by soot. She walked up to Josh and, with as much restraint as she could muster, slapped him across the face. He looked down at her then, slowly, as if released from a trance. Leia could feel her own tears streaming down her cheeks.

"There's no one alive in there, Josh! But I'm right here and I need you! Our child needs you!"

She saw him turn his head and look back at the blaze.

"It's just . . . we came here with good news. How could this happen?"

Leia had no answers. She just held Josh close. She said what little things she could to try and comfort him, knowing nothing really could.

And she thought of Dane, who was now an orphan. Her heart broke for him and Josh.

9

THE POLICE AND EMERGENCY CREWS had far too many questions. Leia did her best to protect Josh from them. However, there were some questions only he could answer, such as how to contact his father.

Leia told them a modified version of the truth: She and Josh had come to the residence to tell his mother of their engagement and pregnancy. But Black Fox had come to warn them about possible danger inside and made sure they'd gotten to a safe distance. Then, Black Fox went inside to warn his mother. And shortly after that was when the explosion occurred.

Leia felt some guilt for lying to them, but it was more believable than the truth. And it let Black Fox die as she'd lived: a hero. It also made Josh's mother's death an accident instead of what it actually was, a tragic mistake. Any follow up investigation wasn't likely to turn up much evidence to the contrary from the smoldering ashes of the house.

After the emergency workers made sure that Josh and Leia were physically alright, and the police finished their questions, Leia sat with Josh for a while and held him. He was conscious but not very responsive. He looked at the ground or the sky. When Leia asked him basic questions, he would grunt or give one or two-word answers. The blank look in his eyes was the hardest for Leia to see, a reflection of his shock and loss.

Leia pulled her cell phone from her purse and called her parents. She assured them that she and Josh were as well as could be expected. She asked if she and Josh could get a ride, since her car was a blackened husk. Her father arrived in his car less than ten minutes later.

On the way back, she told Dad the truth, all of it. He thanked her for that but Leia was surprised at how choked up he got, especially concerning Black Fox's death. She realized there must have been more to his friendship with Aunt Dana than she knew about. The rest of the ride, Dad was silent, doing his best to stay in control of his emotions as well as the vehicle.

Leia let Josh lean on her in the back seat and she held his hand. She wished she could shield him from this trauma as easily as she had shielded him from physical injury.

At one point, Dad pulled over to a curb and parked the vehicle. He had stopped right next to Digby Park.

"I'm sorry, Leia, I need a few minutes to myself. Will you two be okay?"

"S-sure, Dad. I won't let anything happen."

———————

As Steve walked towards the meadow area of the park, he recalled this was where he had met Dana Fox on a bright and sunny spring afternoon twenty-three years ago. He'd been there to walk/jog down the hike-and-bike trail, which stretched from the tree line to a street which ran alongside Lake Digby nearby.

That day, Dana had approached Steve from behind as she walked up the sloping incline of the trail towards the street level portion. She was wearing a white cap, halter top, shorts and tennis shoes. And while she was clearly making a significant effort to catch up to him, she was neither sweating nor even breathing hard. That impressed Steve when he turned around to see who was approaching so quickly.

"Hey! Muscles!" Dana had said. "Yeah, you!"

Somewhat annoyed, Steve decided to walk towards the young African-American woman.

"What is it?" he had replied.

"I need a workout partner, someone strong like you," Dana had smiled. "You interested?"

"What are you talking about?" Steve had asked.

"Okay, I'll be honest with you, I'm a lot stronger than I look," Dana had admitted. "And there's not too many who can keep up with me . . . but maybe you can."

"I'm flattered but I'm even stronger than I look. I'm afraid I'd hurt you."

"Let's put that to the test, okay?" There had been an almost feral gleam in her eyes.

Before Steve could blink, Dana was behind him. She landed a kick behind his left knee that was much harder than Steve anticipated. It almost left him open for the judo throw she attempted on him.

Dana backflipped off Steve's chest as he reached for her and she landed on her feet in a crouch. She was still smiling, looking excited. People nearby gathered to watch, thinking some kind of contest or martial arts demonstration was going on.

"You're perfect! I've never met anyone as strong as you," Dana had said. "That's incredible! I don't have to hold back!"

Steve scratched behind his head. He wondered if there was more to this woman than met the eye or if she was just insane. Or both.

"And I've never met anyone who could move like you," he had conceded.

Then he saw it. Her eyes were no longer human, they were like an animal's.

She's super-powered—like me!

Dana leaped at Steve so fast that he almost didn't see her coming. He actually felt it when she punched him in the face and again, a heartbeat later, when her claws scratched across his chest, ripping his shirt. She made him look like he was standing still compared to her. As the contest became more intense, people backed further away from them.

Mildly irritated, he put out both arms as fast as he could, and he caught her with his right arm at her waist. He winced as he heard her ribs crack. Then he pulled her close and flew straight up.

"Are you alright??" Steve had asked a moment later.

"You can fly!"

"Yes, obviously."

"I'll . . . be fine," she had replied. "I heal very fast."

"Why did you do this?"

"I told you, I was looking for a workout partner. But I will admit to finding you attractive as well."

With that, she had kissed him.

"Um, I don't even know your name," Steve had said.

He had been a little embarrassed by her forthrightness. Yet he had also been impressed by her confidence.

"I'm Dana Fox. And you, handsome?"

"Steve Hamilton."

"Okay, Steve, what say we set down somewhere away from where we were and talk this over?"

"Talk what over? The workout or—more?"

"That, sir, is entirely up to you," Dana smiled expectantly. "I just put the cards on the table."

Six months passed quickly.

"Are you bored already, *Miss* Fox?" Steve had teased.

They were strapped into their seats and riding a Ferris wheel at the Rapid Heights Amusement Park. It was late afternoon, slightly breezy and cool. The park was surprisingly full for an early Fall day.

"You flew me higher than this the first day we met, *Mister* Hamilton," Dana answered with a wink. "I think we'd have more fun climbing down from here. If we're lucky, the ride will be over in, what, an *hour* at this rate?"

"You wound me," Steve had replied in mock horror. "You do realize Ferris wheels are supposed to go slow? They're supposed to be romantic."

"It's a sweet sentiment," she had admitted. "And I'm happy to be on this date with you . . . but—"

"But the Ferris wheel is too kiddy for you. No problem. You pick the next part of the park we go to. Deal?"

"Deal."

Following the ride, he had walked arm in arm with her. She was leaning against him and both of them were smiling. They were the epitome of a young couple in love.

Many families were there that day, mostly young parents with pre-teen children. Dana seemed happily oblivious but Steve noticed the occasional rude stare. It was clear that some of these individuals were not accustomed, or happy, to see an interracial couple at the amusement park, much less one that was openly showing affection.

What surprised Steve was that the stares came from people of all races, including African-Americans.

"Don't let them bug you, Steve," Dana snuggled into his side, her eyes closed.

"Dana, what?"

"Your heart rate increases when you're tense," Dana shared. "It doesn't take a detective to figure out what's aggravating you."

"I'm sorry. I'm just . . . protective. I can't help it. And I'll admit, I've never seen this side of people before."

"Racism? Yeah, it's not exactly a shining example of humanity," Dana conveyed derisively. "But it is an example I've been exposed to all of my life."

"What do you mean?" Steve had asked.

"As a kid, my mother sent me to the Hogan Academy on the north side. It was prestigious, challenging, and mostly white. There were a number of students who didn't think I belonged there because I was black. I did well in spite of them, but I put up with a lot of bullying and harassment, too. Then a lot of us ended up going to Digby University together. I still see a few of them but they've learned to steer clear of me now."

"How did—how do you deal with it?" he had asked.

Dana stopped and turned to look right at Steve.

"I deal with it by understanding that my worth as a human being has nothing to do with the color of my skin or my DNA, even though I'm proud of both," she had replied. "It's about how I choose to carry myself, which is with respect and dignity, and the decisions I make while I live."

"I agree with you. About all of that."

"You know what else, love? I choose to do my best to not waste my time on the haters. And neither should you."

"Alright, fair enough. On a different note, do you think we'd survive the burgers at that stand over there? I'm starved."

Her stomach had gurgled a little then, almost as if responding to his statement.

"No. But there's a Burger Empire about three miles from the park. I spotted it on the way here."

"You knew we'd be having this discussion, didn't you?"

"Do I know my man, or do I know my man? C'mon! I'm starving, too!"

Ninety minutes later, when they arrived back at Steve's apartment in Digby, he couldn't believe how much of a mess they'd left earlier. On the coffee table in front of the couch, there were two open pizza boxes, lonely except for a few partially uneaten crusts still inside and next to them, a mostly empty two-liter bottle of soda on its side. Another empty soda bottle was on the dark blue carpet in front of the television set. The sink was full of unwashed cups, dishes and silverware. Steve's "to do" laundry now occupied three overflowing hampers near the washer and dryer towards the back of the apartment.

Dana had playfully put her arm around Steve's neck and laughed.

"Maybe we should call you 'Super Bachelor,' huh?" she had chided.

"Very funny. You gonna help me clean this up?" he had replied.

"Oh, I could probably handle the laundry and the dishes, SB."

"Okay, that works," Steve chuckled. "Thanks."

Steve took two steps forward. Then he stopped and scratched his head.

"I wonder if this is what being married is like?" he imagined. "You know, splitting the chores, keeping up a place?"

"I wouldn't know," she had answered. "I don't ever plan to marry . . . or have kids."

"Really? I didn't know you felt that way."

"It's no secret or anything. My folks were married but didn't love each other."

"Why'd they get married then?"

"For my father, it was business . . . maybe even family politics. I think Mom just wanted a kid out of it . . . and that's what she got."

"My folks weren't perfect either, but I always thought they loved each other," Steve had admitted.

"Lucky you," Dana smirked.

Steve watched Dana walk towards the washer and dryer. Then she stopped and turned quickly towards him.

"Don't tell me, you want to get married someday?" she had asked.

Steve was picking up the pizza boxes and the soda bottles. He didn't turn around or answer.

"You do, don't you?" she had continued. "And I bet you want kids, too."

Steve placed the trash next to the wastebasket, since it was already full. Then he turned to look at Dana.

"Is that wrong of me?" Steve had asked, sincerely.

"No, I suppose it isn't," Dana had replied. "People have different dreams for their lives."

"I'm sorry if mine upsets you. I just—"

At that moment, Dana briskly walked over to Steve and put her right hand on his chest. He knew it was her gentle way of getting his attention and telling him to shut up. He picked up on the cue and responded appropriately, turning all of his attention to her.

"I love you," Dana had said, looking directly into Steve's eyes, almost hypnotically. "And I'm willing to compromise, to a degree."

"Really? How so?" he had asked.

"I still won't ever get married," Dana had responded, almost emphatically. "But for the man I love . . . I'd have his child."

Steve looked at Dana for a few moments, absorbing what she'd just said. Then he gently pulled back and sat down on the couch, facing away from her.

"What's wrong?" she had wondered.

"Maybe I'm selfish," he had replied. "I know what it took for you to come to that compromise. I've dated before but you're the first woman I've ever loved. So, a part of me is very happy you said that."

Dana seemed surprised by his sudden revelations and the feelings behind them. But her eyes told him she knew how conflicted he was.

"Does that also mean a part of you isn't happy with what I said?" she had asked.

"I don't think either of us is ready to become parents any time soon," Steve laughed. "But as incredible as it would be to have a kid with you, I don't want to just be a DNA donor."

"What makes you think that's all you'd be?" Dana had responded, crossing her arms, the ire rising in her voice. "You say you know what it took for me to come to that compromise, but I don't think you do!"

"Dana—"

"Does a marriage license automatically make a relationship better?" Dana had sounded insulted. "I'm offering you something way deeper and you're saying it's not good enough?"

"No, that's not what I'm saying at all."

"What are you saying then?"

Steve looked down at the floor, his still-conflicted emotions swirling inside. He sighed.

"I guess I have more of a traditional background with my folks, so that's what makes sense to me," he had continued.

"Can't you and I just be happy together? I'm committed to this relationship—to you, Steve!"

"And I'm committed to you, too! I—forget I said anything."

Dana fumed at that but took a deep breath. He had watched her walk to the other side of the couch and pick up her purse. Then she headed to the door. Before exiting, she looked back at Steve with tears welling in her eyes.

"I won't take back any of what I said to you, Steve. And I'll leave you to clean up your own mess."

With that, he watched helplessly as she walked out.

Several months later, Steve and Dana had breakfast at a local cafe called Javalaya. It was just after sunrise, so the cafe wasn't too crowded yet. The air conditioning made the cafe cooler than the morning air.

Javalaya had been in business for about ten years and the owners had recently renovated the place. So, there was still a hint of new paint smell blending with the stronger aroma of coffee, eggs, and meats. Someone was smoking a cigarette not far from the door as they waited for a city bus. Cars and pedestrians passed by. Every now and then, one of the pedestrians would come in for a cup of coffee or something tasty on the way to work.

This morning, Dana looked uncharacteristically timid as she spoke to him. She had worn a new sleeveless blue blouse with a darker blue vest and hip-hugging blue jeans. Her hair was down and pulled over her right shoulder. She also had on makeup which her near-tears were threatening to affect.

Steve had on a black t-shirt, a white jacket, and blue jeans. His hair made it evident that he had showered recently.

"Are you sure?" she had asked him. "We don't have to rush to a decision, do we?"

"I don't see how drawing things out will help," he had replied. "I respect you too much to do that. And I don't want to damage what we're trying to forge in . . . the special group we're forming."

"Did I do something wrong? Did I drive you away?"

"No, I don't think so, Dana. I care for you a great deal. I just . . . our views on a number of things are just too different. I know I can't change you, so I won't make that effort. I think it's more honest to agree to disagree and move on."

"Steve, please . . . can't we just—"

"I love you, Dana," Steve had interrupted. "And because of that, you'll always have a part of my heart. It's just that . . . I can't love you on your terms. I tried. I want to be with you! I wish I could, I really do . . . but . . . if we stay together, we're just going to keep fighting. We'll make each other miserable. I can't do that. I'm sorry."

Dana took a sip of water and looked down. As she put the glass down, Steve could see her hand was trembling.

"So am I. But you feel the way you feel, I can't change that," Dana admitted, slowly and deliberately. "I'll get over you."

"Dana, if this is going to be too difficult, tell me and—"

"No," Dana interrupted. "This dream is more important than our relationship. It—it could change the world for the better."

Dana looked up and locked gazes with Steve. She was teary-eyed but she looked serious, determined.

"I *want* to do this with you," she had emphasized. "Let's forge this team. I know we can make it happen!"

"Alright," Steve had admired. "Then I'll introduce you to a couple of friends of mine. One of them I think is a good candidate and the other has potential."

"Tell me about them."

"The one I think is solid is a technical genius and master inventor. His name is John, but he goes by the codename Silver Knight."

"He sounds interesting. What's he made so far?"

"You mean, besides a super-advanced suit of armor and an orbiting satellite base?"

Dana finally grinned again. Steve was relieved to see that.

"He's in," Dana nodded. "What about the other one?"

"He's got abilities a lot like mine. He's quite the tactician and he helped John and me create the satellite," Steve had continued. "His name is Ed, but his codename is White Knight."

"Two knights and a crusader. Kind of makes Black Fox sound out of place and boring."

"Dana, listen to me. I think if something happened to every other member of this team, you'd still be standing. We need you."

He saw Dana contemplate his words for a moment, taking occasional sips of water. Then she placed her hand on top of his on the table. It was a habit of hers, but Steve didn't mind this time.

"Alright, I'm in. Let's put this team together!"

The memory ended, leaving present day Steve with a flood of bittersweet emotions.

He slammed his right fist into his left palm with such force that a shockwave sent the branches and leaves of the nearby trees blowing outwards for a few seconds before rebounding back into place. Tears welled in his eyes.

Not wanting to be overwhelmed any further by his grief, Steve got on his knees and prayed. He couldn't tell if he spoke out loud or was only thinking. What mattered more was not holding his grief inside. He wanted—needed—to reach out to his Lord for comfort, so he could have peace and be able to help his daughter and her fiancé.

The tears flowed freely, as did his feelings of loss and regret for not being able to protect Dana Fox or his daughter from this disaster. But there was also absolution and healing. He hadn't known about this confrontation between Black Fox and Malevolence. He'd tried to prevent it. And he couldn't be everywhere at once. It didn't take away the loss but it assuaged some of his guilt.

Steve regained his composure. He returned to his vehicle and drove Leia and Josh to his house.

Sue met them as they arrived. Steve saw her take look at everyone's faces and a whiff of the air around Leia and Josh. Then she looked as if she understood pretty much everything. He was glad she only offered her sympathy for what they'd experienced and welcomed them inside.

Steve watched as Leia helped Josh to her room. Steve spoke with his wife and Tanya in the living room. He struggled getting the words out, but he managed to tell them what happened in detail. Sue gripped one of the couch cushions tightly, closed her eyes and a single tear flowed down her right cheek.

Tanya was less reserved.

"How can you just accept all this so quietly?" Tanya demanded. "Am I the only one who sees that this was Aunt Dana's fault? And now, people are dead!"

Sue looked at their daughter for a moment with silent fury. Then she calmed herself.

"We see it, too, Tanya," Sue admitted. "But we see a bigger picture here. And we knew Aunt Dana a lot longer than you. We didn't agree with her methods but we understood her. She was trying to protect people from a threat. She just made a mistake in the way she did it, and she paid for that mistake with her life."

Tanya just looked at her mother then went upstairs to her room.

"I'm sorry about that, Dane," Sue said.

The wall shadows came together and formed Dane Fox.

"Just tell me one thing," Dane asked. "Do you think she suffered?"

"I don't think so," Steve replied. "From what Leia told me, it was quick. She probably didn't feel anything."

"Thank God for that small blessing," Dane sighed.

Dane looked towards the window but even from this angle, the depth of his grief and shock was written all over his face.

"Dane, you're not alone," Sue said. "You've always been a part of this family."

"I know," Dane near-whispered. "But . . . why didn't she take me? This one time, why?"

"She must have known how dangerous this confrontation would be."

"She kept me out of harm's way. Right to the end, she protected me."

"You were always first to your mother, Dane," Steve interjected. "She loved you more than anyone."

Dane's eyes began to tear up and he looked down.

"She didn't love me enough to stay alive," he lamented.

———————

"Do you want to get some rest?" Leia asked. "I can go downstairs and let you—"

"Don't leave me," Josh grabbed Leia's hand. "I can't stand to be alone with my thoughts right now."

"Alright," Leia sat down next to Josh on her bed. "I'll stay with you as long as you need."

Josh smiled but it was distant, vacant and haunting. Leia kept wishing she could find some way to help ease this deep loss, the wound in his heart.

"You're the only person who really knows me," Josh shared. "The only person who loves me as much as . . . as she did."

Leia smiled nervously. She was unsure how to respond to that, even though it made her extremely happy to hear him say those words.

"My parents didn't think they could have kids," Josh continued. "They tried for years. And almost ten years after they stopped trying, I came along and surprised them. By then, Dad had a pretty high-level sales position, so he was always traveling to other countries to make multi-million-dollar deals. He was in Singapore when he got the news about Mom's pregnancy. He was in London when I was born."

Leia listened with curiosity; Josh rarely talked about his father.

"It's not that I don't get along with Dad. But I never got to know him like I did Mom. And it's not really his fault. His job pays well and he's always provided for us. He just . . . couldn't be there. Everything was me and Mom."

Josh turned towards Leia and she could see his suffering through the look in his eyes.

"I don't know what I'd do if you weren't here."

"Have you called him yet, your dad?"

"No. The police will get ahold of him. I don't think I could handle it. I have no idea what to say."

———

Dane kept looking in the direction of Leia's room.

"Is something wrong?" Steve asked. "Worried about Leia?"

"I'm more worried about—what was his name—Josh?"

"I don't understand."

"My mother's actions led to his mother's death," Dane continued. "I want to offer my condolences but . . . somehow I don't think it's the time."

"You're right, it isn't," Sue said, walking up to him. "But you'll know when it is the right time, and then maybe you and he can have a talk."

"That could be a long time," Dane shook his head.

"Yes, it could be," Sue said. "But your heart is in the right place. You're dealing with your own loss, yet you're thinking of others."

"I can't help it."

Steve was pleased to see Sue put her hand on Dane's shoulder, offering comfort.

"That's what makes you her son. She did a terrific job raising you. You're a good man, Dane."

"I don't feel very good. I feel lost."

Steve had been sitting down on the couch listening. He stood up and walked across the room to Dane and Sue.

"It's going to be alright," Steve said. "Maybe not right now and maybe not for a while. But someday."

"I'll hold onto that idea, sir. Because right now, I just can't see it."

"Your father was an incredible man, Dane, and I was proud to call him one of my closest friends. I could never replace him, any more than Sue could replace your mother. But we love you, and we want to help you however we can."

"That . . . means more to me than you know, sir. Mother told me when I became eighteen that I was a man. She explained and showed me the risks of putting your life on the line to stop people from doing evil things."

Dane began to pace slowly as he expressed his thoughts.

"She—she even told me that she wouldn't always be there, that one day she might perish fighting against evil," Dane continued. "But I don't think I ever understood that it could really happen. She didn't teach me how to live without her!"

"That's because no one knows exactly when they're going to die, Dane. You can't teach your child how to live without you," Steve replied. "It's just something that everyone has to learn on their own. It's never easy . . . and it shouldn't be easy. Every life is precious and when one is absent from us, of course we miss them."

"My father died in a car accident when I was ten years old," Sue interjected. "I adored him, all the things we did and the time he spent with me and my sisters. My mother changed after he died. She became withdrawn and an alcoholic. So, in a way, it was like we lost both parents. My sisters and I only had each other to cope with what happened.

"My mother almost died from alcohol poisoning a few years after that. We despised her so much because we were too young to understand her suffering. She'd lost the man she loved and didn't have as good of a job as he did. She had to work two jobs to pay the bills and provide for us. She drank to forget her loss and to keep going, even though it was killing her.

"I wouldn't go see my mother when she was in the hospital. But one of her friends did. And that friend helped her see that she didn't have to continue suffering like she was. She helped my mother see that she was fighting a losing battle and that she needed help. She could have God's help, through His Son, Jesus."

"My mother didn't believe in any of that," Dane replied. "She respected you and Uncle Steve as dear friends and former teammates. But she never understood your choice to—"

Steve raised an eyebrow at that. Dane stopped himself.

"To what?" Sue asked. "It's okay, you can tell us anything."

"To use Mother's words, she never understood your choice to leave behind your responsibilities as crime fighters to settle down and be normal people," Dane replied.

"I see," Steve responded. "Knowing your mother as I did, I can understand why she saw things that way. We tried to explain our decision to her more than once but we had to agree to disagree about it."

"Can you try to explain it to me, sir?" Dane asked. "Because if you had been there today, I can't help but think that things might have turned out differently."

Steve considered Dane's words a moment before answering.

"Let me tell you what would have happened if Sue and I had been there today, Dane. I would have survived the explosion but my wife would be dead along with your mother and Josh's mother."

"You might have talked Mother out of using Silver Knight's device?"

"Maybe," Sue replied. "But what good would that have done? How much did your mother tell you about Malevolence?"

"Only that she was Leia's biological mother, a very powerful and dangerous woman. A formidable opponent."

"That's an understatement. The only thing that kept Malevolence from either killing or enslaving us all was that she went into hiding after she gave Leia to Steve and me to raise. She couldn't read your mother's or my mind when we were in were-animal form, but she could turn anyone against us or use her telekinesis against us."

"She is very dangerous," Dane realized. "I had no idea she had that kind of power. I can better understand why my mother wanted to protect me from her, especially given what . . . what ended up happening."

Everyone was silent for almost a minute. Then Sue spoke up.

"The AR-MEN were never going to come together again as a team, no matter what the threat was," she continued. "Actually, the day Steve came home and told me that John—that your father—had died saving the team from Killer Knight and that our satellite home was destroyed, I got scared."

"Why?" Dane asked.

"If my husband and your mother were the strength that helped forge The AR-MEN, then your father was the glue that held us together. And when he died, everything started to fall apart."

"What do you mean?"

"Steve wasn't the same anymore. For the first time since I'd known him, he became vengeful. He hadn't been able to stop Killer Knight, which led to your father sacrificing himself. Steve started treating every villain as a potential Killer Knight. He stopped holding back, sending every criminal that survived to the hospital . . . but several others he simply killed to silence their threat."

"I told myself I was justified," Steve admitted. "That I wouldn't allow anyone else to die like Silver Knight had . . . that, if anyone would make the sacrifice, it would be me."

"As Crusader, he became more and more reckless, more out of control," Sue added. "I had decided to quit being a model and superhero so I could be a stay-at-home mom and raise Leia. But too many times, Steve barely made it back home. He may have ended whatever threat there had been but the personal cost was high, too high."

"I was focused on end results more than anything," Steve said. "Your mother couldn't be active in The AR-MEN while she was pregnant with you. And my other teammates, Flamia and Medsnake, were still recovering from the injuries they'd received fighting Killer Knight . . . so I was on my own."

"Sometimes, he had horrific injuries. I had to do my best to patch him up and wait for his own healing abilities to bring him back to me," Sue said. "It tore me apart to see him like that. And it infuriated me that he didn't care enough about himself. We were heading to a breaking point."

"What? You mean, you were going to divorce?" Dane asked, surprised.

"Not only that, I was ready to raise Leia by myself, since that's what I was doing anyway," Sue confirmed. "It wasn't what I wanted but I didn't know what to do anymore. I wanted an escape and I was ready to do anything to get it."

Dane looked like he was becoming overwhelmed. He stepped back a moment and looked at the ground.

"Three significant events: Leia's birth, my father's death and my mother being pregnant with me—and everything changed for all of you. It's . . . incredible."

Sue smiled, even though it was bittersweet. She placed her right hand on Dane's left shoulder. She looked at him with a mix of emotions and experience in her eyes. In that moment, Sue looked older than her years but there was something reassuring in the gesture.

"There's a saying, 'nature abhors a vacuum,'" Sue asserted. "People are like that, too."

"Yes, ma'am."

"But the birth of a child does change everything, and it can be so wonderful, Dane. If you have kids someday, you'll understand."

"I've been pretty sheltered my whole life," Dane admitted.

"There will be time for love and for family someday, if you want that," Sue assured him. "There's no need to rush."

"Yes, ma'am," Dane agreed, breaking a small smile.

Steve watched as Dane walked across the room. It looked like he was collecting his thoughts once more.

"How did you and Mr. Hamilton resolve your problems back then?" Dane asked.

"Good question. A lot of that had to do with my mother, believe it or not. By the time Steve and I were having so many problems, my mother had become like a completely different woman. Through the power of the Holy Spirit, she was able to quit drinking. She found support and friendship through her church and had new purpose in her life. She was finally able to put the needs of others over her own."

"Sue's mother had been supportive of our marriage all along," Steve agreed. "Despite any misgivings she may have had about Sue being so young when our marriage started, she gave us her love and trust."

"I didn't believe in her yet, that she'd truly changed. I knew she wasn't drinking but I had resented her for so long, I didn't know how to love her anymore," Sue said. "So, I kept her at arm's length from me, Steve and Leia . . . that is, until I was ready to move out and take Leia with me. I wasn't very rational; my only focus was Leia. I couldn't see that I was about to ruin my life."

10

NINETEEN YEARS EARLIER

Twenty-year-old Sue Hamilton looked out the front window of the duplex she and Steve had been renting for the last year and a half, visually verifying what she already knew in her mind: her truck was packed with the essentials she and Leia would need to live on their own.

Sue looked at eleven-month-old Leia, who was nearly asleep in her arms. The clock on the wall showed it was 9:42 p.m.

Steve might be home soon or he might not come home at all. He was either risking his life to fight super-powered criminals or endangering their lives because he couldn't hold himself back anymore. Either way, knowing how obsessed he was with justice, it pained her that she and his daughter couldn't be his main priority.

Sue cuddled the groggy child and kissed her forehead.

Regardless of Steve's state of mind, she had made a commitment to Leia: she would raise her, like she had every day since this precious girl had come into this crazy world. Sue wasn't a superhero anymore, but she knew she would protect Leia with her life, if need be.

Leia's father wouldn't be happy with them leaving but she couldn't stand it anymore, bringing a child up in such an unstable environment. Leia deserved better. They both did.

Sue walked back to the bedroom to retrieve her purse from a table. As she entered the room, she looked at herself in the full-length mirror. Her hair looked like it hadn't been combed in two days and was barely contained by a yellow hair tie that had squeezed an unruly ponytail out the other end. She looked like she hadn't slept in at least a day. Her black sweat pants hugged her thick waist and had baby food stains on them that were probably peas, carrots, and some kind of fruit. Her yellow t-shirt was inside-out, sporting an unintended midriff from now being too small . . . and Sue really didn't much care.

"Up and coming supermodel," she chuckled.

She had embraced motherhood, but she had expected the man she married to help her raise this child and be fully involved in their marriage, like he had been before John died. Had Silver Knight's sacrifice robbed Steve of his sanity? His love for her? Sue buried her head in her adopted daughter's chest to try and escape that thought but peace eluded her once again.

Releasing a weary sigh, Sue forced herself to reach inside her purse and grab her keys. Then she put her purse over her left shoulder and walked to the front door with her child.

Outside, it was warm and muggy, and Sue thought she caught a flash of lightning in the distance followed by a low rumble of thunder. As she fidgeted to lock the door, she heard footsteps behind her, a woman's footsteps. She recognized the woman's scent immediately.

"Mija, where are you going?" the woman said.

"Mamá, what are you doing here?"

"I tried to call but the line was busy."

That had been intentional. Sue had left the phone off the hook, in case Steve or anyone else called while she was getting ready to leave.

"I was worried about you and your family," her mother continued. "Very worried."

"I'm kind of in a hurry, Mamá. We need to go."

"Where are you going? Your truck—are you moving? You're leaving Steve?"

Sue said nothing. She didn't have the will to deflect her mother's questions or confront her. She was too tired, too spent.

"Mija, turn around and look at me, okay?"

Ten seconds later, Sue turned around.

Her mother was a short, thin woman in her mid-forties with shoulder-length black hair, deep brown eyes, a narrow nose and thin lips. She was wearing a dark blue dress. Stress and years of alcohol abuse made her look nearly ten years older than she was.

But what gripped Sue's attention the most at that moment was the look in her mother's eyes, not just tears but genuine sorrow. It wasn't pity, it was something much more profound.

"I haven't been there for you in years. I was a terrible mother and I know it's probably too late for apologies. But Sue, I am so sorry!"

"Why are you saying this now, Mamá?"

Sue could see that her mother was struggling with her words, but she also looked determined. After what seemed like an eternity in seconds, her mother spoke.

"Because you're about to make a huge mistake. And more than anything, I want to prevent that, if I can."

"How is me moving out and protecting my daughter a huge mistake? Isn't that what parents are supposed to do?"

Sue knew she was rubbing proverbial salt in her mother's wound, but she couldn't help it. It had been so hard to come to this decision. Why was her mother, of all people, standing in her way now, at such a critical time?

"Yes, that is what a parent, a mother, is supposed to do. And that is what I'm doing for you right now."

Sue stumbled back a few steps and was glad the front door was there for her to lean against. "What are you protecting me from, huh?"

She was surprised that her exhaustion was actually blurring her vision.

"What will your husband do after he finds out you've left with the baby?"

'I'm sure he'll track me down and demand I give Leia back."

"And what will you do then?"

"I'll fight him for Leia!" Sue said, with as much conviction as she could muster.

Her mother looked at her with eyes that had the kind of wisdom which came from bitter tears and loss, with heartache that one hopes never to experience. Then she looked down and closed her eyes, as if silently praying. There was no ego, no pity, only concern and a deep love that Sue had never seen before.

"If you fight him, he'll kill you, mija. That child is more important to him than you realize."

"What?" Sue said, her eyes wide with surprise.

"He may be doing things the wrong way right now, but he's doing them for you and Leia."

"What are you talking about?"

"If you abandon your husband, you'll lose everything, including Leia."

"No!" Sue said, squinting her eyes in denial.

Just then, Sue's strength failed her, and she fell to her knees. Sue grasped Leia as tightly yet as safely as she could, holding the baby close to her, but she was fighting a wave of vertigo. Her mother squatted down and put her firm right hand on Sue's quivering shoulder, doing her best to hold Sue up while offering her open left hand.

"Please, let me hold Leia. Sue, you're about to pass out!"

Sue handed Leia to her grandmother. And then she collapsed.

Sue woke up six hours later in her bed and realized she was in feline form. Steve was with her in the room, looking extremely worried as he gazed out the window at the ongoing thunderstorm.

"Hey," Sue said weakly.

Steve's mood immediately brightened as he turned to look at Sue.

"Hey yourself!" Relief brimmed in his voice. "I got home right as you passed out. I brought you inside."

"I'm surprised you didn't take me to the hospital. Oh wait . . . was I like this the whole time?"

Steve nodded.

"You weren't just exhausted. You were sick with a high fever, too. When you're in human form, you heal at a normal rate, and you'd pushed yourself way past healthy. You could have died."

Sue didn't know how to react to that. She knew he was right.

"Fortunately, your body seems to have a fail-safe point where you shut down and your full powers kick in automatically to heal you, but that also means changing into feline form."

"My mother must have loved that."

"Your mother put Leia to bed and helped me with you. She's in the living room asleep right now."

"She wasn't freaked out?"

"She had a lot of questions, of course, but she was more worried about how sick you were. We talked for a long time. She's changed a lot since the last time I saw her. She . . . made a lot of sense."

"What do you mean? What else did she talk to you about?"

Steve looked down and laughed despite himself.

"When she saw that you were Cat, she put two and two together about me being Crusader. She told me she understood why you wanted to leave me, even if she didn't agree with you about it. And she told me that I needed to treat you much better if I wanted to keep you in my life."

Sue didn't say anything. She was still weak and was at a loss for words anyway.

"We talked about a lot more, but I won't go into all that. The important thing is, I realized that she was right about you . . . about us. She was also right when she said that 'seeking revenge is like purposefully keeping your own wound open until you inflict it on someone else, making you as bad as the person who hurt you.'"

"My mother said that?"

"Yeah. I've justified my actions by telling myself I was seeking justice for John . . . but I was only hurting you . . . and us."

Steve got down on his knees next to the bed and lowered his head in shame.

"I'm sorry for everything I've done, Sue, and for all the things I haven't done that I should have. Will you forgive me?"

Sue marveled at her husband's display of humility. But she wanted some reassurances as well.

"What are you going to do differently then?"

"For now, I just want to be with you and Leia. After talking with your mom, I know that you're the most important person in my life. I love you and I want to make you happy again. I want us to be a family."

"Then I forgive you. And I think I need to get some more rest."

Steve gently took his wife's furry hand in his and nodded in understanding. He kissed her hand and continued to look at her with love.

"That's probably a good idea," Steve said.

———————

Her mother stayed the next day to help care for Leia while Steve went to work, and Sue continued to recover. Sue walked into the living room and sat on the couch next to her mother, who had Leia in her lap.

"Thank you for all your help, Mamá."

"You're welcome, mija. How are you feeling now?"

Sue was still having trouble adjusting to this more sensitive and caring version of her mother. She caught herself staring at her, trying to match the face of the woman in front of her with the despairing drunk she had known while growing up. She couldn't. This was someone new.

"Better," Sue answered. "I'm sorry I never told you about this other form of mine, these powers I have. I should be able to turn normal again pretty soon. I guess I went too long caring for everyone but myself and got real sick."

"That is an understatement. You looked deathly when I saw you last night. That is why I was so worried. I was praying for you a lot."

That surprised Sue.

"'Praying?' You never prayed before, Mamá."

"No, I didn't. I was too proud. I thought I would solve everything myself. That was especially true after your father died. I thought I had to be tough for you three kids, so we could survive and make it."

Sue nodded, her mood bittersweet.

"You were tough alright, but we didn't need you to be tough. We needed you to be soft, to help us grieve and move past our hurt and loss. We needed love, Mamá."

Her mother sighed regretfully.

"Yes, I can see that so clearly now. But back then, losing your father was so raw, so painful, I thought all I could do was drink it away. And that didn't leave much left over for you and your sisters."

Sue kept looking at her mother but her mind was reliving memories.

"Sandra and I leaned on each other, but Leticia became like you. Closed off, hard," Sue added. "She watched out for us but I think, as the oldest, she felt like she had to be the strongest. And I don't think she ever really grieved . . . or healed."

"I don't know where she is now. Do you?"

"We haven't spoken in long time, Mamá."

They were silent for a few minutes.

"You're strong, too, mija. I don't mean physical strength, I mean resolve. You found out you had these . . . these powers and you didn't lose your mind. You used them to help people, to save lives. You found other people like yourself, joined a team and saved more lives."

"Steve and Black Fox led the team, I just did what they said to do."

Her mother quietly accepted Sue's modesty but the pride she had in her daughter shone through her eyes and smile.

"Maybe so," her mother continued. "But Steve told me everything about Leia and the woman who birthed her. He told me how much you sacrificed. You know, you would have been perfectly in the right to tell him no, that you wouldn't marry him or help raise his and some other woman's child."

"How could I do something like that? I love Steve. And Leia's mother gave up custody. I'm Leia's mother now!"

Her mother took Sue's hands in hers and gave her a look that was a mixture of humor and scolding.

"I didn't say I think you should have refused him, I'm just saying that there would have been nothing wrong if you had."

"I see."

"I'm also saying that I'm extremely proud of you, mija. Leia is a lovely grandchild and you're a good mother to her."

Sue reverted to human form then. And she felt herself blush.

"Thank you, Mamá."

I can't believe this! I feel like I'm six years old again and I can't help it—I'm so happy my mother said she's proud of me! That's probably because she's never said that to me in my life before. I have to admit, it feels really good!

"Sue, I want to see you and your family happy. But for you to accomplish that, you're going to have to do something you're not used to, something that you may not like."

"What's that, Mamá?"

Her mother squeezed her hands. Sue couldn't fully read her expression.

"As much power as you have, you just saw that it was barely enough to save your life when you got so worn down. And your husband's power didn't protect his mind from grief, vengeance and nearly madness," her mother offered. "What I'm saying is, no one's power, no matter what it is, is anything compared to God's. I think you need to put your trust in Him and His Son, Jesus Christ, instead of yourselves."

I don't recognize this woman. I mean, she looks like my mother but I've never seen this side of her. This confidence and strength. She's living what she's suggesting I do and proving that it's possible.

Sue tried to get up from the couch. She wanted to pace, to physically express the nervousness that this topic evoked in her. But she was still recovering and her strength failed her. So, she sat back down and leaned her back against the couch before she fell on the floor.

"Mija?"

"Sorry, dizzy. Go on, I'm listening."

"Come to church with me some time, you and your husband. Please?"

Whoa! Did my mother just use the word "please" in a sentence? Today is a day of firsts!

"I'll talk with Steve about it."

"Thank you."

———

BACK IN THE PRESENT

"You became a Christian," Dane realized. "And obviously, you and your husband didn't break up. You raised Leia and had another daughter together."

"Yes," Mrs. Hamilton replied with a smile. "Tanya was born five years later."

Dane had been sitting on the couch as Mrs. Hamilton had relayed her and her husband's experience all those years ago. Now he stood up.

"I'm glad that everything worked out for you," he said. "You have the kind of strength to be there for Leia, to help her with . . . everything she's dealing with now."

"We can be there for you, too, Dane," Mr. Hamilton interjected.

"Thank you. I'll probably take you up on that," Dane answered. "But I should go now."

Mr. Hamilton shook his hand and looked at him with what appeared to be fatherly concern.

"Where will you go, Dane?" he asked.

"Home. That's the only place I know."

"Are you sure? We can make room for you here."

"No, you have enough to deal with, sir. But thank you."

"At least let us give you our mobile numbers. We can—"

"That's okay, sir, I have Leia's. If I need to call, I will."

Mrs. Hamilton stood up from her chair facing the couch and walked over to Dane.

"Are you sure we can't change your mind, Dane?" she asked, her worry crystal clear.

"Thank you but no, Mrs. Hamilton. I appreciate . . . everything. Good night."

"Take care, Dane," she replied.

"I will."

11

ANGELA MERRICK WASN'T AWARE OF how long she'd been lying on the floor. All she knew was that she was still half-numb and very cold. She also had a dull throb on the back side of her head.

"You're alive!" a voice said in her head.

Angela tried to shove the voice away from her thoughts. It didn't quite work. The voice was persistent, strong and . . . familiar?

"I wasn't sure after Black Fox used that telepathic scrambler on you, the way it affected you," the voice said.

Black Fox? Dana? Why would she attack me? We're friends.

"Whoa! Wait a second! Am I talking to the same person? Who are you?" the voice wondered.

I'm Angela Merrick! Who are you?

"I'm Leia Hamilton," the voice shared. "I'm your daughter."

That revelation sent a surge of adrenaline through Angela, enough for her to push herself off of the floor and into a sitting position. Memories came to her before she even tried to access them, thoughts of her relationship with Steve Hamilton, her feelings for him. She remembered her concerns about possibly being pregnant, and those concerns being verified by a home pregnancy test and a doctor's visit. But before she could talk with Steve about it, a multitude of voices invaded her mind. There was pain and she was afraid she wouldn't be able to block them out.

There had been another voice within her as well. A very strong, terrifying voice. It had offered to silence the other voices. And she'd been too scared to resist it.

Now she was here, and this new voice said she was her daughter. This girl was named after Angela's favorite character in her favorite movie. Could she really be who she said she was? Angela wanted to believe her.

How old are you, Leia?

"I'm twenty years old."

Twenty? Where have I been your whole life?

"I'm starting to get an idea where you've been. What's the most recent thing you can remember?"

Angela reached deep within herself to find that answer. She trusted this voice. Somehow, she believed that Leia really was her daughter. No matter how improbable that seemed, this girl knew so much. And she worded things kind of like Steve would.

When Angela scoured through her jumble of memories, one stood out.

There was a darkness, a terrible darkness! And such cold! Another woman was with me, an older woman with blond hair. She was scared—so scared! She fell into the darkness! And the darkness—the darkness was alive!? It wanted me, too! But I ran away, as far and as fast as I could. I got away . . . and then I woke up on the floor in some office.

"We have a lot to talk about then. It sounds like you're in your office at Digby. I'll come to you. Just stay there."

Digby College? Why would I have an office there?

"Just wait for me. Don't go anywhere, okay?"

Alright, Leia. How—um—how's your father?

"He's doing well. I'll tell you everything when I get there."

Angela could still feel Leia's presence, even though Leia wasn't talking anymore. Leia had a strong personality but there was also a lot of pain. Angela didn't want to pry so she didn't delve any deeper. She tried to lower her mental volume some.

I must have been shouting in Leia's thoughts. I remember I'd gained the ability to read minds and lift objects, but it's never been this strong before?

Angela saw a purse on the nearby desk. She reached inside and found what she was looking for, a compact mirror. Cautiously, she pulled it out and looked at her face. She recognized herself but it was also like looking at a stranger. Stress lines had etched themselves under her eyes and from the sides of her nose and at the corners of her mouth. Worry lines were evident on her forehead.

It's true! I'm twenty years older. What happened to all those years? Why can't I remember them?

Did Steve and I get married? Did we raise our daughter and then, something bad happened to me? Is that the reason I can't remember?

With my mental powers, did I join the AR-MEN? Was I hurt in a battle?

Angela sighed.

Calm down.

————

Leia could hardly believe what had just happened. She looked down at Josh. He'd finally fallen asleep. Leia stood up, walked out of the room and quietly closed the door behind her. Then she went into the living room where Mom was.

"Something's happened," Leia said.

"What do you mean?" Mom asked.

"I need you to take me to Digby College right now, Mom."

"What's happened?"

"You won't believe me at first, but this is huge. I'll explain on the way there."

"Alright. Let me tell your father and Tanya."

Leia had an inspiration.

"I think Tanya should come, too."

"Why Tanya?"

"I think her being there will help."

Ten minutes later, they were driving towards the college.

"I don't think she meant to reach out to me, but we've already formed a kind of mental bond," Leia shared.

"You're talking about Malevolence, aren't you?" Mom replied.

"Well, Malevolence formed the bond but the voice I heard this time wasn't Malevolence."

"Excuse me?"

"Her tone and her personality were completely different, Mom. So, I asked who she was and she said she was Angela Merrick."

Mom pulled the SUV over to the side of the road and stopped.

"Say that again," Mom requested.

"I believe she's the woman she was before she became Malevolence. She was very disoriented. She was surprised when I told her I was her daughter, but she was utterly shocked when I told her I was twenty years old."

"Wait!" Tanya interrupted. "How could she just revert back after all this time?"

"I have a theory on that, based on what she told me," Leia offered. "She was in telepathic control of Josh's mom when Black Fox used that scrambler on her. I think she couldn't separate from Josh's mom when

Josh's mom . . . died. She was in telepathic contact with her during that experience and it nearly killed her, too."

"So, she nearly died," Tanya considered. "How does that translate into becoming a different personality?"

"Good question," Mom added.

"If Malevolence was that close to death, she might have just retreated inside Angela's mind," Leia continued. "It seems similar to what happened to Angela when she became Malevolence."

Leia could see Mom's eyes widen in comprehension. Tanya still looked confused.

"Angela said she ran away from that darkness, from death, as hard as she could, then she woke up," Leia related.

"You think her true personality reasserted itself to save her life?" Mom asked.

Leia nodded in agreement.

"Wow," Tanya added, looking amazed.

"If that's what happened, it would solve a lot of problems," Mom considered. "It could mean that Malevolence's threat is over. Angela could finally have her life back."

"Yeah, but she'd need some serious help to adjust," Leia replied. "That's why I asked you to come."

"You say she doesn't seem to remember anything from the last twenty years?" Mom asked.

"That's right," Leia replied.

Mom looked down at her considerable belly for a moment. Then she looked at Leia.

"This is gonna be fun," Mom added. "I've more than doubled in size since the last time she saw me. I was a hot model and superhero then."

"You're still hot, Mom," Leia said.

"She's right, Mom," Tanya concurred. "And Dad definitely thinks you're hot!"

"Ahem! Okay, ladies, thanks. You have eased my moment of body insecurity," Mom chuckled.

"So, is it being so curvy that makes you look younger or is it your Cat powers?" Tanya asked.

"Ooh, good question!" Leia agreed.

She smiled at her daughters' encouragement. She released the parking brake, looked over her shoulder to see if the way was clear and pulled back onto the road.

"I think it's a little of both," Mom replied with a grin.

———————

Leia cautiously opened the door to the professor's office. She had asked her mom and Tanya to wait in the hallway.

"Angela? It's me, Leia."

Angela had been staring out the office window but she turned around as soon as she heard Leia's voice.

"Leia!"

Angela looked almost ecstatic as she studied every detail of Leia's face and body. Leia was having a hard time reconciling the woman in front of her with her memories of Professor Doom. They just weren't the same woman!

"My goodness, you're so beautiful!" Angela exclaimed. "You look just like your father. I want to know everything about you."

Then her smiling face became filled with concern.

"And . . . I want to know why I don't remember. There's so much I don't remember."

Leia gave her birth mother a hug, pulling her close. Then she looked Angela in the eyes.

"I'll tell you what I know, but I want to warn you, you might not like what I have to say. You might not believe me. But what I'm about to tell you is the truth."

"I kind of thought you might say something like that. And I didn't even have to read your mind."

Leia spoke for several minutes concerning Malevolence, Angela's pregnancy, and the deal Crusader made with her. Leia also told Angela about her mom and her father and how they raised her.

Angela took all of this information in stride. But it was also apparent that she felt like she'd been hit by a truck.

"I went insane," Angela reasoned. "The reason I can't remember those years is because another personality lived them, not me."

"I'm afraid so."

Angela stood up, but she was shaky and unsure. She leaned against the desk.

"I've lost everything. I wanted to be a scientist. I was so deeply in love with your father. And when I learned I was pregnant, I wanted to be your mother! Instead, I never went to college, I became some kind of villain and I abandoned you and your father. And now, he's married to Sue? Sue had to raise you instead of me? This is a nightmare!"

Just then, Mom walked in the door with Tanya. She looked sympathetic to Angela now.

"It's not all bad, Angela," Mom said. "At least you've come back to us."

Angela looked at Leia's mother and studied her as thoroughly as she had Leia.

"Susan? Is that you?" Angela asked. "You're different."

Mom laughed at that. Somehow, it looked like that made things easier for her.

"It's been a long time," Mom added. "Of course, I'm different. But you don't have to tiptoe, Angela. It's okay to say I'm fat."

Angela continued to look at Leia's mother. It wasn't a rude stare. To Leia, it appeared to be someone trying to steady themselves by identifying with something or someone familiar. Leia could see that this was strange for Angela and difficult for the woman to accept. But she seemed oddly reassured as well.

"I didn't even think that was possible for you," Angela expressed. "You know, with your Cat powers and all."

"You've obviously never had a fat cat before," Mom answered. "It's possible."

"You wear it well. And who's this with you?"

"My name is Tanya," Leia's sister replied, her eyes like lasers focused on Angela.

"You and Steve had a daughter?" Angela asked Leia's mom. "She looks like you but her eyes and the way she speaks are like Steve."

"Yes," Sue confirmed.

"How old are you, Tanya?" Angela asked.

"I'm fifteen. Look, I only wanna know one thing."

"Tanya," Mom warned.

"It's alright, Sue. If Tanya wants to ask me something, I'll try to answer."

Tanya looked like she was struggling to control herself. She was angry, nearly furious.

"If you're all okay now, you're not Malevolence anymore, then who pays for killing Josh's mom and Black Fox?"

Mom and Leia didn't know what to say or do. Tanya had unleashed that out of nowhere.

Angela froze for a moment.

"Black Fox is dead?" she asked. "And . . . I killed her?"

"It wasn't your fault, actually," Leia answered. "Black Fox attacked my—attacked *Malevolence* while . . . she was in control of someone else's body."

"Josh's mother. Whoever Josh is."

"Josh is my sister's fiancé," Tanya offered. "The fa—"

"That's enough, Blunt Girl!" Leia hissed. "Mom, get Tanya out of here."

"Right," Mom replied. "I'm sorry, Angela."

Angela said nothing. She was still visibly shaken.

Mom looked at Tanya in a way that brooked no argument and they walked out of the office. Leia could only imagine the talking to that Tanya would get on the way back to the SUV.

"You call Sue 'Mom,'" Angela said, wiping a tear from her left eye.

"Yeah."

"It looks like she did a wonderful job raising you."

Leia felt bad for Angela. She could see the conflicting emotions on the older woman's face.

"I believe that you would have if you could," Leia offered.

"Would I? Some part of me didn't want to. And that part won out over what I thought I wanted."

"That's not fair to yourself. Malevolence—you—watched out for me ever since I was born. You protected me from a distance. You even saved my life a few times."

Angela was taken aback by that. "I did?"

Leia crossed her arms, trying to find a way to relay her thoughts in a comforting way to Angela. It wasn't easy, there was a lot to consider.

"I think the part that was you had more control over Malevolence's actions than either of us knew," Leia said. "She was angry and jaded, even ruthless, but when it came to me and Dad, I think maybe she tried to do the right thing. Even if she didn't do it the right way."

"What do you mean?"

"What Tanya was talking about. You—Malevolence had taken telepathic control of my fiancée's mother, which was wrong—but she just wanted to talk with Josh. She wanted to introduce herself. And to tell us that she approved of our getting married."

"That doesn't sound very supervillain-like," Angela said, confused.

"No, it wasn't," Leia smiled. "But it is very maternal."

Angela closed her eyes and concentrated.

"Fudge marshmallow cookies?" Angela said, her eyes still closed.

"What?" Leia asked.

"A memory. Sodas in the fridge and fudge marshmallow cookies in the cabinet."

"That's right," Leia understood. "Those were at Josh's mom's house."

"I thought Josh and I should talk," Angela quoted from her memory. "He's going to be your husband. He's the father of my grandchild."

"Yes, she said that," Leia confirmed.

Angela opened her eyes and walked over to Leia. She put her hand on Leia's lower belly.

"You're going to be a mother?" Angela asked.

"I'm still trying to get used to the idea, but yes."

"It's very strange. I remember that feeling, trying to get used to the idea that a baby was inside me. But I don't remember the rest of my pregnancy or giving birth to you."

"Maybe those memories will come back to you. And even if they don't, Dad can tell you. He was with you every step of the way. I think he even took pictures!"

Angela smiled at that and then turned away.

"Your fiancé, Josh . . . my actions as Malevolence led to his mother's death. He'll blame me . . . and he's probably right to."

Leia shook her head.

"No, you're wrong," she countered. "Of course, he's grieving terribly right now but he'll remember what actually happened. You weren't in the wrong here, Black Fox was."

"She was so angry. I remember Black Fox was angry," Angela added. "She hated me!"

"She hated the threat Malevolence represented. Black Fox brought an experimental device that Silver Knight had designed, some kind of telepathic scrambler. It hurt Malevolence and caused your powers to go wild. I used my own telekinesis to protect myself and Josh. But I couldn't save Josh's mom or Black Fox."

"You have telekinesis?"

"That and I can set things on fire with my thoughts."

"Pyrokinesis," Angela said, fascinated. "I've heard of it but I never knew it really existed."

Leia made her eyes glow with flame for a few seconds. Then she let them return to normal.

"You're an incredible young woman, Leia."

"Thanks."

"So . . . Black Fox is . . . was still a superhero. How well did you know her?"

"I knew her as Aunt Dana growing up, but we lost touch and I only ran into her and her son recently."

"Black Fox had a son?"

"Yes, with Uncle John."

Angela looked shocked and then pleasantly surprised.

"I knew they went on a few dates, that John liked her," Angela said, grinning.

Then the reality of Black Fox's death overshadowed her happiness for them and her smile quickly faded.

"I should go see John, turn myself in."

That's when Leia's smile faded, too.

"You can't. He's been dead for a long time."

Whatever color had remained in Angela's skin pigment drained when she heard that.

"How?"

"He sacrificed himself stopping a supervillain named Killer Knight. He saved Dad, Aunt Dana and two others."

Leia watched in stunned silence as Angela's grief burst like a dam. Her mind flooded with memories that weren't hers: a teenaged Angela meeting Uncle John in elementary school; then she had a brief crush on him in high school. Leia could feel every one of Angela's emotions battering her—Angela's love for John, no longer romantic. It was more like he became her own brother. She held deep respect for his accomplishments, who he'd become. And Angela also loved Aunt Dana. Leia's mind was flooded with years' worth of their conversations in a handful of heartbeats. Angela had been Aunt Dana's best friend for a long time. The deaths of Uncle John and Aunt Dana, combined with Angela's own loss of two decades and control of her own life, left her nearly inconsolable. Leia watched her collapse and wail like a lost soul.

As Leia experienced all of these emotions in her mind and heart, she fought to hold her own self together. She focused on the moment and the problem in front of her. She held Angela in her arms and stroked her hair gently, speaking occasionally to try and be reassuring. Most of all, she told Angela that she wasn't alone, that she would help her.

Other professors and staff came to see what was wrong. They were speechless and completely stunned to see Professor Angela Merrick having an emotional meltdown.

12

MISHA BREYER WAS NOT ACCUSTOMED to seeing the third-floor office area congested with people, much less the semi-mad panic that seemed to have erupted today. At first, she thought she heard a woman screaming but then the only sounds she could hear were the students and faculty trying to see what had caused the commotion in the first place. And people started talking among themselves.

" . . . would've thought that was Professor Merrick?" one man said.

"That student seems to have calmed her down," another man added.

"They kind of look alike. Are they related?" a female student asked.

"Isn't that—oh, what's her name—Leia something?" a male student wondered.

"Leia Hamilton?" Misha inquired.

"Yeah, that's it!" the male student replied. "She's the one who calmed the professor down."

That was odd, Misha thought. Leia despised that woman. Misha waded through the slowly dispersing crowd until she saw them for herself. Leia was on her knees and Professor Merrick had buried her head in Leia's shoulder and was—was that woman crying? Leia looked not only sympathetic but concerned for the other woman's well-being.

And at that moment, Misha saw it: the resemblance between Leia and Professor Merrick that the other student mentioned. It was uncanny! They had the same eyes, forehead, lips, and hair color! Misha wondered how she'd missed it before. She'd seen the two of them together, when Leia turned in or picked up papers or when they'd both gone to Professor Merrick's office to ask questions after class.

The tension! Leia never wanted to be anywhere near the woman, and the professor always seemed so guarded. That was more distracting, and entertaining, than what was right in front of her eyes.

A few minutes later, the professor recovered her composure and looked at Leia. Tears were still in her eyes, but was that a smile on her lips? Misha did a double-take and tried to hear what was being said.

"Thank you," Professor Merrick said. "After all I've done, I know I don't deserve your kindness."

"That wasn't, um, you," Leia replied. "I'm just glad you're you now."

"I'm so glad I got to learn about you. I hope I can get to know you and . . . your family better."

Leia went into her purse and pulled out a scrap of paper and a pen. She wrote something on it and handed it to the professor.

"This is my cell number, in case you need it," Leia continued. "Or you can contact me the other way. Either is fine. You can contact me any time."

"I doubt I'll contact you at any time. You need to take care of yourself, especially now. But I'll be in touch."

"Fair enough."

The women stood up and hugged. Then the professor went back in her office, closed the door, and Leia started to walk towards the stairs. Misha went running after her.

"Hey! Leia, wait up!"

"Oh hey, Misha!" Leia answered, half-distracted.

"You want to tell me what all that was about? Not just the drama but why do you two look so alike?"

Leia stopped and chuckled at that. She seemed so different to Misha today, more relaxed, surer of herself. Had something happened to cause this?

"You noticed that, huh?" Leia asked. "May as well tell you then. It'll come out soon enough anyway."

"What will?"

"Professor Merrick is my birth mother."

Misha's jaw dropped.

"Get out! Seriously? She's your mother?"

"Mom is my mother. Professor Merrick gave me half her genes."

It took a second or two for Misha to literally shake off her disbelief. "How'd you find out? Did she tell you?"

"Yeah, she asked me to come here to talk, so I did."

Misha put her hands on her hips, genuinely curious. "Why the drama then? Shouldn't this have been all happy and stuff?"

"I had to give her some bad news. A couple of her old friends that she lost touch with died. She was close to them once, so she took the news pretty hard."

"Oh. The professor is more human than she seems."

Misha slowly nodded in comprehension.

"Yeah."

Misha followed Leia as she walked at a leisurely pace towards the other end of the hallway.

"So, what happens now? Do your folks know that she contacted you?"

"Yeah, Mom drove me down here with Tanya. They're waiting for me in the car."

"Why didn't you come in your car? In fact, what happened to you yesterday? You missed your shift and didn't call in. You never do that!"

Leia stopped and looked away a moment, as if collecting her thoughts, deciding what she was going to say to Misha. Then she sighed.

"I'm sorry about that. I was with Josh at his mom's when—"

Leia looked troubled, haunted, like she was reliving a memory that was truly terrible. Misha could see that Leia was being strong for the professor, for her birth mother. But who was being strong for Leia?

Misha hugged Leia and held her for a moment, quietly supporting her friend.

Minutes later, Leia recovered her own composure and smiled at Misha. Her eyes still had a fragment of that look in them but at least she looked strong enough to handle it now.

"I need to tell you a few things," Leia continued. "You deserve that. You've been a good friend to me."

"Coffeehouse?" Misha asked.

"Too public. But I know just the place."

The stairs to the roof were poorly lit and the door at the top appeared to have been padlocked. But with one touch from Leia, it unlocked and she opened the door. For some reason, Leia brought the padlock with her.

"Okay, you've got my undivided attention," Misha assured Leia.

"Yesterday, Josh and I went to his mom's after Josh asked me to marry him. I said yes, of course."

Misha smiled brightly with that news. "Oh, wow. That's so cool, Leia! Congratulations! But I don't understand . . . that's good news . . . right?"

"Yes, it is. It's what I've wanted for a long time."

She narrowed her gaze. "Then I don't understand?"

The wind picked up and blew Leia's and Misha's hair wildly.

"What are those? They look like bone?" Misha said, pointing at Leia's head.

"They are bone. They're horns."

She wanted to say, "This is a joke, right?" but Leia's serious expression answered that question. Misha became a little fearful. She didn't want to freak out but that was becoming difficult.

"I'm pretty sure I've done your hair more than a dozen times, girl, and those were never there," Misha semi-joked. "How on Earth did you grow horns?"

"A lot has happened to me recently, Misha. I'm about to take you into my confidence about some pretty heavy things. Tell me now if you don't want to know."

Misha crossed her arms and cocked her head. "Who are you talking to, Leia? I may seem like a ditz at parties but I care about my friends . . . and you're obviously going through a lot. So, all I'm gonna ask is that you don't kill me, make me your zombie slave, or steal my soul or anything. Then we're cool."

"That's my Misha. Don't worry, I'm not a demon. Your soul is safe. Now, relax, I'm going to give you a little show!"

Leia tossed the padlock in the air then pointed at it. As gravity started to take hold of the padlock, it moved in the same patterns as Leia moved her arm. She made it dance and zoom in the air like a jet. Then she sent it on a rapid collision course with Misha, immediately stopping it two feet in front of her face.

"How are you doing that, Leia?"

"With my mind. But that's not all I can do."

Leia made the padlock return to her hand. Then she crushed it and showed the mangled metal mess to Misha. And somehow, she made the metal burst into flames. She dropped it on the roof to burn itself out.

"Are you a superhero or something? I thought this kind of stuff only happened in movies or comics!"

"I have the powers but I can't be a superhero. I have other priorities now that are more important."

That piqued Misha's curiosity.

"What do you mean, other priorities? You mean Josh? You said he proposed to you, but—"

"I'm pregnant, Misha. Josh and I are going to be a family."

"Wow! I'm really happy for you! Congratulations again!"

"Thanks."

"I'm not sure I could handle all this as well as you have. Super powers, an engagement and learning you're pregnant all in a few days! Does Josh know about your powers and . . . the horns?"

Leia chuckled. But it didn't look like she was very happy.

"Yeah, I showed him. I had to before I could accept his proposal."

"That was brave of you. He could have bailed. Some people might even see it as justified. Not me, of course."

Leia's eyebrows rose in amusement and she managed a genuine smile. "Of course. Well, I gambled that he'd love me more than he'd fear me."

"Well, you won the bet, so good call. How much have you told the folks, yours and his?"

Leia's expression soured again.

"What? What did I say, Leia?"

"My folks know everything," Leia said, her eyes closed and voice shaky. "It's complicated . . . but both of my parents have powers, too. That's why I have powers."

"Your dad and Professor Doom?"

"Mom does, too. She and Dad were on a superhero team once. So, they completely understood my circumstances."

Misha contemplated her friend's words.

"A team? But as far as I know, there's only been one superhero te— your folks were AR-MEN??"

Leia nodded.

"Leia, do you realize how intense this is? I like to think I'm understanding, and you did warn me this was heavy stuff, but . . ."

"I haven't gotten to the worst part yet. Can you handle it?"

Misha looked at Leia and she saw it again. The pain behind Leia's eyes. Whatever memory was torturing Leia was worse than anything she'd already told Misha. At the same time, Misha's own conscience was telling her that she couldn't turn away from her friend when Leia so clearly needed her right now.

"I can handle it, Leia. Just tell me."

"So, yeah, my folks were superheroes. And . . . my birth mother is . . . or at least she was a supervillain."

"Okay, that's not a big stretch of the imagination."

Leia told Misha about what happened at Josh's mother's house, including the explosion and deaths.

"Oh! Oh, Leia—oh, no. No! That's—that's—I am so sorry!"

Misha hugged Leia and let Leia slump and lay her head on her left shoulder. Misha could finally start to understand a small portion of the burden her friend had been carrying. It was more than she could possibly have managed on her own. And while Misha had no superpowers of her own, she did know how to be there for her friends.

"How's Josh?" Misha asked after a long pause.

"He's taking this hard. He was very close to his mom. In fact, I need to get back to him. But given all that's happened, I didn't want to keep you out of the loop."

"Thanks. I'm glad I could be here for you. And I will continue to be here for you, Leia. But scoot now, your man needs you."

"Yes, ma'am."

"Take the night off. I'll cover for you again. If anyone asks, I'll make something up."

"You just want my job," Leia chided, finally smiling again.

"Am I that transparent?" Misha returned the smile. "Now go! Really."

———

Leia spread her arms and her body lifted off of the roof. Then she sparkled with flames, surrounding but not touching her.

Misha's eyes widened at the sight of Leia's levitation. She was literally speechless.

Leia pointed herself in the direction she wanted to go and leaned forward. For the first time, Leia Hamilton took flight.

This is amazing! I can't believe it! This is really me, this is really happening! Oh! There's Mom's car. Okay, Leia, slow your descent. Good. Now just . . .

Leia landed feet first about one hundred paces from Mom's car. Unfortunately, she nearly shattered that part of the street in the process. Mom and Tanya emerged from the car and ran towards Leia.

"Are you alright?" Mom asked.

"Yes. I'm fine. Everything's fine."

"Good. I'm glad to hear that, because do you have any idea how stupid a stunt that was?"

"I'm starting to. At least nobody was hurt."

"True, but somebody's going to have to pay to fix that road. And if you didn't have your father's invulnerability, you and my grandbaby would not have survived that."

Mom had her stern scolding expression on but Leia could easily read the fear and worry behind it.

"I'm sorry," Leia added. "I just wanted to see if I could fly."

"And you can. Now don't do that again till after you deliver your child."

Leia sighed.

"You're right. I won't do it again."

Leia looked at Tanya, who exuded excitement.

"What?" Leia asked.

"I don't care what I've said in the past. You are the coolest sister ever!"

"Thanks."

"I can't wait to get my powers!" Tanya added.

"Um . . . " Leia had no idea how to respond to that.

Then she looked at Mom again. Mom looked very confused.

"What?" Leia asked.

"I just said 'my' and 'grandbaby' in the same sentence," Mom answered. "That's very new to me. I'm only thirty-nine."

"I can relate. It's not very real to me yet, aside from the dizziness and nausea."

"Oh, give it a month," Mom added. "It'll seem real enough when you start showing."

13

THIS IS AN AUDIO JOURNAL from Angela Merrick, recorded at 6:30 p.m. on August 14th, 2013. I wanted to do this for my daughter, Leia Hamilton, and . . . and her father, Steven.

I've been myself for three days now, but I don't know if that will last. If my other persona, Malevolence, resurfaces, I want some kind of way to convey my thoughts and feelings to them in case I don't return.

Leia, my daughter, I couldn't bring myself to tell you what I felt in my heart: that I love you so dearly. I love you more than anyone except your father. I think you've become your father's likeness in so many ways. He's raised you with the ideals that attracted me to him in the first place and I can tell he instilled them in you without trying. That's just the man he is.

But you've become who you are because you've fought for it. You're a young woman forged in fire, a modern warrior woman with a heart. Hold on to that heart; it's what separates you from me. I have all of the same passions, all of the same wants as you. I just don't have the inner strength to achieve my dreams on my own. I've always known this.

Maybe that's why I made Malevolence. I have to acknowledge my own failings or I'll never have a prayer of making up for them, if that's even possible. From what you told me about what she did, how she behaved, she seems to lack my inhibitions, my limitations. She is everything I aspire to be, yet she attains her desires in ways that are anathema to me. She has no moral center, no sense of good or evil. She just does what she thinks is right and doesn't care about the consequences.

For the harm she's caused, for the lives she's taken, I despise her.

For what she's accomplished, however, I envy her.

Who am I now, really? Who is Angela Merrick? Who is the woman you revived from the depths of Malevolence?

I feel like a woman out of her own time, like Rip Van Winkle awakening from a very long sleep. And I'm no longer the woman I was. I'm not a young adult anymore. I'm almost middle-aged and my child is now the young adult . . . and since she's pregnant with her first child, I guess that makes me a grandmother! It's a lot to take in and process.

So, how am I supposed to pick up these pieces of my life and start again? I don't have the skills and knowledge of Malevolence. I'm a woman with a high school education and no practical experience, even though, ironically, I have a tenured position at Digby College. Am I just supposed to fake my way through being a teacher? I don't even like being in front of people! I quit high school theater after one rehearsal.

I've taken a leave of absence from the college but that's not indefinite. I'll eventually have to come back.

For now, I'm trying to connect with my past again. I can't face Steven yet, not after all I put him through. I'm too ashamed, too frightened. I'm afraid I'll see him and fall in love with him all over again. But he's been married to Sue for so much longer than he ever even knew me. I have to respect that. She's the woman he loves, not me. And, knowing that . . . if I saw him, I know it would break my heart.

Because I'll always love him!

6:47 p.m. - One thing I'll give my alter-ego: she wasn't hurting for money! Between the cash and the credit cards in her—in my wallet, I could go any-where I want and buy almost anything. I don't think I want to know how she came by it, though. But if it helps me till I can get my bearings, then it's money well-spent.

Right now, I'm driving about forty miles outside of town to the community of Punto Verde, California. I've used my telepathy to locate my mother. She and my father used to live in Digby, but a lot can happen in twenty years. I'm just glad I found her. She'll be sixty-six this year. That's so hard to imagine.

I have two brothers, Charlie and Rex, but they must be further away. I couldn't locate them. I couldn't find my father, either. I hope he's still alive.

Okay, this is the address!

After parking by the curb, Angela left her car and walked to the mailbox by the faded wood picket fence. The mailbox had the letters "Merrick," but the "k" was missing. She opened the gate and walked down the curved sidewalk to the front porch of the small white one-story house. There was a wooden table with a half-completed jigsaw puzzle still on top of it. Angela could see a light through one of the curtained windows, a silhouetted form inside.

Excited yet extremely nervous, Angela searched for a doorbell. There wasn't one so she knocked four times on the front door. Fifteen seconds later, Angela heard a muffled voice through the door.

"Who is it?" the older woman answered.

"I'm your daughter, Angela."

Then she remembered her mother's nickname for her.

"It's Angie!" Angela quickly added.

There was at least thirty seconds of dead silence. Then a chain was released on the other side of the door and Angela heard it unlock. The door opened slowly.

Her mother had not aged well. Her once long, jet-black hair was shoulder-length and salt and pepper gray, its luster long gone. Worry and stress lines had etched deeply into the woman's formerly lineless face and age spots had appeared on her forehead and neck. She'd lost weight and looked ill.

But her eyes were still sharp. Angela could sense that her mind was only slightly dulled, as if on a medication. Her mother's eyes narrowed for a few seconds and then opened wide in recognition.

"It *is* you, Angie!" her mother exclaimed. "Where did you go?!"

"I was ill, Mom, mentally ill. Until just recently, it's like I was another person."

"We mourned you, thought you were dead, just like your brothers."

Angela felt like she was going to faint, but she made herself remain standing.

"Charlie and Rex—both? How?"

Her mother motioned for Angela to come inside. Still dismayed by this new revelation, Angela almost lost her footing as she entered the house. She remained standing while her mother sat down on a recliner in the living room.

"They both enlisted after 9/11," her mother continued. "Charlie died in Iraq. Rex died in Afghanistan. It drove your father to drinking, losing his sons after losing you. He died last year of liver disease."

Angela felt not only defeated, she wished she'd never come to this place. She didn't know what 9/11 was but obviously that event had led to her brothers joining the military, perishing in some kind of combat. And her father was dead, too?

"So . . . you were in a mental institution, Angie?"

"No. I developed a different personality," Angela said, not caring anymore how it sounded. "And that other woman lived my life for twenty years."

"Multiple personality, huh? I believe you. But it still doesn't change that you weren't here. And we still thought you were dead. What did you do all this time, you know, as that other person?"

Something sounded seriously off to Angela about the way her mother was talking. She was far too accepting. *Why?*

"You're taking this all pretty well in stride, Mom. I come back 'from the dead,' tell you I had another personality all this time and you're okay with it?"

"I've got terminal cancer, Angie-honey. I didn't bother with chemo and my hospice nurse left before you got here. I'm on so much pain medication, you could tell me you'd become a Greek goddess and I'd probably believe you."

Angela felt like she wanted to curl up in a ball or run far away and never turn back.

Not Mom, too!

"Mom," Angela said, her voice trembling with grief. "How—how long do you have to live?"

"Not long. Maybe a few days. A few weeks at most. Honestly, I'd rather it come sooner than later."

"I'm so sorry, Mom. I wish I could have come sooner."

Her mother looked at her seriously for a moment, then she smiled.

"Angie, I've got some beer in the fridge. Let's talk for a little bit."

"You're going to mix beer with your pain meds?"

"What's it gonna do, kill me?" the older woman replied with a hoarse laugh. "Now c'mon! I wanna hear all about your life!"

Angela told her mother about Leia and her soon-to-be grandchild. She told her what she knew about Malevolence and what Malevolence had accomplished. Her mother seemed pleased to know that their family line would continue. She was happy that her daughter had a job as a professor at a university and had tenure.

But in what seemed a short time, Angela could see her mother losing energy. Maybe the older woman's pain medications were taking effect. Whatever the reasons, her mother's eyelids grew heavier and she began letting her head rest more and more against the soft recliner, unable to hold it up.

Soon after that, Angela helped her mother to bed. She looked at all the medications the poor woman had to take on a daily basis, just to function. Once her mother was asleep, Angela walked around the little two-bedroom house. She sat on the sofa in the living room and looked through her mother's family albums. Then she walked through the house again and memorized all of the pictures on the walls. They were all pictures from simpler, happier times. Most were old enough that she remembered them.

Angela drank some more of her mother's beer. Then she cried for an hour. She mourned the loss of life, the missed experiences and memories, so much time she'd lost with her younger brothers, whom she had helped raise and cherished. She mourned her inability, despite all of the telepathic and telekinetic power at her command, to make her mother whole again.

Angela Merrick felt like a complete failure.

She considered going out to her car and making one more audio journal entry but decided against it. What good would it do? What else could she say at this point. She knew her heart was shattered in a million pieces and there was no way to put it back together. Everything that Angela had known was gone, dead, or dying.

There was the future. But she didn't feel ready, willing, or able to face it.

Inside her mind, Angela woke Malevolence and called to her.

You want to end the pain, even if it means letting me out?

"Yes," Angela said, still crying.

Very well. I will grant your wish.

In that moment, Angela ceded control back to Malevolence to end her mother's suffering . . . and, in a way, her own.

14

LEIA AWOKE FROM A FITFUL sleep, still tired, her eyes burning. It was just after three o'clock in the morning. In the last few days, it had become harder and harder to retain her energy. At first, she thought she'd just overdone it by flying and showing Misha her powers. But that wasn't it; her body was continuing to adapt to its new guest, her child. Her breasts were growing and felt heavier, she had occasional difficulty concentrating and she was perpetually tired. At least the nausea wasn't constant.

She had noticed the development of a slight-but-definite bulge shape to her lower belly area, too. It seemed to grow less slight by the day, at least to Leia.

Wow. That's where my kid is. Hi! I wonder if you're a boy or a girl?

"Would you like to know?" a familiar voice said in Leia's mind. "In a few weeks, I can probably make sure and let you know."

Malevolence?

"Hi, Leia. I missed you."

Where did Angela go? Why are you here?

"My other half found that she wasn't so well-suited for the real world. Tragic, really, though I'm not complaining."

What happened?

"She decided to go on a road trip to try and find herself, but it was a bad idea. She went to find her mother. And she found her. But she also found only heartache and misery.

"At the end, she called on me, woke me from my sleep, deep within her. Angela knew she couldn't make the hard choices. She didn't have the resolve to accomplish what she really wanted. But she knew I could. Angela was in so much pain, so much despair. She'd lost so much that she couldn't cope anymore. So, I helped her."

What do you mean, you helped her?

"I don't want you to blame me or think of me as a monster. I only did what was asked of me. That's all I ever do."

Leia tried to master her emotions.

I don't know who I'm angrier at, you or Angela! You barged in on a very important meeting with Josh's mother, took over her body without her permission, and your presence caused the confrontation with Black Fox that led to both of their deaths!

And Angela—most people don't have other personalities to handle things when life gets tough! I don't blame you for that, Malevolence, I blame her! What she did was unfair, in my opinion—a cop out. You're both parts of one being, one person. I think you're just an extension of her. But it seems like she made you a part that's meant to take the blame for her actions and then you act like you don't care. But you do care, don't you? You care a great deal. Otherwise, why stay vigilant over me, keeping track of me, protecting me by all means necessary all these years, unless you care?

"I never said I didn't care. Concerning you, I care a great deal. I want you to know that."

I understand. What do you want? Why did you contact me?

"You mean, besides out of maternal concern? Actually, I want to speak with your father."

Why?

"That's between me and him."

Not good enough. I'm not going to ask Dad to meet you without a good explanation from you. You want to meet him? Ask him yourself!

"He'll be more likely to come if you talk to him. Leia, your father and I do need to talk . . . about your marriage, about your baby . . . and about what happened at Josh's mother's house . . . and everything since. Would you please ask him to meet with me?"

Leia wrestled with the idea for a minute.

I'll convey the message but it's up to him whether he meets with you or not.

"That's fine. Tell him . . . please ask him to meet me on the roof of the Jason building. I'll be there at eleven o'clock tonight."

And then Malevolence left Leia's mind.

———————

Malevolence watched Steven Hamilton waiting on the rooftop at 10:55 p.m. The moon was out and shining while the evening breeze was cool and pleasant. Steven wore a t-shirt and blue jeans.

She had been there since 10:30 p.m. and had observed his arrival. She drank in his thoughts and appearance.

"This is a familiar scene, Angela. You're here, aren't you?"

"Yes, I am. But you've changed, Steven," Malevolence said directly to his mind, not revealing her location.

She unleashed a sensation like a million electrical needles barely touching him but completely surrounding his body. Thanks to her telekinesis, she knew he couldn't move.

Suddenly, she was behind him, running her left hand down his back. Then she grabbed him with both hands, turned him towards her and kissed his lips like she had when they had been in love. She sensed his heart race, his instinctive reactions but she also felt his thoughts and his will resist her with equal force. Undeterred, she leaned against his chest and continued to fawn over him.

"You're as handsome as ever, but I must say, you're starting to resemble your wife," Malevolence said with a smirk, deliberately gripping his love handles through his shirt.

"I'll take that as a compliment. Angela. Is there a *point* to any of this?"

She raised an eyebrow and smiled mischievously.

"There's *always* a point to everything I do, my forever love, but a girl needs to have her fun, too. And I haven't gotten to play with you in sooo long!"

Steven not only looked unimpressed but almost disappointed.

"You know I can't return your feelings," he replied. "So why do this?"

Malevolence's enthusiasm waned as did her smile.

"Yes, I know. You love the furball now. The mother of your other daughter."

"If you know these things, then why—"

"Because I thought I would enjoy myself before getting to serious business."

Steven struggled against her telekinetic grip to no avail.

"What do you mean, Angela?"

"I'm Malevolence. I do all of the things Angela wishes she could do or the things she's afraid or unwilling to do."

She braced herself for what she was about to tell him.

"Angela was not adapting well to living in the present. Really, all she had going for her was her relationship with our daughter. She made the mistake of looking up her old family. That was the last straw."

"What do you mean? What happened to her family?"

Malevolence stroked Steven's left cheek.

"Dead. They were all dead, except dear old Mom. Pamela Merrick was only dying from cancer."

"What happened to her younger brothers? Her father?"

"Charlie and Rex died in military combat overseas. Her father succumbed to alcohol and grief over losing all his children. Poor Angela. She'd lost her past, you, John and Dana, twenty years with our daughter and then she lost her family, too." Her voice dripped with sarcasm, yet every word was the truth. "She just couldn't take any more. So, she turned to me."

Steven looked like he didn't want to know the answer, but he asked anyway.

"What did you do?"

"I just gave her mother a little push with my mind while she slept. Snapped her neck like a pencil. Death was instant, no pain."

"Why are you telling me this, Angela?"

Malevolence waved her right hand in front of Steven's body and the telekinetic field dispersed.

"Our long-ago agreement was that I keep my nose clean, Crusader. I've just confessed to a murder."

She stared at him, seeing Steven's eyes widen as he realized her intent.

"You know what you have to do," she said. "Kill me."

"What?"

"I won't resist you, Steven. Be as merciful to me as I was to my mother."

She was desperate. They had been her family, too.

"I can't do that," he insisted. "I don't fight and I won't kill anymore."

"I know you stopped being a superhero to become a family man. But you still have your powers. You can still fight."

He was still close enough to touch but she dared not reach out to him. Her pride wouldn't allow her to ask for the solace she dearly craved. Death seemed the only alternative and Steven was powerful enough to end her. It was justice, why was he resisting her?

"As you said, I left that life behind to become a family man," Steven continued. "I'm not Crusader anymore. I'm just a man."

"A man who can lift twenty tons without breathing hard. A man who can fly! How can you say you're not Crusader anymore!"

It had been such a simple idea to lure her old love here and provoke him into killing her. But it wasn't working at all. She could feel the chance slipping away.

"Because I'm not," he added. "If you doubt me, read my thoughts. You have my permission."

Malevolence closed her eyes and concentrated. After several seconds, she opened her eyes, looking surprised, confused and more than a little sad. At first, she wouldn't look Steven in the eyes.

"I knew you took your family to church. I saw that by watching Leia," she related. "But I never read your thoughts or Sue's. It's hard to believe the Judge and Executioner of Criminals has become a pacifist Christian."

He stepped back a few feet, looking perplexed.

"Why is that so hard to believe?" he asked.

"Why? Steven, you were like a god to me!!"

Why did her words sound so strange now? Was it her belief or her desperation talking?

"A god? Where'd that come from?" he seemed genuinely perplexed.

"Are you kidding? You could smash mountains! With that sword of yours, you were unstoppable! You could have ruled the world if you'd wanted to."

Steven shook his head. "I never wanted that."

"I know, but your power is what drew me to you. And even before I knew about your abilities, I knew you had greatness within you. I could feel it. I wanted to be near that, I wanted to feel special like that!"

He sighed. She sensed his frustration building.

"I was never a god," he continued. "I didn't deserve to be worshipped like that. That's not fair to yourself or to me."

"You have your worship and I have mine," she quipped. "That's why I wanted your child, to make your greatness forever tied to me . . . to make my child a demi-god!"

His gaze narrowed.

"Stop this!" he demanded.

"Make me! Shut me up! Silence me! I've defied you! I deserve death!"

She rushed forward with hands raised, trying once more to provoke him into attacking.

"No! I will not kill you!" Steve closed his eyes and clenched his fists.

Malevolence halted her approach and looked at Steven with disappointment bordering on hatred.

"Very well, my love. Then know this: I offered myself to you—to love you and to die by your hand. And you've refused me. Anything I do from now on is your fault, not mine!"

―――――――

Malevolence flew away. Steve took a deep breath and slowly let it out.

"How long have you been there, Sue?" Steve asked without looking behind him.

"The whole time," Sue replied. "I'm proud of you."

Steve followed Malevolence with his eyes as she flew further and further away.

"Thanks. But this is nowhere near over yet. She'll be back."

Steve turned around. Sue was right beside him in Cat form.

"I didn't know she literally worshipped you," Sue remarked.

"There's a lot I didn't know about her. But I believe her. I think she finally told me the truth about why she wanted to be with me and why she agreed to have Leia."

Steve smiled as Sue snuggled against his shoulder. He knew she would feel him trembling.

"Are you alright?" she asked.

"That . . . was really difficult. I had forgotten how seductive Angela could be and how cruel. I knew I couldn't do what she was asking, I couldn't actually kill her, but I let a madwoman go. Again. Anything she does now is my responsibility."

"That's not fair to yourself!" Sue sighed in frustration. "She set up the circumstances. You're not responsible for her actions!"

"Maybe not, but I doubt that will matter to her victims."

"Don't judge yourself, Steve. That's not up to you."

Steve relaxed into his wife's cuddle. He was exhausted now, emotionally and physically. He looked down at the ground and saw an electronic device. A digital voice recorder. He picked it up.

"Malevolence left something for us to find. It looks like a recording device. Maybe she recorded something for Leia."

"Why? That doesn't make sense," Sue wondered. "She's already in telepathic contact with her."

"I don't know. But here it is."

Sue stroked his arm but he could feel her tensing up.

"I think this is something else," Sue considered.

"What do you mean?"

"Despite everything she said, only one thing is true. She loved you then and she loves you now, just as deeply as I love you. She still wants you, but she knows things have changed and she doesn't know what to do. That will drive a person crazy."

Steve nodded. He knew his wife's words were true.

"And unpredictable. I think you're in very serious danger, Sue."

"I've known that. But I think if she really wanted me dead, I'd be dead already. After all, there's lots worse things she could have done than call me furball."

15

MALEVOLENCE WAS AWARE SHE WASN'T alone as she flew through the air.

"How long have you been there, young man?" Malevolence asked.

She concentrated and the shadows on her clothing pulled away from her and formed Dane Fox. She froze his body's movements with her mind and held him close to her body so he wouldn't fall.

"You're the son of Black Fox and Silver Knight, aren't you?"

"Yes, and you're Malevolence, the woman who killed my mother."

Malevolence turned her head and looked at him with a mixture of irritation and dismissiveness.

"Oh, let's not be melodramatic," she countered. "It's true that my telekinesis caused her death but you also know I wasn't in control of that power at the time. So, I don't think I deserve the blame for her death."

"Then who does?"

Malevolence looked away and sighed.

"I'm not heartless. She was my best friend once. Did you know that?"

"No, I didn't."

"I grieve for her. I didn't want her to die. For all of these years, I left her alone because, even though we were no longer friends, I respected her."

She could feel his surprise even though she still wasn't looking at him.

"What? Did you keep track of her like you kept track of Leia?" he wondered.

"Of course. I wanted to know how all of the ones I loved were doing."

"Then why did you stay away? Why did you stay so far away from all the ones you loved? That doesn't make sense to me."

She returned his gaze, her temper starting to flare.

"Of course, it doesn't. You're not me," Malevolence said sharply. Then she sighed again. "I had done terrible things, killed people. I knew I wasn't going to change. And I knew they wouldn't approve. So, I stayed away . . . but I never abandoned them."

She saw Dane raise an eyebrow.

"Your version of having your cake and eating it, too?"

Malevolence couldn't help but grin at that. "What a delightful analogy! I like you."

She and Dane landed softly next to a decadent high-rise building in the new business district of town. Dane had no choice but to follow her mental commands. He walked stiffly behind her.

"Don't worry, I'll handle everything," Malevolence commanded. "Just follow my lead but don't say anything."

They walked in the front door. She let her hair resume its normal raven appearance and allowed her eyes to display their pupils again, no longer glowing. She looked at the Hispanic man in a freshly pressed gray hotel uniform. He had alert brown eyes, close cropped black hair, and a trim mustache. She smiled at him and his eyes took on a glazed appearance.

"This man is with me. His name is Dane Fox and he is my business associate. He is to have full access to my quarters, no questions asked. And I want a spare key made for him."

"Yes, Professor Merrick," the man said. "I'll take care of it immediately."

"Thank you, you're a darling," Malevolence replied with a half-hearted smile.

She and Dane walked to the nearby elevators. After a minute's wait, they ascended to the top floor and entered the Presidential Suite.

"This is yours?" Dane asked.

"I allow myself a few perks. After all, I bought this land and had this hotel built. It's mine. I think I can allow myself the best room in the house."

"You own this? You're that wealthy? How?"

"Ask me no questions and I'll tell you no lies, my young friend."

"I'm not your friend!" Dane exclaimed, sounding as if he was not fully believing his own words.

Malevolence turned and looked at him with a half-grin and narrowed her eyes.

"You could be whatever I want you to be and you'd have no say in the matter," she revealed. "That's the kind of risk you took in approaching me tonight. So, isn't it better to consider yourself my friend than my enemy?"

"I don't know what to think anymore!" Dane answered. "It's all so . . . confusing."

"An honest answer! Now we're getting somewhere."

Malevolence walked over to a wooden cabinet and grabbed what looked like a crystal bottle filled with an amber liquid and put it on the countertop. Then she picked up two glasses from another shelf in the cabinet, placed them on the countertop and poured some of the alcoholic liquid into them. She brought the glasses over and set one of them on a table in front of Dane and kept the other for herself.

"The way I look at it, you came to me for a reason," Malevolence said. "It wasn't to kill me or you'd have taken your shot when you had it. So, you must want information, right?"

Dane didn't say anything.

"I'm willing to accommodate you . . . Dane, is it? I'll tell you whatever you want to know."

"Why? I don't understand your actions at all."

Malevolence chuckled and took a drink of the amber liquid. Then she cast a sideways glance at Dane and smiled.

"You're a lot like her. So direct, forceful. So, convinced you're right, even when you know you're not sure."

Malevolence looked out the tall windows and raised her glass in a toast. She was trying to project confidence to hide just how much she was grieving.

"Black Fox—Dana—you were the most honest woman I've ever met. Long ago, I helped you. And then you were there for me when I needed you. In return, I was your faithful confidante . . . until I pursued Steven and became what I am now," she said, her voice filled with sadness. "I'm going to miss you."

Then she drank from her glass, still staring out the windows.

"What do you want with me?" Dane demanded from behind her.

"You forget, you invited me to your party," Malevolence replied, turning around to face him. "When you caught a ride in my shadows, you entered my world. As Crusader could tell you, that's a very dangerous place. So, I commend your courage and audacity."

Malevolence paced away from Dane, walking back into the kitchen area. She stopped.

"But the real question is, what do you want from me, Dane Fox?"

She turned around and gazed at Dane with curiosity and surprise.

"You're alone now! For the first time in your life, you're without your mother. You know her death was a tragedy but you also know it wasn't my fault, and you don't know what to do. 'Do I continue on as a superhero, even though Mother didn't finish training me?' And you know you're not ready for that. She'd been taking you on missions but she hadn't let you solo yet. So, you wonder 'Do I just become a regular man instead and find my place in this world?'"

Then Malevolence stopped. She looked startled.

"Leia! You like my Leia, don't you? Or you did until you learned about the baby . . . and Josh. You know you can't have her, so you're in a real bind, aren't you?"

Malevolence took another drink and slowly walked towards him.

"You know, we're in the same predicament, really. I can't have Crusader and you can't have Leia. We're both grieving. We're both human beings gifted with extraordinary powers. And we feel all alone in this world."

Malevolence put her arms around his neck and looked at him with pity and intrigue, a bittersweet smile forming on her lips. A spark flew through his body and he could suddenly move again.

"The way I see it, we have an opportunity here," Malevolence continued, her eyes glowing once again along with her red highlights.

Dane looked into her eyes. His emotions were so conflicted. He knew part of what she was saying was completely accurate. And he was afraid of being alone. He felt guilty for his mother's mistake and frustrated by his feelings for Leia. Everything seemed to have led to this moment.

He hesitated briefly. Was this the best of both worlds or a deal with the devil? Was he trying to have his cake and eat it, too, just like her? In the midst of his grief, it was too much to contemplate. So, he made up his mind in that moment, for better or worse . . . and took Malevolence's hand.

She pulled him close, as if to kiss him, looking deeply into his eyes. Their lips were almost close enough to touch and their raw emotions were clear for both to see and feel, like their hearts beating loud in their chests.

Then Malevolence pulled back from Dane.

"No," she whispered softly.

"What? I don't understand!"

"I can't do this to you. Or to her, your mother. I can't claim to honor her memory and also use her son like this."

"You felt the same as I did, I could tell. Why not act on it?"

"Just because you can do a thing doesn't mean you should. It would have been easy to give in to those emotions, yes . . . because we're hurting, both needing something. But someday, you'd resent me for taking advantage of your grief and loneliness, robbing you of something precious."

Dane turned and hit the nearest wall.

"I do find myself genuinely caring for you, Dane. I just want to express that in a better way. Maybe we can help each other through our grief together after all."

"You're talking about being friends," Dane replied bitterly.

"You could have worse friends than me."

Malevolence touched Dane's forehead and he began to lose consciousness. She used her telekinesis to move him to the couch in his drowsy state.

"You won't understand right now," she imparted. "But I will help and protect you. I owe your mother that much and more."

16

LEIA AND JOSH HAD SOME time to waste. A week had gone by and they were at the airport waiting for his father's flight to arrive. They'd just learned its takeoff had been delayed because of bad weather in Chicago; it was running more than an hour late.

Josh had hooked up his earbuds to the headphone jack on the digital recorder.

"Are you sure you wanna hear this?" Josh asked.

"It's from Angela, not Malevolence," Leia replied. "I have to hear it. It might be important, and she wanted me to hear it. But I want you to listen, too."

"Alright."

They each took an earbud and when she was ready, Leia started the playback from the beginning.

Knowing that Angela had correctly predicted that she might not be around much longer made the recording even more painful to hear. At the same time, it was beautiful to Leia. It truly proved that Angela Merrick was a real person and that her birth mother loved Leia and her father. Hearing Angela's understanding of who she was and what she'd become made sense. And it made Angela's mental suicide so tragic.

Leia thought it was over at the point where Angela arrived at her mother's house and she'd stopped recording. But there was a loud click sound and then the recording continued.

Leia, this is Malevolence. I'm sorry. I know you were happy to have Angela back. Truthfully, so was I. But that wasn't meant to be. She's gone now and I'm here in her place.

Angela already said a lot on this recording, so I'll keep this brief. I want you to play this part for Josh. Please. I feel I owe it to him to do this.

Josh, there's no way I can make amends for what happened to your mother. I am so terribly sorry that my actions led to her death. If you want to blame me or hate me, that's fine. I understand.

I do hope you can believe me, at least someday, that I meant no harm to her. I should have just met you and Leia in person, but that's not my style. I went for the dramatic and it nearly got all of us killed. If I had the power, I'd turn back time or bring your mother back from the dead . . . but I can't.

I meant what I told you before we got interrupted. I'm glad you've been so good to my Leia and I will continue to support the two of you—and your child—in any way I can . . . as long as I can. I love you both. For what it's worth, I'm proud of you two. Goodbye.

"I—wow, I honestly don't know what to say about that," Josh said.

Leia removed her earbud while Josh did the same. Leia peered at the portable device and then him.

"She's sincere, Josh. She didn't have to do that."

"I know. I don't hate her. It's just gonna take time to sort everything out."

Leia nodded.

"These last few days, you've kept me from losing my mind, Leia. It's gonna be rough seeing Dad and . . . going to the funeral. But I can do this with you by my side."

"I love you too, cowboy."

Leia lost herself in Josh's eyes for a moment.

"Having things to look forward to helps," he added. "Our wedding, this baby."

Leia looked down with a slight frown and put her hand on her abdomen.

"I don't think I'm looking forward to how big my belly's going to get with this baby," she sighed.

She meant that. The thought had begun to cross her mind more frequently as time passed. Then Josh took her hand in his and kissed it. His gaze went to her abdomen then returned to her eyes, a smile never leaving his face.

"As long as you're both healthy, I'll look forward to it," Josh assured her. "I want to take pictures—lots of pictures! You know, to look back on in the future!"

Leia raised an eyebrow in protest. Then she relented with a shrug.

"If you don't mind whatever expression I have on my face when you take the picture, then you can take as many pictures as you want."

"Deal, love!"

Playfully, she put both hands on her hips.

"Are you saying you'll be totally fine with the weight I'll gain having this baby, Joshua Manning?"

"Yes."

Her lips and expression remained semi-stern but inwardly, she appreciated what he said.

"And if I stay plump because I can't lose the weight from having this baby?" she added.

"That won't lower my interest in you one bit, Leia Hamilton."

For a few seconds, Leia just stared at Josh in disbelief while he beamed at her lovingly. And then she grinned.

"I love you! Now go get me some ice cream, Josh. I'm starving!"

"Any particular kind?"

She stepped behind him, grabbed his shoulders gently and physically turned him around. She reached over his right shoulder and her index finger pointed ahead of him.

"At the stand over there, they have this one called Chocolate Banana Avalanche!" she continued. "I want four scoops, buddy, in a cup!"

"You totally set me up for this, didn't you?" Josh chuckled.

"It's payback, y'know? You got me pregnant," Leia beamed, grinning.

"True."

As he began to walk towards the confection cart, she lightly grabbed his wrist. He turned his head.

"See if they have sprinkles!" she pleaded. "And whipped cream! And hot fudge syrup on top!"

Josh laughed. "Are you trying to gain ten pounds today?"

"It's gonna happen soon enough anyway. May as well get the suspense over with, right?"

Josh laughed again and made a mock bow to Leia. "Thine wish is my command, milady!"

And then he ran for the ice cream vendor as quick as he could. Leia giggled at the sight, just happy to see Josh in a better mood. That was her real objective. Satisfying her craving at the same time was just a nice bonus.

———

Once he'd gone around the corner, Josh stopped and leaned against a wall. As dozens of people walked nearby, Josh closed his eyes and clenched his fists. Images from the day he lost his mother still raged through his mind. Those images collided with the images of Leia being so in love with him and his feelings of pride in their relationship, his happiness at the idea of marrying her and starting a family. He felt bittersweet tears burning in his eyes and wiped them away with his right hand.

Then Josh stood up straight and composed himself.

"Leia, you're the best part of my life right now," Josh said softly to himself. "You may not know it, but you've given me something to live for, to dream about. So, I'm not gonna fall apart. My future's with you and I'm gonna do everything I can to make you happy!"

———————

One hour—and four devoured scoops of whip cream and fudge sauce-covered Chocolate Banana Avalanche ice cream with sprinkles and a healthy dose of playful flirting between Josh and Leia—later, David Manning's flight arrived at the airport. He was one of the last people to depart the plane with his travel bag on wheels. When he saw Josh, he smiled and waved his arms, thoroughly confusing his son and Leia.

Mr. Manning was Leia's height. Leia could easily see how Josh had gotten his lanky build from his father. Mr. Manning's hair was silver and receding and he also had a closely cropped mustache. He was wearing a dark brown business suit but he'd loosened the silky black tie and unfastened the top two buttons of his white shirt. His white undershirt was no longer tucked into his slacks.

A moment later, Mr. Manning briskly walked over to Josh and bear-hugged him. Josh immediately recoiled from his father's presence.

"You smell like a whiskey factory!" Josh criticized, disgusted.

"They offered us two complimentary drinks in first gla—I mean, first class," Mr. Manning semi-slurred. "I had a few more. Whatsa harm?"

"Whatsa harm? You're not making a good impression on my fiancé or me, for that matter!" Josh said.

"You muss be Lisa," Mr. Manning said, extending a hand slightly to Leia's left. "I'm David Manning. Nice ta meet'cha!"

Leia took Mr. Manning's hand and shook it, barely, against her better judgment. And somehow, she managed a fairly pleasant smile for her future father-in-law.

"I'm Leia Hamilton, Mr. Manning. It's nice to meet you, too."

"Look, honey, I don' stand on cere—Sarah? I thought you said your name was Lisa. Oh, wait! You're Princess Leia, right? I remember you now! You're a tall one, ain't ya? Pretty . . . but tall!"

"Dad, let's get you to your hotel so you can sober up, okay?" Josh insisted, taking his father by the arm.

But Mr. Manning swung around to face Leia again.

"Hot dang! I just got it. You're marryin' my boy?"

"Yes, sir, I am."

"Works for me. You're pretty sweet-lookin', young lady! I bet my boy knocked—"

"I'm hitting him," Leia glared at Josh.

"Go ahead," Josh replied, facepalming.

———————

"How's your hand?" Josh asked.

"Not as sore as I hope your dad's jaw is," Leia replied.

"We can find out when he wakes up. Between your punch and all the liquor he consumed, he's gonna be out awhile."

Leia looked over at Josh, who was driving her back to her parents' house. He looked stressed.

"You were very professional with the airport and hotel staff, I was proud of you," she offered. "But I think they knew what was going on."

Josh grimaced briefly.

"Of course, they did, they see this kinda stuff all the time," he chafed. "And it's not my first rodeo with Driving Sales Dave."

"Are you serious? He's done this before? You didn't say he was an alcoholic."

Josh brought the car to a stop in front of a traffic light.

"He saves it for 'special occasions,'" Josh said, making imaginary quotation marks with his fingers. "The last time was the weekend he made it back to celebrate my high school graduation."

"I'm sorry, honey. I didn't know."

The traffic light turned green and Josh proceeded forward again.

"Don't apologize," he continued. "I was too ashamed to share that. Maybe I'd hoped it would go away when he left. And I suppose it did till now."

Leia understood Josh's frustration, but she also understood something else.

"He's suffering, too. He must have loved your mother deeply."

"They were married twenty-nine years. It would've been thirty years in November."

"That's quite an accomplishment."

"Yeah."

She would always side with Josh but she sympathized with Josh's father, too.

"I'm not defending his actions, Josh, I'm the one who knocked him out, but I think you should forgive him."

"He made a complete idiot of himself in front of the woman I love."

Leia nodded. But she wasn't ready to abandon her point, either.

"People have different ways of grieving," Leia added. "He seems like the kind of person who always has a smile for everyone, even if he's not really happy."

"He is like that, yeah."

Then a flash of images cascaded through Leia's mind in a rush. She jerked back in surprise.

"What is it?" Josh asked, concerned.

"I just saw something in my thoughts—I think it was from the connection I have with Malevolence," Leia answered. "It was so fast, but . . . ?"

"What did you see?"

"Dane. I saw Dane. And he's with Malevolence."

17

DAVID MANNING WAS SURPRISED HIS jaw was still attached to his skull, the way it ached when he woke up. Slowly, he sat up from his bed and looked around his hotel room.

He supposed he deserved the way he felt. Who would've thought that girl was so strong that she could lay him out in one punch?

He staggered forward to the bathroom and washed his face. Then he looked at his reflection in the mirror. It was only a little red and not even that swollen. Still, he had seen better days. He wondered what he'd been thinking, getting that hammered on the flight?

Then David gazed at his wedding ring and remembered what he'd been thinking.

He eyed the hotel phone and considered calling room service. There was still one night before the funeral and he had no intention of facing it sober.

"Is this how you want your son to remember you, Dave?" Alyssa said.

The memory was two years old but so clear in his mind. They were in the living room of his house and Josh had stormed out.

"I don't understand, Lys?"

"I think you do," Alyssa added. "Did you come home for your son's graduation or did you just need an excuse to party?"

"For the graduation."

Alyssa was short and well-mannered but she had always possessed an inner strength that David respected. When her eyes and crossed arms relayed her disapproval, he took her seriously.

"Josh doesn't seem to agree with you," she continued. "So, instead of spending time with his father, whom he normally admires, he's probably going to see his girlfriend, Leia. Because at least she respects him."

He attempted to stand to defend himself but gravity and his inebriation had other ideas. He slumped back into his chair before making his point.

"That's not fair, Lys! I had a few drinks on the plane to relax, sure."

Alyssa leaned over and got right in David's face.

"And you had a whole bottle of wine here," she chastened. "Now you can barely stand. How does it look to your son that you can only be around him when you're wasted? How is that fair to him?"

"I'm sorry, Lys. I don't do so well socially outside the work environment."

She wagged a finger in his face, unconvinced.

"Uh-uh! Not buying it, Dave. You're just used to those twenty and thirty-year-old salespeople you're competing with who don't have families and still want to party. You've been away from your family too long."

David Manning turned away from his wife, ashamed as he realized the truth in her words. Alyssa took his hands in hers and looked in his eyes.

"I know you have a tough job, and you're one of the best, in my opinion," she added. "You navigate those 'shark-infested waters' with skills and experience that surpass most of your peers. And you do it for us, to provide for us, because you love us."

"Nobody understands me like you, Lys."

"You have a son who'd like to understand you very much," she continued. "Why don't you go sleep this off and I'll smooth things over with Josh. We'll do something together tomorrow, alright?"

In the present, David viewed the alarm clock on the end table. It was eight o'clock in the evening. He located his cell phone, his son's phone number, and called to beg his forgiveness.

———

Malevolence stood near the wall-length window overlooking Digby, California's bustling downtown business district. She had just showered and was in a white hotel robe.

Who are you really, woman? Is Malevolence truly separate from Angela Merrick?

Twenty years ago, the original Angela Merrick called on me to save her from drowning in other people's thoughts, to use my strength to protect her and fight back against her fears and insecurities. And I did. So, when the immediate crisis was over, why didn't that Angela come back to reclaim her life, especially to experience having her baby?

How many times have I had this conversation with myself?

You are Angela and Angela is you. I just have the traits the original Angela always aspired to. That's why she first allowed me to remain the dominant persona. That's why she's doing it now.

I'm the one who's protected Leia, Steve, Sue and Tanya all these years. I may have allowed myself to accumulate wealth but it was to give me the resources to stay in the shadows. I can do more for them this way.

At least, that's what I've told myself in every conversation I've ever had with myself when this came up before. But I'm not sure I believe it anymore.

Is that why I was I attracted to Dane, his innocence, his naiveté —because I miss that about myself?

He's young enough to be my son.

I think I wanted to touch what remains of your parents, Dane. In you. But I truly don't wish to hurt you.

What is it that I do want? And why don't I know the answer to that?

Leia, what role am I supposed to have in your life, now that you're getting married and having a child? Somehow, I doubt you'll call on me to babysit your son or daughter.

Malevolence sighed.

Leia knows Dane is here and some of what happened. I could feel her reaction earlier.

It was my fault that she received those mental images. I let the Cognac lower my inhibitions. Not exactly a brilliant move, getting even a little drunk, Malevolence. You're a telepath.

Now, Leia's hurt by my actions and Dane . . . what am I going to do with Dane?

Steven, why couldn't you have just killed me like I asked?

"I have no regrets, Malevolence," Dane shared.

He stood about thirty feet from her.

"You can pick up my thoughts?" Malevolence asked.

"I'm used to observing people, and your body language was very contemplative. You looked like you were feeling regret."

"You have no idea the things I regret. If you did, you'd better appreciate what I did for you."

Dane appeared to consider her words before continuing.

"You were right . . . about Leia," Dane said. "She's with the man she loves. I couldn't really let myself believe that before. I've never been in a real relationship before. And I'm not claiming to understand everything now . . . but I have a better idea."

"You can see her devotion to Josh."

"Yes. He's the only man for her. I can see that she loves him deeply and she's quite happy to be . . . carrying his child."

Malevolence felt sympathetic towards Dane. "Still a little hard to take, eh? Understandable."

Dane began to pace for a moment.

"It's not too hard to let her go," he continued. "I met her, fell in 'like' for a few hours then learned she was completely unavailable to me. As one-sided loves go, that's not too bad."

Malevolence nodded. The irony of their circumstances was not lost on her.

"True," she stated. "And then the same thing happens with me. I'm sorry."

She looked down at the city below then up at the moon. Dane walked next to her.

"I don't know if I can look at you and just see a friend. You're an amazing woman."

"I'm also old enough to be your mother," she warned. "You deserve to be with someone closer to your age."

Dane looked down at the city, too.

"I'm not sure I'll ever find anyone who's closer to my age."

"What about that Australian girl, Amanda Franklin?"

Dane sighed. "We'll never see each other," he lamented. "It's not like I can fly to the other side of the world whenever I want."

Malevolence smiled, seeing an opportunity.

"Says who?" she asked. "I could finance that easily. Or I could arrange her move here."

"You'd do that for me? Why?"

Malevolence sighed deeply.

"Oh, let's see, I just messed over one important area of your life and nearly messed over another. I think I owe you a few."

Dane's eyes were tired and unsure.

"I'll have to think about it," he replied. "I really haven't given Amanda any thought recently. I have a lot to sort out."

"The offer is open-ended, Dane, no expiration date."

"Thanks."

Just then, Malevolence felt another inspiration.

"How long has it been since you chatted with her?" she asked.

"A month, I think."

"I have a pretty impressive desktop setup in my office. You're welcome to use it. She's probably online and . . . you have some catching up to do."

"You're right about that."

18

STEVE TOOK A MOMENT TO marvel at the feeling of soaring through the night sky before landing on top of the tallest building in Digby. He didn't normally fly so fast, on the rare occasions he used his powers, but since he was wearing normal clothes and no mask, it seemed a prudent precaution.

The winds howled as they weaved their way between the nearby buildings and over the top of the Dutchman International Tower. Steve sat down against the wall to the stairway entrance for the roof. Ghosts from years past occupied his thoughts.

"John, am I doing the right thing with The AR-MEN?" Steve wondered.

"What are you talking about?" John asked.

Steve Hamilton the Crusader, Tina Yang who was Flamia, and John Covington the Silver Knight were in one of the conference rooms on the AR-MEN's orbiting satellite. John was in his armor, his helmet and Crusader's mask on the hardwood table in front of him. Tina sat in a chair next to his. Her mask was hanging around her neck, surrounded by her long, braided black hair on either side. Steve alone stood before one of the view ports looking at the world below as though he was carrying all of its burdens.

"We've been lucky so far. Aside from a few scrapes and bruises, we've come away from every fight with a victory," Steve disclosed.

"That kind of luck can't last forever. One or more of us could get seriously hurt, even killed."

"Yes, we could," Tina chimed in. "But believe me, the team knows that. You and Ed are mostly invulnerable but the rest of us aren't."

"Exactly! We've hardly any margin for error," Steve added.

"We have a margin for error?" John asked, raising an eyebrow. "That's news to me!"

Steve sighed. Then he sat down in the chair to John's left. The room was half-lit by the glow from the moon and countless, distant burning stars which blended with the smooth wooden wall paneling and the black marble floor tiles. It all contributed towards the solemnity of this moment.

"I just . . . I don't want to be responsible for any of your deaths," Steve admitted.

"So, that's easy enough. We just won't die," Tina said with a wry grin. "Happy?"

Tina's grin faded when she didn't get the response she'd hoped for. She created two small fireballs and began juggling them close to her chest to try and hide her nervousness.

"No one laughs at my jokes," she murmured.

"Let me know when they're funny," John quipped.

"I'll get right on that, metal man," Tina shot back with a sarcastic tilt of her head.

"You don't respond well to criticism, Tina," John replied with a nonchalant expression. "I imagine dating you is a challenge."

"Don't worry, you will never get to find out, John," she answered frostily.

Steve loudly cleared his throat and John quickly turned his attention back to Steve.

"Okay, you don't want to be responsible for our deaths? Fair enough," John conceded. "Tell me . . . why did you form this team?"

Steve was taken aback for a moment. He had to think about the answer.

"Dana and I put this team together to make a difference, to save lives," Steve replied. "It was a way to put our powers and skills to good use, help the world and all that."

"Yes, and you've succeeded. We all believe in those goals," John said. "Don't lose your resolve now."

"Is that what I'm doing?" Steve asked.

"In this case, John's right. You can't have it both ways, Steve," Tina said. "Either the team exists and we fight the bad guys and help with disasters and whatever comes . . . or we don't. Being an AR-Man means putting your life on the line to achieve something incredible."

Ed La Marque walked into the room. He was wearing his White Knight costume, the white hood pulled back and resting on his long white cape. Ed had a muscular, almost chiseled-looking face—long, somewhat narrow and angular—with a broad and flat nose, small but intense eyes and short blond hair in a buzz cut. He was drinking a fresh cup of coffee.

"Tina has a point, Steve-o," Ed suggested, smiling. "It's a risk and a privilege to be on this team."

"Please, Ed, join the discussion," Steve said, motioning to a nearby chair.

"Don't mind if I do," Ed replied.

John stood up and stretched momentarily. He seemed relieved for an opportunity to get a break from the conversation.

"That coffee smells good. I think I'll get some," John said.

"It's a fresh pot, I just made it," Ed replied. "Colombian, I think."

"Um, can I have some, too, John?" Tina asked him.

"How many teaspoons of coffee do you want with your sugar?"

"Two sugars, no cream," Tina replied, ignoring his jibe.

"Right. Six sugars, two creams," John teased.

Tina huffed and abruptly stood up, half-irritated, half-amused, and walked over to John. He was easily a foot taller than her but that didn't matter. John obviously had expected this response but said nothing. He tried to keep a serious look on his face but a smile kept breaking through.

"Let's go get coffee, funny guy," Tina demanded.

"I thought I was metal man?" John replied.

"Shut up! If I have to stand over you to see that you make my coffee right, I will!"

"You do realize that's physically impossible, right? You're shorter than—"

"Move!" Tina snarled, staring him down while pointing to her right, down the hallway.

Then they both started walking down the corridor towards the kitchen. Ed and Steve watched with barely contained delight.

"They're dating, aren't they?" Ed wondered aloud.

"I don't think so," Steve answered. "But they do seem to enjoy flirting."

Ed started tapping a rhythm on the table while Steve was deep in thought.

"That's how it started with you and Sue, right?" Ed continued, breaking the silence.

"No, Sue was a little more direct," Steve cleared his throat again, looking away from Ed.

Ed took a sip of his coffee and waited a moment to see if he would continue.

"Care to elaborate?" Ed added.

"Another time, okay?"

"Let me guess: Sue tracked you to a remote place, either on or off the satellite. Then she claimed you as hers and seduced you?"

Steve stared at Ed for several long seconds without blinking or changing expressions. Then he turned his chair to face the view port again.

"No comment," Steve answered.

Ed took his right index finger and lined it up with his nose, tilted his head to the right a little and then pretended to shoot an imaginary gun at Steve.

"Bingo! Right on target," Ed fired back. "Speaking of which, one of the first things you told me was how risky this whole idea for a superhero team was. I appreciated that because I like to know what I'm getting into."

"I guess I've been looking at things a little differently lately."

"You mean because Angela is having your kid? When's she due anyway?"

"In four months."

Ed nodded and took another sip of coffee.

"Becoming a father does that to you," Ed continued. "It changes things, makes you more protective, more sensitive to your own place in the world, I guess. Sometimes it even makes you question yourself."

"Yeah, I guess you would know," Steve replied. "How old is your son now?"

"Ten months."

"I don't get something. How do you and Sidra both participate in the team? Sue's already planning to leave the team once Leia is born."

"I can respect that. Sue's a fine woman and you're a lot luckier than you deserve."

Steve blushed slightly and nodded.

"Tell me about it! But really, how can you and Sidra be superheroes with such a young child?"

"Two reasons: My sister lives with us and isn't working right now, plus she loves helping care for our son. And Sidra and I are both fighting to make the world a little better for him."

At that moment, Steve and Ed were interrupted by what sounded like a distant scream from Tina. As they both stood up to go see what was the matter, John's voice came over the intercom: *"White Knight! Crusader! Come to Infirmary Three immediately!"*

Steve grabbed his mask and put it on as he rushed out of the conference room. White Knight was nearly to the infirmary already.

When Crusader caught up with White Knight, he was stunned to see White Knight's wife, Sidra, who also went by the code name Medsnake, unconscious on one of the infirmary beds. Silver Knight was inserting an intravenous line into Medsnake's right arm so she could receive fluids and pain medication. He'd already secured her right leg in a brace. Her face was severely bruised and she was bleeding from a split lip. Medsnake was wearing plain clothes.

Standing next to her was Flamia, her eyes filled with shock and concern. At the same time, Flamia was holding Medsnake's uninjured young son, Jason, and doing her best to calm him down as his anguished cries filled the room. Flamia cast a worried look at Medsnake, her best friend.

When Flamia's gaze wasn't on Medsnake or Jason, it turned to the woman in the bed next to Medsnake. But that woman was covered with a sheet, deceased.

"What happened?" Crusader said.

"Sidra was barely conscious when she arrived via the teleporter a few minutes ago but she did tell me a few things," Silver Knight replied. "Mainly, that Hero Hunter attacked her and tried to take her son. Hunter was obviously hired to investigate the team and learn our identities, probably to exploit and use against us."

"He had figured out who Ed and Sidra were," Steve said quietly to himself.

"Sidra said that she fought him but . . . he had on some kind armor that insulated against her electrical powers," Silver Knight continued. "He broke her leg and roughed her up pretty badly. Ed's sister fought him with her bare hands to keep him from getting the baby, but—"

"He killed her!" White Knight lamented, lowering the sheet back over his sister with shaking hands. "He broke her neck and killed her!"

"Sidra told me she focused her full power on Hero Hunter and overloaded his armor," Silver Knight added. "She injured him but he got away."

"Not for long!" White Knight yelled.

Crusader turned to look at White Knight. His friend's dark mood was so palpable, it was almost another presence in the room. White Knight's eyes, which were normally cheerful or teasing, were bloodshot and tear-rimmed, wild-looking in their desperation. His entire countenance had fallen and his breathing was ragged.

White Knight then walked over to his wife and kissed her forehead, taking her hand in his. The pain medication Silver Knight had administered was taking effect and keeping her unconscious.

"Thank you for saving our son," White Knight said. "I'll make sure that Hero Hunter never gets back to his boss with our information. I'm sorry I wasn't there before but I'll protect you now!"

White Knight then turned to Silver Knight.

"Can you triangulate Hero Hunter's position, Silver Knight?"

"I've already got it. Since Medsnake flooded him with her electrical energies, it's leaving a trail based on her energy signature. It's lighting him up like a Christmas tree to our sensors. I'll feed it to your wrist unit."

"Thanks!" White Knight replied.

Then White Knight approached Crusader.

"See, Steve-o? This was a risk," White Knight acknowledged. And even though White Knight was managing a basic sense of composure, Crusader could hear the tears in his voice. "When we put on these costumes and fight the bad guys, sometimes the bad guys fight back. Sometimes they play dirty . . . go after your family . . . your wife, your sister, your child . . . "

Crusader was not prepared for what he saw in his childhood friend's eyes. The desperation and grief was apparent and completely understandable. But as White Knight spoke, his desperation transformed and hardened into singularity of purpose . . . and then it twisted, over the course of several seconds, into madness.

"And . . . that's when they have to die," White Knight said slowly, his grimace turning into a smile. "Surely you see that, right?"

"What? Ed, we don't do that," Crusader warned. "We're not killers!"

"We're not, huh?" White Knight scoffed, getting right in Crusader's face. "We have these abilities . . . and you're saying if they hit us, if they kill us—or a bunch of innocent bystanders—we're not supposed to use our powers to find and stop them, permanently? To break their necks?"

"We have responsibilities! And that means we stop the bad guys and let the justice system deal with them. It's not a perfect solution but otherwise, we're no different from the bad guys!"

"No different," White Knight repeated, considering Crusader's words. "I guess you're right."

"I'm glad you—"

"To stop them," White Knight interrupted Crusader. "I'll have to be like them . . . be ruthless! It is what they deserve . . . yes!"

Then White Knight began making a sound that was part-laughing and part-crying. He seemed to be struggling within himself, his own sense or right and wrong battling his desire for revenge and to protect his family. He looked at Crusader once more, this time with uncertainty and a hint of despair.

"I don't know what's going to happen next," White Knight admitted. "So, promise me, if I don't come back, that you'll take care of Sidra and Jason for me, okay?"

"You have my word," Crusader assured him.

White Knight smiled.

"That's always been good enough for me, Steve-o," White Knight replied. Then his eyes went ice cold and his smile collapsed. He pulled his white hood over his head, the shadows obscuring his eyes and giving him the unsettling look of an executioner. "Computer, execute override command WK725. Teleport me to the coordinates just transferred to my wrist unit, storage protocol Delta!"

With that, White Knight vanished from the satellite. Silver Knight scrambled to the nearest wall computer interface. Crusader heard Silver Knight mutter a curse under his breath.

"What is it? What did he do?" Crusader asked in frustration.

"When Ed helped me code and test the operating system for the satellite, we set each other as system admins, in case anything happened to either one of us; it was a redundancy, a failsafe," Silver Knight answered. "Ed must have used his admin access to build a backdoor for himself to override the computer system. It was probably for emergencies, but he just used it to do a site-to-site teleportation from here to near Hero Hunter's location. He also wiped the coordinates from the satellite computer simultaneously. I can probably pinpoint his location from memory. But by the time I do that, he could do just about anything or even move to another location."

"But you think he's going after Hero Hunter . . . to kill him," Crusader said.

"I have no doubt whatsoever," Silver Knight answered.

"Do what you can. The sooner we find him, the better!"

"I'll stay here with Sidra and the baby," Flamia interjected. "You two stop Ed . . . and Hero Hunter."

"We will, Tina," Crusader assured.

Several minutes later, another voice came over the communication system. It was Black Fox checking in.

"We read you, Black Fox," Silver Knight answered. "Go ahead."

"Silver Knight alerted me about Hero Hunter when Medsnake made it to the satellite," Black Fox continued. "I picked up his scent from the crime scene and closed on his current location."

"What's the situation?" Crusader asked.

"White Knight has Hero Hunter cornered in an alleyway. I'm above them looking down from the roof of the next building," Black Fox replied.

"Be advised that White Knight has gone rogue," Crusader warned. "He's . . . not well, Black Fox."

Black Fox gasped. Then she took a deep breath and let it out.

"Understood. I will attempt to engage them and keep things from escalating too much. But given White Knight's strength, speed and cunning, some backup would very much be appreciated!"

"Silver Knight and I are on our way."

"Roger that. I'll hold him for as long as I can. Black Fox out!"

———————

Hero Hunter had shed the damaged armor and was wearing all-black plain clothes and a black face mask with protective multi-purpose goggles. He had a rather intimidating rifle pointed at White Knight, who was less than five feet from Hero Hunter.

"I can definitely tell that you've been fighting my wife," White Knight said. "Do you want to know how I know?"

Hero Hunter said nothing. Suddenly, his head twitched involuntarily then his left arm did the same thing. He didn't react to the twitches, he just kept his rifle trained on White Knight.

"Every sixteen seconds, your body has muscle spasms. It's a side effect of her electrical powers interacting with your nervous system," White Knight continued. "For the most part, it's harmless and it wears off after an hour or two. But in the meantime, it's pretty inconvenient."

Hero Hunter slowly turned and backed towards the entrance of the alleyway. He never took his eyes off of White Knight, his rifle ever focused on its target.

"In battle, timing is everything," White Knight taunted. "And, unfortunately for you, yours is now off. You can't run, you certainly can't hide. So, you know you have to fight . . . but against me, you can't win."

White Knight vanished. Then he reappeared behind Hero Hunter, relieved Hero Hunter of his rifle with his left hand and brought his right fist down on top of Hero Hunter's right shoulder, shattering it. Hero Hunter screamed from the pain and collapsed to the ground, writhing in agony.

White Knight reached over to pick up Hero Hunter, but Black Fox stepped between them.

"Please, White Knight, enough," she insisted. "He's down. You beat him."

"You know he killed my sister, right? He also nearly killed Medsnake and took our son."

Black Fox mouth gaped in shock and dismay. But knowing the capabilities of who she was facing, she quickly mastered her emotions.

"No . . . I didn't," Black Fox admitted. "I'm so sorry for your loss. But killing him won't bring your sister back. And it won't make you feel better."

"He has information on my identity and Medsnake's, maybe more team member info. Wouldn't you agree that's an unacceptable risk?"

"Maybe it is but that doesn't justify murder. I can't just stand by and let you kill him."

White Knight looked at Black Fox almost sympathetically. Then he spoke into his wrist communicator.

"Computer: execute override command WK725. Teleport Black Fox to the satellite."

But nothing happened.

"Silver Knight already deleted my override command," White Knight realized. "Smart . . ."

"He is that," Black Fox added.

" . . . but unfortunate, too," White Knight continued.

White Knight sped behind Black Fox and landed a number of pinpoint hits at critical nerve clusters, knocking her unconscious.

"I'm sorry, Black Fox, I didn't want to do that. But I know you'll heal up in the next hour or so. I just couldn't have you stopping me."

White Knight picked up Hero Hunter by the neck and held him at eye level. Hero Hunter was still conscious but completely incapacitated. With a flick of his wrist, White Knight broke Hero Hunter's neck, killing him. He stared at Hero Hunter's lifeless body for several seconds, unknowingly holding his breath the whole time. Then he exhaled and slung Hero Hunter's body over his right shoulder.

White Knight looked down at Black Fox's sleeping body.

"You were right. Killing him won't bring my sister back and it doesn't make me feel any better," White Knight admitted. "But I will always protect my family . . . no matter the cost."

Then he leapt up and flew away.

————

Hours later, Black Fox and Crusader sat down in the main conference room on the satellite looking sullen. Neither of them had anything to say for several minutes. They didn't even look at each other. Finally, Black Fox sighed.

"White Knight going rogue . . . it's beyond a security breach, beyond a disaster," Black Fox said. "I don't even know how to categorize it."

"Silver Knight has adapted the computer system," Crusader added. "At least, he shouldn't be able to use it against us now. And I don't think he'll blackmail us with our identities, that was his sore point with Hero Hunter."

Black Fox took off her mask with her left hand, still looking at the table. She gripped the mask tightly and threw it towards the door hard enough for it to bounce and land on the other side of the room. She slammed her right fist against the table and looked at Crusader, her face a contortion of rage and frustration.

"His sore point?" Black Fox fumed. "His 'sore point.'"

Black Fox leaned on the table, her head lowered as she attempted to control her emotions. Then she walked up to Crusader and gently took off his mask.

"Get up," Dana demanded.

Steve stood up and turned to face her.

"Our buddy, Ed, is just as strong as you, Steve! He helped build this satellite and, if provoked, he could turn it into a floating tomb for all of us! So, I'm wondering why my co-leader on this team is still talking about Ed La Marque—the biggest threat we could possibly be facing—as if that man is still our pal?!"

"I'm sorry."

"I don't want sorry, I want resolve. I want a plan to deal with this. Most of all, I want you to snap out of this fog your brain is in! I may not have known Ed since elementary school, but I did know Angela that long, and she did the same thing to me. I know how you feel and I know what you need to do!"

She softened her mannerisms and put her right hand on his left arm. In her eyes, he could see remnants of the love they once shared.

"Ed La Marque is not the same man anymore. He won't hesitate or second guess like we might, his mind is made up," Dana continued. "He will use all of his powers to their fullest while we'll still be holding back to protect civilians or each other. And he'll use every one of our weaknesses against us. He doesn't have to go public with our identities or threaten to blackmail us. All he has to do is show up outside our jobs or homes and attack!"

The hurt and disappointment Crusader felt towards Ed's betrayal was so strong that it was nearly overwhelming.

She took a step forward and looked like she might hug or hold Steve, but she stopped herself when she saw a change in his expression.

"You're right," Steve realized. "We have to protect ourselves and our loved ones . . . because nothing's certain anymore."

"Yes," Dana replied. "Exactly."

"Ed was trying to tell me something along those lines before everything went south. He said being on this team is a dangerous risk . . . but it's worth it for the good we can do."

"Insightful man."

"We have to rally the troops, shore up—"

"Steve," Dana interrupted.

"What is it, Dana?"

When she looked at him now, it wasn't as Black Fox the superhero. She was just Dana Fox the woman.

"In order to rally the troops, I feel like we need to settle something between us," she added. "Otherwise, they might pick up on it. We need to be unified on things."

"You're right," he replied. "So, what do you want to talk about?"

Dana almost collapsed into the nearest chair. Steve hadn't seen her display this kind of vulnerability in a long time.

"I'm happy for you and Sue, so don't get me wrong about that," Dana looked up at Steve and tried to smile. "You found someone who wanted to marry you and . . . well, I like Sue. She's been good to you."

"What's the problem then?" Steve asked.

"It kills me that Angela is having your child!" Dana admitted.

Steve stepped back a few feet. "Oh! Wow. Um, I don't know what to say to that."

Dana looked down at the table, leaning on both elbows from her seated position.

"Before she developed powers, when she wanted to be your girl-friend, it's not like I could say anything. You broke up with me and that was that. I wasn't her mother . . . just her best friend!"

"You felt like she stabbed you in the back and I went along with it."

Dana stood up, a bit unsteady. She leaned against the table with her hands again.

"In retrospect, can you blame me?" Dana asked. "But I don't feel that way anymore. The situation has become much more complex. And I have very mixed feelings about the whole thing now."

"What do you mean? How do you feel?"

"You really want to know the truth?"

"You know I do."

Dana pushed away from the table and began to walk slowly towards Steve.

"Out of respect to Sue and you, I'll never act on my feelings . . . but I still love you. I'll put my pride aside, however, and tell you . . . I'm envious of Angela."

"What? But you said you didn't want kids."

"I told you I would have the child of the man I loved. Unfortunately, you're the only man I've ever loved this much. I may never have children but that doesn't mean I won't be jealous of my former best friend."

Steve looked at Dana with a great deal of compassion. And he smiled.

"For what it's worth, I think you'll find a deeper love with the right man. And you'll be a terrific mother someday."

Dana smiled back. "Thank you, Steve. I'd like to believe that. I really would!"

"Then believe it. You are the most vibrant, alive woman I've ever known. You have so much to offer someone, so don't let me hold you back. Live your life to the fullest and you'll find that true love."

"He says, as he reminds me yet another reason why I love him so much. Fine! I'll be open-minded. For all I know, Mr. Right may be walking into my life right now—"

Silver Knight walked into the conference room just then.

"I'm sorry but I need to borrow Black Fox," Silver Knight interrupted. "It shouldn't take long but it is important."

"Are we finished discussing . . . things?" Steve asked.

"I've said all I had to say," Dana replied. "Thanks."

———————

Black Fox walked off with Silver Knight. He looked at her with some concern.

"Did I walk in on something personal between you two?" Silver Knight asked.

"Nothing to be concerned about, John, just resolving some unfinished business. Steve and I are just good friends."

"Okay, that's good."

"What do you need me for?"

"I need to run a scan to see if either Hero Hunter or White Knight left any miniaturized electronic devices on you."

"Makes sense."

———————

On top of the Dutchman International Tower, Steve's thoughts returned to the present. He lifted his head. Someone else was near him. Whoever they were, they were breathing through their nose, probably louder than they intended. It sounded like someone trying to control their emotions but not quite succeeding. Steve braced himself, trying to be ready for anything before he turned around. But before he could, he heard that voice.

I'm sorry.

This time, Steve whirled around with super-fast reflexes he'd forgotten he had, digging his left foot so hard into the roof's surface that it made a two-inch deep semi-circle as he turned. Nothing could have prepared him for the sight of Malevolence there.

"What's going on?" His hand passed through the woman in a black dress who stood in front of him.

I'm nearby. I'm projecting this image of myself into your thoughts.

At first, he was outraged. She had been listening in on his deeply personal memories and introspections? And now she would probably use that against him—except she didn't. What faced him was not what he was expecting. Instead of the cocky and angry woman he was used to, she was sad and sympathetic. She hadn't gotten her breathing completely under control and even though Steve didn't see any tears, he could tell that she had been crying. Had he ever seen her this way?

I didn't mean to intrude. Your feelings . . . memories were so strong— towards John, Dana, and even Ed, I couldn't help overhearing. It woke me from a sound sleep.

"I'm sorry I disturbed you," Steve growled, still a bit unnerved.

I've never seen these memories . . . I'm still taking them in. I didn't know you and Dana had loved each other so much.

"Yeah."

You were so angry the last time we spoke, I didn't sense how much you were grieving her.

"That was intentional."

The lingering silence was awkward but neither of them averted their gaze from one another.

I didn't know she envied my having Leia. It made me wonder how different our lives would have been if she'd had your child first. You wouldn't have left her, we wouldn't have dated. I wouldn't be . . . me.

"Yes, but then, we wouldn't have Leia, either. Sue and I wouldn't be married or have Tanya. I wouldn't be . . . who I am now."

But Dana wouldn't have died facing me. And you'd have another daughter . . . or son. Dane could have been yours, under those circumstances.

"And then he wouldn't be John's son. I accept that things happened the way they were supposed to. It's painful, yes. I grieve for Dana. She was my first love and a dear friend all these years. But she's gone and I'll move on, just like I did after John and Ed died."

I'm moving on, too.

"Are we . . . having an honest conversation?" Steve asked, half-jokingly.

First time for everything, right?

Steve closed his eyes, chuckled and nodded in agreement.

"I can handle that."

Unintentionally mirroring Steve, Malevolence closed her eyes . . . and then took in a deep breath and slowly exhaled.

"I've always wondered something. If you were such good friends with Dana, why did you even consider dating me?"

Are you kidding? The first time I met you, I was attracted to you. But you were with Dana, so I let that go. When she messed things up, though, you became fair game again.

"Charming."

Hey, unlike Dana, I had absolutely nothing against marrying you—even though that didn't work out for us, either—but, well, we did have Leia.

"Yes. I'm grateful for Leia every day."

Steven, since we're being honest . . . I was going to have her, one way or the other.

"You just put on an act to get some extra benefits out of it? I can't say I'm surprised."

You know me.

Malevolence crossed her arms and looked at the ground.

"You stayed with me and Sue through the last six months of your pregnancy, but I haven't seen you in twenty years. So, I don't know who you are anymore. I only know what you've shown me today."

I know. That's why I—anyway, I know that.

She swept her hair back, but a few stray hairs fell back across her forehead. She sniffled and appeared to wipe a tear from her right eye.

Steve pondered Malevolence's words. His grimace softened. Hints of a smile started to tug at the corners of his mouth. Then a half-laugh escaped his lips, sounding more like escaping air than a true chuckle. But the nature of this conversation had made it impossible for him to stay angry.

"We're both pretty awful at communicating . . . back then and now . . . aren't we?"

Yeah . . . we are. We're not doing too bad right now, though.

"Back then . . . a part of me didn't want you to go after Leia was born. I didn't want to separate you from our daughter."

That's sweet but it would never have worked. It would have put far too much strain on your relationship with Sue.

Steve remained silent, allowing the fullness of his revelation to dawn on Malevolence.

You—or at least a part of you—still wanted to be with me, even if it cost you your relationship with Sue? I had no idea!

"I was a very different person then. I'm not proud of that but we're being honest. And you were having my daughter."

I see. Well, thank you for your honesty.

"If you'd known that, do you think it would have changed anything?"

Probably not. I'd have been flattered, probably quite moved . . . but I was such a hothead . . . and stubborn . . . back then. Most of all, I didn't want to taint my child with what I had become . . . cold, cruel . . . a killer. I truly felt that Leia would be better raised by you . . . and your wife . . . no matter how much I loved her.

Steve was still having some trouble accepting what he was hearing. Malevolence sacrificed custody of her daughter to protect Leia? Malevolence had depended on Steve to raise their child correctly? This was not the Malevolence he knew.

Through their temporary telepathic bond, Steve could feel what Malevolence felt: Sadness at the avoidable loss of life over the years. The loss of possibilities that could have been but never were and never could be. A wish to comfort Steve but not knowing how. And most of all, feeling older than her forty-two years.

You didn't get to say goodbye to any of them. John, Dana, Ed—they all died in catastrophic explosions, so there were no bodies. You couldn't even view them at the funerals.

"No, I couldn't," Steve said somberly.

Malevolence reached out in sympathy to Steve. But then, Malevolence's image shifted and blurred.

"What just happened?" he asked.

Malevolence's image continued to shift and shimmer for several seconds.

Dane, don't! Yes, I do, but—you can't just—I'm in the middle of—

Malevolence gasped.

"Dane? Did you just say Dane? Dane Fox is with you?"

Yes.

"You know he's Dana's son, for crying out loud! And you—it hasn't even been—don't you have any decency?"

Steven, you don't have all the facts. Let me—

"No, I don't think so. This conversation is over."

And with that, Steve Hamilton abruptly turned his back on Malevolence and flew away.

———————

It had been a long time since Malevolence felt defeated like this. She was somewhat numb. They had been connecting and relating, getting along, for the first time. And now that connection was gone, destroyed like so many other parts of her life.

Dane put his hand on her right shoulder. She saw a look of concern in his eyes.

"I messed up your conversation with Mr. Hamilton, didn't I?" Dane asked. "I'm sorry."

Malevolence forced a smile for Dane's benefit.

"You had no way of knowing," Malevolence answered. "I'm not angry. Mr. Hamilton and I just have a bad history."

Malevolence sighed.

"And I really am awful at communicating with him! Even when I'm trying to put the past aside and help him with his grief, I somehow manage to mess it up."

"I'm pretty sure it takes two people to communicate," Dane said. "Don't be too tough on yourself."

Malevolence looked out the window at the night sky.

"Maybe the only thing he and I will ever have in common is our daughter," Malevolence said, answering Dane's unspoken question. "I think that's very sad."

19

THE FUNERAL STARTED AROUND ELEVEN o'clock the next morning at the Digby Funeral Home. The solemn, closed casket service was attended by more than one hundred people, including Josh, his father, Leia, and her parents. The remainder were from Alyssa's family, friends from the neighborhood, her church and her job.

Only about one-fourth of the guests came to the graveside burial service. The cemetery's grounds were very well-maintained and spacious. The numerous trees and bushes, abundant living greenery, were proud guardians standing tall over the property. The overcast sky and cool wind offered a sense of solemnity and calm for those attending, almost exclusively family and Alyssa's closest friends.

Leia hadn't been to a funeral since she was a young child. All she could think to do was just to remain close to Josh and offer whatever comfort she could. He was so quiet, not exactly distant but she could tell he was re-living many memories of his mother; she hoped they were good ones.

The service was almost over when she sensed Malevolence's presence. She briefly glanced over her shoulder and saw Malevolence and Dane at a respectful distance. Leia forced herself not to engage her birth mother in mental conversation. She couldn't stop Malevolence from attending but she didn't have to like it.

Malevolence being there was like having a fine tea cup at the edge of a table. It was bound to break sooner or later and Leia did not want that. At the same time, Malevolence hadn't technically done anything wrong.

Leia looked over at Josh and gently took his hand in hers. She saw him manage a hint of a smile.

Once the graveside service was over, Mr. Manning turned to his son and Leia.

"I know we—I know I started things badly yesterday," Mr. Manning confessed. "I'd like to make it up to you. Can we go somewhere and talk? I'd like to learn more about this girl you're going to marry."

"Leia, are you okay with this?" Josh asked.

"Yes. Yes, I'm fine with it," Leia answered. "But first, I'd like to introduce your father to my parents before they leave, if you don't mind?"

Josh nodded his approval and looked to his father.

"Not at all," Mr. Manning replied.

———

Two and a half hours later, David had taken his son and future daughter-in-law on a scenic drive in the countryside.

"There's a little town about ten miles from here named Harken. That's where I was grew up," David said. "I think the population hit one thousand a few years ago, but I'm not sure about that. The community was nice enough, but I spent my teenage years planning my escape. I succeeded after I earned a scholarship to Digby College. And while I was earning my business degree, I met Josh's mother."

"She was going to Digby, too?" Leia asked.

"She was my top rival in class, actually," David replied.

"I never knew that," Josh said.

David viewed the lush green hills under the hazy sky. With one hand gripping the wheel and the other tapping nervously on the seat.

He was proud to have his son with him but frustrated that he didn't know what to say or do around him. So, he relied on instinct and tapped into his wealth of personal stories.

"We didn't talk about it much, it was kind of a sore spot for a while," David shared. "More for me than her, I think. I can admit it now, that she was better than me. She had fresher ideas and well, more cut-throat tactics than I was willing to use."

"Mom? Cut-throat? Are we talking about the same woman?" Josh asked.

David let loose with a belly laugh, his first in a long time. It felt good. In the rear-view mirror, he saw Leia smiling. Was she glad for him? That was nice.

"You two didn't know that Alyssa Denton," David continued. "I may have been Driving Sales Dave, but she was called Ice Witch Lyssa. And anyone who tangled with the Ice Witch usually lost."

"She must have hated that title," Josh rolled his eyes.

"Hated it? She's the one who made it up!" David said. "She wanted to intimidate the other students . . . and it worked, for the most part."

"Except for you, right, Mr. Manning?"

Continuing to catch glances through the mirror, David noted that the young woman's smile was infectious. She certainly was pretty and had been very supportive of his son. They seemed closer than ever.

"Leia, please, call me Dave."

"Alright . . . Dave."

"You might say I felt the need to answer her challenge," David boasted.

"How did you answer her challenge, Dave?" Leia asked, now grinning.

David relaxed some. He had pulled one of them in. Now it was time to weave words and have fun.

"That's a funny story, actually," David replied. "Because in the classroom, I proved I could match her strategy for strategy, tactic for tactic, and I thought that would be the end of it. Game over."

"But obviously it wasn't," Josh added. "What happened?"

"Your mother challenged me to a drinking contest," David said.

David heard Josh lean forward in the back seat and Leia's soft giggle. Noting the stop sign ahead, he slowed the vehicle and prepared to brake.

"Really? Now that is funny!" Josh said. "Who won?"

"Actually, about halfway through, as we got more and more relaxed, she asked why we were rivals to begin with," David recalled. "And I told her I was going for the best grade in the class by challenging myself against the other best student. And that's when she told me she was doing the same thing."

"Then what happened?" Leia coaxed.

"We told each other how much we respected each other," David said. "Then she reached across the table and pulled me into a kiss. That's when we started going out."

"You got that from your mom?" Leia blurted, turning to look at Josh.

"Hey, you're learning about this at the same time as me," Josh said.

David chuckled. Seeing his son and Leia interact reminded him of his early years with Lyssa. Had they been this young and carefree, too? He nodded, silently answering his own question.

"Who knew daring was genetic?" Leia considered.

"So, how soon do you two plan on tying the knot?" David asked.

"Right away," Josh answered.

David noted in the mirror that Josh turned to look to Leia, as if for guidance. She smiled at Josh and quickly nodded her approval. Then Josh looked towards his father.

"Leia's pregnant, Dad."

David blinked a few times. The news was abrupt but not a complete surprise. He remembered Lyssa telling him about the first girl their son had brought over to their home back in grade school. He knew their history. Seeing them together now, he was happy for his son.

"Ah. Okay. Well then . . . congratulations!" David said slowly. He smiled. "You two do make a fine couple. Friends since you were in single digit years, going out since high school. Now you're gonna marry and make me a grandfather. Yeah . . . I'm just fine with that."

"Thank you for not being upset," Leia said, somewhat bashfully. "I know this is kind of sudden."

"Leia, if there's one thing I learned from Josh's mother, it was to adapt to things."

"Thank you, sir—er, Dave," Leia replied.

Passing a roadside sign with a lawyer's advertisement, David had an inspiration.

"In fact, I can help you get the right documents and I know a Justice of the Peace who owes me a favor," David shared. "You two just fill out the paperwork. We'll get you married in no time at all."

"So, when do you have to get back to work?" Leia asked.

"Oh, I'm taking a leave of absence from work for a while. I've got months of vacation time built up and I'm taking it. I may have missed Josh's birth but I'm not going to miss his wedding or the birth of my first grandchild."

"Dad, that's great! That means a lot to me."

They were interrupted by Leia's belly announcing its hunger rather loudly. It caused her to blush bright pink with embarrassment.

"Well, we've obviously been out and about too long," David acknowledged. "Mama here needs to eat, as in, like, yesterday! So, Leia, tell me what kind of food you want and I'll take us to a restaurant. It's on me."

Leia gave it about three seconds of thought.

"Steak!" she declared.

"Ah! A woman after my own heart," David replied. "We'll go to Guenther's Chopping Block. It's not far from here and it's got the best steak for a hundred miles"

"Oooh! I heard that place was amazing!" Leia gushed. "Can we really get in there?"

"Who do you think got them their meat connection?" David said proudly. "Guenther's an old friend of mine. I introduced him to his wife."

"Is there anyone in or near Digby that you haven't met or made a deal with?" Josh asked.

"There's an old fortune teller on Third Street who played hardball with me," David replied, grinning. "But I heard she retired a year ago and closed shop."

Ninety minutes later, they left Guenther's happy and quite full.

"I have to say, Leia, I'm impressed with your appetite," David praised. "You're going to have one very healthy kid at this rate. You just might want to balance it out with a little exercise."

"She said she's trying to get the first ten pounds over with this week," Josh shrugged.

"I think I exceeded my goal with that, but it was so worth it!" Leia smiled with her eyes closed and patted her stomach. "That was truly exceptional. Not just the steak and garlic mashed potatoes but that peach cobbler a la mode was off the charts!"

David smiled as Leia leaned against Josh, who had his arm around her as they walked to the car.

"It's Guenther's wife's recipe," David said. "And a lot of moms kind of go overboard with the first pregnancy. Alyssa gained sixty pounds with you, Josh."

"She did? Mom never said anything about that."

"We'd wanted a child for so long, you see," David continued. "So, when Alyssa found out she was pregnant, she was extremely protective. She made sure she ate all the right things but she didn't go out except when she had to and she was worried that exercising too much might cause a problem. Like I said, protective."

He pressed a button on his keychain that unlocked the SUV rental.

"I guess I can understand," Leia said. "The pregnancy must have been like a dream come true for her."

They entered the vehicle and buckled up. David started the engine before continuing.

"It was. She was thirty-five and we'd already given up on having kids. She never said anything to anyone about this, but . . . when you've been together as long as us, you understand things about your spouse. I could tell that even though she never got rid of all of the pregnancy weight, she kind of considered it a badge of honor."

Leia and Josh nodded.

"So, am I dropping you off at your apartment, Josh, or Leia's parents' house?"

Leia made eye contact with Josh and pointed at him.

"My apartment," Josh replied.

"Sure thing."

———————

A few minutes later, Leia closed the apartment door behind them. Josh sat down on his couch. Leia joined him.

"How are you, honey?" Leia asked.

"I'm still kind of overwhelmed," Josh took Leia's hand in his. She smiled at that. "I think I'm gonna feel this way for a while . . . which is yet another reason I'm so glad I have you."

Leia gently squeezed Josh's hand, looking into his eyes with a mixture of pure love and sympathy. A trace of bitterness appeared in those eyes but when he looked at Leia, he couldn't maintain any of it, it just melted away. Only some sadness remained and it was in conflict with his joy.

"Mom's gone, Dad's back, and he's finally trying to be a dad. You're pregnant and we're getting married very soon," Josh returned Leia's gentle squeeze.

"At least your dad didn't drink at dinner," Leia considered.

"Yeah, I wonder what the story is behind that. He did a complete about-face from last night and he's being . . . consistent now. I'm not used to it."

"But it's good."

Leia changed into some sweatpants and a t-shirt she'd left at Josh's apartment previously while Josh fixed some tea in the kitchen segment of his efficiency.

"Oh wow!" Leia exclaimed.

Josh turned to see Leia by the wall mirror. The lavender t-shirt she had on, which had fit her just a month ago, was clearly tight on her now. But what riveted their attention was Leia's well-defined baby bump. She was over halfway through her fourth month and now there was a gradual outward curve from just under her bust line to right below her waistline. She placed her hands around her baby bump.

"You hadn't seen this before?" Josh semi-joked.

"Well, to be honest, I was trying not to pay attention. The morning sickness hasn't been as bad, I've had more energy and I wanted to concentrate on you."

"I don't think you can ignore the baby anymore," Josh said, putting his hand on her belly.

"Nope. Kiddo's just gonna get bigger. I guess I just needed a reality check. I'm really pregnant with your baby, Josh Manning."

He pulled her into an embrace and she certainly didn't mind. Stepping back, he looked at her abdomen and then at her eyes.

"Yes, you are," he added. "I hope it's a girl."

"You do? Why?"

"I don't know, I guess I hope she'll get her looks from you."

"Like you're Quasimodo or something?" Leia intimated, laughing.

"No, I know I don't look like Quasimodo . . ."

He was silent for a few seconds.

"Ever since Mom died, I've been hoping we'd have a little girl."

He didn't have to explain. She knew exactly what he was saying.

"That's beautiful, honey. I hope it's a girl, too."

"I won't be disappointed if it's a boy," Josh added.

"I know," Leia said.

Leia cupped her hands around her bump and looked at it, marveling. Josh put his hands on hers.

"Wow," Josh said. "Look what we did."

"Yeah, wow. Love me?"

"I love you," Josh said, looking up at Leia.

They didn't need words in that moment. Then reality invaded. Leia closed her eyes and looked down. She stepped back and sat in one of the chairs.

"We need to start thinking about names," she contemplated. "And other prenatal stuff."

"Oh yeah. Those are important."

"So, by February or March, she'll be born," Leia added.

"Less than five months. That's not really a long time."

She tried to imagine their future. She could envision Josh holding their baby in his arms and later, running around to play with the girl or boy.

"No, not really. How do you feel about being a dad?"

She had to repress a giggle when Josh's eyes widened like a deer caught in headlights. Then he pondered her question more seriously.

"It's exciting," he affirmed. "But it was kind of surreal until today."

That seemed an honest enough answer to Leia, even though it was also vague.

"And now?" she prompted.

"Now it's real," he answered. "It's very real."

"Is that good or bad?"

Josh seemed to snap out of his brief dazed state and smiled.

"It's good! Are you kidding? You're her mom. Together, I feel like we can do this. And our folks are behind us, so it'll be alright."

Leia looked at Josh and grinned, but said nothing for several seconds.

"What?" he asked.

Leia leaned back in her chair and laughed.

"You just can't admit that you're terrified, can you? Is that a guy thing? It's cute."

"Well . . . yeah," Josh said, returning her smile.

She stood up and walked over to Josh, wrapping her arms around his shoulders. She dreamily gazed into his eyes.

"Don't feel bad, I'm terrified, too. But it's okay, for all the reasons you said."

"Yeah it is."

She heard herself sniffle and became a little self-conscious.

"I'm completely crying, aren't I?" she asked.

"Like Niagara Falls," he replied.

"I'm happy, Josh. I'm just happy."

"I know."

Then he kissed her like she was the only woman in the world. And in his world, she was.

20

THE NEXT FEW DAYS WERE a jumble of paperwork and making wedding preparations. Mom and Dad volunteered to have the wedding ceremony in their house. It was large enough and the number of guests was small enough that, given how quickly everyone wanted the event to take place, it would do nicely.

Mom and Tanya had cleaned and decorated the house while Dad mowed the lawn and trimmed the hedges. Misha had taken Leia shopping for her dress and to have her hair styled. Josh and his father bought a suit for Josh, an impressive engagement ring for Leia as well as wedding bands and made arrangements with a Justice of the Peace.

The day of the wedding came. It was set to take place at five o'clock in the evening at the Hamilton's home. Most of the twenty-five guests had arrived early and were seated. Leia and Mom were in Leia's room making final adjustments and waiting for the right moment to enter the ceremony.

"Want some coffee?" Mom asked.

"For once, no. I'm nervous enough. Besides, I'm supposed to cut down on that for the baby, right?"

"Smart girl. Well, you may be nervous but I think you know everything's going to be just fine today. You're marrying the man you love."

Leia smiled. "Yes, I am."

"Then there's nothing to worry about. Just take some slow, deep breaths. I'm going to make sure your dad and the JP are ready. I'll come for you in a few minutes."

Ten minutes later, Mom returned. She slowly walked Leia to where Dad was waiting in the hallway near the living room. Leia proudly took her father's arm and smiled every step of the way as they approached Josh and the Justice of the Peace, a middle-aged barrel-chested man with dusty red hair, a handlebar mustache, and impressive sideburns. Despite his gruff look, he had a kind, grandfatherly smile and eyes. He was wearing a simple gray suit with a collared white shirt and black tie.

Leia beamed with joy as she took in the sight of her handsome soon-to-be husband in his black tuxedo with white ruffled shirt and black bow tie. His hair was slicked back in a way that complimented his cheeks and drew attention to his eyes, which were entirely focused on his bride-to-be. He looked nervous but very happy.

Leia felt the same and wondered how her dress looked to everyone else. She'd insisted the dress be off-white and as comfortable as possible while also maintaining a somewhat demure look. The result was white chiffon lace that ran from above the bust line to her neckline and formed sleeves that ran to just below her elbows. The dress flowed freely below the bust, deflecting attention from her baby bump and allowing better ease of movement.

The ceremony itself was straightforward and didn't take long. A few questions, an exchange of wedding bands, a declaration of marriage, and the bride kissing the groom. Everyone laughed then clapped when she pulled him into the kiss. The reception was a flurry of pictures taken, gifts given, various conversations, and generous servings of cake and fruit punch.

"Congratulations, Leia," Misha declared. "You're officially a married woman!"

"I know, right?" Leia replied, switching to a whisper. "A week ago, I officially look pregnant and now I'm officially married."

"You've got the bump already? I wasn't sure," Misha whispered back. "Can I touch it?"

"Later, okay? Not everyone here knows I'm 'with child' yet," Leia added, using her fingers to indicate quotes.

"Ahhh, I get it. Just don't 'conveniently forget,' okay?"

"Don't worry, I won't. Like you'd let me forget, once I've agreed to something."

"You've got that right."

———————

David walked outside to smoke a cigarette. But before he could light up, he noticed a woman looking into the window of the Hamilton house. Curious, he walked up to her. As he got closer, he noticed that her jet-black hair had glowing red highlights. She seemed to be concentrating deeply on something and not aware of his presence.

She startled, apparently now mindful of him. Her highlights faded. She turned around and looked at David.

"Can I help you, miss? Are you looking for something or someone?" David asked.

"You're the husband," the woman answered, looking pained. "I see. You're here for the wedding."

"How would you know that?"

"I'm also here for the wedding. My name is Angela Merrick. I'm Leia's birth mother."

"You're—I don't think I saw you inside with the other guests?"

Angela's facial expression was a blend of mild embarrassment and genuine frustration. She ran a hand through her hair nervously.

"Leia's father and I don't really get along anymore," she replied sheepishly. "I didn't want to cause any trouble."

"I think I understand," David nodded. "But perhaps it would be best if you left. I don't know where Leia's dad is but I'm sure he'll come out here sometime."

"Perhaps you're right. I'll go now. It was nice to meet you, David."

Angela walked down the sidewalk, turned a corner and disappeared.

"How did she know my name was David?" he asked himself, scratching the back of his head.

"Are you alright?"

Steve startled David.

"Oh! Mr. Hamilton! Wow, I didn't see you walk up just now."

"Thanks for getting Angela to leave. I was concerned I might have to say something to her. And call me Steve, please."

Now it was David's turn to feel a bit awkward. Leia's father had an intimidating air about him.

"She said she didn't want to cause any trouble, Steve. She your ex-wife?"

Steve seemed clearly upset, both by Angela's coming to the event and David's question. However, he could also see Steve working hard to remain calm and host-like. In all fairness, Steve was mostly succeeding.

"Ex-girlfriend," Steve added. "She's Leia's mother."

"She did say she was Leia's mother. At the risk of being rude, can I ask what happened?"

Steve's hard eyes and frown gave David his answer.

"Today, we're celebrating our children's wedding, Mr. Manning. Let's not ruin it with bad memories."

David could appreciate that. He tried to ease the tension with a smile of his own. "Ah, I get it. No problem. And call me Dave, okay?"

After acknowledging that, Steve excused himself and went back inside. David spent a few moments pondering the mysterious raven-haired woman whose highlights had briefly glowed red. There was something unusual about her, more than met the eye. And whatever her mystique turned out to be, it was enough to spook a big man like Steve Hamilton. There had to be some kind of odd, uncomfortable history between the two of them.

David pulled his mobile phone from his shirt pocket. He dialed a ten-digit phone number that only he and a handful of other people knew.

"Ross, this is Dave Manning. I need to call in a couple of favors. Yeah, it's important; it's for my kid."

David listened for two minutes straight before replying.

"Fine, then. I'll consider all debts paid after this. But I need you to find everything you can on a woman named Angela Merrick. I think she's local. I know it'll take time to get the info but if you could bump this in priority, I'd appreciate it."

There was another brief pause as David listened.

"Thanks, Ross. I knew I could count on you."

David ended that call and began another.

"Kelso, this is Manning. I need some of your friends on stand-by, if you know what I mean? Money's no object. Right. Excellent. I'll let you know. Later."

———————

Ten days later, David met with Ross at a 24-hour diner halfway between Digby and Harken. It was three o'clock in the morning. David was dressed like a local, with blue jeans, t-shirt, and baseball cap. Ross was Vietnamese, fifteen inches shorter and wore a blue jean vest over a white t-shirt and dark blue jeans. They sat down at a table and ordered coffee and pancakes. Ross had a folder-sized envelope with him. He handed it to Manning.

"You were right to be concerned about this one, Dave. The government has a file a mile long on her. I only got copies of the most relevant parts, along with copies of significant photo evidence."

"What makes her such a threat?"

"She's a tough target, tougher still to bring in alive. She can read minds and move any size object with her thoughts."

"What?" David said in a hushed tone. "What put her on the radar originally?"

Both men halted their conversation as a waitress brought them each a cup of steaming hot black coffee.

"The government took an interest in a group of self-proclaimed 'heroes' with superpowers a little over twenty years ago," Ross answered. "Angela Merrick was the girlfriend of the leader of those heroes, a guy who called himself Crusader. His group was called The AR-MEN."

"I remember them."

Ross nodded and took a sip of his coffee. David did the same.

"Merrick didn't have any powers at all when we first investigated the team," Ross continued. "Then, out of nowhere, she demonstrated off-the-scale telekinesis and telepathy. She began controlling local crime bosses, killed a few of them, intimidated scores more. She was setting herself up as the central authority for the entire region. But before she could get any further, this supervillain who had started calling herself Malevolence, dropped off the radar. The government thinks that maybe she got wise to her trail and found some way to throw them off her scent."

"Her trail?"

Ross nudged David's arm. The waitress was heading over with their pancakes. They both assured her of their satisfaction with the coffee and food before she left to attend to others.

"The government had a liaison working within The AR-MEN. He was one of them, called himself Silver Knight," Ross reflected. "He informed the government of the general activities of the group and the government left the group alone."

"Smart guy."

"Yeah, unfortunately he died a while back. And the group broke up soon after that."

That raised more questions in his mind.

"If this Malevolence disappeared back then, how does she have such a large file?" David asked.

"She didn't completely disappear, and the government had more than one trail."

Over the next forty-five minutes, Ross shared with David the reports on Malevolence: That she became pregnant with Crusader's child. And Crusader took her into his home until she had the child. David quickly put the pieces of this puzzle together in his mind. Crusader was Steve Hamilton. His child with Malevolence was Leia. Steve's wife was Cat.

But that part of the family was innocent enough. Steve and Sue had stopped being superheroes to raise Leia. And Leia had fallen in love with Josh. The only wild card remaining was Malevolence, right?

"Merrick surfaced again about three years ago, as a statistics professor at Digby College," Ross added. "My sources believe she did this to get close to her daughter, to make contact with her."

"Why, after all this time?"

"That's where this gets weirder, Dave. Her daughter has powers of her own."

"Excuse me?"

"Look at these," Ross pulled some additional photos from the envelope.

David Manning reigned in a feeling of nausea as he looked at what appeared to be small bone horns in Leia's wind-blown hair. But he couldn't hold back a gasp as he viewed a series of photos that showed Leia moving a small object—was that a padlock?—through the air. Then he saw a picture of Leia closing her fist and the padlock imploding.

"I've seen enough," David pushed the photos aside.

"I'm sorry, Dave. I just did what you asked."

"Just answer me this, Ross. Is there any indication the daughter has the same personality, the same goals as her mother?"

"I'd have to say no, based on the evidence. You're worried because she married your son?"

"She's pregnant, Ross. That . . . thing is carrying my grandchild."

"She's not a *thing*, Dave. Until about two months ago, she didn't have these powers. And there's no indication she's anything like her mother."

Ross stared hard at David for a few moments. David then looked down and took a few more sips from his coffee. He'd have to get a to-go box for the untouched pancakes.

"What are you planning to do, Dave?"

"Leia's innocent in all this. It's not her fault who she got her genes from. And her dad was a good guy. I used to admire Crusader."

"I think a lot of people felt that way. So, what are you going to do?" Ross repeated.

David put his coffee cup down. Then he looked at Ross.

"May I keep these?" David pointed to the materials from the envelope.

"Yes, that's the standard arrangement."

"Thank you."

"Dave . . ."

"I'm going to do my government a service, Ross. I'm going to eliminate Malevolence."

21

"ONE MONSTER PEPPERONI WITH ANCHOVIES!" Leia shouted over her left shoulder.

"MP with fishies, got it!" Misha replied with a smile from the kitchen.

Misha had been keeping an eye on Leia and her interactions with the customers all shift. Despite all of Leia's powers, her best friend could only handle so much. She had become much more protective of Leia over the last couple of months.

"Welcome to Skippy's! What can I get for you?" Leia said to the next customers, an African-American couple in their thirties. The woman was very pregnant.

"A large pepperoni pizza," the man said.

"And some of your cheesy bread," the woman added.

"If you don't mind a recommendation, try adding some spinach and roma tomatoes to the pizza," Leia suggested. "It's good for mom here and it tastes amazing!"

The woman nodded enthusiastically at her husband.

"Deal," the man replied. "Add two bottled waters and that'll be all."

"Great choice! That'll be $24.72."

"How far along are you, miss?" the woman asked while her husband handed Leia a credit card.

"Fifth month," Leia rubbed her noticeable belly with her left hand while she swiped the card with her right.

Misha had to admire Leia's fashion sense. Since the standard Skippy's uniform had become very restricting to Leia, she had begun wearing her name tag on a white blouse that flowed evenly over whatever skirt she chose that day. Today's was dark blue. The clothing choice complimented her but also left no questions as to her pregnancy.

"First baby?" the man asked Leia.

"Yes, sir."

"Us, too! How long have you been on your feet today?" the woman wondered.

"Four hours," Leia answered, steadying her back with her left hand and returning the man's card with her right. "Two to go!"

"You don't even look tired!" the woman said, amazed. "When I was five months, I'd get winded at the slightest exertion!"

"I'm stronger than I look," Leia replied meekly. "Believe me, I feel it. But working keeps me active."

"I drag handsome here to go walking with me every day. Though we've had to cut back a little recently. I'm due in a few weeks."

Leia carefully looked to make sure she wasn't holding up customers. And there was a break for the moment.

"Boy or a girl?" Leia asked.

"We're having a boy!" the man beamed. "How about you? Do you know yet?"

"We just confirmed the other day, at the doctor's office, that it's a girl!" Leia shared, looking enthusiastic.

"Aw, you look so happy! I'm happy for you," the woman replied.

"Thank you so much! I'm happy for you, too," Leia added. "Good luck in a few weeks!"

Misha and Leia watched the couple walk cautiously towards a booth. The husband moved the booth's table slightly forward to accommodate his wife's condition. Misha enjoyed seeing Leia happy, but she also felt the need to return her attention to work.

"So that's one large pepperoni with spinach and roma tomatoes and two bottled waters . . . right?" Misha stood behind Leia with her hands on her hips.

"Um, yeah," Leia replied, clearly embarrassed. "And a cheesy bread."

"Cheesy bread, got it. Well, I guess I can understand."

"That's me and Josh in about five months," Leia said blissfully.

"I know that pregnancy makes a lot of changes in the body, Leia, but I don't think it can change the ethnicity of both parents."

Leia threw her Skippy's hat at Misha, who blocked it reflexively.

Misha reached down, picked up the hat off the floor and handed it back to Leia.

"Thanks," Leia said.

"No worries. You don't need to be bending down like that, Mama. But you really should put your hat back on."

"Why?" Leia asked.

"Your horns are showing," Misha whispered.

"Oh!" Leia responded. "Right! Good for business. Got it. Thanks."

The remaining two hours passed without incident. Misha offered to drive Leia home, as she always did.

"Doesn't Josh have a car?" Misha asked.

"Yes, but he works till one in the morning on the other side of town," Leia replied. "Mom said she could get me. You don't have to do this all the time."

"I don't mind. Outside of work and school, I don't do that much."

Leia nudged Misha's shoulder. "What about your bustling social life?"

"Sometimes it bustles a little too much. Do you think I want to end up an alcoholic or—"

Misha stopped herself from saying the word "pregnant."

"I used to have fun with them, but I've been happier spending time with you," Misha corrected herself.

"Awwww, I appreciate that. What about your family?"

Misha sighed. "My brother, Len, and his wife, Sarah, have been visiting my folks this month. They're from Ohio, where my brother moved for his work, and they brought their two kids. So, I've just been hanging out here in the meantime."

Misha spied a look at Leia. She could see her friend's confusion and concern on her face.

"You don't get along with your brother?" Leia asked.

"I'm crazy about Len and his wife, but their kids are little—"

Misha stopped herself from saying the word "beasts."

"They're a little spoiled," Misha continued. "So, they do whatever they want, as loud as they want. I can't stand it."

"Their parents don't discipline them?"

"My bro works sixty hours a week, and Sarah is kind of timid. She doesn't like confrontation, so she doesn't do it at all."

The truck ahead of them stopped suddenly as another car pulled in front of it from the next lane. Misha had to brake quickly. She looked over to Leia, who nodded that she was okay.

"Well, that doesn't sound very healthy," Leia responded after a moment. "For her or the kids."

"Now you see why I'm not visiting right now," Misha huffed. "And I hope you and Josh learn from their example and raise your little girl right."

"Wow, yeah. There have to be some kind of rules and consequences for breaking those rules. My folks taught me that and I agree with it."

Misha nodded. They drove along silently for a minute before Misha turned and looked at Leia.

"So, tell me, Leia, honestly . . . were you and Josh using any kind of protection at all?"

Leia focused on scratching an itch on her belly.

"That would be a no then. Were you *trying* to get pregnant?!"

"No! It's just—I . . . told him not to worry about it."

"You implied you would take care of the birth control?"

Leia turned her head to look at Misha and nodded.

"Wow. Leia, you did get pregnant on purpose."

Leia looked down. Misha couldn't tell if Leia was just embarrassed or ashamed.

"I didn't think it would happen so soon," Leia responded. "I was three months pregnant when I found out, and Josh and I had only been together for four months."

"You could have gotten pregnant on the very first time. It happens to a lot of women."

Misha wanted to pull over so she could give Leia her full attention but they were on a busy road with a surprising amount of traffic for this time of night. She would just have to manage as best she could.

"It's like when Josh and I decided to become more serious, I romanticized it too much," Leia continued. "I wanted to know him, all of him. And if that meant having his baby, that was a risk I thought I was ready to take."

"I'm sorry if this sounds harsh, Leia, but that wasn't smart. And it was kind of mean. You were gambling with your future and you misled Josh."

Misha heard Leia gasp. There was silence for a few seconds.

"I know," Leia admitted. "I should have been honest with Josh. I didn't give him a choice in this."

"He's not blameless, either. He had a choice," Misha added. "This may sound old-fashioned but you two could have gotten married first, you know."

Leia sighed.

"It may sound old-fashioned but you're right, Misha. We ended up getting married anyway."

Misha was pleasantly surprised to hear that. "Josh is a good guy. He loves you and did the right thing."

"Yes. My Josh is a good guy."

Misha smiled.

"What you and Josh have is pretty incredible. The pregnancy part scares me silly but I'm happy for you. I think I'll wait a few years for that kind of love, maybe a decade, I dunno. That is, if I don't scare off my future husband. I'm not a romantic like you, I'm too practical."

"Says the party girl."

Misha forced herself not to grimace at that remark. How could Leia be so thoughtless with her words sometimes? Misha could only blow off so much. She breathed in slowly through her nose and exhaled through her mouth. It calmed her slightly.

"Have I partied since you told me about the baby?" Misha asked.

"No. I've actually been surprised by that," Leia replied. "Why did you stop?"

"I've been wor—wanting to help you. And honestly, the party scene was starting to bore me."

Misha heard Leia scoff at that, even though she couldn't look over to see her expression.

"Well, aliens have obviously abducted my best friend and left some kind of clone in her place," Leia mocked. "So, do I call you Misha 2 or Zoglorxx?"

"Very funny," Misha rolled her eyes. "But I'm serious. I guess your situation made me realize that there's more to college life than parties. I suppose I should thank your kid for that someday."

"That's sweet."

"There's only one downside to it all," Misha began. "Between my decreased activity, Skippy's leftovers, and all our late-night snack conquests, I've gained more than just the satisfaction of being a good friend to you."

In her peripheral vision, Misha could see Leia nodding in understanding.

"Ah! That may be true," Leia acknowledged. "But who has revolutionized her fashion style and wardrobe to accommodate that modest increase with advice from her pregnant best friend, who *also bought* that wardrobe? Why, you have!"

"Modest increase? Tell that to my hips!"

"Turn in there, woman!" Leia said, pointing ahead and to the right. "Mama Leia demands sustenance!"

Misha pulled into the parking lot and gently rolled to a stop before the giant neon sign in front of the building.

"The twenty-four-hour Pancakeria?" Misha noticed. "This place got me through freshman year. That's when I learned of their Festival of Flapjacks!"

"Yep! This is the Home of the Blueberry Banana Flapjackalanche!" Leia announced.

"Ah! You're aware of that," Misha said, imitating Leia as she exited the vehicle. "Six thick, tasty blueberry-banana pancakes covered in homemade blueberry syrup, served with four eggs, toast and orange juice."

Leia unbuckled and opened the car door. She soon was at Misha's side and they walked towards the restaurant entrance.

"I want that. However, you know I'm just going to devour that, go home and sleep for nine hours. That's probably not too good for me, I'm thinking."

"You definitely shouldn't eat that whole thing," Misha agreed.

"You're right. I'll give you half!"

Misha raised an eyebrow as she opened the door for Leia.

"What? Girl, don't you believe in to-go boxes?"

"It's not as good the next day," Leia pouted. "You have to eat it with me."

"Do you know what eating half of that will do to me?"

"You're such a good friend, Misha. I love you!"

Leia looked at Misha with the most ridiculously large and cute puppy dog eyes and blinked several times. Misha tried hard to resist Leia's gaze but her defenses broke down by degrees as the staring contest continued. Finally, Misha's walls fell and she hung her head for a second. Leia hugged Misha and thanked her profusely. Misha couldn't help but smile at Leia's sincere enthusiasm.

"It's a good thing I have a best friend who will continue to finance my fashion revolution," Misha glared at Leia. "Apologize to my hips now."

"Don't mention it," Leia smiled. "And I'm sorry, Misha's hips. I promise I'll make you look fabulous!"

Satisfied, Misha led Leia to sit down at a booth close to the entrance. Their waitress made pleasant conversation with them and took their order. Misha got out her mobile phone and snapped a quick picture of Leia.

"What are you doing?" Leia asked.

"Preserving the memory," Misha replied. "You already know how this ends. We may as well have fun taking pictures along the way."

Ten minutes later, the waitress returned with a tray full of steaming hot goodness and set it down on the table in front of Leia, who salivated as she grinned at it. Misha looked at it in awe.

"It's perfect!" Leia exclaimed.

Misha smiled and took the next snapshot with Leia enjoying her first bite of the monstrous breakfast extravaganza. She and Leia only ended up taking eight pictures.

The waitress took the last picture. It was Leia and Misha asleep, their arms and heads on the table, with relaxed grips on their forks and only a small remnant of pancake, egg, and toast bits littering the plates in front of them. Their orange juice and water glasses were completely empty.

22

DAVID MANNING SAT IN HIS hotel room and lit another cigarette. The talking heads on the television debated ardently about some political topic he cared nothing about. It had been like this since the night he met with Ross at the diner, two months ago. He was waiting. Always waiting.

Of course, David had visited his son and daughter-in-law several times a week and stayed in touch with friends and other colleagues via social media, either on his phone or laptop. But the nights were the most difficult, the most boring. Television held little appeal but made good white noise. Streaming music was enjoyable, when he was in the mood for it. But David was a people person. Ironically, there were very few people he wanted to be around these days, outside of family.

His mobile phone rang with a special ringtone he'd assigned.

"Kelso! What've you got for me?" David asked.

"It's all lined up, just like you wanted," Kelso replied. "We even got the special insurance you ordered."

"Alright! Great work, Kelso. When can we move in?"

"I have surveillance on them. There's a car on the way to pick you up now."

"Excellent," David looked at the shotgun lying on his bed. "I'll be ready."

Twenty minutes later, there was an insistent knocking on David's hotel room door. When he answered, he beheld a short Hispanic woman in her mid-forties. She had short, dark brown hair and was dressed in black leather except for her gray blouse. She was also wearing sunglasses, even though the sun had set an hour earlier.

"Manning?" the woman asked with a gruff, almost angry voice that was barely above a whisper.

"I'm Manning, yes. You're the driver?"

"I'm the insurance," she answered, turning to leave. "Let's go."

"Now just a moment," David protested, reaching out to grab the woman's arm.

He didn't see her move. He only felt the air rush past his right arm, watched the lower half of his sleeve disappear and saw five bloody lines scrawl across his forearm. He started to cry out but thought better of it. He just gripped his arm and looked at the mysterious woman in amazement and fear.

"That was your only warning, Manning," the woman said. "I let you keep your arm. Be grateful, shut up and let's go."

This time, David did as he was bidden without question.

———————

Leia had started calling Malevolence "Mother" in recent weeks. Malevolence would never be Mom but she was Leia's birth mother and she was trying to be a part of her life. So, Leia decided to honor that. She had seen how much this simple distinction had meant to Malevolence.

Leia and Josh had never been to Mother's penthouse suite before. Leia wore a flowing pink maternity dress which complimented her now-six-month pregnant belly. She also wore a white dinner jacket. Josh sported a gray suit. Mother looked surprisingly festive in an orange satin dress with black sash and matching dress shoes.

"You're early, Leia," Mother noted. "I almost didn't have time to finish making dinner."

"You cooked?" Leia said, clearly impressed.

"I admit my culinary expertise is limited, but I have been known to make a casserole now and then. Contrary to legend, not all super villains have staff waiting on them hand and foot. I chopped off their hands and feet!"

Mother laughed but Leia stared at her in annoyance and Josh was frozen solid.

"This is why I was a villain and not a comedienne," Malevolence said.

"Why not? You'd have slain your audience!" Josh uttered.

Leia looked at her husband as if he'd just grown a third eye.

"I like him!!" Mother said, clapping and laughing. "He's funny!"

"He's just full of surprises," Leia pasted on a fake smile, hitting him on the back hard enough to knock the wind out of him. "That's my Josh!"

"You should loosen up, Leia," Mother replied. "I know you can't have wine but how about some fruit water or soda?"

"Fruit water is fine for me and Josh, too," Leia acknowledged, sitting down on one of the chairs Mother had placed at the dinner table.

"Sure!" Josh agreed, coughing and trying to regain his bearing. He chose to sit down, too.

"Thanks for the dinner clothes, Mother," Leia added.

"I wanted something to show off your natural glow, darling," Mother replied.

"So, make your eyes look like they're on fire to really bring it out, hon—" He was cut off by Leia planting her elbow into his left ribs.

He grabbed his side and doubled over, crying out in pain.

"Josh, what is it?! Did I—" Leia said.

"Far be it for me to interfere in your marital bliss, Leia, but you just fractured your husband's third and fifth ribs. You must be getting stronger."

"No! I didn't mean to! Josh, I'm so sorry!"

"I'm dulling his pain receptors telepathically but he's going to need bedrest and real pain meds to recover," Mother said. "He knows you didn't mean—"

Just then, Mother fell quiet, appearing to listen to something Leia couldn't hear. Her demeanor shifted to one of ice-cold fury; her eyes glowed and her red highlights lit up, indicating she was at full power.

"What's wrong?" Leia asked.

"Dane has spotted . . . uninvited guests," Mother responded. "I'd recommend you leave but they're too far inside the building. I'll have to protect you; you protect your husband."

"Alright. Any idea how many?"

"At least twelve. And they're heavily armed. Probably mercenaries. They won't cause trouble until they get here but they're also blocking the normal escape routes."

Several minutes later, one large rugged man dressed in all black kicked in the front door and fired two rapid bursts from his semi-automatic rifle into the suite before charging in. He was bald, had pale, weathered skin and a merciless expression as evident as the scars on his arms. Another large and identically attired man with a long face, squinted eyes and long blond hair tied in a ponytail rushed in behind him. Two more came crashing in through the wall-length window: a dark-skinned man with a trim, athletic build, close-cropped black hair and a bright burn scar on his cheek, and a very muscular, brown-skinned woman with short, dreaded hair and a small but jagged scar across her nose. Each wore a gun belt and had a rifle strapped to their back, a pistol ready in their right hands.

Almost immediately, all six were lifted several feet into the air and pulled into a semi-circular pattern. Their guns twisted into various shapes and fell to the ground while the expended bullets were flying in circular patterns near the ceiling. None of them could move anything except their heads and they all looked down. Mother walked slowly towards them, a terrifying grin on her face.

"Welcome to my home. I am Malevolence. I'm having a little party this evening but your names weren't on the guest list. That's okay, though, we'll just improvise. You're all five-year olds, and there's a TV in the back room playing back-to-back episodes of your favorite childhood shows. There's also cake and punch. It'll be lots of fun! Now go play, kids!"

Mother gently lowered them back to the ground and released them. Leia watched in amazement as six grown adults eagerly scampered to a furnished but otherwise empty guest room and began acting like little kids at a birthday party.

"It's scary that you can do that," Leia stated.

"They'll live. Keep a shield up around yourself and Josh, no matter what—"

A rifle butt slammed into the left side of Mother's head with a loud crack. Stunned and bleeding, she crumpled to the ground in pain. David Manning stood over her.

"Dad?" Josh exclaimed.

"Sorry, Josh, they didn't tell me that you two were here," David replied. "All I want is Malevolence."

"Why?" Leia bristled. "What has my mother done to you?"

As soon as the words left her mouth, Leia realized what she'd said and regretted it.

"You mean, besides killing my wife?" David snarled. "It took quite a lot of digging but I got to the truth about her, you, your family . . . everything."

"Dad, that wasn't Angela's fault! You've got to stop this!" Josh squinted from the pain. "Why did you hire these -- these thugs? Call them off!"

"Josh, I'll get you and Leia out of here safely. I like Leia and I want you two to have a happy life. But Malevolence is another matter."

Leia steadied herself and rose to her full height. She allowed her eyes to glow with flame, and she pointed at him accusingly.

"Then you have a problem with me! I won't let you kill my mother in cold blood."

David took aim at Leia's mother who was unmoving on the floor.

"Don't do this, Mr. Manning!" Leia shouted. "I won't let you!"

"Dad, please! You're aiming at a defenseless woman!" Josh screamed. "What is wrong with you??"

"She's a monster! She's a monster!" David shouted back. "I have to do this!"

As David was about to pull the trigger, Mother lifted her head. Blood was trailing down from where she'd been hit, forming twin inch-wide trails from the left side of her hairline; it flowed to her cheek and over her left eye, which was only half-open. She lifted her right hand and pointed at Manning's gun, which flew from his hand and disassembled in mid-air before landing across the room in pieces.

"Leia, now!" Malevolence said with great strain, fighting to stay conscious.

When David turned to look in Leia's direction, her right fist connected with the left side of his jaw. He was unconscious before he hit the ground.

Leia was angry and disappointed but also extremely confused with her father-in-law's actions. How could the same man who'd been so supportive of their marriage and pregnancy hurt her birth mother and nearly kill her?

Then Leia saw that Josh had passed out from his own pain. She went to him, sat on the floor right next to him. She rested Josh's head on her lap and stroked his hair.

"Are you alright?" Leia asked her mother.

"I've probably got a concussion, I'm bleeding pretty badly . . . and it really hurts. Beyond that . . . I don't know. I was fortunate to . . . disarm Josh's father. I can't concentrate enough . . . to use my powers right now. And we're still in danger."

"I'll protect us."

"You've done a great job of that, but don't get cocky. There are ways to kill telekinetics . . . and despite your power increase, your pregnancy makes you vulnerable."

"I'll be extra-careful."

"Before I was injured, Dane told me he knocked out four of them. I stopped six . . . and you stopped Josh's father. That makes eleven."

"There's still one more. What will we do?"

Dane crashed through the roof, a silhouetted female figure on top of him. His costume was slashed in several areas. He was unconscious and bleeding from his mouth and had a deep gash on his chest. Both of them landed across the room from Leia, Mother, and Josh. Then the woman's arm raised so quickly, it was almost invisible and began descending in a slashing motion towards Dane.

But it stopped just short of Dane's head, and the woman couldn't make it move. Furious, she looked up.

Leia briefly caught a view of herself in a landscape wall mirror. She was a wonder to behold: a pregnant woman in a pink evening gown with flaming, pupil-less eyes, full horns, and glowing with power. Her right hand was fully extended, and she was standing in front of Mother and Josh.

"I don't know who you are, but I won't let you kill my friend!" Leia growled.

Leia could see the woman clearly now. Set on either side of her head were cat-like ears in the midst of her short, dark brown hair. She also had feral, brown feline eyes and light brown fur. Her nose was human, but her teeth were all animal. Her hand, still in the killing pose, had razor sharp claws at the end of each finger.

And Leia recognized her.

"Aunt Leticia?" Leia said, stunned. "You're a cat like Mom??"

"You're Leia," Leticia replied. "The girl my sister raised?"

"That's right! How can you be an assassin??"

"Nothing personal, kid. But you're not blood-related to me, so don't think I won't end you. Let me go and you'll live to have that baby!"

"I don't think you can hurt me. And I mean that literally."

"Maybe I can't hurt you," Leticia added, pressing a button on her belt with her free hand. "But I can damage this building!"

The rest of the ceiling exploded. Leia had to focus her telekinesis on protecting her mother and husband from the falling debris. And Leticia took that moment to leap towards Mother, attempting a killing strike.

Leia saw a blur to her left via her peripheral vision. She felt the air rushing towards the three of them and, without changing her stance, instinctively lashed out with her mind to keep the threat away.

Only this time it wasn't a telekinetic shield she formed.

It was a moving wall of fire!

Leticia was struck with the force of a missile, enveloped in flames, and ejected from the building while still fifteen stories in the air. If she felt anything before she died, it had to be surprise.

Leia mentally threw the debris she'd been holding across the room, away from her family and Dane. She ran towards the just-made hole in the wall, her mouth agape, and desperately looked for her aunt. When she saw the broken and still-burning corpse on the ground, she screamed from the depths of her soul.

Leia had never wanted to hurt her aunt, much less kill her! She didn't think about how desperate the situation had been, how she was the only one between Aunt Leticia and her birth mother or that she had acted in self-defense. Leia only knew that she had brutally slain a member of her family, Mom's sister, her aunt. She had taken a life and that could never be undone.

She was still screaming when Mother took her by the hands and looked in her eyes.

"You have to calm down, Leia," Mother pleaded. "I know what happened just now is . . . the most terrible moment in your life! It makes you feel like a monster—like you're the worst person in the world. That woman is dead and yes, you did it. But you have to think about your baby now, Leia. She needs you to be calm . . . or she'll be in danger! Do you understand me?"

Leia's screams turned into sobs as she began to calm down. She backed away from Mother, leaned against an undamaged part of the wall, and slowly slid to a sitting position on the floor. She allowed herself to revert to her normal, human appearance.

Leia cradled her arms around her belly. "I understand."

———————

Moving slowly and unsteadily, Malevolence was forced to retrieve her mobile phone from across the room. Through the fog of her vision, she somehow remembered Steve's phone number and called to tell him what had happened and that Leia really needed her parents. Steve flew with his wife to the scene before police and emergency crews arrived.

Malevolence, now using her identity as Professor Angela Merrick, fought to stay conscious just a while longer, so she could speak with the police. She fabricated a unique story to explain what had happened.

She told them that the superhero, Shadow, who had continued in the legend of his mother, Black Fox, had uncovered an assassination plot against the State Governor, who was in town for a political event —she'd picked up that tidbit from David Manning's mind, something he'd watched on television recently. Unfortunately, the assassins chose to fight back against Shadow and that battle had concluded at this high-rise hotel, impacting Professor Merrick and her visiting daughter, son-in-law, and her son-in-law's father.

The final assassin, who appeared to have super powers, chose to go out in a blaze of glory rather than surrender. To Malevolence, it was laughable fiction but she managed to convince them it was the truth, since the truth was far less believable.

The emergency crews wanted to take everyone to the hospital for medical treatment and observation. Malevolence resisted the idea but she had no choice in the matter after she finally passed out from her injuries.

———————

She saw that Ross was smoking a cigarette below the No Smoking sign. He stood by the storage door to unit #199 at the back end of the self-storage facility lot. The lighting around this part of the facility was minimal but enough for her to see him as she walked in his direction with a barely noticeable limp she had long since gotten used to. Her lustrous red hair blew across her round face in the wind. Her mood and clothing matched the cold weather. She dwarfed Ross' height by more than a foot and she was not happy.

"Do you think you'n your people coulda foun' any worse—any more *public*—way t'mess this up, Ross?" she said with more than a hint of Scottish accent. "Your mission was a complete disaster!"

"I warned them what to expect with Malevolence and Shadow, Sidra. But we didn't know about Leia Hamilton's capabilities."

The crescent moon was partially obscured by clouds this evening and the wind's bite was frigid. Sidra La Marque just stared disapprovingly at Ross for a few moments, her arms folded over her soft and profuse stomach.

Then her frown relaxed. She exhaled, releasing her tension.

"I like you, Ross, so I'll smooth things over . . . this time," she added with a lilting tone. "But headquarters isn' happy aboot losing this many agents in a night, including a super-powered one. The regular agents still think they're young children! They're a complete loss! And Leticia . . . "

"I know. I guess you could say they paid for their failure," Ross said sadly.

"No, they paid for *your* failure!" Sidra shouted, pointing at him. "Leia is the daughter of Crusader 'n Malevolence! Didja think she'd be a pushover?"

"I thought Leticia could handle her," Ross responded. "I thought Leticia was perfect for the job."

"You . . . thought wrong," Sidra said, clenching her teeth in anger and regret.

Now Ross stared at Sidra for a moment.

"The way you're going to smooth this over . . . is by eliminating me, isn't it?" Ross asked.

"I promise, y'won't feel a thing, Ross," Sidra answered.

"Can I ask you something?"

"Sure. Why not?"

"What was it like, being a part of the AR-MEN back then?"

"The best years of m'whole life," Sidra replied with a wistful smile. "A shame it had to end, but it did get me this job, so no complaints."

"You're a true believer in the government, aren't you, Sidra?"

"Just b'cause you'n I dated a few times doesn' mean you're privy to all m'secrets, Ross."

"I suppose it doesn't matter," Ross said, his hand shaking a bit as he lowered his cigarette and exhaled smoke. "Mind if I finish this?"

Ten minutes later, Sidra walked away from the storage facility lot, the air still sparkling with electricity around her. She heard a footstep behind her—or was that someone landing? Either way, she wasn't alone.

"It's done," Sidra said.

"I could tell," another woman replied. "Electrocution leaves a certain . . . odor."

"It's been a while, Tina. What can I do for you?"

"We're to drop surveillance of Malevolence and the surviving AR-MEN to a bare minimum. We're not stopping altogether but it's time to lay low."

"For how long?"

"HQ wasn't specific, so until we hear otherwise."

Tina Yang may have been five years younger, noticeably slimmer, and eight inches shorter than Sidra La Marque, but her presence and expression made it perfectly clear that she demanded respect. Her straight jet-black hair was short and stylish, with bangs parted on the right. It mostly concealed an old knifing scar.

Tina walked slowly and deliberately towards Sidra, the chilling wind rustling her closed midnight blue jacket. The moonlight shone off of her black boots but she seemed to be radiating her own slight glow. As she got closer, Sidra started to feel the heat envelope that surrounding Tina's body.

"Show off," Sidra said.

"I thought you might like to warm up," Tina replied.

"Just like old times, eh?" Sidra scoffed, a trace of bitterness evident.

"Like you said, a shame it had to end," Tina added. "I miss those days, too, sometimes."

"We were better people then," Sidra looked off to the distance. "With a better purpose."

"How's your son?" Tina asked.

"Jason's fine. Jus' turned twenty-one last September. And no, he hasn't shown any sign of havin' any powers, which is jus' fine with me."

Tina's eyes widened slightly and she raised an eyebrow.

"That's surprising to hear."

"Is it? Havin' powers drove my husband t'madness an' got him killed. The world doesn't need another Killer Knight."

Tina nodded soberly.

"Fair enough. Tamara is fourteen now and Jill is seventeen. Neither have shown signs, either."

"Maybe the next generation is bein' spared."

Tina sighed derisively and her brow furrowed.

"I doubt it. Leia and Shadow would seem to be evidence to the contrary."

Sidra shrugged, her gaze now focused on the ground.

"How are you, Sidra? I mean . . . really, how are you?" Tina asked, her formerly icy gaze showing actual concern.

That caught Sidra off-guard and she looked up, confused.

"You look really stressed . . . and you've lost weight," Tina added. "Honestly, I've been worried about you. What's wrong?"

Sidra narrowed her eyes.

"You're concerned that m'personal matters'll affect m'job performance. Well, y'don't have t'worry aboot that. M'fine."

"Good. I'm glad."

There was a tension that still lingered in the air.

"I should ne'er a given Ross permission t'work wi' Manning. Not against Malevolence. It was a d'saster waitin' t'happen."

"I signed off on it, too. I trained Leticia myself. I . . . regret their loss."

"D'ya ever regret the path we've both chosen?"

"A dangerous question," Tina warned, her expression grim but tempered by familiarity. "Are you sure you want to ask?"

Sidra just looked at her expectantly, with a mixture of impatience and mild amusement at the discomfort Sidra knew she was causing her colleague.

"We were John's fail-safe, in case anything happened to him," Tina said. "But I don't think either of us had any idea where that would lead."

"'Where that would lead,'" Sidra echoed with a bitter chuckle.

Then all traces of humor left Sidra's expression and she walked within an inch of Tina, whose own expression completely masked whatever emotions she was feeling.

"Malevolence is na th' only monster in these parts," Sidra said, looking right at Tina.

"We do what we do to protect the citizens of this country and the world," Tina replied dispassionately. "It's not radically different from what we did in the AR-MEN."

"I used to tell myself that, too," Sidra interjected. "But I doubt I would have killed my man to cover his mistakes when I was in the AR-MEN!"

"Your man, when you were in the AR-MEN, was every bit as powerful as Crusader and the second deadliest psychopath in the world!" Tina seethed, incredulous. "Your being married to him didn't stop or even slow his destructive slaughter. When you saw that, you were even in a position to—you could have stopped him before he attacked the satellite! We didn't have to go this route! You could have—"

Tina stopped and folded her arms across her chest and turned away, only the rasping wisps of warm air coming from her mouth betraying how much pain she was still venting. Sidra didn't feel Tina's heat envelope anymore, figuring Tina was too upset to maintain it. Sidra had never seen Tina get this roused before.

Likewise, Sidra could feel her heart pounding in her chest and resounding in her ears. Tina's words had cut her deeply. There wasn't one minute of any day that this truth hadn't haunted Sidra these last two decades. It had taken years of therapy and the love of her son just to keep Sidra from ending her life many times.

Sidra backed up a couple of feet from Tina. She lowered her voice and her tone softened, enveloped with sadness borne for so many years.

"He was na that way when he started out. D'ya remember? He was a gentle, funny man . . . a good husband and father. He was a hero. But the day I was attacked and his sister, Cassandra, died, it changed him. It changed him so much."

"I remember."

"I was too blinded by m'love f'r who he had been . . . seein' ev'rythin' through the eyes of a new mum. I missed the chance t'end his suff'rin' before he took us all down this road."

Tina turned and looked at Sidra then. Was that sympathy in her eyes?

"You were there for me then. Y'helped me through m'loss when he and John died," Sidra said. "I . . . I never thanked y'properly f'r that."

"We were friends then," Tina replied with evident sadness. "We . . . were like family."

Sidra leaned against one of the storage doors, feeling a little drained by the confrontation.

"We were more human then, too," Sidra added. "We hadn't compromised that part o' ourselves just t'survive yet."

"We were still very young and naive. We thought we could change the world."

Sidra clenched her fists. "And instead, th' world changed us . . . inta the very monsters we swore t'fight."

"That was the only way to win," Tina answered, her voice a hushed whisper, heavy with regret.

"Maybe so," Sidra conceded. "Still, the price was so high. Too high."

"Maybe so. But what's done is done. We are who we are now."

"Aye. That we are."

"Goodbye, Sidra." Tina mustered a bittersweet smile.

"G'bye, Tina," Sidra replied, mirroring Tina's expression.

Tina then turned and walked away from Sidra, even her slight glow eventually disappearing in the distance.

Sidra closed her eyes and chuckled to herself.

"You ne'er could lie to me, Tina. You can fool the rest of the world but not me. Maybe y'still have some o' that humanity left in there somewhere."

Sidra looked up at the moon for a moment. Then she shivered in the cold and put her hands in her coat pockets, walking away in the opposite direction from her former friend.

The next morning came more quickly than Malevolence expected. As her vision cleared, she saw that Steve was in the room alone with her. She put her hand to the bandage surrounding her forehead like a headband. It was still sore to the touch on the left side where she'd been struck and she could feel some kind of medication dulling the rest of her pain.

I was hurt worse than I realized!

Malevolence tried moving her head from side to side. Her neck was very stiff, and each movement brought new and unpleasant sensations that ranged from pinpricks to electrical jolts. Malevolence thought she could sense Steve's thoughts, but it was like listening through water, she couldn't make out the words. That's when she realized he was actually speaking out loud and that she was experiencing some vertigo.

"Are you alright?" Steven asked.

"I'm glad I'm in a bed, whichever Steve said that."

"Do you want me to get the nurse? I can—"

"No, I'll be fine. I was attempting humor again. It just never seems to work."

There was an awkward silence for a few seconds.

"Why are you here?" she wondered.

"You called us, remember?"

"No, not that. I mean, why are you in my room instead of Leia's?"

Malevolence had to keep her eyes closed half of the time. The vertigo wasn't abating and the pain medication was enhancing that particular sensation.

"I wanted to thank you," Steve replied. "You did your best to protect Leia, Josh, and Dane. I may not approve of all your methods but you didn't kill anyone, either."

"That's . . . quite an admission from you," Malevolence tried to remain perfectly still, her eyes still closed. "I'm honored."

"You also helped keep Leia calm when she was very upset. You probably prevented a miscarriage."

"I get it, you're grateful. Look, Steven, the moment Leia and Josh entered my home, they were under my protection. Dane, too."

"Right . . . Dane."

"You've made your feelings clear on that, so let's not discuss him, okay?"

"Alright."

Malevolence turned away from Steve in the bed, squinting in discomfort as she immediately regretted the sudden movement. Steve started to walk towards the door, understanding Malevolence's silent message for him to leave.

"I do wish I could have spared Leia from killing," Malevolence added. "The first time you take a life, it . . . changes you."

"I know," Steve said, reflecting her somber tone.

Steve turned again to leave, but stopped, still facing the door.

"Why did you come back into our lives?" he asked. "What happened last night . . . with Leia . . . probably wouldn't have happened if you'd just stayed away."

Malevolence, still turned away from Steve, opened her eyes again slowly. Tears escaped but no sound proceeded from her trembling lips. In this moment, the hurt inflicted by his few spoken words dwarfed her physical injuries. It took many long seconds for her to regain enough composure to speak again.

"You're right." Her voice was hoarse and tired, even a little shaky. "David Manning was afraid of me. He hired people and attacked because of me. He was so scared that he was willing to become a criminal to 'protect' his own dreams, his family. And in a way, I can relate."

"How do you mean?"

"All of my life, Angela has been scared. She was always told she wasn't good enough by her father and half-ignored by her mother. As the oldest child, she helped take care of her brothers while her mother drank and her father worked so he could avoid his problems at home."

"You never told me any of this."

"She was ashamed of it. After you and I made our arrangement, after Leia was born, I had a choice to make. I moved away as we agreed, and all I had to do was start over . . . but I couldn't."

"Couldn't . . . or wouldn't?" Steve pressed.

Malevolence bit her lip and squinted again in response to Steve's verbal dig. She cleared her throat to buy a moment while she steeled herself towards more conversation.

"You're more bitter than you let on, Steven. Or perhaps realize."

"Perhaps," Steve said defensively.

"The semantics are irrelevant anyway. I chose to observe and protect Leia, even if from a distance."

"But you're not at a distance anymore."

The stress from the confrontation was wearing on Malevolence, increasing her pain and soreness, amplifying the vertigo. And at that moment, Malevolence felt her own bitterness surge to the surface.

"How long, Steven? How long was I supposed to live in exile, stuck between two worlds and not being a part of either of them? Did you just expect me to find an office job, meet a nice guy, make a new family and forget my old one?"

Steve turned to face her then.

"I was no longer an ordinary woman! Even people who didn't know what I was cowered near me because they sensed it. They *knew* I could kill them with a thought! I've had zero chance at a normal life, so why shouldn't I try to grasp a little bit of happiness by getting to know the child that I gave birth to? Or are you telling me I'm not good enough to be in her life?"

An alarm went off on Malevolence's monitoring equipment. Her nurse, a short and athletic, thirty-something Nigerian woman with shoulder-length black hair entered the room immediately in response to the alert. She took about two seconds to look at the two of them and sense the tension between them.

"Sir, I need you to leave the room right now," the nurse insisted. "You are putting my patient at risk."

Steve opened his mouth to say something but seemed to think better of it. He walked toward the door but paused as glanced back at Malevolence as the nurse helped her lie back down.

23

AS STEVE EXITED ANGELA'S ROOM, Sue was standing outside with her hands on her hips and looking annoyed. She took his right hand in hers and dragged him towards the break room down the hall. Then she closed the door and lightly punched him in the left shoulder.

"I thought you were going to wait for me before going in there!" Sue said, exasperated.

"I only wanted to thank her . . . but it . . . didn't . . . um—"

"You must not be thinking clearly. Did you forget who you were going in to see? The last time you saw her in person, she called you a god and asked you to kill her! How did you think this would go any better?"

Steve sighed.

"I messed up pretty royally. I'm sorry."

"Yeah, you did," Sue also let out a sigh. "Apology accepted."

She paced the room for a minute and Steve looked out the window.

"You two have too much history. You know better. You're vulnerable to her. And vice-versa."

"Yeah. She said I was more bitter than I realized."

"Evidently, you are! And it's time for you to acknowledge that and let it go."

"You're right."

Steve stared out the window in the direction of the rising sun. His lack of sleep and the stress over what Leia, Josh, Dane, and even

Malevolence had been through collided with his regret in mishandling his conversation with Malevolence. He felt weary and ashamed for being so aggressive towards the woman he once loved, the mother of his firstborn child, while she was still in the hospital recovering from serious injuries. His actions were at odds with the person he knew himself to be. He realized he had been fighting shadows of his own past, all by himself; no wonder he was making mistakes! In his thoughts, he humbled himself before his God and Savior and prayed for help, guidance and forgiveness.

Sometime later, Steve looked through the break room window and noticed a flock of birds flying in formation nearby. They moved across the sky like dancing silhouettes in the morning light, enjoying these moments without a care in the world.

Sue pulled him close and hugged him. He melted into her arms and allowed himself to release tears and feelings he'd been bottling up for more than twenty years.

———————

Leia didn't expect to wake up in a hospital room connected to cords and an intravenous line. She heard the electronic representation of her baby's heartbeat on its own monitor. From the light coming in the window, she could tell it was morning but couldn't determine much else. Her vision wasn't entirely focused and she felt lethargic.

Leia also didn't expect Tanya to be the first person she saw. Tanya was asleep on the couch next to Leia's bed but Tanya startled awake at the first sound of motion from Leia.

"Sis, you're awake! How are you feeling?" Tanya looked concerned and relieved at the same time.

"Groggy. What happened?" Leia asked.

"The nurse gave you something to help you sleep. He said it was safe for the baby. Mom and Dad said you were really upset last night. They said something bad happened at Malevolence's place."

"Yeah, something bad happened."

Leia's mind replayed the events of the previous night in a rush. Tanya held her sister and gently stroked Leia's hair.

"I'll be here for you, Leia," Tanya soothed. "No matter what happens."

Leia could sense Tanya's presence, but she was so gripped by her own emotions that she couldn't focus on anything else. It took several minutes for Leia to return to coherence.

"Josh and I, we'd been invited over for dinner at—my birth mother's place," Leia began, her voice just above a whisper. "It was fine at first, then . . . it wasn't. My—I've gotten stronger. I've gotten stronger and I hurt Josh. Didn't mean to. But before we could help him, a group of people rushed in with guns, tried to kill Mother—Malevolence—while I protected Josh."

To Tanya's credit, she kept her own composure. Her eyes would occasionally widen but she wanted to be strong for Leia.

"Mother stopped them with her powers but didn't kill them," Leia continued. "But Josh's father snuck up and hurt her, was gonna kill her. He hired those people who attacked us. Between me and Mother, we knocked him out. Then—she showed up."

"She? Who?" Tanya asked.

"Aunt Leticia," Leia confirmed. "She was a cat-woman like Mom."

Tanya's body tensed, her expression soured, and she involuntarily snarled.

"Why was *she* there?" Tanya asked.

"She was also hired by Josh's dad to kill Malevolence," Leia replied. "She tried, but I—"

Leia couldn't complete the sentence. In her mind, she saw it all again in slow motion: the wall of fire hitting Aunt Leticia, consuming her in fire before it knocked her out the nearest window, shattering the glass. She relived the awful uncertainty of her aunt careening through the air for a number of seconds before gravity took hold.

"I killed her, Tanya!" Leia sobbed. "I killed Aunt Leticia with my powers! I didn't mean to but she's dead! She's dead and I killed her!"

Tanya gently embraced her sister and held her close.

"Shhhhh! Calm down, Leia. I'm here. You're safe with me. I won't let anything happen. I love you. I will always love you."

Even through her guilt and shame, Leia felt her sister's genuine compassion and affection for her. She had never needed it so much as now. She held onto it like a life preserver, a beacon of hope and sanity. At that moment, her sister's presence was all she knew, all she wanted to know. She was Leia's hero.

Eventually, Leia opened her eyes again.

"You feeling a little better now?" Tanya asked.

"Yeah, thanks. Thanks for everything."

Tanya smiled at that. "You're my sister."

Leia nodded slowly. "I think I can talk about it a little more . . . now that you know."

Tanya nodded as well. "I can't believe Josh's dad hired those people to kill Malevolence. What's going to happen to him?"

Leia wondered if the police had arrested Mr. Manning. Her memories after her aunt died were a haze.

"I don't know. I was pretty out of it after . . . everything," Leia answered. "I only know that I knocked him out."

"You're a hero, sis! You saved everybody!"

"I didn't save Aunt Leticia," Leia began to cry again.

Tanya held her sister again, occasionally stroking her hair. Leia wondered if she was hearing things. Was that congestion or was her sister actually purring? Tanya's words interrupted Leia's thoughts.

"Let me tell you something about Aunt Leticia, Leia. She's always scared me, ever since I was a little girl."

"Why? She . . . always looked bored to me, like she didn't want to be at family functions. And I know she avoided me because I wasn't Mom's biological child."

Tanya's muscles started to tense, even as she continued trying to calm her.

"There's that, but there was more," Tanya added. "I could always sense her hostility, like an electric charge in the air. And she had a smell that just set me on edge."

"You smelled something from her that made you edgy? How does that work?"

Tanya pulled back from Leia, still sitting on the side of the bed. She lowered her head and chuckled to herself, a slight irritation evident in her voice.

"I'm not totally sure," Tanya continued. "But you know how some animals, when they get around each other, just don't like each other? They've never met but if they get too close, they warn each other off with a growl or they start fighting. It's kind of like that."

"Wow, I had no idea. Maybe you've got some of Mom's cat genes in you."

"I hope so. I've never seen anything so amazing as Mom in her cat form!"

"Yeah," Leia said, smiling at that memory.

The door slowly opened, and their mom peeked inside.

"Oh good, you're awake," their mom interjected.

"Speak of the feline!" Tanya said. "Hey, Mom! Could you tell we were talking about—"

"Cork it, Tanya," Leia inserted with a smile. "Hi, Mom."

Mom looked around the room for a second, assessing the readouts from the monitors.

"You want me to turn up the lights? It's a little dark in here," Mom asked. "I guess they did that so you could sleep."

"Leave them, I may go back to sleep. I'm still a little loopy from the meds they gave me."

"If that's what you want to do, that's fine, but you might consider getting something to eat first. Are you hungry at all?"

"I feel like I should be. Maybe I will order something in a few minutes. Is there a menu with the number to call for service?"

"Tanya, would you go ask one of the nurses out there for a menu?" Mom winked.

"Sure, Mom," Tanya replied.

Tanya walked out of the room and Mom pulled a chair to the side of Leia's bed and sat down. She took Leia's hand in hers and looked at Leia with sympathy and concern. It was obvious that Leia had been crying.

"How are you, really?" Mom asked. "You don't have to hold back. Tell me everything."

"Mom, Aunt Leticia was there last night," Fresh tears welled in her eyes. "She had powers like yours."

"What? Why was she there? I knew she had powers like mine. She developed them a few years after mine appeared. I'd stopped her from using them for petty theft a few times, but . . . I don't understand why she'd—"

"She was an assassin. She'd been sent to kill Malevolence."

Mom gasped. Her eyes widened in comprehension.

"Her power would be well-suited to that!" Mom said. "Did Malevolence stop her?"

"No, Mom," Leia replied somberly, closing her eyes in shame. "I did."

"What—what happened?" Mom sounded as if she dreaded the answer.

Leia looked at Mom with her eyes wide open for several seconds before answering.

"Mom, I . . . killed her! I killed her."

"What?" Mom responded in a hushed whisper, slowly shaking her head as though denying the facts. "No . . . wait—what do you mean, you killed her?"

Tanya re-entered the room with the menu.

"Mom, she told me. Please don't make her re-live it again," Tanya pleaded.

"Tanya, what?" Mom answered. "I don't understand."

"I know she was your sister and you loved her, but she was a willing part of this attack. Leia stopped her from killing Malevolence and everyone there."

Mom looked bewildered, even agonized, as she opened her mouth to say something but couldn't. She looked down, shut her eyes and gripped her thick arms as if holding herself in place. Leia watched Tanya take a step forward. It looked like Tanya wanted to comfort their mother like she had Leia. But their mom looked up at Tanya and raised a hand for her to keep back. Tanya did as she was bidden but still looked concerned.

Mom looked sadly at Leia. She was quiet for a few more seconds, looking as if she might be collecting her thoughts, figuring out what she wanted to say.

"Tell me something," Mom asked. "Even if Leticia took the assignment to kill Malevolence, why she was willing to kill you? She knew you're my daughter."

"No, Mom, I was never your daughter to Aunt Leticia. Since I didn't come from your womb, it didn't matter to her that you raised me from birth. She told me that, and that she would end me if I got in her way."

Mom looked at Leia helplessly for a while. She was clearly hurt to hear what Leia had said but not offended.

"I . . . accept what you say, Leia. The facts speak for themselves, don't they?"

Mom managed a slight smile as she touched Leia's right cheek with her left hand. She was crying now.

"Leticia once asked me why I chose to marry your father, a man I'd only been dating a few months. She wanted to know how I could take responsibility for another woman's baby, knowing that child wasn't my own."

"What did you tell her?"

"The truth. My heart wouldn't let me make any other decision. Any man who would go to such lengths to guarantee that his child would make it into this world . . . was a man worthy of my love. And I knew that child would be very special."

Leia was proud of her mother. She didn't know what to say but she was glad to hear this.

"And what did she say to that?" Leia asked.

"She said I was weak and a fool. She told me I should have more pride in myself, that if I wanted a child, I should get pregnant. She told me that Steve and his girlfriend were just using me and that I should escape. I disagreed rather harshly with her and we . . . were never really close again after that."

Leia could see what a painful admission that had been for Mom. She knew Mom and her sister had been very close growing up. She couldn't imagine the loss Mom must now be feeling.

"Mom, I'm sorry. I didn't know that."

"Honestly, many times, I've wished I could have been the one to carry you inside me instead of Malevolence. When she was living with me and your father, all throughout her pregnancy, I was so envious, so jealous. But for your father's and your sake, I held my peace and did my best to support them. And that paid off, because I got to raise you. I wouldn't trade that for anything. I'm so glad you and your baby are still alive after last night!"

Leia managed a smile. Mom gently hugged Leia and Tanya hugged Mom from behind. That moment lasted several minutes.

Then Tanya let go of Mom and stood back a few feet. Mom took both of Leia's hands in hers.

"I'm sorry you were put in the position where you had to make a life or death decision like that," Mom said. "I . . . understand what you're going through."

Leia picked up on Mom's word choice and sad expression, which was a reflection of her own. For the first time, Mom looked older than her thirty-nine years to Leia and she understood why.

"When you were a superhero, did you have to kill? Did Dad?"

"Yes. We both did. And it wasn't always so clear-cut as what you went through. Some of those people didn't have to die. But hindsight is always one hundred percent. And it's useless if you don't learn from it."

"How did you live with it back then?"

"That was a different time and we were different people then. After I . . . killed, I would continue to remember what happened. I would relive the whole thing in my mind over and over until enough time passed that it wasn't active in my thoughts. Then I would only see it now and then . . . and in nightmares."

Leia sighed and slowly nodded. "I think it'll be like that for me, too."

Mom shook her head at Leia.

"It doesn't have to be. I mean, yes, you'll always remember what happened last night . . . and you should. But you can have a better hope for the future and your family's future."

"You're my family, Mom. You and Dad and Tanya."

Mom smiled but there was a mild scolding behind her gaze, teasing yet firm.

"Do I need to remind you that you've gotten married and are having a little girl?" Mom declared. "You and Josh are your own family now. You're still a part of your original family, of course. But you need to start thinking about this new family you and Josh have started."

"You're right, we are our own family now. Wow. That's—wow."

Then Leia caught Mom's underlying message.

"You're talking about what you and Dad believe, aren't you? You think that will help me, too?"

"Yes, I do. The Lord brought me and your father back from a worse situation than yours. At one point, I was willing to leave him and take you with me."

"You never told me that, either! It was that bad back then?"

Mom sat down in a chair next to Leia's bed. She looked emotionally drained but still determined.

"I wanted to wait until I felt you were ready for me to tell you about this, but yes, it was that bad," Mom added. "However, The Lord sent someone to help me back then, to convince me that I was about to make a big mistake. I listened to her and I got the help I needed. And I was able to help your father the same way."

"How?" Leia said, curious for the first time about this aspect of her Mom's past.

Mom pondered her thoughts a moment, locking her fingers together on top of her stomach.

"When I gave my life to Christ, He sent His Holy Spirit into my heart and it changed who I was," Mom answered. "It was like becoming a brand-new person, even though I had all my memories from before, but I wasn't alone anymore. Christ was there, helping me and teaching me. He gave me a strength that wasn't in my muscles. It was in my spirit.

"I still had a lot to learn. I'll always be learning ways to be a better person," Mom continued. "But I have hope that I never had before. And I have a guide book in the Bible."

"I guess I never related to what I heard in church."

Mom nodded and smiled slightly.

"I understand. The Lord can show us our need for Him at any time but you're only coming to a crossroads now," Mom added. "You've made some serious life decisions. You have responsibilities you didn't have before."

"Yeah, I get reminded of that every minute of every day," Leia replied, caressing her pregnant belly. "Now, I'm a mom like you."

Mom leaned forward in her chair and placed her hands on top of her legs. "Yes, you are. But that's only one part of who you are. You're truly your own woman now and I'm proud of you. I want you to know that."

"Thanks, Mom. A lot has happened in a short time."

"That's life, Leia. You get used to it after a while."

Leia could feel her smile falter. Guilt returned.

"I do need better control over my powers, Mom. Last night, before the attack happened, I . . . I hurt Josh. I just meant to nudge him but I cracked a couple of his ribs."

"Oh! I thought that happened in the attack."

"I'm afraid, Mom! I'm so strong, I could kill him next time. And once our baby is born—"

"I understand, Leia. And you're right to be concerned."

Leia looked down for a moment. Then she looked up at Mom.

"Can . . . can the Lord help me control my powers?" Leia asked.

"Yes, I have no doubt about that, Leia. But we can talk some more later. I think you should get some food now . . . and some rest."

Leia nodded, closing her eyes. Then she wondered something.

"Alright, but . . . Mom, how's Josh? Have you seen him?"

"I saw him. He's going to be okay, Leia. He's in a room on the third floor."

"Are they gonna let me go today? There's nothing wrong with me."

"I think so. The doctor will want to make sure you and the baby are okay, then she'll probably release you."

Mom asked Tanya to stay with her sister a while longer, which Tanya gladly agreed to.

24

LATER THAT DAY, LEIA AND Malevolence were released from the hospital around the same time.

Leia didn't know whether her husband would be awake or not as she opened the door to his room. The sun would be setting soon and the lights in his room were about half-lit. The sounds of his monitors were being drowned out by the television playing a commercial. The back of the bed was inclined some to allow Josh a better view of the TV and more of a sitting up position. As it registered with him that the door had opened, Josh slowly turned his head to face Leia and his expression completely brightened.

"Heyyyy!" Josh said, weakly. "M'glad you're here!"

She came to his side and gently put his right hand on her belly.

"Where else would we be?" Leia replied. "The doctor gave us a clean bill of health, so here we are."

"Heh, good," Josh added, smiling with his eyes half-open and looking happily at Leia's face. "Sorry, the pain meds're making me a little goofy. Um, are you gonna refer t'yourself in the plural for the rest of the pregnancy?"

"Yes. It's me and your daughter in one body. So, we're an 'us' for now."

Josh tried to shift his position to see Leia better. Leia winced seeing his obvious pain.

"I feel terrible about this," Leia shared, losing a lot of her joviality.

"Hey, I'll be fine," Josh reassured her. "The doc said I'll heal up in a few weeks."

"A few weeks. I just wish I hadn't done this."

"Leia . . . baby . . . I know you'll be more careful. So, I'm not worried."

"I'm so in love with you, Josh! You're a part of me—all the time—and in my heart. We're a family now."

"I love you, too, Leia. Yer right. We're a family. Yer all the family I need."

She just held him in a tender embrace for several long minutes. Then she lifted her head in surprise.

"She's doing it again!" Leia said happily.

Leia pressed Josh's right hand firmly over her lower part of her belly.

"It may be hard to tell through this dress I'm wearing but can you feel that?"

"I feel something. What is that? Is that her?"

"Yep, that's your daughter. She's kicking, letting us know she's awake and saying 'hi' to us."

"At six months? Wow!"

"It's nearly seven months now. So, what's her name, Dad?"

Josh observed Leia's abdomen for a few seconds then looked up at Leia's face and nodded with a satisfied grin.

"I think we should each pick a name then we'll figure out the order of the names. I want to give her my mom's name."

Leia nodded her approval. "Alyssa is a pretty name, I'm good with that."

"How about you?" he asked.

Leia sat down on the side of his hospital bed as she pondered an answer to his question.

"I want to honor Dad somehow, but we can't name her Steven. How about Stephanie?"

"Stephanie Alyssa Manning?"

"Stephanie Alyssa it is! But she'll go by Alyssa."

"You hear that?" Josh asked, speaking directly to Leia's belly. "You're Alyssa. Stephanie Alyssa Manning. Are you cool with that?"

"She kicked again!" Leia said excitedly.

"We seem to have a consensus then, Mom."

Leia blushed.

"What izzit, Leia?"

"Oh . . . it's just . . . that's the first time you or anybody has called me 'Mom.'"

"Well, I think you better get used to that, cuz that's what Alyssa's gonna call you."

"Yeah . . . you're right. Wow."

Just then, Leia saw her Aunt Leticia in her mind once more, the woman's eyes as the wall of flame hit her. Leia almost lost her balance and had to lean on the bed for support.

"Leia? What is it?" Josh asked soberly.

"Bad memory," Leia answered. "I'm okay."

Josh didn't look convinced. "I don't think you're okay at all," he continued. "Were you thinking about . . . last night?"

"Yeah. My aunt was one of the assassins. She had cat powers like Mom."

"I could hear a lot of it, but I didn't understand everything that happened. I'm just glad you and Alyssa are safe."

"Oh! I thought . . . in a way, I was hoping you were unconscious."

"I know things happened quickly, that it was over very fast. I heard you scream before I passed out."

Josh slowly and carefully reached up and took her left hand in his right hand. Leia felt like she could spend eternity in the oasis of her husband's love. His eyes told her he wanted to console her and make everything better if possible. Understanding that, all she could do for the next minute or two was smile. When she spoke again, the specter of her aunt's death was temporarily banished.

"Okay, next consensus! We all want Daddy home!"

"Daddy, huh?"

"Every little girl needs to call their father 'Daddy'. She can call you Dad when gets to be a teenager, if she wants to do that."

"No argument here. Hey, why don't you go home, change clothes, and get some rest. You can bring me some regular clothes tomorrow for when the hospital releases me."

Leia deliberately narrowed her eyes and pouted. "I don't want to leave you now, Josh. I just got here."

"You don't have to leave right now, silly. Of course, I want you by my side as long as possible. But I was trying to think about your folks and your sister, too."

Leia sighed as she relaxed a little.

"No offense to my parents and sister but we need to think about this family first," she interjected. "I can always call Misha for a ride home."

"And another free late-night meal?" Josh said, raising an eyebrow.

"I got paid this week. I'll treat her for once," Leia replied.

"Why do you drag that girl along when it's you that's hungry?" he chuckled.

"Misha's been a super-supportive friend. She's like another sister to me."

"That's great! Not too many friends are like that. I hope you tell her that and do things in return for her."

Leia grinned and started running one of her hands through Josh's bed-disheveled hair.

"I do! And I buy her new clothes whenever she asks for them. I get her really cute stuff."

"So . . . does she know what happened last night?"

Leia lowered her hand back to her side and leaned against Josh.

"No," she answered. "She's gonna freak when I tell her. But I owe it to her to tell her anyway."

"Leia, at least go call her and let her know you're okay. Friends do that, you know. You can give her the details when she picks you up."

"A—alright."

After she stood up, she began stepping towards the doorway. But then, she stopped and lowered her head, ashamed.

"A real friend would have called her already . . . and a real friend owes her a decent explanation," Leia conceded. "You win. I'll go spend some time with her and tell her what happened."

"That's my Leia!"

"It's gonna reek being apart from you till tomorrow."

"I don't want to be apart from you, either, but I'm an adult, I think I can handle a night in the hospital by myself. I'll be okay."

"You totally set me up for this, didn't you?"

Josh tried to look serious but couldn't maintain it. "Yes, but for a good reason," he laughed.

"Fine. But just for that, I'm getting Misha to take me to *La Cuchara Grasienta* tonight!"

"You say that like it's a threat," Josh replied, snickering.

"Not at all," Leia smiled as she walked back towards him.

Josh put his hands to Leia's face and softly pulled her into a long kiss. A couple of minutes later, their lips parted and Leia stood woozily with a goofy smile on her face.

"Well . . . as long as we understand each other," Leia said.

"We do," Josh answered. "Have a fun time."

Leia leaned close and gave him a quick kiss.

"Get better, my husband."

"I will. Hey, I've still got my phone. Text me when Misha takes you back home, okay?"

Leia waved her hand as she started to walk towards the door, happy and still drunk from their kissing. Josh quickly grabbed his mobile phone, silenced his natural reaction to the pain from that action, and turned on the video app.

Leia spied his actions and decided to play along. She slowly turned around, her hands on her hips and imagined that her hair was blowing in the wind. Then thanks to her telekinesis, her hair began to move as if it really were air-blown and her dress rippled in accordance. She smiled at Josh and slowly walked a few steps forward, imitating a runway model.

"Have I told you that I think your powers are awesome?" he asked.

"Nope! Not even one little word," she replied with a fake pout.

"Well, I think your powers are awesome!"

Leia winked at Josh and headed towards the door again.

"Give my best to Misha!" he added.

"Alright," she replied.

Leia didn't know until now that it was possible to love a man without limits. She could feel her love, admiration and desire for Josh Manning continuing to grow. She smiled at him but was at a loss for words.

Josh waved, giving her the permission she needed to leave. It was much harder to get her feet to go along with the idea. But a few seconds later, somehow, they did.

———————

Malevolence moved somewhat unsteadily through the hospital. Physically, she was well enough to be released with only a bandage on her head covering the twelve stitches needed to close her wound. Other wounds were not so easily seen.

Between the pain in her head and the mild medications given to her to reduce that pain, Malevolence still couldn't concentrate enough to use her powers. She wasn't used to feeling so vulnerable. At the same time, she was determined to see Dane and learn his condition, so she pressed on, despite her own insecurities and challenges.

Malevolence had learned the location of the Recovery Unit from one of the hospital's elderly volunteers. The Recovery Unit was one step below Intensive Care without being a regular hospital room. It allowed the patient more attention from nurses and doctors and closer monitoring of their condition. As Malevolence stood in front of one of the nurses at the unit, a short, petite blond in her early twenties, her patience was wearing thin.

"I don't think we have anyone here by that name, Ma'am," the nurse said.

Malevolence looked at the woman as if she were an idiot.

"You might try spelling my friend's name right. It's 'D-A-N-E F-O-X,' not 'D-A-N F-A-X,'" Malevolence insisted.

"You can see my screen?" the startled nurse replied.

The young woman had her monitor turned at an angle where Malevolence could see half of it, enough to tell that the nurse had mangled the name's spelling. But Malevolence was a creature of habit and the nurse had given her a welcome outlet for her frustrations.

"You don't want to know what I can do, honey," Malevolence warned. "Now look his name up properly and tell me where he is . . . because at this rate, I can see you developing an obsession with plaid. Really ugly plaid."

The nurse gulped and fumbled nervously at her keyboard to perform a fresh search. When she did look up at Malevolence, her eyes were fearful.

"He's in RU Room 28 . . . Miss," the nurse offered. "Down this hall and on your right."

"Much better!" Malevolence replied. "Thank you for your assistance."

Malevolence walked over to Dane's RU room. He was unconscious or sedated and every vital sign was being monitored. He had bandages on his chest showing from underneath his hospital gown. There were bandages on both his arms.

He was under my protection! If Leia hadn't killed the woman, I would hunt that assassin to the ends of the Earth for doing this!

A male nurse entered the room to check on his patient.

"Hi there," he said, quietly. "I'm Pete. I'm Dane's nurse for the day shift."

"I'm . . . Angela, Dane's friend. How is he?"

"He's doing a lot better, actually. There seemed to be a poison in his system last night, but we can't find any trace of it now. And his lacerations are healing very rapidly. I've been a nurse for fifteen years and I've never seen anything like it."

"His mother was the same way," Malevolence shared. "Healed extraordinarily fast."

"How fortunate for him that he inherited that then," Pete replied. "It's up to the doctor but I imagine he'll be here for a few more days, mostly for observation and recuperation."

"A few days? That's not bad. I can't wait for him to wake up."

"The way he's doing, I imagine he'll be conscious before too long."

Pete verified Dane's temperature and blood pressure and excused himself from the room to go check on another patient. Malevolence walked up to Dane's bed where he was still lying unconscious, a light snore escaping his lips.

So, you have some fox in you after all! Your mother would be pleased.

She sat in a chair by his bed and admired him as the waning sunlight's rays entered the room through his window and gently illuminated Dane Fox. She wasn't aware how much time had passed when Dane opened his eyes and groaned in discomfort. Malevolence was just happy he had returned to consciousness.

"Malevolence . . . what happened? Are you alright?"

"I'll be fine . . . and so will you, Dane," Malevolence answered, taking his hand. "Leia saved us all. We're at the hospital."

"Leia did? That's amazing. But somehow, I'm not surprised."

"You were hurt the worst, but you're healing quite well now. The nurse said he's never seen anything like it."

"Healing? I heal fast? I didn't know that. I guess I inherited werefox powers after all."

Malevolence continued to hold Dane's hand and felt more than simple concern or compassion for him. Even in this short time, he had become dear to her.

"Dane, I'm just so glad you're going to be alright. I'd like to discuss something with you, if you're up for it.

"Alright."

"I know I could never take your mother's place, but . . . I've come to care deeply for you, like a son. I offered you your own room in my home and it's . . . been my intention to protect you."

"What are you trying to say?"

"I know you're an adult but I'd like to make our relationship more official. I'd like to legally adopt you."

Dane smiled. He even closed his eyes and chuckled a little, then regretted it. Malevolence regretted that she couldn't control his pain.

"I'd like that. I've felt our friendship mature, too. At first, my feelings were romantic but it didn't take long to get over that," Dane admitted. "You've been a good friend, I've come to respect you a great deal. And as hard as it's been, I've come to accept that both my biological parents are dead."

Despite the physical discomfort it caused him, Dane reached over and took both of Malevolence's hands in his.

"You've been the closest thing I've had to family, in a time when I really needed that. I'd be honored to join yours," Dane answered.

"I'm glad you feel that way," Malevolence added. "Being there for you, having you live with me and share my life, it's changed me for the better."

"I'm not sure what you mean. I've just been myself."

"You're being modest. You've helped me come out of a carefully guarded shell to experience life again. For the first time in twenty years, I'm not alone anymore. You accept me for who I am, as I do you."

"You've been misunderstood and endured a lot, but you're an incredible woman. You're kind, resourceful, protective and even generous. If I've been able to help you in any way, I'm glad."

She grinned widely at his acceptance. The look he gave her was reassuring. She then looked at him and chuckled.

"What is it?" Dane asked.

"Well, I think I'm going to have to make a new identity for myself. It's about time to leave Angela Merrick behind and well, I don't think they'll put Malevolence as a name on the adoption papers unless it's my legal name . . . and I'm not too interested in pursuing that."

"You have a point. So, what do you want to be called?"

"You know, after all this time being um, me, I don't exactly know."

Dane had a thoughtful look on his face. It was gentle and inquisitive yet confident and loving.

"Ah-hah-lee," Dane said.

"I beg your pardon?" Malevolence asked.

"Ah-hah-lee—it's Swahili for 'Chance.' It just came to my mind and it's perfect for you."

"You know Swahili?"

"It's a hobby of mine, yeah."

"How do you spell 'ah-hah-lee?'"

"A-J-A-L-I. I feel like—like life has given you a second chance, at so many things. What do you think?"

"Ajali. Ajali. Chance in Swahili," Malevolence said, looking out the window. "What would my last name be, dare I ask?"

"Something simple."

"Like Fox?" Malevolence interjected playfully, turning to look at him. He smiled in response.

"Nice, but what are the chances of my adoptive mother having exactly the same name as me?"

"Hm, you have a point. What about Free?"

His eyes and nod signaled his acceptance of the idea.

"I like it!" he added.

Facing away from Dane again, Malevolence lowered her head and expressed her happiness in a smile and silent tears.

"Ajali is a good name, Dane. Tomorrow, I'll start the paperwork to legally change my name from Angela Merrick to Ajali Free. And I'll begin the adoption process. So, I guess you can call me Ajali from now on."

"It's nice to meet you, Ajali."

"This will take a little getting used to . . . but thank you."

Ajali looked at Dane with a little concern. "Are your grandparents still living?"

"I don't know about my father's parents, but my maternal grand-mother is still alive," Dane answered. "She lives in San Diego, but . . . she never liked me. She tolerated me because I'm her grandson."

"Charming woman. What's her name? And how old is she?"

"Wendy Fox. I think she's sixty-two or sixty-three now. Why?"

"Just curious about our family."

Ajali pressed the nurse call button. A moment later, she explained to Pete that his patient was awake and needed pain medication. Soon,

Pete arrived to administer the medicine and then left to respect their privacy.

"You're going to get very groggy soon, Dane," Ajali told him. "Go ahead and sleep."

"Alright."

Ajali kissed his forehead and quietly walked out of the room, filled with new purpose and hope.

She felt like she'd been half-dead for the last twenty years. She knew she had purpose but no personal fulfillment or growth. But now, things were different. She had finally taken a stand for her own future. And she knew Dane wanted the future she was offering, as her son. In her mind, she wondered about the irony of a supervillain and the son of two superheroes becoming a new family. She had never imagined she would get a second chance to be who she was originally supposed to be. She had heard of such things before but never given it much thought. She supposed for the first time that perhaps things did happen for a reason.

Then she began planning a short flight to San Diego.

25

MISHA WAS COMPLETELY SPEECHLESS. AND for once, Leia was quiet with her head lowered and no smile on her face. Neither of them even seemed to be aware that they were in the loud, bustling environment of *La Cuchara Grasienta #4*, even though they were surrounded by other restaurant patrons sitting at nearby tables and booths, wait staff walking around, and a five-member Mariachi band performing on the stage in the middle of the restaurant.

None of that mattered to Misha and Leia.

"She's dead?" Misha whispered. "And *you* killed her?"

"Yes," Leia also whispered. "I couldn't let her murder my birth mother."

"I need a drink, something really strong."

"Misha, what was I supposed to do? Josh's dad hired those thugs, including my aunt, to kill Malevolence."

Misha looked skeptical, slightly shaking her head.

"That doesn't sound like the man I met at your wedding," Misha added. "Did he say why he wanted her dead?"

"He called her a monster! He hit her in the head with his rifle and was going to shoot her, but she disarmed him. Then my aunt crashed through the ceiling, having cat powers like Mom and she wanted to kill Malevolence, too!"

Misha gripped the table when Leia revealed that.

"Your aunt's a feline assassin?" Misha blurted.

"Yeah and she was gonna kill anyone who got in her way, even me."

Trying to remain calm, Misha leaned forward to keep her voice down. Leia leaned close to listen.

"But couldn't you just, I dunno, put a shield around you, Malevolence, and Josh?" Misha whispered.

"Things were happening too fast, Misha. She even blew up the roof—"

"She blew up the roof?" Misha exclaimed, wide-eyed and pale-faced.

"I was already shielding them from those debris when she went after Malevolence again. I barely had time to react."

Misha sat back in her chair, putting one hand to her temple and closing her eyes. She took a couple of breaths and then looked at Leia again.

"So, what happened?" Misha asked. "How did she die?".

Leia told Misha how her Aunt Leticia perished at her hands.

Misha looked nauseated. Staring at Leia, Misha stood up, looking hurt, like someone who felt betrayed. With a near-panicked expression, Misha squeezed out of the booth they were in and stumbled past the other customers till she made it to the building's entrance.

With some difficulty, Leia followed her.

Once outside, Misha ran hard. When she turned a corner, Leia could see the tears streamed down Misha's face. Several blocks later, Misha slowed, panting hard. She stumbled and tripped onto the sidewalk, badly scraping her right knee and both her hands when she used them to break her fall.

Leia was having trouble keeping up and she wanted to see if Misha was going to actually leave her or come back and apologize.

Her friend took neither action. Misha cried, beat the sidewalk and, not seeing Leia nearby, cursed at her friend at the top of her lungs.

"How can I help you when you're the one with the power to stop bad guys with your mind?" Misha screamed. "What am I compared to that?"

"You're my best friend," Leia said.

Leia hovered about five feet in the air. She mentally extended her horns fully and caused her eyes to glow with fire. She pointed at herself.

"I've shown you this part of me before. I've shown you what I can do. So why are you afraid of me *now*?"

Misha briefly looked up at Leia and then looked down.

"How did we get to this point? How did my best friend become a killer?"

"Do you think I haven't asked myself those questions, Misha? You didn't know my aunt, but I grew up with her. She was my family! I'd do *anything* to change what happened but I can't! It doesn't work that way. I wasn't trying to be a hero! I wasn't in costume chasing after her, cutting her down in cold blood. Josh and I were invited over to dinner at my birth mother's place. I was in a pink maternity dress, for crying out loud! My husband was in a suit. Paid killers broke into Malevolence's place with guns and attacked. Aunt Leticia would have torn us all to pieces if I hadn't stopped her! So, tell me, Misha—buddy, best friend—why does my *keeping people alive* give you the right to curse my name and run out on me, huh? I'd really like to know that!"

Leia was crying now too. She lowered herself to the ground, willed her horns to shrink down, and let her eyes return to normal. She reached into her purse and pulled out her wallet. She took out two twenty-dollar bills and tossed them within a few feet of Misha, who was still on her knees on the sidewalk. Then Leia took out a ten-dollar bill and did the same time with it.

"This is for dinner. I even covered the tip," Leia said, her voice now hoarse, her tone sad and spent. "Since you freaked out before we could enjoy it, you get to take home all the food. I don't want it anymore."

––––––––––

Leia turned around and walked away. It was then that Misha noticed for the first time that Leia's walk had started to become a waddle.

Misha shifted her position and sat against the wall of the building next to the sidewalk. Still crying, Misha looked at the moon and the city lights. Then she looked at her friend who hadn't even gotten a block away yet.

"Leia, how did this happen to us?" Misha said to herself in a soft voice. "Why did things have to get so complicated, with super powers and hired killers and super villains? What are you??"

Misha shook her head vigorously in frustration.

"Misha . . . you're being an idiot," she continued. "That answer is right in front of you. She's your best friend . . . who's six months pregnant . . . can fly . . . stop bullets . . . set people on fire . . . and then send them falling to their deaths."

Misha shook her head again, as if trying to throw off unpleasant thoughts.

She knew Leia had saved her birth mother, her husband and her baby from mercenaries. How was she wrong for that?

"It's called self-defense, Misha," she told herself.

Leia could have played it safe, too. She didn't have to tell her anything at all about the attack at her mother's place. If she hadn't done that, everything would have stayed the same, wouldn't it? She could have kept Misha in a safe little fantasy world Misha enjoyed so much, the one where Leia didn't use her superpowers around her and thought she was fooling her by dragging Misha everywhere to eat food with her.

In actuality, Misha knew Leia really did think that. As if she wouldn't know Leia felt insecure about gaining weight from the pregnancy. Leia wanted a buddy to share in all the fun.

Misha shrugged. She didn't mind helping her best friend through her vulnerability.

"So why can't I help her now?" Misha asked herself. "She shared that information with me because . . . because . . . that's what best friends do. It's not always going to be fun and games. Sometimes telling the truth is a lot harder than telling a lie. Telling the truth brings consequences. She knew she might lose me as a friend over this . . . and she told me anyway. Then I freaked out on her. I folded on her. I treated her like a criminal. No, worse. I treated her like a monster!"

Misha remember how much it hurt Leia when Josh just looked at her like he was scared. Misha had cursed her name. She had screamed at her, acted completely terrified of her and didn't bother to hide it. She had treated Leia like she was a monster! A demon!

"And she's pregnant!" Misha derided herself. "How could I do that to her?"

Misha slapped her legs, as if that would instantly give them strength.

"C'mon, Misha!" Misha grunted, forcing herself to stand. "It's not too late!"

Misha's knee was bleeding pretty badly. She didn't care. Her legs felt like they were made of jelly and she was lightheaded. Finally, a surge of adrenaline hit her and she limp-ran after Leia. She had to switch between a limping jog and a limping full run to make any kind of headway, but she had at least gotten close enough to call out.

"Leia! Wait!" Misha shouted. "Please! Wait for me!"

Misha was so focused on getting Leia's attention that she didn't realize she had limped into an intersection. She heard a bus horn blare and turned in time to see its headlights, mere feet from her.

And then she was flying. Leia's arms were wrapped around Misha from behind and Misha's lower back could feel the bulge of Leia's belly. When Misha turned her head and looked up, Leia's expression was one of relief. Leia's eyes weren't glowing and she wasn't displaying her horns.

Moments later, Leia descended to a rooftop. She helped Misha steady herself once they landed.

"Thank you for saving me," Misha offered.

"I couldn't let you die like that," Leia replied, her voice cracking on the last word.

Misha looked at Leia standing right in front of her.

"That's who you are, isn't it?" Misha asked.

"Excuse me?"

"You're nearly seven months pregnant, Leia, but since I was foolish enough to run in front of a moving bus, you flew in front of that bus and rescued me!"

"I had to. I couldn't lose you!"

Standing unsteadily, Misha put one hand on her hip and pointed at Leia with the other.

"What about your baby, Leia? Am I worth your child's life?"

"My baby wasn't in danger. I had a telekinetic shield around myself. I pulled you inside it when I grabbed you."

"And if your timing hadn't been perfect, your shield would be down when the bus hit and we'd all be dead!"

Leia sighed and nodded.

"You're not a superhero, Leia. I think you know that. You just care about people, especially your family."

"You're part of that family, Misha. You're like the older sister I always wanted."

"I feel the same way, Leia. You're the sister I wanted, growing up with only brothers. I'm sorry for the way I treated you tonight. I'm ashamed that I behaved that way towards my best friend. My sister. You didn't deserve it."

"It's okay, Misha. We're all okay."

Misha's expression softened and she allowed herself a smile.

"Leia, you may not be a superhero but . . . you're my hero. You're the bravest woman I've ever met."

Leia stepped forward and hugged Misha. They cried together for a while.

"We need to get you seen by a doctor, Misha. Your knee is still bleeding."

"I guess driving to the hospital isn't an option then . . . if we could even make it to my car."

———————

Leia conceded Misha's point with a nod of her head.

"Yeah, you aren't driving and I don't think you want me behind the wheel of your precious Mustang," Leia interjected. "Especially since I don't know how to drive a standard."

"Looks like we're taking 'Air Leia' then," Misha replied.

"Alright, just hold on to me from behind. Hold on tight."

Misha did as Leia suggested. Leia spread her arms and they slowly lifted off the ground, no longer feeling the pull of gravity. She was lifting the two of them gradually, gently lifting them a hundred feet straight up.

Then Leia gave a slight push with her thoughts and they started moving northward.

"Isn't the hospital in the other direction?" Misha asked.

"It's a two-minute detour," Leia insisted. "I am not leaving all those enchiladas behind! Me and Alyssa need food!"

"Who?"

"Josh and I named our baby today. She's Stephanie Alyssa Manning . . . but she'll go by Alyssa, after Josh's mom."

"Alyssa. I like it! And please, get the food. I can wait outside a minute. And I'll pay for it."

"Why? I said I'd cover it tonight."

"Your cash is still back on Third Street. Drama queen."

26

ONE WEEK LATER, AJALI FREE was walking through a suburb of San Diego. With only the limited information Dane Fox had provided, it had taken three hours to locate Wendy Fox's home in a city with over three million people.

The upscale townhome was in a quiet neighborhood full of families. Ajali stood across the street trying to decide whether to go talk to the woman. The fall breeze was made even more chilly by the city's proximity to the ocean, even at this distance. She was glad she'd brought an overcoat and dressed for the weather.

Ajali was so lost in thought, she didn't hear a woman walk up behind her.

"Can I help you?" the woman asked. "You look kind of lost."

When Ajali turned, she was surprised to see Dane's grandmother. Apparently, she was out for a morning jog. Her mostly black hair had a few gray streaks and was pulled into a ponytail. She was trim and appeared to be in very good health; the years had clearly been kind to her.

"I'm just visiting the city," Ajali replied. "I'm looking for Wendy Fox."

"Well, that would be me," the older woman responded.

"I need to talk with you about your daughter and grandson. That is, if you have some time?"

Wendy Fox looked at Ajali with suspicion for a few seconds. Then she relaxed a little.

"Let's cut to the chase, shall we?" Wendy said quietly, yet with some menace. "You know my grandson. His scent is all over you. So why are you here?"

"You have powers, too?" Ajali wondered, trying to keep her voice down but not entirely succeeding.

"Don't look shocked, dear. I wouldn't have given you the time of day if I hadn't put a few of the pieces together. My abilities are fairly low level, but I use them to my advantage."

"I see."

"Let's go inside and talk. I'd like to know how you know Dana and Dane."

Wendy led Ajali past the entrance gate and they went inside her house. She grabbed two mugs from a kitchen cabinet.

"Do you drink coffee?" Wendy asked.

"Please. I take it black."

"Well, we have something in common already. What's your name, miss?"

"Ajali Free," she answered, earning a raised eyebrow from Wendy.

Wendy brought the two steaming cups to the living room and offered one to Ajali, who was already sitting on the couch. Wendy sat down beside her. And she smiled, somewhat insincerely.

"My daughter and grandson have been out of touch with me for several months. That's not like them. I figure you know what happened or you wouldn't be here."

"Yes, I do. Did . . . did you know Dana was the superhero named Black Fox?"

"I suspected so, yes. I saw the news footage over the years. Even through that mask, it looked like her."

"Yes, the mask," Ajali reflected.

Ajali reached into her purse and pulled out the damaged Black Fox mask and handed it to Wendy Fox.

"Your daughter is dead, Mrs. Fox. She died about four months ago."

Wendy Fox took the mask with both hands and looked at it, turned it around. Her hands began to shake and her arms seemed to lose strength. The mask fell into her lap and Wendy squinted her eyes in grief.

"How?" Wendy asked a moment later.

"She was in a gas explosion. There was no possibility of survival. But she was trying to save lives."

Wendy Fox took the metal mask and hugged it close to her chest, her eyes beginning to shed tears.

"You loved her . . . very much," Ajali said quietly.

"She was my child! Of *course,* I loved her."

Wendy's expression suddenly looked very haunted and pained.

"But she probably died thinking I hated her."

"No. She didn't think you hated her. You could say anything about Dana and she would have forgiven you. She just didn't know why you couldn't accept her son."

"How on earth could you know that??"

"I'm a telepath. And I was there when she died."

Wendy Fox stared at Ajali in disbelief for a minute, tears still streaming down her face.

"You were there? And you survived! Tell me what happened."

"I'll just say this: Your daughter was true to herself. She knew the situation was dangerous, so she kept her son away, protected him. And she didn't suffer. It was all over in a few seconds time."

"So, Dane's okay! But why didn't he contact me?"

Ajali could feel her temper flaring. "Based on what he's told me and his memories of you, I'd say it's because you'd never shown any interest in his life and you disrespected his mother in front of him," Ajali said, a protective edge arising in her voice. "Why do you think he'd turn to you now?"

Wendy sighed and looked downward.

"I suppose you're right," she conceded. "But I was never angry with him or Dana. It was Dane's father I had a problem with. He fathered a child then disappeared. I guess I was disappointed that Dana chose a man like that."

Ajali brow furrowed and she twisted her mouth, trying to hold herself back from what she wanted to say. Was this woman so ignorant that she'd insult John, too, without knowing the facts?

"Did you ever ask her what happened to Dane's father?" Ajali offered in a barely civil tone.

Wendy considered that for a few seconds before she answered.

"I asked Dana once, when she learned she was pregnant. I asked if the father would be there for her and help out with her child. But she would just close herself off, cry and shake her head."

"That's because she was still traumatized. He died saving her life. Dane's father was Silver Knight."

Wendy Fox was silent for a while after that.

"I wish she would have told me that. She never said much to me."

"Dana was all about actions, not words."

"She got that from her father. He was like that. How is Dane?"

Ajali took a sip of the still-hot coffee. It helped settle her frayed nerves some.

"It's still a fresh loss, but he has her strength," Ajali replied. "He's managing."

"Where . . . where is she buried?"

"In Digby Cemetery. I took care of it."

"Thank you."

Wendy looked down at the ground for a few moments, collecting her thoughts and absorbing all of this information. Then she looked up at Ajali.

"I lost—no, I *wasted* so much time with Dana, and now she's gone. I don't want to lose any more time with my grandson. But . . . then again, he probably doesn't want to see me now."

"Why don't you let him decide that? I can get us tickets to Digby and we can be there by tonight."

Wendy continued to stare at Ajali. It wasn't offensive, just intense.

"Who are you really, Ajali? How do you know Dana and my grandson? And why is his scent so strong on you?"

"I'm really just Ajali Free. Dana was my best friend for a long time, but we drifted apart."

"And Dane?"

"Um, yes, Dane. I felt responsible for Dane, so I took him in. With his consent, I'm in the process of formally adopting him."

Wendy Fox took in a strong whiff of air, closed her eyes, and seemed to be thinking. Then she opened her eyes in surprise and looked at Ajali in disbelief.

"That would explain the unfamiliar environmental scents. They're from your home. A high-rise hotel?"

"Your powers aren't as low level as you made them out to be. You're a full were-fox, aren't you?"

"Yes, although I really prefer my human form. But let's not change the subject. Do you have children of your own?"

"I have a daughter his age. She was raised by her father and step-mother, but we've recently reconnected."

"I can tell. You weren't nervous until you started speaking about her. Then your heart sped up some and your breathing quickened. You're proud of her and excited to be in her life."

"Not low level at all," Ajali said under her breath.

Wendy stood up and looked at her with a slight smile.

"I'll go with you to see Dane. I owe him that, and a lot more. If he'll let me, I'd like to start over with him."

Ajali nodded in satisfaction.

"Give Dane that opportunity and he may very well give you that chance."

27

JOSH SAT ON HIS HOSPITAL bed, wearing his clothes from the night of the dinner party, half-watching the business report on a local news station. He was waiting for his discharge papers to be completed by his nurse when his father walked in the door. Josh saw him but said nothing, instead slipping on his black dress shoes. Slowly and carefully, he pushed himself off of the edge of the bed and stood up, grateful that the oral medication was lessening the pain from his still-injured ribs. He wished they could do the same for his heart regarding his father.

The midday sun's rays shone through the blinds and across the room, lining the television set and the walls, competing with the room's electrical lighting.

Standing in the doorway, his father's face showed a mixture of concern, hesitation, and nervousness. His dress shirt and slacks were flawless, as if recently ironed after being perfectly folded. But Dad's face was unshaven, his eyes had dark circles underneath and his hair looked like it had barely been tamed by a comb in the last few days. He smelled of cigarette smoke as he walked into the room.

"I'm glad you're doing well enough to be released," David said.

"Thanks," Josh replied.

"All I had was a bruised jaw and a mild concussion, so they let me out yesterday."

"Look . . . Dad . . . "

"You have every right to be furious with me, Josh. Go ahead. Say whatever you want."

"Alright. Well, since you offered, did my wife finally knock some sense into you?"

His father chuckled at that, but there was no happiness in his voice.

"No, she just stopped me. What finally knocked some sense into me was getting someone else killed."

That surprised Josh. He tried to contain his reaction, not sure whether he could trust anything his father said.

"What are you talking about?" Josh asked.

"Oh! I thought Leia told you."

"Told me what, exactly?"

"About Leticia Sanchez, her aunt."

"Leia told me her aunt was one of the mercenaries you hired, that she's super-powered."

"She's dead. Your wife had to kill her to protect you, Shadow and . . . Malevolence. I checked with some friends of mine at the newspaper. They gave me the song and dance Malevolence sold them—which was pretty clever, I have to say, especially since it didn't implicate me—that was a surprise. Anyway, I put two and two together."

"You're lying."

Then Josh remembered the sad look on Leia's face when she was thinking about her aunt before. Josh had been much too sedated to decipher the fullness of his wife's emotions at the time but now it made more sense. Knowing the type of person Leia was, Josh couldn't imagine the grief it would cause her to be responsible for a death, particularly a family member. Just realizing her burden created a wound in his heart. He felt determined to help her come to grips with that pain and loss.

"You know I'm not lying, Josh; I can see it. I guess Leia didn't want to put that on you yet. She really is a sweet girl."

Hearing those words caused Josh's anger to suddenly surge.

"She wouldn't have had to do anything like that if you'd just stayed out of things!" Josh erupted. "I wish you'd never come back! You did less damage when you were just a drunk who visited on special occasions!"

"You're right," Dad answered. "My actions led to all of this. I know that now."

Josh simmered with hostility and glared at his father.

"Look, Josh, I know you may never speak to me again after this, and I guess I can't blame you . . . but hear me out, okay? My actions may have been wrong but I only wanted to protect you . . . and Leia . . . from that monster, Malevolence."

Josh made a sound of disgust.

"Malevolence accepted me as Leia's fiancé from the first time she . . . met me. She was a criminal but she treated me with respect, like a son-in-law. She even bought me this suit, invited me and Leia to her place and cooked a casserole. You, on the other hand," Josh said with a near-snarl. "You hired a bunch of armed creeps and a super-powered killer. You sent them to Malevolence's place without knowing all the facts! You endangered my wife, my child and me! You're lucky you don't have a lot more deaths on your conscience! So, you tell me, 'Dad', who's the real monster here?!"

"Josh—"

"Get out!"

"Son, please—"

"Get out of this room and out of my life! I mean it!"

Dad looked sadly at his son, resigned to the inevitable.

"You're going to be a father soon. You'll understand better once your little girl is here," Dad insisted as he turned to leave. "You'll do anything to protect her."

"I will never be like you! I'll protect my daughter in my own way . . . starting right now. Go."

"When you've had a chance to process all this, you know how to reach me."

"That may be . . . quite a while."

"Fair enough," Dad responded as he walked out of the hospital room and his son's life.

———————

Leia had been approaching Josh's room, ready to take her husband downstairs to where Mom was waiting with the car, when she couldn't help but overhear most of the conversation between him and his father. In a way, Leia admired David Manning for his courage in coming to see Josh, knowing that he would probably get this kind of reaction. Truthfully, Leia was upset and hurt by David's actions, too, but she could understand them.

Leia only wanted to comfort Josh. Beneath the fury and indignation, she could sense the deep and lonely hurt in his voice. Josh felt like he had been betrayed in the worst way possible by his only surviving parent. Leia knew the toll it was taking on her husband to drive away the man he had spent his whole life wanting to get closer to—the father he'd wanted to pay more attention to him, to be proud of him. It was heartbreaking, even though it was necessary at present.

Josh still needed time to heal from his mother's death, more than he needed to heal from his injured ribs. He was still getting used to his new roles as husband and father-to-be. But David Manning had made his son's struggle to establish and grow into these roles considerably harder.

"Sometimes the only way to move forward is to turn away from the past," Josh had once told Leia. It was something his mother had taught him and that seemed to be exactly what Josh was doing. Leia was determined to be there for him and support him, no matter what.

The room's door opened, and David Manning exited. After closing the door, David immediately turned his head to the left and made eye contact with Leia. Leia did not move and said nothing. David looked down and let out a sigh. Then he looked up again with a sad but sincere smile.

"I'm sorry, Leia, for everything. I'm just glad he's got you."

Leia motioned for David to come to her.

"Let's go for a little walk, Mr. Manning."

They walked down the hall and stopped at a walkway between hospital buildings that was lined with a row of blind-less windows that faced the cityscape. The sun's glare was fierce but neither of them seemed to notice or care.

"I don't know how long it'll be before Josh will be ready to see or speak to you, but he doesn't hate you. And neither do I."

"Thank you. That's . . . more than I deserve."

"He's going to be very protective of our daughter," Leia said, gently touching her belly with her left hand.

"It's alright, Leia. With you two as her parents, she's gonna be one amazing kid. Even if I never see her, there's a certain satisfaction in knowing your family is going to go on, to survive."

Leia studied David's facial expression for several seconds.

"Josh will probably get mad at me for telling you this, but we named our daughter Alyssa. Stephanie Alyssa Manning."

David suddenly but gently pulled Leia into a hug.

"Thank you," David said in a whisper, his tears evident in his voice.

Then David released Leia and pulled back a bit, looking at her with a joyful smile and renewed life in his eyes.

"You just gave an old guy like me reason to live. Now go see your husband. I'll get out of your hair."

"Take care . . . David."

"I can see why he chose you. You're strong . . . and beautiful . . . but you're also sensitive and very kind. It's a good, and rare, combination. He's going to need you."

David looked down for a few seconds and scratched the back of his neck.

"It hurts to admit this, but Josh is right. I became more of a threat to my family than your birth mother ever was," David said, not looking up.

"David . . ."

"I didn't see what was right in front of me. You and Josh aren't kids anymore, you can watch out for yourselves and you've . . . you've built a relationship with that woman. You're her daughter, after all. Your children will be her grandchildren, too. There's no reason for her to harm you."

"I'm glad you see that now."

"I just saw what she'd done in the past and the incredible power she has. I let my fear of that power control my actions. I should have trusted your and Josh's judgment. I'm sorry that I didn't."

"My mother's power is scary! I don't blame you for your concern. But yes, you should have trusted us. You should have trusted Josh. He's really the one who's been hurt the most in all of this—no disrespect to you or your loss, sir."

"No offense taken. I know you're right. Josh was so close to his mother. I know it must've crushed him to lose her, especially . . . the way it happened."

"It's still crushing him, David. He depends on me so much because he doesn't have her anymore. I'll do anything for him, I don't mind at all. It makes me feel like I'm helping him . . . but it's going to take a long time for Josh to heal."

"Yes. I think it's going to take a long time for all of us to heal, Leia. But I feel like between you and your folks, my son's in good hands."

Leia didn't know how to respond to that, so she just smiled.

"You've been there for him all along, since grade school."

"It's the other way around, sir. Josh came to my rescue and he's the one who wanted to be my friend. Every day, he found a way to make me feel special or beautiful. I loved him before I even knew what love was. And I gave him my heart because I wanted him to have it. I felt like we belonged together and I knew that he felt that way, too."

"You two were just meant to be then. Heck, you probably know him better than I do."

"I don't know about that," Leia protested.

David sighed. The stress of the confrontation with his son and its consequences could be seen in his furrowed brow, his bloodshot eyes and the deepening lines on his face.

"It's alright," he continued. "I knew after Josh was born that I was making sacrifices in order to provide for him and my wife. But I'm only now figuring out that it wasn't worth it. I cheated myself out of time with my only child and I can't get that time back, the experiences I missed. I don't know my son very well. And I can't blame anyone but myself."

"So . . . what will you do now?"

"I'll do what I do best. I'll go back to work and put the pieces back together, reinvent myself and try to do better. I guess I'll learn to accept the things I can't change and all that. And if Josh ever decides to forgive me and let me back into his life . . . well, a man can hope, can't he?"

"Always," Leia said softly.

"Take care, Leia. You just keep doing what you're doing."

Leia watched David Manning walk away. She had no more words for her father-in-law. Each of his steps looked like they took serious effort. She could not imagine the burdens David must feel responsible for. But at least he seemed to finally be taking responsibility for his actions. She respected that.

"I'll send you pictures—on your cell phone," Leia blurted out. "Of Alyssa!"

David lifted his arm to wave acknowledgment of Leia's words, but he didn't look back and kept going. Leia felt a sad sense of relief when her father-in-law entered an elevator and the doors closed behind him.

———————

Leia recovered her composure and made sure she was exuding confidence as she walked into Josh's room. Josh's anger vanished the moment he saw her. She sat down on the bed right next to him, wrapped her right arm around him and leaned into him, looking into his eyes.

"Ready to go, handsome?"

"I'm ready but the paperwork isn't. It shouldn't be long, though."

"Alright, I'll keep you company."

"Music to my ears," Josh replied, using the remote control to turn off the television. "If I had to listen to one more lawyer commercial, I was gonna lose it."

"Awww, we can't have that. Poor guy. All cooped up for two whole days in a hospital and forced to watch cartoons, reality shows and the Financial Network."

"Don't forget the Always Depressing, All-The-Time News stations!" Josh said with a wink.

She looked at him in feigned, over-the-top "distress."

"Oh nooo! That's terrrrible!" she exclaimed.

"I don't think you're taking me seriously."

"No, I'm not. So! My husband, what do you wanna do when we spring you from this place?"

"Well, since you asked—" Josh answered with a hungry look in his eye.

But he leaned too far forward and gasped, wincing from pain.

"Easy, Baby!" Leia gasped, using her arms to help him sit up straight again. "You're going to have to take it easy while you heal!"

"I'm . . . starting to get that," Josh responded, his voice a harsh whisper.

"There's no way you're walking all the way to Mom's car like this," Leia said, starting to stand up. "I'll make sure they get a wheelcha—"

"Don't. Don't leave me," Josh pleaded, holding onto her hand.

Understanding his feelings, Leia leaned into a very gentle and close hug with him. She rested her chin on his shoulder and ran her fingers through his hair.

"I can't leave you, Josh. I'm yours, remember? And you're mine. I've been together with you since we were kids. For better or worse. Mother of your future brood. All that!"

"What? Where did future brood come from?"

"Oh, you're in for it, mister! After Alyssa, I'll want two boys and another girl to make our family complete."

"You want three more kids?"

"Uh-huh! Right away. Back to back. Just think, honey: I'll be pregnant for years!"

Josh stared at her knowingly, having figured out what she was really doing.

"You're joking," he acknowledged.

"Took you long enough to figure it out, genius!" Leia grinned and patted him on the head.

"You totally played me!"

"Like a fiddle," Leia gloated.

"Wow. So, you don't want more kids?"

"No, I totally do! But I don't want them back-to-back and I don't have a set number that I want to have."

Josh sighed in relief, looking almost offended at first. Then he laughed, loud and long before settling down and turning towards Leia with love in his gaze.

"Thank you, Leia! I needed that. I really needed that! The whole world can fall apart but if I spend five minutes with you, everything is perfect again."

Leia kissed Josh on the lips.

28

DANE WAS SURPRISED THAT AMANDA Franklin was waiting for him as he stepped off the plane in Perth, Australia. She looked genuinely happy to see him. He'd half-expected her to be in her cosplay attire but she was smartly dressed in a flowing light blouse and slacks, wearing glasses. She'd also cut and styled her hair. Meeting her in person for the first time, Amanda was taller than he'd anticipated, and she'd gained some weight since their last video chat but that didn't matter to him.

They didn't speak before embracing. When they eventually pulled back and looked at each other, she was crying.

"I'm so sorry about your mum, Dane. And I'm sorry I haven't been there for you like you've needed."

"It's okay."

"No, it's not. It's really not! I know we've only chatted in text and videos over the web but you really mean something to me."

"I feel the same about you."

"I know we never said this out loud but I'm your girlfriend . . . aren't I?"

"Yes, you're my girlfriend."

She smiled, looking relieved.

"Dane, I've been too guarded with my feelings. I was too focused on my interests and having fun to bring much depth to our chats, our time together. I let fear of rejection paralyze me but I don't want that

298

anymore, I want to be more real with you . . . because I love you. I love you very much and I'm so glad you're here!"

Dane smiled, too. Her sentiments brightened his spirits.

"I've wondered about your feelings, but I think I was scared, too," Dane admitted. "Just not for the same reasons."

"The way I feel about you scares me sometimes," Amanda said. "I've never felt this way before. I've been in bad relationships before and for a while, I didn't want to be in any relationships. But then I met you through the games and I started to look forward to the times you'd be online. I enjoyed our friendship and I'd feel sad when you had to go. I'd miss you until I saw you next."

"It was the same for me."

"What changed everything for me was when you told me that your mum—your sweet mum who I saw only a couple of times through video—had passed. You couldn't go into any detail, but you looked so . . . so frail and hurt and lost . . . my heart really went out to you. I wanted to be there comforting you and I wasn't able to. I couldn't stop thinking about you, I wanted to help somehow. I still do."

Dane could feel his emotions rising to the surface. They welled within him, threatening to explode in waves of either sadness or joy or some combination of the two. The look in Amanda's eyes was compelling him to reach out to her, to hold her and tell her everything.

"I—thank you for that, Amanda," he replied, feeling a tear run down his cheek. "I'm . . . grateful . . . for everything."

"When you told me you were coming here from the States just to see me, I got so excited and I knew I had to get it together, do things different. I want to do right by you, Dane."

What did she mean by that, he wondered.

"Do right?" Dane repeated.

"I know there's things you feel you can't talk about with me," Amanda shared, taking his hands in hers. "But I want to know everything about you. I need you to trust me with your secrets and your feelings. I want to be the one you go to, the one who helps you and shares your burdens."

Dane looked at Amanda, assessing how serious she was and whether she was being truthful. He sensed no deception, only love. It surprised and relieved him.

"We have a lot to talk about then," he said, after kissing her hands.

They walked out of the airport hand-in-hand on the way to her car.

––––––––––

Thirty minutes later, they arrived at Amanda's apartment. She lived on the third floor in a modest flat with no roommates. Dane was quietly impressed at the thorough job she'd done making the place not only presentable but clean and smelling of scented candles. The living room centerpieces were two large bean bag chairs whose tops were shaped like cat heads, one black and one white, with a coffee table in front of them which included a gaming console as well as remote controls for the wall-mounted flat screen television and stereo system. The room was lit by several candles in various locations, tucked away into relatively inconspicuous holders.

"Nice digs," Dane praised.

"You really like it?" Amanda asked.

"Yes, I do. You did a great job decorating here."

"Thank you. Mi casa es su casa. How long can you stay?"

"Ajali said that's up to me. I can book the return trip whenever I want."

"Ajali? Who's that?"

"The woman who's adopting me."

Amanda raised an eyebrow at that.

"You're twenty-one years old. Why do you need to be adopted?"

"Ajali used to be good friends with my mom. She's also kind of rich. So, it's to make me her legal beneficiary."

"How do you feel about that, Dane—you know, becoming someone else's son?"

"I'm fine with it. I'll always be my mother's biological son . . . but I'll be gaining more family than I've ever had. She has a daughter named Leia who'll be my new sister. And my sister has an incredible father, step-mom, and half-sister. Leia just got married, too, and is having a baby in a few months."

"Wow, that is a lot of family! Congratulations."

Dane looked down for a moment and there was a brief awkward silence.

"What is it, Dane?"

"I have several things I need to tell you . . . and I don't know how you're going to react, so I'm kinda nervous."

Amanda put a hand on his shoulder and gave him a reassuring smile.

"You can tell me anything," she added. "I can keep secrets. And maybe I can help."

"This will change things and you may regret it. If you're not sure, tell me now and I won't think any less of you."

He wasn't sure how to take her confused look. He noticed his heart beating a little faster. He wanted to tell her everything but he felt like she deserved to make an informed choice.

"What? Is this about your mom or about you?" she asked.

"Both," he replied.

"What, do you have a criminal past or something? Drug habit? Whatever it is, I can handle it. Tell me."

"No, it's nothing like that. I'm sorry, I didn't mean to alarm you," Dane said, embarrassed at how he'd phrased things.

Amanda nodded, clearly relieved but not backing down, either.

"No problem. This is obviously significant. You can take your time."

Dane relaxed, letting out a sigh. It took him a few more seconds to say what he'd been guarding so closely.

"My mother was Black Fox."

"Black Fox? The superhero?"

"Yes."

Amanda slightly tilted her head, looking bewildered and yet contemplative. Then her eyes widened, as if she'd had an epiphany. When she gazed at Dane again, it was with a new understanding.

"Your internet alias—and you being Black Fox's son—you're Shadow? You're a superhero, too?"

"Yes."

"You have super powers?"

Dane gestured with his right hand towards Amanda's wall shadow. It left the wall and alighted atop his hand. With his left hand, he made his own shadow dance with hers on the wall. Then he snapped his fingers and both shadows returned to normal. Amanda was equally delighted and speechless for a few seconds.

"What a beautiful power!" she exclaimed.

"You're not scared?" he wondered.

"How could I be scared of you, Dane?"

Dane chuckled. "This also allows me to conceal my identity. And because I'm part-werefox, I can heal very fast."

Her eyes narrowed. He knew this would be a lot to take in.

"Were . . . fox?" she asked. "Like a werewolf, except a fox?"

"Yes. My mother was a full werefox. That's where her powers came from. It's passed down in our family."

Amanda sat down on one of the beanbag chairs and shook her head briefly. She leaned back, closing her eyes as she exhaled.

"Incredible," she turned her head to look at Dane. "Thank you for trusting me with this."

He sat down in the white beanbag chair next to her.

"Like you said . . . you're my girlfriend. I didn't feel like I could keep this from you anymore."

Amanda stood up and Dane did the same. Her eyes locked on his with a confident satisfaction as she pulled him into a passionate kiss which Dane did not resist. The kiss felt right, warm, comforting. He ached inside when it was over; he hadn't known how much he'd needed to feel loved by her.

She then further surprised him by going down on one knee, looking up at him, nervous yet hopeful. She took out a small box and opened it, revealing a ring. It looked more like a promise ring than an engagement ring but it was beautiful, made of white gold; there were no jewels on it.

"You probably thought I asked your ring size awhile back for a cosplay outfit but the truth is, I want a future with you. Even knowing all you just told me about being Shadow and a werefox and all that, it's worth any risks to me. So, Johnathan Dane Fox, will you marry me?"

For Dane, time itself seemed to freeze and he felt a rush of excitement and terror wash over his body. He heard his mother's voice in his mind: "When you fall in love—and you will fall in love—it would be better to find someone who also has powers. If they don't have powers, they'll have to be a special person to accept and love you, despite your gifts."

He looked down at Amanda, who had pinned all her hopes and dreams on this very moment, on him, and knew this woman was special. She accepted and loved him for who he was. Dane thought of Ajali, who had encouraged him to visit Amanda here on the other side of the globe, and he wondered what she would think of this moment and the decision he was about to make. Then he smiled.

"Yes, Amanda Claire Franklin, I will marry you!"

She hugged him tightly. Then she kissed him a couple of times. He let her place the ring on his finger. It was a surprisingly good fit.

"I know the guy normally does this thing but I'm different."

"You're Australian!" Dane said in a fake Australian accent.

"You got that right, mate!" Amanda replied with a wink and smile.

That made them both break into a nervous fit of laughter, which was as relieving as it was spontaneous.

"What do you want to do next, Dane?"

"We should tell your parents. And I need to call Ajali and let her know."

Dane took a step forward but hesitated before looking back at Amanda.

"Is something wrong?" she asked.

"There's something I should tell you about Ajali."

She walked over to the kitchen area and grabbed a couple of glasses from the cupboard.

"Sure. What is it?" she wondered as put one of the glasses beneath the ice dispenser on the refrigerator. Dane waited for her to finish dropping the small frozen cubes into each receptacle.

"Ajali has powers, too," he shared. "She's a telepath and telekinetic."

"Seriously?" she responded. "Wow, but—"

"And she used to be a supervillain . . . until recently."

"What?"

Dane sighed. He knew Amanda would be surprised but her wide-eyed expression showed him she was stunned, even dismayed by this news. Still, he had gone this far. He had to tell her the rest.

"Have you ever heard of Malevolence?" Dane asked.

With that revelation, all the color drained from Amanda's face.

"I see you have," he continued.

Amanda gripped her arms and tried to remain calm despite her fear. "Dane, she's a murderer!"

He nodded. "Yes, she has killed people."

"Lots of people!" Amanda added.

"Years ago, yes," Dane conceded. "She was a different person then. She'd just gained her powers and she was unstable."

Amanda slowly shook her head in disbelief. "You're defending her? I know she's offered to adopt you and she's rich, but—"

Dane stepped closer to her. He was determined to diffuse this situation. Somehow, he had to make Amanda understand.

"I'm not defending what she did back then or because she's rich or any of that," he insisted. "I'm defending who she's become now."

Amanda slammed her palm on a countertop. Her eyes pleaded with him. "Couldn't she just be fooling you, making you see what she wants you to see?"

"She has the power to do that . . . but she wouldn't."

"How can you be so sure of that?"

Dane stretched forth his hand to try and assure Amanda but she stepped back. However, she didn't look away from him.

"Her daughter, Leia, wouldn't stand for it," Dane declared. "And Leia's father certainly wouldn't. He used to be the superhero called Crusader."

Amanda's jaw dropped at that.

"Wait, a superhero and a supervillain had a child together?"

Dane nodded.

"It's a long story but let's just say they were dating before Malevolence's powers emerged, before she became a supervillain."

"That sounds like a story you'll have to tell me sometime."

"I'll let her tell you, if she's willing," Dane soothed. "I want you to meet her."

"I don't know, Dane."

He gently pulled her hands from their protective grips on her arms and held them together in front of him.

"That's kind of my point: there's a lot you don't know about Ajali," he said. "She's not Malevolence anymore. She's a mother and about to become a grandmother. She's making peace with her past. Can't you at least give her a chance? If you don't believe in her, then believe in me."

Amanda looked at Dane and offered a weak conciliatory smile.

"Alright, Dane, you win. Besides, I suppose I shouldn't start on the wrong foot with a future mother-in-law who could fry my brain."

"Or make you think you're a five-year-old."

"What?"

He hadn't meant to share that. Now he had to explain it.

"Um, well, those were criminals anyway."

"'Criminals?'"

"Assassins, actually."

"They were trying to assassinate Malevolence?"

Dane nodded. "While Leia, her husband, and I were there. But we all survived."

Amanda looked aghast for a moment. Then she stopped and pointed at him, smiling. "You almost had me there for a moment! You're messing with me! That didn't actually happen, right? She didn't do that?"

Dane did not laugh or give any hint of changing his story.

"Actually, she totally did do that," he confirmed. "But it was to avoid killing them."

"Well, did it wear off? Are they okay now?"

Dane sighed. "I really don't know. But Ajali saved a lot of lives that night, and her daughter saved mine."

For the second time, Amanda shook her head. Dane felt bad for her but he had also warned her about what he was going to say. She leaned against one of the walls and looked at the floor.

"Assassins, telepaths—how do you deal with it, Dane?"

"I was trained for this ever since I revealed my powers to my mother as a teenager. She trained me for all kinds of things since then."

"I see. That doesn't sound very safe."

Dane leaned against the wall next to Amanda and took her hand in his.

"It's not. But Mother always told me it was my responsibility, as someone with powers, to protect everyone else. She truly felt that was the right thing to do, even though it cost her life."

Amanda turned her gaze to Dane.

"And how do you feel about it?" she asked.

"I think it's a noble ideal . . . but it's also not realistic. I've seen another way. Leia's father married another superhero and they left that life behind to raise Leia. They also had another daughter together. The world has continued to exist without them stopping every criminal and they've provided a stable home for their family. That's what I want."

"Stability or a family?"

"Both."

She pushed off the wall and faced Dane, who did the same. She held both his hands and smiled at him.

"You're a wise man, love. Now I know I made the right choice."

"How about you, Amanda? How do you feel about kids?"

"Honestly, I never gave it much thought before I wrestled with my feelings for you."

"And now?"

Amanda kissed him again and her eyes gave him his answer.

We should get married very soon, Dane thought.

29

ONCE AGAIN, LEIA FELT ANXIETY as she smelled the smoke and felt the rush of hot air before the fireball erupted in front of her. It didn't matter that she knew this was a dream—no, a nightmare—she couldn't stop it, couldn't escape into a waking state. For all intent and purposes, she was in Josh's mother's house right after the gas main had exploded. Except this time, Josh wasn't with her and she didn't know what to do.

"Why, Leia? Why didn't you save me, too?" Alyssa Manning asked from behind Leia.

Leia couldn't turn to face her. She didn't want to see the burned, skeletal corpse of her mother-in-law, somehow animated and speaking to her. The raspy voice with sincere, sweet tones was torture enough.

"I wanted to be at your wedding, to be there when my first grand-child was born," the corpse said. "But instead, I died. I was only ten feet away from you and you let me die!"

"She's not real, this is just a dream," Leia closed her eyes.

Leia felt the corpse's physical presence shuffle closer to her back and began to feel nauseated at the stench of burned skin and bone. It was both terrifying and repulsive.

"I thought we were friends, Leia," it said. "I took you into my heart when I let you date my son. I accepted you and was thrilled to learn you're having a baby with my Josh. So just tell me, when I was in danger, why didn't you save me?"

"It wasn't like that!" Leia shouted, still refusing to look at the corpse. "I didn't know how to control my powers yet! It was tough enough just to save Josh!"

Leia shivered as the temperature felt like it dropped dramatically in just a few seconds. She turned and the corpse of Alyssa Manning was nowhere to be seen, along with the burning remains of the house. Leia was disoriented and somewhat dizzy. She could only tell she was inside another building.

"I know you couldn't save Alyssa or me," another female voice said from nearby.

Leia's heart sank as she realized the voice belonged to Black Fox. Leia now recognized that she was in Black Fox's house. She turned and saw the silhouette of Black Fox in the unlit hallway outside the room she was in. Black Fox walked out of the shadows, looking entirely normal, except for the dented and soot-covered mask. That, and there was no mercy in her feral eyes or the sharp teeth she bared.

Leia didn't know how to react to this setting or Black Fox's presence. She just felt her anxiety rising and a deep, foreboding sense of dread and despair.

"What I do want to know is, why did you let Malevolence anywhere near my son?" Black Fox asked. "Do you know what a slap in the face that was to me?"

Black Fox had never been in one of Leia's nightmares before. Instinctively, Leia knew she couldn't run from or fight her. There was no point; she was dead.

"I'm not your son's guardian, Aunt Dana! Both he and Malevolence are adults. They chose their relationship with each other!"

"That may be true, but he trusted you. I think he was even starting to love you, but you ignored him! Without me, he's lost. And you know how Malevolence is! She just snatched him up because she could. What were you thinking?"

"I could never have loved Dane! I've been with Josh for years. Dane's a good man but Josh is the only man I'll ever love!"

"I know that, Leia. But you didn't even *warn* Dane about Malevolence. And you certainly didn't protect him!"

"I didn't even know that Dane befriended Malevolence. I still don't know what their relationship is. I'm his friend but I can't control what he does."

"Really? Are you sure about that?"

"Your problem is with Dane, not me. Why don't you ask him why he chose to hang around with Malevolence?"

Black Fox stared at Leia in cold hatred for several seconds.

"You're such a disappointment," Black Fox said, her voice becoming animalistic as she gritted her teeth.

The sun saber in her right hand came to life, extending a blade of flames from its golden hilt. In the next two seconds, Black Fox rushed from across the room to where Leia was standing. And despite Leia sending the command to her brain to activate her telekinetic shielding, she was shocked as she felt the burning sword begin to slice through the left side of her abdomen.

In that instant, Leia's eyes opened wide and she screamed as loud as she could. Her telekinetic powers tossed the pictures on the walls into the kitchen of their apartment. The moment Leia cried out, Josh was instantly awake and trying to help her, despite his grogginess. It took ten minutes before Leia could even speak. She had stopped shrieking after she realized she was awake but the trauma was still present in her mind. She wrapped her arms around her pregnant belly, hugging it as she cried. She closed her eyes, whispering "not real" and "just a dream" over and over again like a mantra.

Josh held her and reassured Leia that she and the baby were fine. It was another half hour before she calmed down. And even though it was four in the morning, she knew they probably weren't going back to sleep again. Josh made her some decaffeinated tea. As she sipped the hot liquid, she felt her nerves relax a little more. She let out a deep sigh.

"Sorry, Josh, that one was the worst nightmare yet."

"You were okay for a while but now, it's worse than ever. That's four evenings in a row, each nightmare getting progressively stronger."

"You're worried. I am, too."

"Was it . . . my mom again? Or your aunt?"

"Last night, it was my aunt," Leia said, her hands starting to tremble. "But tonight, it was your mom and Black Fox. The part with your mom is always the same. But Black Fox was—her sword—she was—"

Leia found she couldn't finish her sentence. She lost the strength in her hands and the teacup fell and spilled on the carpet.

"Leia! Stop thinking about it! Focus on me!"

Leia's concentration abated, and she looked into Josh's eyes. Then she broke into tears and sobs. Josh held her as close as he could and let her cry.

"So, do you and Mom plan on having any more kids?" Tanya asked matter-of-factly, as she spooned some salsa onto her Denver omelette.

Steve had to make a concerted effort not to accidentally spit out his coffee when his daughter asked that question.

"Where did that come from?" he asked.

He had taken Tanya on a father-daughter breakfast to *Diner Du Jour* in the northern part of Digby this Saturday morning. It was just after ten o'clock. At Sue's suggestion, they were wearing matching clothes: black jackets, white t-shirts, blue jeans, and tennis shoes.

The diner had plenty of customers, but it wasn't packed or overly noisy. Steve and Tanya's table was in a less-crowded corner next to a large window facing a mini-shopping district, where families had already lined up to take advantage of deals on a variety of products and services.

The restaurant itself was something of a local legend landmark, known for its quality food and customer service over the last fifty years. The interior was very clean, the light blue walls decorated with pictures of national and international celebrities who had visited the diner during its history.

"Oh, come on, Dad!" Tanya continued. "Everyone seems to be having babies right now except you and Mom."

"Since when does your sister count as everyone?" Steve responded, nonplussed.

"Look, I know Leia's about to make you a granddad but you and Mom are still young. I really think you should have another baby. Or two."

"I appreciate the compliment—*compliments*—really, I do. But I'm just wondering, is there a particular reason you're suggesting this?"

Tanya looked at her father thoughtfully for a moment. Then she took a bite from her omelette and washed it down with some orange juice.

"Leia's married. She's moved out and she and Josh are doing their thing and that's cool. But it made me think about me being your and Mom's only kid—you know, that you two had *together*. And then I thought, there's really no reason you couldn't have more kids!"

"Have you already talked to your mother about this?" Steve asked, taking in a forkful of gravy-sopped biscuit and reaching for his glass of water.

"Of course! And she said I should talk to you."

"Nice deflect, Sue," Steve murmured under his breath.

"Oh, she wasn't deflecting," Tanya replied, looking down at her plate as she cut another piece of omelette while still chewing her food.

"You've got your mom's hearing," Steve countered with a hint of sarcasm, mildly annoyed.

"Mom made it pretty clear that she has mixed feelings about having more kids. But she also said that it was something that you two had to be in agreement about. That's why she said I should talk to you."

"I guess that's fair."

Tanya looked at her father, patiently waiting for a response.

"We've considered having more kids over the years, Tanya. I would usually bring it up, making the same suggestion as you, that it would be good for you to have another sibling. Your mom thinks about that a lot, too."

"But you've obviously decided against it each time. Why?"

"Because with your mom's cat powers, there's actually a very good chance of having more than one child in the pregnancy."

"Oh, you mean like twins?"

Just then, their waiter, a tall and thin bald man with a trim beard of auburn hair, stopped by their table to see if they needed anything. Steve asked him for another coffee. The waiter went off to get it.

"No, more like quintuplets or maybe more," Steve answered. "At least, that's been the concern."

"You're worried about having five kids at once?" Tanya asked, her tone somewhere between amused and surprised.

"Yes."

Tanya started laughing, almost uncontrollably, but she quickly reined herself in to just a few more semi-giggles.

"Mind if I ask what's so funny?" Steve asked, genuinely perplexed.

"Well, let's see if I understand this," Tanya said very quietly. "You and mom are both super strong and fast. You can fly, she's got hyper senses. You both heal fast and you're pretty invulnerable. When you were superheroes, you faced perils, trauma, injuries and death from all kinds of villains and natural disasters . . . but what *worries* you is having several babies to raise at the same time?"

Steve looked at her for a minute, stunned by the simplicity and truth in her logic. Then he put his left hand over his eyes and started chuckling. He slowly ran his hand down his face then used it to pick up his glass of water and take a drink.

"It does sound kind of minor, when you put it like that."

"Dad, I know it's not cheap to raise kids and it takes a lot of time and effort, but . . . I think it'd be worth it."

Steve smiled at his daughter and drank down all of his coffee in one shot. Then he put down the coffee cup and signaled the waiter with his hand, asking for the check. Then he turned his attention back to Tanya.

"I'll tell your mom about our little conversation. And, who knows, things might be different this time. Now, what say we go get you those clothes you wanted?"

"Sounds like a plan. And Dad, thanks for hearing me out."

A few minutes later, Steve paid the bill and the two of them left the diner. They headed down the sidewalk towards Tanya's favorite fashion stop, their walk the exact same to anyone watching them.

———————

The wall clock at the Hamilton's showed that it was just after nine-thirty in the morning. Sue poured two cups of coffee and then added a teaspoon and a half of sugar and a teaspoon of creamer to each cup. She was still stirring Leia's coffee as she brought the cup to her, being careful not to spill any on herself or Leia, who accepted the cup and saucer. She took a sip from it before putting the cup down on the dinner table where she was sitting.

"It's decaf," Sue said.

Sue couldn't help but notice the dark circles under her daughter's eyes. Leia looked like she'd tried to manage her hair but there were numerous loose strands standing in defiance of her attempt. Leia's black t-shirt had obviously been put on in haste, as it was a size too small on her and exposed several inches of her belly once she sat down. The gray sweat pants she was wearing fit her but smelled musky, probably from sweat.

"Thanks, Mom."

"This must be serious if you had your husband drop you off here first thing of the morning. Thanks for calling first."

"Actually, it was Josh's idea. He did his best to help me, really, but . . . "

"Sometimes you still need your old Mom, huh?"

Leia looked at her with a raised eyebrow.

"You're not old, Mom. I imagine you'll still look hot, even when you're eighty. And I never stopped needing you."

"Eighty, huh? I'm having enough trouble with forty and impending grandmotherhood. Let's not talk about eighty."

That surprised her daughter.

"You don't want to be a grandmother?" Leia asked.

"No, that's not it, honey. I just didn't expect to be one for several more years."

"I wasn't planning to be a mom yet, either," Leia replied, shrugging then pointing to her belly with both hands. "But here we are."

"You must not be too bad off if you can still joke."

"I guess," Leia said, looking away and not sounding convinced.

Sue walked behind Leia and gave her a tender hug. Sue would never tell Leia this, but she knew precisely why her daughter loved her hugs. That's why she gave them freely when Leia needed them, even now when she didn't ask for them. Sue had learned to read every cue from Leia's body language.

Sue recalled that eleven years earlier, Leia came home from school one afternoon bruised and bloodied from another fight, the day Leia met Josh.

Josh had helped Leia inside the house until she sat down in a chair and introduced himself to Sue like a proper little gentleman. Sue appreciated his kindness to her daughter and wondered for a moment, with his charm, what kind of interesting friend Josh would be to Leia. Sue had assured Josh that Leia would be fine, that she would take care of her, and Josh left.

The moment Sue had closed the door, little Leia wrapped her arms around Sue's waist from behind and was holding her as tight as she could, almost like she was gripping onto her mother for dear life. Sue turned around and picked Leia up and gave her a full hug. Leia put her head on Sue's shoulder and cried and sobbed and told her everything that had happened. Sue just listened and stroked Leia's hair and acknowledged her from time to time until Leia relaxed.

Then the nine-year-old girl snuggled her head into Sue's chest and squeezed her hands around rolls on either side of Sue's belly and giggled, the way she had when she was half that age. Sue had never heard Leia sound so content.

"This is the best feeling in the world, Mom! All the bad things go away when I can hold onto you like this. You're so soft and comfortable. I wish I could stay here forever!"

Now, in the present, even though her daughter was twenty years old and with child, Sue knew that a part of Leia would always find comfort in a simple hug from her. The thought made her smile but she also knew that Leia needed more than a hug to help her this time.

"Bad dreams, I take it?" Sue queried.

"Last night, Black Fox started cutting me in two in my dream," Leia said, sniffling.

"That's . . . pretty bad. How long has this been happening?"

"Off and on since Josh's mom died but they got worse after . . . Aunt Leticia. And this week, the dreams have been getting worse. They're so awful and intense, I don't know how much more I can take. I can't concentrate in class and I'm exhausted by the time I get to work. I'm a mess from not getting enough sleep, but I'm also afraid to go to sleep."

"I get it. Yes, you do need my help. Don't worry, Leia."

"Thanks, Mom. Tell me what I need to do."

"Come with us to church tomorrow. With Josh. I'd like for you to talk with the pastor about your dreams, about . . . everything."

"What if I have another nightmare again tonight?"

A woman cleared her throat behind them. Her voice was immediately familiar.

"I can help with tonight," Ajali said, standing behind both of them.

"Angela? What are you doing here?" Sue demanded.

"Sorry for the intrusion. I let myself in," Ajali answered. "Angela is gone. Dane gave me a new name. I'm Ajali Free now."

"Ajali?" Leia repeated.

Ajali shrugged.

"New life, new name," Ajali declared. "I've been aware of your nightmares, Leia, since I healed from my injuries. And for a single night, my power can suppress them."

"You'd do that? Why?" Leia questioned.

"I'm no psychologist but you've been through so much recently, it's not surprising you're having bad dreams. I guess I just want to help in a way that only I can. That's why I'm offering to hold back the nightmares tonight."

"Thank you. I don't know what else to say."

"Your thanks is enough."

"You have my thanks, too, Ajali," Sue mentioned. "And I wish you and Dane well on the adoption."

"Wait! What? Adoption?" Leia looked in astonishment at Ajali. "You and Dane are adopting a kid?"

Ajali crossed her arms and looked at Leia.

"Um, no," Ajali answered flatly. "I'm adopting Dane."

"Oh! Oh . . . wow. Sorry. I guess I misunderstood your relationship."

"Apology accepted. You've been dealing with a whole lot, so I understand."

"She was so opposed . . ." Leia whispered.

"What's that?" Ajali asked.

"In the nightmare, Black Fox was so angry that you two were, um, together and that I hadn't done anything to keep you apart. She was even willing to kill me over it."

"Do you—did you really feel that guilty over me and Dane, Leia?" Ajali sounded somewhat hurt.

Leia couldn't look Ajali in the eyes. Instead, she looked at the ground.

"I see," Ajali considered, slowly backing up. "Well, like you said, you misunderstood our relationship."

"Ajali, I know you've been used to doing things how you please over the years," Sue interjected. "But when you come to my house, either call or knock first, okay?"

"Sure," Ajali replied, with a mixture of amusement and sincerity.

Sue followed Ajali with her eyes, smiling but with arms crossed, until Ajali walked out the door.

30

JOSH HAD WOKEN UP EARLY for once. He looked over at Leia sleeping deeply. He was grateful to see her at peace instead of tossing, turning, and moaning. He rose and put on some jeans and a t-shirt. Locking the door behind him, he quietly slipped outside.

He walked to the parking lot and sat on the hood of his car, looking at the dawn sky and the moon shining above. A cool breeze soothed his skin.

"I miss you so much, Mom!" he spoke as if she were nearby. "You were taken, right in front of me, and I'm having a really hard time getting over that. I keep feeling like, if you were still here, you would have kept Dad from doing those awful things. Then Leia wouldn't have had to kill her aunt to protect us and she wouldn't be having these nightmares."

Even though he knew his mother wouldn't answer, it felt good to talk to her. It made him hope that somehow, she could at least hear him.

"You would have loved our wedding, Mom, I know it. You would've spoiled Leia more than me—well, just as much as me, anyway. You'd have bought her so many clothes and anything else to make her feel loved and accepted into our family. You'd have told her every embarrassing story about my childhood and I wouldn't have minded a bit.

"You'd have loved your granddaughter's name. You . . . just would've loved your granddaughter."

Josh allowed himself to cry.

He couldn't hold it in; he'd held it back for so long already. The tears continued to flow, and his breathing became ragged gasps then sobs.

Leia's arms surrounded him. She helped him stand up from the slumped state he'd been in on his car hood and pulled him close into her embrace. He felt such gentleness and warmness from her even as the bulge of her stomach pressed against him. It was like both she and his daughter were trying to comfort him.

Without a word, Leia walked her husband back inside their apartment and they sat on the bed. She looked into his eyes and he could tell she understood everything he was going through and that she had known it all along. Drained by his emotional release, he found bliss in her strong arms holding him while he surrendered to sleep.

Josh woke again, still in his wife's embrace. He looked up and smiled at her. She was asleep in the bed with him, still sitting up. The night stand held a half-empty cup of water and Josh saw a few remaining Pop Tart crumbs on Leia's mouth, chin, and hair. He realized she had used her telekinesis to fetch a late-night snack without disturbing him.

Josh relaxed and enjoyed looking up and admiring his wife, who was still wearing a robe over her night clothes.

This is paradise. This is what I always wanted with you, Leia.

With every bit of gentleness, he could muster, Josh slowly sat up and got out of bed, so he could look at Leia from a few feet away, a different perspective. He heard her snort and mumble a few incomprehensible words, and then she began to softly snore as she adjusted to his absence.

Josh sat in a nearby chair. His eyes absorbed her every line and curve, noting how much her body had changed since becoming pregnant. It amazed him.

Mom would be proud.

———————

The alarm clock began playing music from a local pop radio station. Leia stretched her arms and let her body slide downward into the pillows on the bed. She shifted to several more positions, trying to get comfortable and not completely succeeding. After that, it took her several seconds to get her bearings before she opened her eyes.

"Josh?" Leia uttered, her eyes only half-open.

"Hey there, hon," he replied from the nearby chair.

"How long have you been sitting there?"

"Long enough," he answered, smiling. "Great view."

Leia sprawled across the bed on her back and looked up at Josh, making him look upside down. Her hair was strung across her face and flowing over the bed in front of her.

"Oh yes, this is so flattering," Leia said.

"You are super cute," Josh added, now grinning. "And beautiful."

"Only you could think that," Leia sighed.

Josh looked at the alarm clock.

"What?" Leia wondered.

"We'd better start getting ready."

"'Getting ready? Oh, right! Today, we're going to my folks' church."

"You still want to do this?"

"Yes, I really do."

"Alright then. I'll be there for you all the way."

"That's all I ask."

An hour later, Leia gave Josh directions on how to get to the church. They passed her parents' house on the way.

She looked at Josh, who was relaxed but still had a serious expression on his face.

We'll have to get a bigger place soon, Leia thought. *And we'll make that our new home.*

As they turned the corner, Leia told Josh to turn left at the next stoplight. The church was at the end of that block.

The church was a long one-story building. It was at least twenty years old but had been re-painted recently, giving it a fresh and well-cared for look. The landscaping was crisp and well-kept; the parking lot did not show much wear and tear. While larger than some church buildings, it could not be confused with any megachurch Leia had seen.

She had attended this church as a child and stopped during her teen years, but not because of any philosophical or personal conflicts with either the congregation or the pastor. Leia had just been absorbed in her own experiences away from the church. At the same time, she had been feeling more and more connected to Josh and those feelings continued to blossom.

Leia and Josh arrived early but there were already cars there and people entering the church. Leia thought she recognized a few of the people her age. Josh parked the car and opened Leia's door and helped her steady herself as she got out of the vehicle, which she was grateful for.

"Two more months of this, Leia. If you think it's challenging now—" Ajali interjected from behind Leia.

"Malevolence?" Leia asked in a harsh whisper

Ajali wore a light orange blouse with a white skirt and matching jacket. Her hair was tied back. Behind Ajali, Dane was wearing a pin-striped gray and white suit that made him look very dashing. There was another young woman with them that Leia didn't recognize. She had shoulder-length red hair and wore a light blue dress.

"Remember, it's Ajali Free now, Leia," she added in an amused whisper. "Besides, ex-supervillains can't go to church?"

"Leia, Josh, there's someone I'd like you to meet," Dane interrupted. "This is Amanda Franklin, my fiancée."

Leia did a double-take but allowed herself a smile and extended her hand in friendship.

"This is a happy surprise! It's nice to meet you, Amanda, I'm Leia."

"The pleasure's mine," Amanda replied, accepting Leia's handshake then Josh's.

Mom walked out of the church and towards them. She looked cautious, especially towards Ajali, but not unpleasant. Mom walked and gave Leia and Josh hugs. She then warmly welcomed both Ajali and Dane before being introduced to Amanda.

Leia and the others followed Mom inside the church and towards the sanctuary where the morning service would be held. Mom introduced Leia and the others to several friends before finally sitting down towards the front of the sanctuary. Leia and Josh sat down to Mom's left while Ajali, Dane, and Amanda sat to her right.

Leia was not surprised when Mom looked across the aisle at Dad with an expression that said "I've got this. Stay back." Dad acknowledged Mom's cue with a polite nod and walked out to the foyer area. Leia figured that since Dad and Ajali had such a turbulent history, he was probably going to calm himself and pray before the service started.

Leia had not been to this church in several years, but she still remembered the subdued lighting and listening to peaceful instrumental hymns being played at a low volume over the sound system. She looked around at the people, some she recalled, and others were new to her. They spanned all ages and ethnicities. Those who were having quiet conversations seemed to be enjoying themselves while others who were still finding their seats seemed in good spirits. Leia perceived only acceptance and goodwill.

———————

Soon, a thirty-something, tawny-brown-hued man in a black suit and tie walked up to the microphone stand in front of the podium. He announced that the church service was about to start and asked everyone to refrain from further conversation and turn off their cell phones or put them on silent.

After waiting a few moments for people to comply, he welcomed everyone to the church service and asked everyone who was able to stand up and join him in singing a congregational hymn. Following that, there were some announcements and prayer requests for the sick or those recovering from illnesses or surgery.

Then the pastor, a dark-skinned man in his mid-forties, introduced himself and explained that there was going to be a change in the morning's service. He said that originally, the program would have started with several songs by the choir, but he was compelled by the Holy Spirit to do things differently this morning.

The pastor spoke briefly concerning the history of the church's ministry and its mission, which was to tell the world about the life, death and resurrection of Jesus Christ, the hope He offers to everyone. The pastor asked a few people to come up and share their testimonies of how their lives had been changed by The Lord's love, mercy, and the gift of salvation.

One young woman walked down from the choir stand to the podium and spoke into the microphone. She was short and thin, moving quietly, humble in her manner. Despite being perhaps in her mid-twenties, the look in her eyes and the premature stress lines on her face gave her the gravity and presence of someone who had lived longer. And yet, there was also a sweetness and a determination in the way she carried herself that was remarkable. Out of slight nervousness, she swept aside her brown bangs and looked at the audience.

"Hello, my name is Macey Turner and I barely made it to adulthood. Both of my parents were alcoholics who were physically and emotionally abusive to me for all of my life. By the time I was old enough to go to school, they had destroyed my self-esteem. Because of the way they spoke to me and treated me, I learned to fear and distrust everyone. Before I started high school, I had attempted suicide numerous times. The few friends I did have tried to help me to escape my life by either running away or using drugs . . . but that kind of escape is only temporary and doesn't bring security or peace. I always had to wake up and go home to my parents, who were resentful and ashamed of me. I used to think it would have been better if they'd never had me, if I'd never been born. That's why I wanted to die—I thought that was the final escape.

"The day that I'd finally worked up the resolve to jump off of a building, I was eighteen years old. I was a high school dropout, just learned I was pregnant by a guy who didn't love me, and I was too poor and scared to have an abortion. But I didn't want to make my child face my parents and I didn't think I was a good person to have as a mother, so I was going to kill us both and, in my mind, stop the suffering.

"I'd picked the time and place and was on my way there when I ran into a former classmate, Sheela Collins. We hadn't exactly been friends but she was the closest I'd come to one in my life. She was nice to me and seemed like a good person. She must have seen something in my face or in my eyes that day because she became very concerned for me. She asked if we could talk and when I didn't respond right away, she offered to just listen. I didn't know why at the time but I decided to trust her and tell her everything, all my hurts and worries. I told her about my baby and what I was planning to do. Once I started sharing, it was like a door had opened and I couldn't close it. I cried and screamed and let out feelings I'd kept trapped inside me since I was a child. It didn't solve my problems but it helped me feel better. I hadn't known how much I'd needed that or how good it could feel.

"Sheela invited me to stay with her for the next two days at her parents' house and I got to see what a real family was like for the first time. Her parents were quiet and kind of reserved but they loved Sheela and her younger brother, Kyle. They talked to and listened to each other. They didn't drink or do drugs and they were interested in their kids' lives. They wanted them to do well. And they made me feel welcome in their home. They didn't judge, look down on me or try to lecture me. They just let Sheela be a friend to me and that's what I needed more than anything.

"After those first couple of days, when I asked Sheela why she was doing so much for me, she told me that the Lord had let her see that I was suffering, and she wanted to help me. But she knew she didn't have all the answers, she was just trying to be a friend. She told me about the Lord Jesus and invited me to come to her church anytime. There was no pressure and she told me it was up to me; if I didn't want to go, it wouldn't change anything between us. But I felt indebted to her and agreed to visit her church.

"It didn't take me long to realize that the Lord was offering a solution for all of my problems; I didn't have to go it alone like I had my whole life. Even if I hated myself and was ashamed of my choices in life, Jesus loved me and wanted to help me. So, I gave my life to the Lord Jesus Christ, and He healed my heart and my mind. He gave me the strength to move out of my parents' house and take control of my life. The Holy Spirit filled me and granted me the help I needed, that my child needed.

"That was six years ago. It can be hard being a single mom but I can call my pastor for prayer and advice anytime. I have a new family, all of my brothers and sisters in Christ. And I've been able to forgive my parents and move on with my son. I have a job, a car, a place to stay. But most of all, I have hope. Please keep me and my son in your prayers, thank you."

Leia looked on this young woman in amazement. Her eyes brimmed with tears.

She couldn't imagine facing any of what she had gone through, especially recently, without Mom or Dad. She couldn't think of a time they didn't love or support her. And yet, Macey Turner never had loving parents. Leia tried to comprehend Macey's experience, how her parents had hurt her in every way, to the point she didn't want to live, and she didn't want her baby to face the same thing she had.

Leia looked down and protectively caressed her belly, as if trying to reassure her unborn daughter.

A few other people shared similar experiences. Some seemed to have had good lives with incredible potential but inside, they were lost and alone, craving something more, which led them to make choices that sabotaged their own lives and dreams. No pleasure satisfied them for more than a short time and then they wanted something else, leaving them feeling anxious and desperate—empty. Losing more ground towards their goals, they all came to a crossroads in their lives. But each had met or knew someone who was a Christian, who had shared with them what Jesus Christ had done for them once they accepted him into their heart. They each had been blessed and their lives had changed for the better because of Him.

Leia's own experiences were so different from theirs—after all, how many people had superpowers?—but she related to their pain and desperation. She had overheard words about Jesus and the Bible when she was a child and even through her teen years, in church and at home, but they'd only been words, other people's opinions. Now, she was curious. And even though every real-life story she was hearing was different, their needs were the same. She knew that she needed that same hope.

Minutes later, the pastor went into his sermon about Christ's love, forgiveness, and the power Christ has to change lives, just as He had with those who had shared their testimonies. The pastor read and explained scriptures from the Old and New Testament to reinforce the points he was making.

When the pastor finished, he gave an invitation for anyone seeking the Lord. Leia stood up and, with Josh's help, made her way to the front of the sanctuary. This was what she'd been seeking: forgiveness and change, better control over her life!

The pastor looked at Leia curiously and smiled.

"This salvation you're talking about—the forgiveness and everything," Leia said, teary-eyed but determined. "I want it! I really want it."

It was a deep, almost instinctive feeling that she couldn't ignore.

The pastor talked briefly with Leia and read her some scriptures. He motioned for her to sit down in a chair and to pray and invite Jesus Christ into her heart. Leia did everything that the pastor said.

In her seat, Ajali not only viewed everything with her eyes but was listening to Leia's thoughts, too. And what she saw in Leia's thoughts nearly overwhelmed her. Ajali sensed that Leia had a new inner strength. Something had fundamentally changed in Leia's mind, heart and even her soul.

Ajali could detect that Leia felt understood and loved in a way she had never experienced before. It differed from the love of Josh or her parents. Leia believed she felt the presence of the Holy Ghost within her for the first time. She was at peace.

When Leia opened her eyes, she was crying but she wasn't sad. When the pastor asked how she felt, after getting a little choked up, Leia said she felt like Jesus was in her heart. She felt happy and free!

Ajali walked up and hugged her daughter, followed by Josh and Amanda. She was very relieved that Leia was so joyous and cheerful. Leia told everyone that Ajali was her birth mother. By this point, Steve, Sue, and Tanya had joined them as well. The whole church celebrated Leia's decision.

31

THE NEXT MORNING, WHEN LEIA opened her eyes for the first time, she felt that something wasn't quite the same. She ran her right hand over her belly then touched her face. She ran her fingers up the side of her head and then just above her forehead. That's when she knew.

"They're gone!" Leia exclaimed. "I can't believe it!"

As Leia scooted herself off of the bed, she saw her husband groggily lift his head from the pillow and look in her direction. She entered the bathroom and turned on the light. She deliberately parted her hair and stared at herself in the mirror. She heard Josh's footsteps approaching her.

"What's gone?" he asked.

"My horns! They're completely gone!"

"What? Wait . . . that's good, right?"

"Yes, that's good! That's very, very good!"

"What about your powers? Are they still there?"

Josh's wristwatch lifted up from the table across the room and flew over to him. It dangled in the air above his hand until he took it. Leia smiled at him.

"I feel just as strong as before, but I feel like I can control it better, like most of the time my power is automatically in normal mode until I need more strength or power."

"That's . . . amazing, Leia. You think it's because of what happened at the church yesterday?"

"Well, that's what it feels like. I know I didn't do this. It . . . it must be the Lord."

"Wow! I've always been kind of a skeptic of religion but I can't argue with results."

"This isn't religion, Josh, this is—this is God working."

"Like I said, I can't argue with results. I'm just happy for you."

"Thanks. I don't know if I still have power over fire. But even if I do, I don't want to ever use it again, not after what happened last time."

Josh held Leia close. Remembering that night was always difficult for both of them.

"So, am I looking at a future superhero—that is, once you have this baby?"

"No. Misha was right. I'm a wife and mom now and that has to take priority. Besides, my own Mom showed me that leaving behind the life of a superhero in order to be a good wife and mother is no bad thing. She never regretted it . . . and neither will I."

"That works for me, but I'm selfish. I want you near me as much as possible!"

Leia kissed her husband and then looked at him with a wry smile. "You do, huh?"

"Absolutely!" he said.

"Prove it, cowboy!"

———

Dane and Amanda sat at the top of a hill overlooking part of the city. It was almost noon and there was a moderate December wind blowing.

"How long have you been standing back there, Ajali?" Dane asked without looking back, startling Amanda slightly.

"Long enough to enjoy watching you two for a bit," Ajali responded. "How did you know I was here?"

"I picked up your scent in the wind. I don't think I have near the fox in me that Mother did but it's there. I've noticed it a lot more since I got out of the hospital."

"What you have is perfect," Amanda added, putting her arm around Dane. "It helped you survive and I'll always be grateful for that."

"I'll second that emotion," Ajali agreed. "Why don't you both come back home, we can talk on the way."

Dane and Amanda walked over to Ajali and they all began heading southward.

"Okay. There's something I'd like to talk to you about," Dane mentioned.

"There is?" Ajali wondered.

"I told Amanda this already, but I've decided not to follow Mother's path. I'm not going to be a superhero. And I think maybe I was never meant to be one."

"Well, I certainly won't try to change your mind," Ajali offered. "But what made you come to this conclusion?"

"You and Amanda," he continued. "This life that we're all building together, you as my adoptive mother and her as my soon-to-be wife. I really understand Steve and Sue's decision to just be a regular family."

Ajali raised an eyebrow at that but balanced it with a genuine smile.

"How does that make you feel about your mother's decision to remain a superhero?" Ajali asked.

"I understand that, too. She tried really hard to find a balance. She'd lost Dad and she wanted to honor his memory, his sacrifice. But she never neglected me, even if it meant losing sleep or missing the occasional patrol of the city. She always watched out for me and let me know I was loved and precious to her."

"You had the best of both worlds then," Ajali praised. "My mother would get so drunk, she'd barely remember she had a daughter."

"I had a pretty normal mum. No complaints, really," Amanda said sheepishly.

They walked along in silence for several seconds before Dane continued.

"Mother did her best under tough circumstances," he added. "But in the end, being a superhero only got her killed."

"She knew the risks when she put on the mask," Ajali acknowledged sadly. "She was the most valiant and honest woman I've ever known."

"You miss her, don't you?"

"I miss her a great deal," Ajali answered, her voice cracking on the last word. Dane could tell she was fighting back tears.

He looked at her reassuringly.

"Tell me more stories about my mother. How did you two meet?"

"I'd like to know that, too!" Amanda inquired.

Ajali brushed a tear from her right eye and cleared her throat. They started walking again.

"Dana and I met when we were girls, maybe ten years old?" Ajali said. "I would run errands for my parents, just to get out of the house. And my folks were so in their own worlds, they wouldn't really notice how long I was gone."

Dane looked at Ajali sympathetically.

"It's alright, Dane. That was a long time ago, it doesn't bother me anymore," Ajali continued. "I would just walk for a long time or ride the bus. I took in the sights around me and formed stories. The old man who played checkers at the table outside the bookstore—the one who always wore a dark suit and fedora hat—was he actually a time traveler? Had he been a knight in medieval times but he grew tired of warfare and came to our time to get away from that? Was he here just to live out his remaining years as a gentle, grandfatherly figure, available to anyone who wanted to play checkers with him while drinking a cup of coffee? I was always fascinated with history."

"That's some imagination," Dane said, clearly impressed.

Amanda nodded in agreement.

"I met your mother in that bookstore," Ajali mentioned. "I was just hanging out with nothing better to do and not feeling particularly imaginative when she walked in. And in that moment, she completely inspired me!"

"What do you mean?" Dane asked, genuinely curious.

"Well, your mother looked a lot different back then. She had shorter hair, was very shy but at the same time, she was very stylishly dressed. That was probably her mother's doing. She was also quite plump, the most adorable girl I'd ever seen. I felt like there were a thousand stories behind her sad and reserved eyes. I knew right then that I had to get to know her."

Dane stopped and looked at Ajali in amazement.

"Wait, are we still talking about my mother? I can't imagine her shy or plump! She was always so extroversive and athletic."

Ajali chuckled at Dane's lack of life experience.

"We're talking about when she was a child, before she ever developed her powers," Ajali gently insisted. "She had issues with her parents, just like me, and she chose to avoid conflicts and retreat inward. A lot of people do that."

Dane nodded at that.

"She probably thought I was crazy when I introduced myself and asked to be her friend," Ajali added. "Your mother wasn't exactly the trusting sort."

"Yeah, that never really changed," Dane confirmed. "But obviously, she trusted you. She became your friend."

"Not at first," Ajali revealed. "I had to get past her walls of self-protection and give her a reason. I told her that I needed her help, that I had all these stories in my head about the people and places around me but I could never write them down. To the girl I was, writing my thoughts down would get in the way of the creative process and I was all about the creative process."

"And that worked?" Dane asked.

"She asked me to prove it, to tell her some stories about the people in the bookstore," Ajali replied. "So, I did. She loved the story about the old man playing checkers!"

Ajali stopped again and smiled. Hers was a wistful smile and she almost looked like she might lose her composure again. But then she recovered and looked at Dane and Amanda as if to say "I'm okay" and they started walking again.

"I don't think I've ever told anyone about my friendship with Dana, not in detail like this. It hurts, because I remember why I loved her so much . . . but it's also kind of healing. It's nice to share the memories with others."

"I'm grateful to listen to you talk about my mother. She never talked much about her past, except for her time with Dad and when she was in the AR-MEN."

"I don't know why but in those early days, I always wanted to pull Dana out of that cold and lonely place in her mind that she always seemed to be," Ajali continued. "In a lot of ways, my own circumstances at home were worse than hers but I focused on helping my friend any way I could. I know I annoyed her a lot with my pushiness and crazy ideas but gradually, she came out of her shell and became a more confident and outgoing person."

"Then I guess I have you to thank for that," Dane remarked. "It was that confidence that led her to act on her feelings for Dad and pursue him."

"You'll have to tell me those stories, Dane," Ajali said. "I only knew that she had a crush on him."

"Gladly." His eyes lit up. "Hey, do you have any pictures from those days?"

Ajali's smile became a wide grin.

"I actually do," she replied. "We'll have to go to one of the storage facilities where I keep my old stuff."

"One of?" Amanda queried.

"What can I say, I'm a pack rat," Ajali admitted. "You never know when your old things may come in handy, like thirty-year-old pictures."

Ajali put her arms around Dane and Amanda as they continued down the sidewalk. They were rapidly approaching her building.

"When can we go there?" Dane asked. "Now you've got me really curious."

"Let's go inside for a little while and warm up first since we're already here," Ajali insisted. "We can go tonight, okay?"

"Fair enough," Dane replied. "And thank you."

"Yes, thank you . . . Mum," Amanda added.

"I should be thanking you two," Ajali winked at Amanda to show that she appreciated the compliment and respect. "I wouldn't have thought these old memories would be useful anymore, but you're showing me that they are."

They entered the building they called home, closing one door but opening the potential to countless others.

32

MISHA OFFERED LEIA A HOT cup of herbal mint tea which Leia gratefully accepted. Leia was sitting on a very plush couch at Misha's apartment. Misha sat in a chair facing Leia, took a sip of her own tea, and put the cup back on its saucer on the table in front of her.

"I'm glad you told me," Misha remarked.

"I hope I haven't made you uncomfortable," Leia said.

"It's obviously been a powerful experience for you. And hey, if it got rid of the horns, I've got no problem with it. If you can be comfortable with me being Jewish, I can be comfortable with you being Christian."

"You know I've always been cool with you. You're my best friend."

"I'm the same with you. That'll never change, Leia."

Leia smiled at that and took another sip of the tea. Misha followed suit.

"Josh is also thinking about becoming Christian. And believe it or not, I think my mother is giving it serious thought, too."

"Josh, I can understand. He'll follow you anywhere. But Professor Doom?"

Leia adjusted her position on the couch until she found one that was more comfortable. At nearly eight months into her pregnancy, that was becoming a challenge. She looked at Misha with some disapproval.

"You're not really being fair to her, Misha. As Malevolence, she did many bad things, but she also never had a life of her own. You don't know what she went through growing up. She didn't have mental problems for no reason."

"Alright, maybe I don't know about her past. Maybe I only know what she showed me."

"Has she committed any crimes in the last six months, Misha? Killed anyone? Stuff like that?"

"Not that I know of, but she is a telepath."

"You are so not funny right now," Leia said, rolling her eyes. "Like I said, she didn't have a good relationship with her family. And when her powers manifested, she couldn't handle it and created the Malevolence personality. She did some terrible things but she spent most of the next two decades just watching out for me. She became Professor Doom to be near me to protect me. After all this time, she doesn't have to do that anymore. I'm a grown woman, with powers, and I can protect myself. She's finally free to live her own life and that's what she's doing."

"By adopting the son of the woman she kil—" Misha faltered as Leia glared at her. "By adopting the son of the woman who her powers killed? How is that okay?"

"Actually, it's a big deal. She's taking responsibility for what happened, in her own way. She feels the need to provide security and stability for Dane, both emotionally and literally. And she's extending the same to Dane's fiancée."

"That's . . . pretty amazing, actually. Go, Dane, huh?"

"Yeah, I'm happy for both of him and Amanda. And Professor Doom, too!"

They shared a short giggle then both were silent for a moment.

"I'm happy for you, too, Leia."

"Thanks. Where did that come from?"

Misha briefly looked at Leia seriously and then looked down, smiling.

"You've grown up a lot this past year. I really wish you'd been spared all that heartache, pain, and stress but you've come out of it better. You're a stronger woman inside now."

"I've been a spoiled brat and I dragged you into the middle of my mess."

"Hey, sister, I don't go anywhere I don't *want* to go. And the spoiled brat thing was an act. I knew that all along."

Leia stared at Misha.

"You were insecure, I could see that," Misha continued. "You were dealing with some crazy stuff . . . and being pregnant, too."

"True."

"I wanted to be there for you in any way I could. Although sometimes, it felt like I wasn't doing anything at all."

"Your company was everything to me. Especially all the late-night conversations."

"And meals," Misha added, not quite under her breath.

"Yeah," Leia replied with an embarrassed smile. "There were a lot of those."

Leia squirmed a bit at the awkward silence that permeated the room for a moment.

"But I didn't mind," Misha interjected. "You'd do the same for me, if I were in your place, right?"

"You mean if you sprouted wings, could fire eye beams and learned you were carrying twins?" Leia laughed.

"Um, not the powers. I just meant the meals," Misha confirmed.

"Oh! Would I get fat for you if you were the one who was pregnant and had cravings all the time?"

Misha facepalmed at her friend's blunt response.

"Um . . . yes, Leia. I'd really like to know that."

"Well, sure I would, in a heartbeat!" Leia grinned.

Leia then looked at Misha with a confused expression.

"What?"

"Well, as an incentive, I bought you cute clothes," Leia added.

"And?"

"You have no fashion sense. What incentive would you give me to eat all that food?"

Misha fumed with indignation. Leia stared at Misha expectantly for several seconds before pointing at Misha and erupting in laughter.

"I totally had you there! You should have seen yourself!"

"Ha-ha. Hilarious. Really."

"Oh, come on, you're not really mad, are you?"

"Me, mad? Nah!"

Then Misha grinned mischievously and Leia's smile collapsed.

"You're totally going to get me back for this, aren't you, Misha?"

"Totally . . . because that's what friends do, too."

Leia took a final sip of her tea, looked at Misha and smiled.

"Thanks for being my best friend."

"I'll always be there for you," Misha said. "And your kids."

"Do you know something I don't?" Leia added, slightly tilting her head.

"You'll want more kids with Josh. I don't see Alyssa being an only child."

Leia sighed mildly and relaxed.

"Que será, será," Leia answered, raising her tea cup towards Misha as if making a toast. "Whatever will be, will be."

33

"WHY DID WE COME HERE?" Josh wondered.

"I wanted to . . . because we've come full circle," Leia answered.

It was twilight and she held his hand as they walked off the curb and down a gradual grassy slope to the elementary school playground.

"This is where we first met," she continued, looking at the playground. "In a few weeks, Alyssa's going to be born. And if we stay here a few more years, this is where our daughter will go to school."

"Huh! You're right. Who'd have thought . . . the scrawny boy with glasses and the strong, fighting tomboy would end up together, married, and starting a family."

"Well, I thought! You set the stage that day, cowboy. Now you're seeing the results of your handiwork."

"Excuse me? We were nine years old. What are you talking about?"

Leia put a hand to Josh's cheek and looked at him blissfully.

"You won my heart that day, Josh. Don't think little girls don't think ahead because they do."

"I don't doubt it, especially knowing you. But are you saying, even back then?"

She lowered her hand from his cheek to his arm and continued to look at him.

"When you made it clear you weren't like the other boys, that you wanted to help me and were even willing to fight for me to protect me, it was a done deal. My little self said, 'He's mine!'"

"Seriously?"

"That lasted until the first time you made me mad. But I never let myself get far from you. And when you finally asked me to be your girlfriend, I didn't exactly put up a fight."

"No, you didn't."

"That's because, deep down, I already knew I wanted to be with you," she added. "You'd earned a place in my heart."

They stopped between the swings and the slide and Josh gently pulled Leia into a hug from behind her, his hands wrapped around her abundant belly. She put her hands around his. They absorbed the love of that moment, not having any words to properly express what they both felt, for each other and their child.

But then the moment passed, and Leia sighed as reality intruded on her thoughts.

"The world hasn't exactly become a nicer place since those days," she considered. "Alyssa might find herself fighting with the children of some of our old bullies."

"Then I feel bad for any children who try to fight her," Josh answered. "Something tells me she'll more than hold her own."

"You're probably right! That said, I'm glad Ajali has mellowed since my childhood days. Those kids won't have to face the wrath of Granny Malevolence!"

"No, but now that I think about it—" Josh started to say.

"Leia?" a woman's voice said from close by.

Leia and Josh turned to see an Asian woman in her early twenties with a toddler-aged boy in hand. She seemed familiar to Leia and Josh.

"Yes?" Leia answered.

"Wow! I'm not surprised you don't remember me. I'm Jenny. I was Jenny Cho back then."

Leia stared at the woman for a moment until she recalled where she knew her from. Then everything made sense.

"You looked familiar to me. How have you been, Jenny? I don't think I've seen you since middle school?"

"Yeah, my family moved to Seattle. I came back here to go to college."

"And start a family, I see. He's a handsome little guy."

"Thanks. His name's Kenny, like his father. He just turned three."

"Congratulations!" Leia offered sincerely.

"Looks like you're about to have your own," Jenny noted. "Congratulations to you, too."

"Thanks. You may remember my husband, Josh?" Leia said, looking proudly at Josh.

Jenny's jaw dropped open.

"*This* is the same Josh from when we went to school here? Skinny Josh?"

"Guilty as charged," Josh answered, grinning.

"Well, you guys were inseparable, even back then. I guess I shouldn't be too surprised. He defended you when we—"

Jenny's smile faded and was replaced by a more somber expression. Then she walked up to Josh and looked him in the eye.

"I wish I'd had your courage back then," Jenny said. "I always admired you for fighting for her, whether in words or deed. She needed someone like that."

Then Jenny faced Leia.

"I'm sorry I never stood up for you back then, Leia. I knew the boys were wrong to do that, and they were so . . . cruel. But I was more worried about them and what the other girls thought of me. I let that keep me from doing the right thing . . . and from being your friend."

"I'm sure you made other friends back then," Leia replied.

"Making friends doesn't always mean you make the right friends. It took me a long time to realize that. And I regretted never being a good one to you. When I recognized you just now, I knew I had to tell you that."

Leia looked at Jenny and her little boy, who was now dragging his mother's hand, wanting to go to another part of the playground. Right then, Leia saw an opportunity. She reached out and put her right hand on Jenny's left shoulder.

"That took a lot of courage, Jenny, and I'm grateful. What say we give friendship a fresh go? Anyone who's willing to do what you just did is someone I'd like to know better."

"I'd *like* that! I'd—I'd really like that," Jenny said, her eyes tearing up as she smiled. "Can we keep talking over by the slide? Kenny seems to have his heart set on it."

"Yeah."

Twenty minutes later, Leia and Josh watched as Jenny walked home with her son. Josh had his arms around Leia's shoulders from behind and her tears began to flow.

"Are you alright?" Josh asked.

"Yeah, I'm fine, baby. I just didn't know how much I needed something like that. It was very . . . healing."

"And you made a new friend."

"No, I regained an old one. She was my best friend in third grade."

"Oh! That was a year before we met."

"Jenny abandoned me when the rest of my friends did. That hurt me more than the rest of them put together."

"Wait, are you saying I was the *only* friend you had back then?!"

"Yes, Josh, that's what I am saying. You were the one who stood with me through everything. You never let me go, never turned away, no matter how rough things got."

Josh nearly lost himself in Leia's eyes once more. They were so inviting but they also had experienced their share of pain and loss.

"I guess I kind of knew that, but I just wanted to be your friend," he answered. "I was so focused on protecting you and getting to know you that I didn't see the big picture."

He could feel her relax and heard her exhale slowly through her nose.

"That's alright, Josh, that's exactly where I needed you to be at that time. And I treasured you and your friendship for that. That's why it was easy to become your girlfriend and then . . . more. That's why I did my best to stand by you, no matter what."

"My future was always going to be with you, Leia. I've known that for a long time. I love you."

"I love you, too. Now and forever."

"Now and forever."

Leia turned around and put her arms around her husband and squeezed. He could tell she was taking care not to use too much strength. She pressed her lips against his and leaned against him. Josh didn't want this moment to ever end.

Minutes later, they turned and took one last look at the playground before returning to Josh's car.

"So many memories there," Josh remarked.

"Yes, but no regrets," Leia added.

"No regrets."

"Before you know it, our baby's gonna be born. We're gonna be able to hold her in our arms!"

"And change her diapers and feed her and rarely get sleep."

"Comes with the territory, cowboy," Leia said, putting his hand on her belly.

"True. I think I can get used to it."

Leia looked Josh in the eyes lovingly, kissed him, and they walked home.

34

AJALI HAD BEEN WITH HER daughter for the more-than-twenty-seven hours it took for her granddaughter to be born. She had done her best to ease her child's pain and marveled at sharing this birthing experience through her telepathy. Even now, she was in contact with her daughter's mind.

Leia discovered a new form of happiness and awe when the nurse handed her newborn daughter to her wrapped in a pink blanket. The child, who weighed nearly eight pounds and was twenty-two inches long, was equally tired. Beside Leia, Josh was as close to the two of them as humanly possible, a grin spreading ear-to-ear beneath his sleep-deprived eyes.

"Look at her, Josh! Isn't she incredible?"

"Yes. And like I hoped, she looks more like you than me."

"We don't know that for sure, silly. She's going to change a lot, especially the first year. She doesn't even have hair yet."

The baby stirred and tried to move around, making weak crying sounds that made Leia feel more protective and even more in love with her child. Leia could also feel Josh's love for his daughter, hear the happiness in his voice, and see the excitement in his eyes. Leia didn't think it was possible to love this man more than she already did. But as she watched him carefully yet proudly hold his daughter, Leia found a new and deep reservoir of devotion, trust and the purest love for her husband.

Ajali's own mild exhaustion made it almost impossible to tune out everyone else's thoughts and emotions. She knew she might regret it later but for now, she couldn't help it.

Sitting in a chair about five feet away was Misha. She was equally sleep-deprived but overjoyed for her best friend

"They're in their own world right now but I'm glad we can share in the happiness," Steve shared.

"You were exactly the same way with Tanya," Sue said, elbowing his ribs with a sly smile. Steve's return look and smile were his acknowledgments of his wife's truth.

He was the same with Leia, too, Ajali thought to herself, smiling proudly. *I remember that vividly.*

But Ajali's smile faded when she also remembered how soon she'd decided to give Leia up and walk away. That loss would always haunt her because it had been her choice.

"Don't think you're getting out of babysitting the granddaughter," Sue said, looking right at Ajali. She was attempting to cheer her up. "We love her already but we get breaks sometime, too."

"Oh, I know I'll have my hands full," Ajali said. "Between Leia's daughter and now Dane—"

"Dane? What are you talking about?" Sue asked.

"He's waiting for the right time to tell me, but I've known that he and his wife, Amanda, are expecting," Ajali replied. "It might even be twins, though I'm not sure about that, since it's early on."

"Wow! Congratulations, Ajali," Sue beamed. "I think being a grandma already agrees with you. You've got that glow."

"No, that's all Leia," Ajali joked. "I just look old enough for the part."

"I don't see any gray in those hairs," Sue quipped.

"No, you don't," Ajali said with a touch of bravado and a smile, teasing her hair as her red highlights lit up in the midst of her jet-black hair. "And you won't!"

"Show off," Sue chuckled.

Ajali chuckled back. She was happy for her daughter and everyone present.

"Y'know, if you ask me, getting heavier was one of the best things that ever happened to you, Susan," Ajali replied, amused to finally get a chance to poke fun at her past rival.

"And how do you figure that?" Sue asked, a genuinely perplexed look on her face.

"Well, for one thing, it's the perfect post-hero secret identity," Ajali answered. "No one would possibly suspect you were The Cat."

"Okay, fair enough," Sue acknowledged.

"But more importantly, you found the best love test in the world for Mr. Muscles here. And it paid off. Based on the time I read his thoughts on the rooftop, I can absolutely verify that he truly enjoys you as you are now."

"Is that your attempt at tactfully saying he prefers me fat?" Sue asked, smiling.

"Yes."

Sue put her left arm around Steve's waist and pulled him closer to herself. He didn't appear to mind.

"I could've told you that," Sue continued. "We know everything about each other."

"I think it's wonderful that you two have that kind of openness and sincerity in your relationship," Ajali agreed. "And who knows? Maybe I'll find love again someday."

"You will," Sue insisted. "You really have changed, Ajali. You're more open and you let people in. It'll happen."

Ajali appreciated Sue's well wishes towards her. When had they become friends?

"He'll have to cook, though. I'm doing good to make casserole; otherwise, I have someone else cook," Ajali declared with a shrug.

"You always were practical. I remember you made our budget when we were living together, before your powers emerged," Steve admitted.

"Wait, *she* made a budget for you two back then?" Sue asked.

"I also picked out the apartment," Ajali added. "And I made him go get a job to pay for it. That way, he only had to focus on me when he got home."

"You let her do that?" Sue looked sternly at Steve.

"Um, it made sense at the time?" Steve answered, shrugging.

Ajali enjoyed watching Steve and Sue together. She'd come to appreciate them much better as a couple. Sue was every bit as practical as Ajali had been, but Sue demonstrated her love more openly and in subtler ways than Ajali knew how to. Sue picked up on the tiniest physical, verbal and emotional cues from her husband and addressed them with maternal precision and care.

Ajali looked at her daughter and saw the woman—the life—she'd hoped to have two decades ago.

I wanted that so badly then, for Steve to fawn over me the way Josh does Leia. But when I saw his love was only for his daughter, I had to try to accept that . . . even though it broke my heart. Steve and Sue did such an incredible job of raising Leia. And now, Leia has a husband and a daughter of her own. I couldn't be prouder of her!

"I guess I'm a little late," a voice said.

Wendy Fox entered the room. She gave a respectful nod to everyone, especially Leia and Josh. She mouthed the word "congratulations" to them and left them to their cooing over their newborn while she walked towards the rest of the family.

"Mrs. Fox?" Steve asked.

"Please, call me Wendy. Ajali called me when Leia went into labor. I got here as soon as I could to show my support. After all, we're family now."

"You're right," Sue agreed, taking Wendy's hand. "We're family. It's so good to see you, Wendy! It's been too long."

Sue quickly sniffed the air. Then she looked in amazement at Wendy.

"I never knew she got it from you," Sue noticed. "Instead of the suit."

"And I never knew you were The Cat until now," Wendy said. "Imagine my surprise. I guess these old senses have gotten keener with age."

"I've noticed the same thing," Sue added. "You'd think it'd be the opposite."

──────────

Leia looked across the room. As she saw these very different people from such different backgrounds and experiences come together to celebrate being a part of one big blended family, it filled her with a different kind of joy and satisfaction.

She closed her eyes and smiled, inwardly saying a silent prayer of thanksgiving for these many blessings in her life. Her life made sense to her now and she loved everything about it.

Leia turned all her attention to the beautiful little baby girl in her arms, loving her more by the second. She knew the days and years ahead might pose challenges but she also knew she could handle them. And the rewards ahead would make them all worth it.

EPILOGUE

THE DOOR OPENED WHEN SHE exerted a little force to it and Tanya walked onto the roof of the hospital. She didn't know whether she was more impressed with the Healthflight helicopter sitting on the helipad or the gathering storm clouds overhead. She pulled her mobile phone from her purse and dialed a number.

The wind picked up and she could smell the moisture in the air. After several seconds, her friend answered.

"Hey, it's Tanya. Yeah, I finally got phone reception, Krissy. I had to come to the roof but I can hear you pretty well. Can you hear me?"

Tanya walked around restlessly, listening to Krissy.

"I'm at the hospital 'cause my big sister is having a baby. No, I don't wanna see all that gross stuff, I just wanna see the baby . . . but it's been taking a while. That's why I called, I'm going crazy here!"

Lightning flashed across the sky and ten seconds later, a fierce rumbling of thunder followed. A light rain began to fall.

"Oh, this reeks! It's starting to rain! If I have to go back inside, I'll lose reception. Hey, wait, do you have this on speaker phone? I can hear C.C. in the background with you! Stop laughing at me! I—"

Tanya had been backing up slowly without looking where she was. One of her feet felt nothing beneath it. She attempted to put her right foot back on the roof but the water that was now coating the rooftop made it slick underneath her other foot. She staggered, trying to keep her balance.

The next flash of lightning was so close that it was blinding to Tanya. Thunder exploded immediately overhead, and a strong gust of wind battered her left side, knocking her over. Her mobile phone bounced onto the roof. She screamed as she fell.

Adrenaline surged within Tanya, her terror intensifying as her descent speed increased. In desperation, as she came close to the side of the building, she clawed at it with both arms, using all of her strength. There was a painful jolt to her arms and then her left side hit the wall. But her fall was now slowing. A few seconds later, she stopped.

The cold rain helped her regain focus as she cautiously opened her eyes. First, she noticed that her senses were much more acute. Even on this dark and storm-filled evening, Tanya could see much further than she ever had before. And the smells from the ozone in the lightning discharges, the oils released by the rain, the gasoline from vehicles, and the pungent odors exiting dumpsters in the area all assaulted her at once. The nearby thunder was deafening and the light rain sounded like an amplified Geiger counter.

Tanya concentrated past all that and noticed that her hands had gripped into the side of the building. Above her hands, she saw the ten claw lines trailing almost halfway down the building.

Her arms were lightly covered in wet brown fur. Gravity and some slight discomfort from the back of her blue jeans indicated that she had a long, thin furry tail. Raindrops deflected off of her ears and Tanya realized they were on the top of her head, not the side. And Tanya smiled.

As quickly as she could, Tanya pulled herself up the side of the building by using the embedded claw marks as hand holds. When those ran out and she still had about one hundred feet to make it back to the roof, she noticed the windows to either side of her. Since the window to the left was closer, she stretched her left arm as far as she could and then used her fist to smash a hole into the wall. She grabbed onto that hole with her right hand and stretched to the left and repeated the step. Once she got close enough to the window, she gripped on to the two handholds and swung her legs around towards the window before letting go and her momentum carried her through the glass and into the twelfth floor of the hospital.

Tanya bounced off of the floor with her left hip. She crashed into a vending machine, breaking its glass and toppling it as she landed unceremoniously on her plump belly. That knocked the breath out of her before the right side of her face smacked hard onto the floor. A second later, the vending machine fell on her back, stealing consciousness from her.

As her senses slowly revived, Tanya could hear the wind rattling the shredded remains of the blinds. She felt that her whole body was soaking wet and she was covered in glass. But she wasn't hurt! She was just a little stiff and sore.

Tanya heard the clattering of several footsteps approaching, people alerted by the tremendous clamor. She surprised herself by easily getting to her knees, tilting to one side, and letting the vending machine roll off of her back. Unsteadily, she rose to her feet and heard glass shards fall to the ground. Her right shirt sleeve had caught on the window and was blowing in the blinds, leaving Tanya's thick, furry arm exposed with not a single cut, bruise, or broken bone on her entire body.

Tanya ran. She was so fast that she didn't touch anyone as she sped around the corner and down the hallway towards the stairs.

Excited by this new rush of energy, she leaped from the top of one set of stairs to the next lower level. She kept going until she reached the hospital basement.

Tanya sat down at the bottom of the stairwell and hoped no one would come down there anytime soon. The adrenaline rush now fading, Tanya felt spent, frustrated, and confused. She leaned forward and rested her head in her hands.

That's when she felt her feline snout and whiskers.

Tanya concentrated and tried to think about appearing the way she had before this transformation occurred. Nothing happened. Then she imagined the cat-like features fading away. Still nothing.

"I didn't change back either when my powers first manifested," Mom admitted.

Mom walked down the stairs from the first floor towards Tanya. Her expression was a mixture of concern and pride.

"Mom? How'd you know? How'd you find me?"

"Krissy called me in a panic. She thought you'd fallen off the building. I asked Ajali to find you and she did. Are you alright?"

"This is really weird, Mom. I'm a cat like you but I'm strong like Dad and I can't be hurt."

Mom smiled at her but Tanya could see her concern.

"Best of both worlds, huh?" Mom shared.

"I was so happy when I figured out that these are my powers!" Tanya continued. "They finally happened! But I can't enjoy them if they never turn off. I'll be a freak."

"If it's any consolation, if I use my powers for too long, I run the risk of staying in Cat form for either an extended time or maybe permanently."

Tanya looked at her mother to determine if she was being serious. There was no doubt that she was.

"So, I could be stuck like this?" Tanya asked.

"I won't lie to you, mija, your body might think this is what's natural. It might want to stay that way."

"So, if that's true, what do I do? How do I see my friends or go to school or just go outside?"

Mom stretched out her hand to Tanya and helped her to stand up.

"Tell you what, let's focus on what we can handle," Mom offered. "Let's call Krissy and let her know you're alive. Then we'll get you home and you can decide if you want to tell your friends what's happened to you."

Tanya nodded. That seemed reasonable.

THE END

ACKNOWLEDGMENTS

I'd like to acknowledge and thank my God and His Son, Jesus Christ, for their presence and power in my life. They inspired me to take elements and characters from a comic book story I wrote and drew over thirty years ago and novelize them in the present day. I'd also like to thank my wife and children for their love and support over the last several years. Special mentions to Tantz Aerine, Centcomm, Allyssa Maldonado, Valerie Wilmoth Tullos, Shadow Castner, and Jackie McFadden. Many thanks to my family and friends who encouraged me in writing this novel.

I want to thank my publisher, Ambassador International, who welcomed me into its family during the February 2018 #FaithPitch Twitter event. I have met and become friends with some wonderful people. They have been open and very encouraging to me, all with a humble and Christ-centric focus on worship, praise and fellowship. For that, I am very grateful.

This novel is special to me because it may be the last story I ever write with these particular characters. The AR-MEN was my first creative endeavor, a comic book I hand-drew and lettered, starting in 1980 when I was only ten years old. I continued the comic through the year 2000 and created one final issue (#147) in 2006. None of it was printed or sold; it was a labor of love. And as in this novel, there was more than one generation of heroes, villains, and supporting characters.

I wanted this novel to be explore those characters and develop their personal stories and histories, in a way that the comics didn't. I feel like I succeeded. I took some liberties with those stories and histories but I feel that I remained true to the characters and what they represented.

This novel also had spiritual elements. I'm no preacher or minister but I am a nondenominational Christian. I wanted to weave the spiritual into the story without being preachy or blunt. You can let me know whether I succeeded in that or not. I had to be true to myself and I feel that I accomplished that.

Lastly, I was inspired by National Novel Writing Month (nanowrimo). I wrote the first draft of this story during November 2013, surpassing the minimum 50,000-word requirement. It took some years to revise the draft into a final manuscript. Then it went through more edits through my editor at Ambassador International (thanks, Daphne!), but it was so worth it. I'm happy with this novel and I hope you enjoyed it as well.

ABOUT THE AUTHOR

Allen Steadham created comic books and webcomics before he started writing novels. He has been married to his wife, Angel, since 1995 and they have two sons and a daughter.

When not writing stories or drawing comics, Allen and his wife are singers, songwriters and musicians. They have been in a Christian band together since 1997. They live in Central Texas.

For more information about
Allen Steadham
&
Mindfire

please visit:

allen@allensteadham.com
www.allensteadham.com
www.facebook.com/jaspecfiction
@Mindfirenovel
www.instagram.com/allensteadham

For more information about
AMBASSADOR INTERNATIONAL
please visit:

www.ambassador-international.com
@AmbassadorIntl
www.facebook.com/AmbassadorIntl

If you enjoyed this book, please consider leaving us a review on
Amazon, Goodreads, or our website.